# Qua

Book One in the Quantum Series

By Douglas Phillips

Table of Contents

# 1  Space

Sergei Koslov floated a few centimeters above his seat, enjoying the last few minutes of weightlessness. Soon enough, he would be back in the crushing gravity of Earth. Wobbly legs would be a small price to pay for the innumerable pleasures of returning home.

He glanced out the window. The gentle curve of Earth's blue-and-white horizon stood in sharp contrast to the blackness of space. Sunlight magnified the natural beauty of oceans and clouds, but it was the night side that revealed the lights of civilization. More than anything, Sergei missed the energy of a city at night—any city. He'd passed over most of them in the last three months.

*Home. Almost there.* The only thing separating him was a fiery ride down through the atmosphere.

Sergei and his two companions were wedged shoulder to shoulder in a space no larger than the backseat of a small car; cramped, but bearable for the short ride down from the International Space Station. A pencil gently tumbled in the air. Anton Golovkin grabbed it and secured it with a clip. In the center seat, Jeremy Taylor confirmed the computer trajectory, his reach to the control panel extended by means of a small stick.

A voice in their headsets interrupted the soundless cabin. "Soyuz, ISS. *Kak pashyevayesh?*"

Sergei keyed his microphone and replied in English, "Doing well, ISS. We're enjoying every minute. The view is much better down here. How are things with you, Nate?"

There was a slight delay in Nate's response. "Sergei, my friend. In your haste to get home it appears you've left something behind. A music CD? On the cover, there's a photograph of a beautiful young woman wearing a red scarf and… well, not much else."

Sergei laughed. "You found it quickly, Nate. A gift, to help you Puritans in America better understand the finer things in life. I hope you will enjoy."

"*Spasibo*, Sergei, very generous... I think. When I get home, I'll send you some of my favorite decadence from the West. Your view of me might improve."

The Russian glanced over at his two companions and lifted his hands in the air. "Nate Erasco? Decadence? Not possible."

"Tell it straight, Sergei," Jeremy said. "But you'll miss that Puritan. You know you will."

Three months aboard the International Space Station had been a life-changing experience that was now coming to an end. Jeremy was right. Sergei would miss waking up each day to the incredible view from orbit. He'd miss the comradery of the ISS team, especially the Americans, even Nate. Back on the ground, Russia and America were worlds apart.

Sergei shifted to his role as Soyuz Mission 74 commander. "ISS, six minutes until descent burn. Changing to frequency 922.763."

The voice on the other end also changed tone. "Copy Soyuz, 922.763. *Bezopasnoye puteshestviye*—safe trip, guys."

Anton pressed a key and a checklist appeared on his display. Each man flipped their helmet visor down, pulled on gloves and locked them in place.

Sergei peered once more through the small Soyuz window. Their orbital height had decreased substantially, and their speed of eight kilometers per second was now obvious. The clouds, ocean and land below raced by at high speed as if predicting the drama of atmospheric contact that would come soon.

Sergei reached out and pressed a button to engage the reentry sequence. From ports on Soyuz, tiny jets of nitrogen shot out into the silent vacuum of space, nudging them into perfect retrograde position for the final burn. A countdown clock appeared on the computer display, and as the clock reached zero, the big descent rocket behind their backs ignited and shook the spacecraft with a deep rumble. Sergei and Jeremy bumped fists. The deceleration was immediate, and they were pressed into their padded seats. A few minutes later, the burn stopped as quickly as it had started.

"Descent velocity within target envelope," Anton called out. "Six minutes to atmospheric contact."

The computer displayed a large yellow light, and two loud bangs reverberated from behind their seats, followed by two more ahead. Jeremy visibly twitched at the sound of the explosive bolts.

Sergei looked out the window to confirm their separation from the forward docking module and the aft rocket. The discarded parts would never make it to the ground, destined to become globs of melted metal, disintegrating in the intense heat of reentry. Their capsule would take the same path, but thermal shielding would make all the difference.

Sergei shifted in his seat, anticipating the final, but most dangerous leg of their journey. *Home. Nearly there.*

Five heart-pounding minutes passed until the first shudder rattled the spacecraft. The top of the atmosphere.

The bumps increased, and a minute later, their seats were shaking violently. The three men briefly held gloved hands and smiled through their helmet visors. The bounces were frequent and strong. Larger jolts caused the entire cabin to rattle like an old pickup truck on a washboard road. But their smiles didn't fade. They had been through worse, and home was within reach.

Sergei keyed his microphone, his voice jittery from the bumps. "Moscow, Soyuz. Atmospheric contact, descent normal. We're picking up light chop."

In his headset, a Russian voice replied. "Soyuz, Moscow, confirmed atmospheric contact, altitude one-seven-four kilometers, up range seven-two-zero kilometers. Status is green. See you in a few minutes."

Sergei's fingers dug into the armrests on his seat as the jolts increased in ferocity.

~~~~~~~~~~~~~~~~~~~~~~~

Far below, on the flat, dusty plains of western Kazakhstan, a lonely Russian soldier stood outside his truck. He lifted his sunglasses and gazed upward. A beautiful day, and warm by Kazakh standards, with only a light coat needed to protect from the chill of the wind. The soldier picked up his binoculars and scanned the sky, looking for the object he expected to appear at any minute.

His job was simple: visually confirm reentry and contact the operations commander at Korolyov Mission Control. Radar and GPS would do the rest, providing descent vectors and computing the exact landing site, where recovery teams would be waiting. Soyuz landings were good, but with somewhat older technology, Russia still employed ground observers just to be sure.

The soldier's patience paid off as he noticed a thin contrail high in the atmosphere, streaking west to east at high speed. He grabbed his radio from the truck's seat and spoke with pride and excitement. "Moscow! Moscow! Soyuz reentry visual confirmation at Caspian Station."

The response was loud and clear. "Caspian, Moscow. Confirmed sighting. Maintain contact."

He lifted his binoculars and located the tip of the contrail once more. But now, something was different. The air at the tip began to shimmer, as if looking through the heat above a fire. The shimmer intensified, making the air opaque and partly obscuring the view. He squinted.

4

An intense flash of blue-white light, blindingly bright, exploded across the sky. Reflexively, the soldier dropped his binoculars and covered his eyes. Seconds passed as the brightness faded. A massive sonic boom shook the air and the ground.

His hands shaking, he lifted his binoculars and searched again. The long white contrail lingered in the high, thin air, marking the reentry track. But the contrail ended abruptly, and beyond it there was no spacecraft. No movement. No parachute. Nothing but empty sky.

The spacecraft was gone, as if it had never been there.

Confusion overwhelmed the soldier. *The blue flash... what? The boom... an explosion?*

He dropped his binoculars and for a full minute scanned the sky with his own eyes. He could pick out the remains of the contrail, wisps of white but nothing more. A minute later, a demanding voice burst from his radio.

"Caspian, Moscow. We have lost radar contact. Report!"

The soldier picked up the radio, collecting his thoughts before keying the microphone. He shook his head and kicked the tire of his truck.

*"Blyad!"*

## 2 Ground

At NASA's Goddard Spaceflight Center in Greenbelt, Maryland, Communications Specialist Dana Tunney pulled her headset off one ear and stared at the computer display. She rubbed her tired eyes and ignored several blinking lights. Equally neglected were the cup of cold coffee and half-eaten donut on her desk.

Her shift supervisor stood by her side, peering over her shoulder. She pointed to the screen. "Roscosmos reported simultaneous loss of radar and radio contact at altitude one hundred seventy kilometers. It's been twenty-five minutes and they've heard nothing. Nothing through the global network either. No telemetry, no voice."

The supervisor leaned in closer. "You were monitoring, right? What was the last transmission from Soyuz?"

She swiveled to face him. "All was well. They had just hit the top of the atmosphere. They were reporting some turbulence, but systems were normal and the descent trajectory looked good. But then... it just disappeared. Radar, communications, telemetry... everything. I'm continuing to monitor the comm frequency. Moscow is transmitting, but they're getting nothing back."

"Major malfunction?"

She sighed. "Yeah, I'm afraid so. Something big."

"Did it break apart? It must have burned up, right?"

"It sure as hell is pointing to that." She rubbed a hand across her forehead. "Good God, it's another Columbia disaster." She felt a chill as she recalled witnessing the space shuttle disintegrate on reentry. The fatal accident was years ago, but memories were still strong for those who were closely involved. And now the nightmare was repeating. Her mind played out the grotesque view of a spacecraft breaking apart, the burning pieces streaking across the sky and marking a path of destruction and death. And then, something clicked.

"Weird," she said softly, her eyes still focused on the display. "They're not tracking debris." She looked up at the supervisor. "Radar should have picked up debris for several minutes after the loss of radio contact, but the Russians are saying that the radar contact disappeared. One minute it was there and the next... gone. That doesn't make sense for a reentry breakup."

"It might be the Russian high-altitude radar. It's not exactly reliable. Have they reported any debris on the ground?"

She leaned back in her chair. "Well, they're mobilizing teams across a wide area of Kazakhstan, but it will be hours before we get any reports. At this point, everyone's assuming catastrophic structural fail—" But she didn't complete her sentence. She held up her hand, pulled her headphones tight over her ears and stared straight ahead.

"What? You're getting something?" the supervisor questioned. "Put it on speaker."

Dana looked up, her face pale. She reached to the panel, switched communications from headphones to speaker and turned up the volume. The static was continuous and loud, like ocean waves crashing on a beach. But out of the noise, a faint voice could be heard. It was hard to make out, mixed with so much static. But it was a man's voice, and he was clearly speaking Russian.

# 3  Americans

Daniel Rice ran down the dark residential street in Vienna, Virginia, extending his stride to avoid puddles from the recent rain. The Gear watch on his wrist displayed 5:30 a.m., and Billie Joe Armstrong poured a live version of "Warning" into his earbuds. He was in the zone. Every portion of his body moved in unison, and the running was effortless.

Since hitting forty, Daniel made sure that exercise was part of every day. The effort had paid off. He was fit, and stronger than when he was thirty. A morning run was his first choice for summer months, but now, in September, rain became a more frequent obstacle. Weekend skiing was a winter favorite, but that was last year. His new job had included a transfer from Seattle to D.C. From one Washington to another, but the two cities couldn't be more different.

The move was a major step forward in his career, reporting to the president's science advisor, Spencer Bradley, who had been a mentor to Daniel over many years. The day after Bradley was picked, he'd called Daniel and offered him a job. "My go-to guy," Bradley had said. "The president may not know it yet, but he needs you." Daniel's decision was easy.

In midstride, his phone erupted with a ringtone that told him Bradley was calling. It also meant his run would be cut short. He slowed to a stop, took a few deep breaths and touched his watch.

"Rice here." His voice was scratchy on its first use of the day.

"Daniel, sorry to wake you. We have a critical situation."

"I'm awake," he said between the panting breaths. "What's up?"

"Sorry to intrude, then. I hope whatever you're doing is as good as it sounds."

Daniel laughed. "I hate to burst your fantasy, Spence, but I'm just running. If you need me, I can be back home in five minutes."

"Four would be better," Bradley suggested. "The topic is confidential, so I'll fill you in when you get here. I'm sending a car, and pack a bag—you may need to catch a flight. How soon can you be ready?"

"Just send the car, I'll be ready. Your office?"

"Nope, Situation Room."

"White House? It sounds like a big deal."

"It is."

Daniel hung up. The White House wasn't unknown territory. He had already worked on several programs that involved the president, including a working lunch once. But a classified science program? That was rare. Closer to nonexistent.

Twenty-five minutes later, Daniel was home, showered and dressed in a dark business suit and blue tie, his standard choice when meeting with higher-ups. He glanced in the hallway mirror and brushed his fingers through his hair. *A bit grayer every month. No worries.*

He walked into the kitchen, where a striped tabby rubbed his chin against the edge of the island counter. "Don't worry, Darwin, I didn't forget you." He poured some food into the empty dish. The cat looked at the dish and back up at Daniel.

"What, not good enough for you? Ungrateful wretch." He bent down and scratched behind the cat's ears. "The vet says it's better for you. Get used to it, my friend, it will make you strong." Darwin rubbed the side of his face against Daniel's hand and purred.

"Hey, buddy, I have to leave. I might be gone overnight. But if you're lucky, Janine might stop by." Darwin's chin-rubbing intensified. "Yeah, you like Janine, don't you? I don't blame you. Maybe you can curl up on her lap. Lucky bastard."

He slipped on a lightweight overcoat, grabbed his laptop case and stepped outside. A hint of the rising sun was just beginning to show towards the east. Clouds from the passing cold front lingered over northern Virginia, but through a break he spotted Jupiter, shining brightly. If his telescope had been set up, he would have seen a nice arrangement of Jupiter's moons, with Io and Europa on the left, Ganymede and Calisto on the right. The four Galilean moons were his usual mental connection whenever Jupiter was in view.

On other nights, he identified the brighter stars and noted their distances from Earth: Sirius 8.6 light years, Procyon 11.5, Aldebaran 65.2, and on it went. There was no point to the mental exercise. It was nothing more than a checklist, a routine… an obsession, and it didn't end with astronomy. When in Salt Lake City or Los Angeles or Seattle, the routine switched to naming the surrounding mountain peaks, including their elevations. On any flight, it was a careful notation of every adjustment to ailerons, flaps, or landing gear. At breakfast, he estimated the atomic composition of his cereal or the diffraction of sunlight through the glass of orange juice.

Would the science inside his head ever stop?

*Probably not.*

A black SUV pulled up to the curb. The window rolled down and the interior lights came on. Daniel saw the familiar face of one of the Secret Service agents at the White House.

"Hey, Julian, how are things?"

"Doing well, Dr. Rice," the large man behind the wheel replied. "Good to see you again. Sorry for the short notice."

Daniel climbed into the backseat. "Not a problem. Just missing a bit of my morning run, that's all. What's the scoop?"

"Sorry, sir, I have no information. All I know is I'm taking you to the White House. An aide will get you to the conference room where they're meeting. There's a fresh scone in the box if you'd care to eat while we drive."

"Thanks, Julian, I knew you'd come through." Daniel reached into the box and pulled out the desiccated pastry. For the OSTP science team, scones were a *thing*. Daniel went along with it.

"So, it sounds important. Who's at this meeting?"

"Not at liberty to say, sir."

"Ah, that's what I love about working for the government. Be ready to go at a moment's notice, but we're not going to tell you the subject matter or even who you'll be meeting with." Daniel patted Julian on the shoulder in a friendly gesture. In truth, he had no complaints about his job.

"Yes, sir, it certainly keeps you on your toes."

Even at six in the morning, the traffic inbound to Washington was building rapidly. Julian made it as far as Arlington and then flipped on the emergency lights for the remainder of the drive. Ten minutes later they drove through the west gate of the White House.

Daniel hopped out, stretched both arms, and for a moment allowed the surroundings to soak in. The soft light of dawn lit the columned entrance to the West Wing in a pink glow. He looked up at the graceful building added to the White House in 1902 by Teddy Roosevelt and occupied by every president since. Anyone would be impressed by this historic place, and Daniel certainly was.

A Marine guard opened the door and Daniel walked into the marble reception area. The ground floor was for the president, visiting foreign dignitaries and members of Congress. The second floor provided work space for the president's staff. The basement was for everyone else.

"This way, sir," the Marine said, leading Daniel down the steps. They ended up in a dimly lit hallway and turned into the Situation Room, bright and already full of activity.

11

Several men in various military uniforms sat on one side of the long conference table, leaning toward each other in quiet conversation. On the other side of the table, Daniel recognized Augustin Ibarra, NASA's Administrator. Older, and balder, Spencer Bradley was seated next to Ibarra, and both were in conversation with a tall, well-dressed woman who clearly had their attention. Daniel recognized her from photos—the president's national security advisor, Christine Shea.

On the other side of Ibarra sat a young woman whose focus was on the notepad in front of her. She was petite, with short dark hair and glasses, and she wore a dark business suit. Daniel didn't recognize her, even when she looked up and made eye contact.

As Daniel walked in, Shea broke off her conversation and spoke directly to him. "Welcome, Dr. Rice, glad you could join us. Please have a seat, we have much to cover."

"I'm happy to help," Daniel replied and took the seat next to Bradley.

Shea walked to the front of the room. "Everyone... let's catch up." The side conversations died down and all eyes turned toward her.

"Four hours ago, at two a.m. our time, a Russian Soyuz spacecraft carrying three astronauts, an American and two Russians, from the International Space Station was reported destroyed on reentry over Kazakhstan. Russian ground controllers at Korolyov tell us that everything was running smoothly up to the moment when they lost radar and radio contact. They're still researching the cause of the failure, but they believe the spacecraft broke up rapidly, or possibly exploded. The Russians have teams deployed now to search for debris and remains, but so far, no word on any recovery. The initial assessment is that all three on board were killed."

"The American was Jeremy Taylor," Ibarra added. "NASA has already contacted his wife."

There was little reaction in the room, but for Daniel, it was entirely new information. He realized that by now the story was probably showing up on news sites and TV channels around the world.

Daniel scanned the room. The president's advisors, NASA representatives and military leaders sat around the table. They would all be needed for the coming investigation. But Daniel's purpose at the table was unclear. He provided oversight for government science programs. A spacecraft accident simply wasn't his domain.

"That's the basics," continued Shea. "However, as we were just beginning to discuss, there's more to this story. General Stanton?"

A white-haired man in an Army uniform leaned forward and cleared his throat. "Well, first let me caution that we're only a few hours into this and information is sparse. The Russians might have key details they've neglected to pass along to us. But from what we know so far, their story doesn't add up. Soyuz is two tons of metal, yet they're claiming their high-altitude radar didn't track any debris. Nothing. They said the Soyuz descent vehicle completely disappeared off radar."

"And what would you expect to see?" Bradley asked.

"Something. More than something, a lot. A blizzard of radar contacts. That's what makes no sense. When Columbia broke apart in 2003, our facilities tracked debris all the way across Texas and into Louisiana. Hell, hundreds of people saw it from the ground. Debris is part of any uncontrolled reentry, and it's a no-brainer to track it on radar. That's how you find it when it hits the ground."

The general glanced at Shea and waved his hand as if answering a question he knew was coming. "Yeah, yeah, it could be misinformation. It could be a Russian radar problem, or some other technical issue. Hell, I'd be willing to cut the Russians some slack, except for the communication Ibarra's guys picked up. That's pretty goddamned screwed up."

13

Augustin Ibarra elaborated. "Our people at NASA Goddard were monitoring the S-band communication. That's standard protocol, they monitor all near-Earth communication twenty-four hours a day via satellite relay. Just after three a.m., nearly an hour after the Soyuz event, they picked up an audio transmission, a broken conversation in Russian. It was too faint to make out much, just a few words that didn't mean anything."

"What's strange about that?" Bradley asked. "Maybe a Russian CapCom?"

Ibarra nodded his head. "Right. Our people thought the same thing. That frequency is reserved for transmissions between space and ground. We use it for our missions, and the Russians use it for theirs too. All radio transmissions are picked up by ground antennas or geosynchronous satellites and put on a communications network, and our people at Goddard are tapped in to that feed. At first, they thought the voice was just a Russian ground controller still holding out hope. But they looked at the source signature, the metadata on every transmission. It wasn't coming from Russian Mission Control. The voice was from Soyuz."

Christine Shea shook her head. "A voice, coming from Soyuz, *after* it supposedly blew up. Or should I say, after it disappeared." She looked directly at Spencer Bradley.

There were several glances around the room, and Daniel saw the tell on Bradley's face. After many years working together, Daniel knew him well. Bradley was holding back, hiding something.

Shea looked up at the ceiling as if staring through the floor to the Oval Office above them and took a deep breath. "If we don't get this right... the president is going to have a fit."

Shea leaned forward with both hands on the table. "Ladies and gentlemen, it's time for action. This is an event that we need to fully understand, and we're not there yet. I believe there are three avenues we must investigate. The first and most likely possibility is that we're looking at a failure of the Soyuz spacecraft on reentry. Whether all aboard were killed is a separate question. NASA will take the lead, in cooperation with our Russian partners at Roscosmos. Augustin, any comments or questions about this part?" She looked over at Augustin Ibarra and he shook his head.

"The second is the possibility of an act of terrorism or war, that Soyuz was taken out by a missile or bomb. Ukrainians? Russian separatists? Who knows? While this may be unlikely, I want to know for sure. General Stanton's team will investigate, jointly with the Russians." Stanton nodded in agreement.

Shea paused again and took a sip of water. "The third possibility is also unlikely, but I want to investigate it just the same. This one's politically awkward because it involves a classified program right here in the United States."

Shea looked at Bradley and continued, "This program is an advanced scientific study run out of Fermilab in Illinois. It's called Diastasi. It's on the cutting edge of high-energy particle physics, and, at the risk of sounding crazy, they make things disappear. Literally, disappear. The descriptions we've heard of the Soyuz *disappearance* seem to me to have similarities, and I'm not a person who believes in coincidences."

Daniel felt the energy in the room shifting, and like everyone else, he was puzzled by Shea's statement. Daniel knew about the work at Fermilab. Buried under the ground in Illinois was the nation's largest particle accelerator, a place where protons smashed into atoms, creating exotic particles like neutrinos.

Daniel perked up as he heard his name.

"We're asking Dr. Rice to investigate this third possibility," Shea continued. "Let's keep this one quiet—no contact with the Russians, please. There's no reason to stir up a hornet's nest if we can investigate on our own and rule out any linkage to Soyuz."

She turned to Daniel. "Dr. Rice, I know we're putting you on the spot here, but I'm equally confident that you are the right person to help. Dr. Bradley can provide further details. Spence, can you get this investigation rolling?"

Bradley stood up, and Daniel followed his lead.

Ibarra held up a hand. "Before you go, gentlemen, I have a request." He turned to the NSA and lowered his voice. "Ms. Shea, you raise a concern about a secret program. A program NASA is not involved in and had no prior knowledge of, but which could have caused a major spaceflight disaster? I can't tell you how many alarms are going off in my head right now."

Shea nodded. "Augustin, I completely understand, but remember that I'm only speculating. We don't know if there's any connection— that's what Dr. Rice will investigate. It will probably be nothing."

Ibarra settled back into his seat. "I'm sure you're right, but the scenario is unsettling. NASA needs to know about any program that has the slightest potential to impact space operations." He exchanged glances with the woman sitting beside him. "I had intended for Ms. Kendrick to work with Roscosmos, on your first scenario. But, given the circumstances, I think it would be better for her to join forces with Dr. Rice and Dr. Bradley."

All eyes in the room moved to the unfamiliar participant at the table. She carefully removed her glasses and nodded in acknowledgment.

Shea turned to Bradley. "Any problems, Spence?"

"None whatsoever. We're happy to include her," Bradley responded. "Are you ready to go, Ms. Kendrick?"

The young woman stood up and grabbed her notebook. "I am, thank you, Dr. Bradley."

Bradley ushered them from the room and closed the Situation Room door behind them, and the three stood in the quiet hallway.

She reached out to shake hands. "Marie Kendrick, NASA Special Operations. It's a pleasure to meet you, Dr. Bradley, Dr. Rice."

"Nice to meet you, Ms. Kendrick." Bradley held her hand for a moment. Daniel knew the routine. She was young, maybe twenty-eight or twenty-nine. Fresh-faced, no lines around her eyes, no battle scars. Daniel had witnessed Bradley's approach to hiring, with only the most experienced people making it through. From the looks of things, even collaborators got the same treatment.

Bradley pointed to a NASA pin on her suit lapel in the shape of an eagle. "You've flown in space?"

She showed a puzzled look as she touched her lapel. "Oh, the pin. No. The eagle signifies NASA flight operations. In my case, seventeen training missions on the MD C9-B, better known as the Vomit Comet. Wild in its own way, but not in space."

"Training, I see." Bradley nodded. "You know, I've always wanted to do one of those zero-G flights. Does it live up to its reputation, Ms. Kendrick?"

"On the first flight, nausea is guaranteed. But you get used to it. And please, call me Marie," she asked.

Bradley nodded, his balding head glinting under the hallway spotlight. "Very good, Marie. Glad you could join us."

She had apparently passed inspection. Daniel held out his hand. "Daniel Rice, it's a pleasure having you on this investigation, whatever it is. I'm afraid I'm clueless. A classified program, potentially tied to a space disaster? Technology that makes things disappear?" Daniel turned to Bradley. "What the hell was that about?"

Spencer Bradley took a deep breath, his cold stare alternating between Marie and Daniel. "They say teams are built on trust. So, trust

17

me when I say you're not going to like this next conversation." He pivoted and waved a hand. "Follow me."

# 4  Russians

The black BMW raced down the motorway northeast of Moscow, parting traffic with its blaring horn. Nearing the city of Korolyov, it passed a large rocket standing as a monument along the side of the road. Korolyov was one of the *naukograds*, cities built during the Soviet era as showcases for science and technology. Modern Korolyov was less a showcase and more an industrial city, with new European companies displacing rusting Soviet factories, long since closed.

The car exited the motorway and sped down a broad, tree-lined street into an unassuming neighborhood of low-rise office buildings and apartments. It screeched to a halt in front of a row of flags from multiple nations. The sign in front was modest. *Tsentr Upravleniya Poletami*, commonly known as TsUP, the Russian spaceflight center.

A large man in a business suit stepped out of the car and hurried through the entrance. He displayed his security badge, walked through a metal detector and turned down a hallway marked *Mission Control* in both Russian and English.

He passed through a second security station and stepped into a cavernous room filled with rows of desks, computer displays and people in motion. A forty-foot tall video screen stretched across the room's far wall. Its world map provided multicolored orbital tracings, along with live video feeds from space and ground.

A group gathered around one of the workstations, and the large man headed their way. A young man wearing a headset waved him over. "Director, I'm glad you are here. The transmission is continuing even now."

"Have you identified the source?" the director asked him.

"Yes, sir. It is Soyuz, there is no question. We have been receiving for more than thirty minutes, but they are not hearing us."

"Put it on speaker."

The group gathered close to listen. The Russian voice coming from the speaker was clear at times, but broken by static.

"... correcting for descent anomaly ..."

"... orbital height above the disc varies ..."

"... receive your transmissions. We have checked our equipment ..."

"... we see the fire, has Earth ..."

The voice faded. They listened for another minute, but the speaker returned nothing but static.

"It has been this way," the young man said. "A break, followed by a transmission, followed by another break. We are hearing some of the same words. We think they are repeating. With time, we may be able to fill in the blanks."

"Still nothing on radar?"

"Nothing, sir. Radar is blank. They are not there, yet they are."

"Any idea what he means by the fire?"

"I don't know, sir. Something they are seeing either in space or on the ground?"

"Keep monitoring and provide a transcript of the full recording to my desk once you have it all," the director told him. "Is this transmission on the global network?"

"Yes, our partners in the United States and Europe are receiving the same thing."

"Good." He turned to the group of people standing nearby. "I want all department heads in my office in ten minutes. This is now a rescue mission. Our first task is to determine Soyuz's location. In the absence of radar, this will require creative thinking and full participation from our partners."

The director eyed each person in the group, their faces blank. He abruptly turned on his heel and left, leaving only the sound of static still scratching from the speaker.

# 5 Quantum

Daniel followed Bradley out of the West Wing and along the path to the Eisenhower Executive Office Building. The ornate building looked as if it belonged in Paris, not Washington. Classically French in architecture, with roof dormers and dozens of chimneys, it was called ugly by some but named a National Historic Landmark by others.

Their strides along the concrete path revealed an urgency. Daniel's newest partner kept in step, her pace just shy of a jog. "It's nice your office is located so close to the White House," Marie said between breaths.

"Proximity may be its only virtue," Daniel replied. "*La Bastille* will wear you down, particularly on those cold January mornings as you wait for the Jurassic-era heating system to kick in." Marie looked up, smiled weakly and refocused on the ground.

Bradley led them past the inoperable elevators and up marble stairs to the second floor. They passed through an oversized doorway, a sign displaying *Office of Science and Technology Policy*. A reception desk stood in the center of the room, and behind it a woman looked up from the pastry box she had just opened.

Bradley spoke to her even as he opened the adjacent door to his office. "Janine, we're going to need to get Daniel and Marie on a plane to Chicago. Commercial if practical, but get them there quickly. And please let Director Park know they're coming and will have full security clearance. On second thought, don't worry about Park, I'll call him myself."

"No problem, Dr. Bradley, I'll get the transportation," Janine answered. She stopped what she was doing and turned her attention to Daniel, now standing at her desk. "Good morning, Daniel. How are you?"

"Morning, Janine. Suddenly busy, and just barely past breakfast. Perhaps an indicator for the rest of the day?" Daniel flashed his best early-morning smile, and Janine responded with one of her own. OSTP had some top-notch people, and Janine was one of them. Her beautiful smile was just a bonus.

"Our newest colleague," said Daniel, gesturing to Marie, who had caught up and was breathing heavily.

Marie reached out to shake hands with Janine. "Hi, Janine. Marie Kendrick, NASA Operations. You'll probably need my info to book flights?" She pulled her government badge from its clip and offered it to Janine.

Janine held up her hand. "Not really needed, thanks, Marie. I'll get you both on a military flight. Much faster and no boarding passes. You'll like it."

"That's okay?" Marie asked. "Didn't Dr. Bradley just say—"

"Pay no attention to what the boss actually says," Janine laughed. "I know what he really means when he says 'quick,' and it doesn't include having you wait in TSA lines."

The two women exchanged a look, acknowledging their common experience. Daniel was oblivious to the female connection happening right in front of him. One of the unspoken wonders of the world is the ability of women to identify allies, five seconds after they've met. Daniel was thinking of more mundane things.

"Janine, this trip is short notice—well, no notice at all, really. I hate to ask, but is there any chance you could locate someone to feed Darwin again for me? I'll leave a key."

He got the answer he was hoping for. "I'll do it myself," Janine said, looking directly into Daniel's eyes. It was a sweet look, bordering on romantic. She held out her hand, and Daniel handed over his house key. "Don't worry about kitty cat," she continued. "As I recall, he likes me."

23

Daniel squinted. Was she reminding him that she had been at his house before? A suggestion of interest? *You're reading too much into it,* he thought. *She's offering to take care of your cat.*

"Thanks, I owe you one. More than one," he said. The quick exchange was all they would get as Bradley stepped out of his office with a glare that made it clear their time for pleasantries was up.

Marie leaned into the desk. "Nice to meet you, and thanks for your help."

Janine flipped the key a few times in her hand. "My pleasure. Have a good trip." Marie and Daniel disappeared into Bradley's office and the door closed.

The office was relatively small for a top advisor to the most powerful person on the planet. Just a desk, a bookcase and a few chairs, with a view out the window to traffic on Seventeenth Street below. Working for the government didn't come with luxury.

Bradley swiveled his chair around and wrote on a notepad as he talked. "You'll need to be at the airport soon, so I'm just going to get you started. When you get to Fermilab, you'll be meeting with the director, Jae-ho Park, and he'll give you more. Park is an enigma, but nothing a bit of strategy can't overcome."

"Difficult?" asked Daniel. He had seen it before. Science facilities around the nation were in regular communication with Washington, but resentment at being audited could still be strong.

"I wouldn't say that," Bradley countered. "He's cooperative enough, but highly protective. I can help grease the skids, but I want you two already on a plane when I make that call. Otherwise he'll spend the entire call arguing about why you don't need to be there."

"Do we need to be there?"

"Yes." Bradley sighed heavily. "Yes, you do."

"Something tells me this is no ordinary story. Spence, I realize my knowledge of every government program is not one hundred percent." Daniel raised an eyebrow. "But it seems my exclusion from this particular program is intentional."

"You're right on that, but don't feel bad. Until this morning, even the vice president was an outsider. The security is tight. I'll catch you up. It's fascinating stuff, but it transitions into the realm of science fiction pretty quickly. When Shea mentioned they make things disappear, she wasn't kidding."

"Okay," Daniel chuckled. "Tell us all about the invisible ray gun."

"We'll get there. But first, particle physics. Marie, are you familiar with Fermilab?"

"I've heard of it," she answered. "It's near Chicago?"

"Yes, Batavia, Illinois. It's the principal laboratory in this country for high-energy particle research. They have a long history of major discoveries, mostly related to quarks and neutrinos." Bradley's eyes darted between them. "How about string theory?"

Daniel answered. "Well, it's the idea that all matter is made up a fundamental building block, even smaller than a quark. It's just a mathematical idea, though, not yet proven. Proponents say that string theory could unite the Standard Model with the Theory of Gravity, giving us the so-called Theory of Everything."

Marie raised both hands. "Sorry, I don't suppose you might have a copy of Particle Physics 101 that I could borrow? My background is in space operations. Very much Newtonian physics, velocities, acceleration, orbital mechanics. A smattering of Einstein. We don't have much need for anything more exotic."

Daniel knew the feeling. His scientific education was deep, but his career had wandered across multiple disciplines, and there was always a situation where his subject knowledge was thin. It was natural

25

to feel intimidated when everyone else in the conversation seemed to be an expert.

"No problem," Bradley continued. "Space operations... that's dealing with the logistics of space flight?"

Marie sat up higher in her chair. "Well, it's a lot of things— training, planning, people and hardware. In my case, it's all human spaceflight. For example, recently I've been working with engineers on some ISS design improvements. We have a lot of private companies involved these days, and frankly their engineers don't have the same level of experience that you see in the NASA family."

"Family?" asked Daniel.

"Yeah, it really is," she said. "Astronauts, their spouses, their kids, their parents. It's surprising how close you get. We think of ourselves as an extended family."

"And the guys in Soyuz? Jeremy Taylor?" asked Bradley.

"Yeah, both Sergei and Jeremy," she said, looking down. "We're pretty close." The emotional connection was obvious. Daniel wondered how she might be handling the real possibility that both men were dead, or soon would be. He hoped she was ready for whatever lay ahead.

"Everyone is doing their best to help," Bradley said as carefully as he could. Marie stared at the floor and nodded.

She lifted her head, and her eyes fixed on Bradley. "I know they are," she said, her voice steady. "Thank you, Dr. Bradley. If you can help with the physics, I'll be in a better place to contribute."

"I can do that," Bradley replied. "I'll give you the thirty-second summary of string theory, and I'm sure Daniel can fill in the rest later. Okay?"

Marie nodded.

"Let's start with atoms. Protons and neutrons with orbiting electrons, right? But as small as they are, these particles are composed of even smaller bits. Quarks and leptons. They're like Lego blocks; put a few quarks together and you have a proton."

Bradley gestured as he talked. "That's the matter side of the universe. In addition, there are four fundamental forces, the strong and weak nuclear forces, the electromagnetic force, and the gravitational force. In quantum physics, forces are represented by a particle called a boson. For example, a photon is a type of boson that transmits the electromagnetic force. The Standard Model pulls all of this together into one theory of matter and force." He paused and raised both eyebrows quizzically.

"Keeping up so far." Marie smiled.

"Okay. Now, here's the twist. Gravity, one of the four forces, seems to be different, and physicists have struggled for years to understand why. This is where string theory comes in. It resolves the question by suggesting that gravity is *not* different and can be integrated into the Standard Model like the other three forces.

"According to string theory, quarks and leptons and bosons are all made up of an even tinier bit, a one-dimensional string that vibrates in different ways to represent each particle. If string theory is right, then gravity combines with the Standard Model and forms what they call the Theory of Everything."

"Very nicely explained," said Marie. "I've read about some of those concepts, but you do a good job of putting it together into a coherent story."

Bradley momentarily stopped and rubbed his shiny head. "Very kind of you. At my age, I'm glad I can still communicate. But now the story gets strange. Do you recall the discovery of the Higgs boson in 2012?"

"At the CERN facility in Switzerland?"

"Right. It was big news at the time, transcending the scientific world and spilling out into public journalism. There was plenty of excitement, even though the average man on the street had no idea what a Higgs boson was. But the discovery wasn't just Higgs—there was more, much more."

Bradley paused, eying Daniel and then Marie as if he was ready to spill the beans. "It wasn't well reported or even understood at the time, but on top of the Higgs boson, the CERN project team found the elusive string itself. No longer just a mathematician's dream, it suddenly became real. String theory, and all that it implies, is real."

The jumble of science, ever-present in Daniel's head, made a connection. "Spence, that's huge. It's the dimensional mathematics in string theory, right? If there's evidence that strings are real, then the dimensional mathematics would have to be real too."

Bradley smiled broadly. "It's your specialty, Daniel, finding the relationships. Precisely why you're the right person to lead this inquiry. The quantum world can get very strange. Location becomes a probability not an exact coordinate, and particles can become entangled like twins that think alike. String theory has its own bizarre world because the mathematics only work when string vibrations occur in more than three dimensions."

He turned to Marie. "You've probably heard of extra dimensions? A fourth dimension?"

Marie shrugged. "Well, I know physicists sometimes use time as the fourth dimension."

Bradley nodded. "They do, yes. But string theory involves mass, energy and space, not time. So, when physicists talk about extra dimensions, they're talking about space. We're all familiar with a three-dimensional world, right?" He gestured towards the sides of the office. "We say that this room has three dimensions, walls and ceiling, each perpendicular to the other. If we talk about a position on Earth, we use three descriptions, north and south, east and west, up and down. In mathematics, we use the *x*, *y*, and *z* axes. Now, what if there was a fourth dimension—a fourth dimension of space?"

Daniel shifted in his chair. He started to say something, but held back. Bradley was walking straight off the crazy cliff. If it was coming from anyone else, Daniel might have laughed it off and walked out. But coming from Bradley, even crazy could start to sound plausible. He watched to see how Marie might react as Bradley continued his plausibly crazy explanation.

"What if there were another dimension, perpendicular to the existing three? I can't point to this direction, because I'm a three-dimensional person and can't move my arm into a fourth dimension. I can't see it because my eyes are also stuck in this three-dimensional world. But mathematically, it's a simple matter of just adding a fourth axis. In fact, string theory doesn't stop at four dimensions. It postulates a world of ten dimensions, three of which we see and seven that are hidden to us."

"Mysteriously hidden dimensions? To tell you the truth, it sounds more like some religious cult," Marie said earnestly.

"Reality doesn't always conform to our idea of what's normal," countered Bradley. "The evidence uncovered in 2012 demonstrated that string theory is the true representation of particles at the quantum scale, including the bizarre notion that strings support ten quantum dimensions."

"Why do you say *quantum* dimensions? Are they submicroscopic?" she asked.

"Precisely. Strings are unimaginably small. If a single electron were enlarged to the size of the Earth, a string would still be a speck of dust too small to see. These seven extra dimensions that I was talking about? For all practical purposes, they don't exist, they're too small. But at quantum scales, they're as real as anything else."

He paused, looking around the room as if strings might be floating in the air. "The universe is often stranger than we expect and sometimes stranger than we can imagine."

Daniel sorted through the concepts Bradley was presenting. Physicists had long speculated that string theory might be real, yet no more than a curiosity. The quantum world often stipulated rules that applied only to infinitesimals. Even still, confirmation of string theory would be an enormous achievement. His natural skepticism kicked in.

"Spence, I get it. But if strings were found in 2012, how come it's not big news? Come on, that's huge. I read a lot of science journals, and nobody's mentioning it."

Bradley nodded in agreement. "Just as the universe is mysterious, so are governments. The initial evidence was incomplete. Scientists discussed among themselves, but before any results were published, both the US and Europe decided to classify all projects. They instructed project scientists at CERN and Fermilab to continue to study but not publish until further directed. There were a few leaks to journalists, but without confirmation, those stories died quickly. I think everyone expected the classification to be lifted, but so far that hasn't happened."

Daniel put the pieces together. "So, Christine Shea thinks that this classified work on string dimensions has somehow caused Soyuz to disappear? What does she know that you haven't told us?"

"She's speculating," said Bradley. "Let's be cautious about this. There are other more conventional explanations, and we'd all be wise not to jump immediately to the craziest idea. Let's pursue this rationally and see what we find. It may amount to nothing."

Something flashed on Bradley's computer, attracting his attention. "It looks like Janine has you on a military flight out of Joint Base Andrews. A car will pick you up out front. We've only got a few minutes... but hang on, something else... it's from Shea." Bradley clicked and read aloud.

"She says: 'Attached are recordings from Goddard and Australia. No radar contact, voice only. Unusual, to say the least. Continue your investigation with all speed.'"

He clicked again, and his computer speakers came to life. Bradley turned up the volume. The sound was mostly static. Faintly in the background, a few Russian-sounding words could be heard.

"The voice might be Sergei," said Marie. "It's hard to tell with so much static, but it does sound like him. From what I could hear, he's saying 'contact... lower frequency... world... repeat.' Not terribly meaningful."

"You speak Russian?" Daniel asked.

Marie nodded. "Well enough."

Bradley replayed the audio again, and all three strained to hear anything else in the recording. Marie shook her head, still uncertain. "If Soyuz is the source, it must be Sergei."

Bradley nodded. He clicked again, and they listened to a second audio file. Daniel stepped closer, and Marie pulled her chair up to the edge of Bradley's desk. The audio was still broken by static, but the words were crisper, and this time in English. The voice was American, and the man's tone was clearly distressed.

"... not receiving, but we will continue to transmit until..."

"... orbital decay likely to continue as we are..."

"... all three discs come into view at times..."

"... Mission Control, Soyuz, repeating at..."

Marie gasped as the last statement was spoken. She looked at Daniel. "It's definitely Jeremy Taylor," she said, beaming. "I'm sure of it."

31

Bradley pounded his fist, and pencils bounced on the desk. "They're alive."

Marie's expression changed. Her eyes cast down and she shook her head as if something was still wrong. "Two different transmissions picked up on both sides of the planet," she said slowly. "It shows that Soyuz is still in orbit. So, why no radar contact?"

"Maybe they landed in Australia?" offered Daniel.

She shook her head. "Even a landing would have produced a radar track. We've got pretty much worldwide radar coverage, even out over the Pacific. I don't see how we could have missed it. And the Australia transmission proves they made another orbit. It blows away the theory that this was just a Russian radar failure. The Australians couldn't find them either."

"Going forward," Bradley said, "I think we have to assume they're still in orbit. This is looking like a rescue mission—NASA and Roscosmos will take the lead. But our task hasn't changed. We still need to know if the Diastasi program at Fermilab had anything to do with this. If we're lucky, we're chasing down a dead end, and NASA will find Soyuz the old-fashioned way. But if we're dealing with something more bizarre, it's our job to figure that out, and soon."

He picked up a pencil and poised over a pad of paper. "Marie, how much time do you think they have? Oxygen-wise."

Marie shook her head slowly. "There's the rub. They separated from their service module hours ago, so... the air in the cabin plus a few emergency bottles. Twenty-four to thirty-six hours, at least that's what the Soyuz manuals will tell you."

"Could they stretch it?" asked Daniel.

"Maybe, a little. But the longer they stretch, the more carbon dioxide build-up becomes an issue." She exchanged a serious look with

Daniel. It was clear there were several ways this could end, and few of the outcomes were positive.

Bradley wrote a few numbers on the pad and punctuated them with the pencil point hitting the paper. "The clock is ticking."

Janine opened the door. "The car is here to take you two to Andrews."

"On your way," Bradley said with the wave of a hand. "I'll send a few more documents about the program by email, and I'll make sure that Dr. Park is ready for you when you arrive. Good luck, and let me know if there is anything I can do on this end. Remember, you have the full resources of the president at your disposal."

# 6 Darkness

The cabin was still and quiet, the violent shaking of reentry now a remote event in the past. Sergei lifted his helmet visor and removed his gloves. He peered outside through the single small window. The view was unlike anything he had ever seen.

"Where do you think we are?" Jeremy asked.

"Not where we're supposed to be," Sergei answered.

They were still in space, of that much he was certain. But this space was anything but normal. In one direction, a single brilliant light and a field of stars filled the view, stretching infinitely to the left and right, up and down. In some ways it was a normal view of the sun and stars, but different... somehow, separated.

*As if we're next to an enormous wall, with stars painted on it.*

The view in the opposite direction was just as startling because there was nothing but black. No light. No stars. Darkness. With nothing in the foreground, there was also no sense of depth. He couldn't tell if he was viewing a nearby black curtain, or whether the darkness continued forever.

The spacecraft slowly rolled and the view changed. Another shape came into view, embedded within the wall of stars. A great slash of blue color, elliptical in shape, but so narrow as to be pointed on either end. As time passed, the width of the blue ellipse narrowed further, becoming needlelike, as if it might disappear altogether.

The view fit no perception of what space looks like. Any view across space, in any direction, invariably includes a measure of randomness. This view was jarring because of its uniform geometry. A wall of stars with a definite edge.

Anton checked his display once more. "Still no telemetry, no ground transmissions of any kind, no GPS, no satellite relays. We have no position data. We could be anywhere."

As Anton spoke the words, Sergei felt a chill. A commander must always know the location of his ship. But beyond a GPS readout, humans feel their position using a built-in sense, an internal gyroscope. It was a comfort that could only be identified once it was lost.

*I am nowhere.* The feeling was more than disorienting, it was terrifying.

"Full system check," Sergei ordered, both to his crewmates and to himself. If nothing else, it would provide an opportunity to participate in routine. All three men pressed buttons on the control panel and noted information in their displays.

"Heat shield is intact," reported Anton. "And it's still hot. Two-one-three degrees."

"At least the reentry wasn't our imagination," said Jeremy. "Cabin pressure is good, $CO_2$ scrubbers are online and clear, oxygen normal at forty percent."

They continued with their readouts. Primary navigation computer, communications equipment, and on and on. All systems were working normally.

Sergei flipped a switch to connect his headset to their communications radio and pressed a transmit button on his armrest.

"*Moskva, Sayuz, sdelanny.*"

The cabin was quiet as they waited several seconds for a response. Sergei tried again.

"*Moskva, Sayuz. Peredachu na 922.763. Otvechat.*"

He held his breath, listening. Sergei dialed another frequency.

"Houston, Soyuz. Transmitting on emergency frequency 927.0. Respond."

He checked his display. A self-test confirmed the radio was working. The three men looked at each other, and the continued silence

35

brought with it the full realization of their situation. They were alone. For reasons none could understand, they were lost and completely alone.

Above Sergei's left shoulder, the view outside was still the same. A vast wall of stars and a long thin splash of blue. It was a view as gloriously stunning as it was bizarre. Except for the star wall, the rest was nothing but a dark void.

~~~~~~~~~~~~~~~~~~~~~~~~

The human eye is naturally attracted to contrasts of light and to movement. The eye does not perform well in darkness. Had there been more light, or had Sergei's eyes been receptive to a broader range of the electromagnetic spectrum, he might have noticed something else out in the darkness. Away from the stars, away from the light, the dark void was not entirely empty.

A single angular object, a wedge shape, drifted across the dark space. The wedge was black, imperceptibly different from its surroundings. Black upon black. Its surface was a near-perfect absorber, and with no reflection; even its shape was difficult to determine. If the wedge had been between Sergei's eye and the wall of stars, he would have noticed its negative space as it blocked out the stars behind it. But it wasn't. Floating in the darkness, the wedge provided no clues as to its origin, its size or its purpose. It was simply there.

The wedge remained stationary for several minutes. Then it rotated slightly, and near one end, a small red light appeared.

# 7  Insight

Early-morning sunlight arrived at the bedroom window, making the shade glow. Branches outside shifted in the breeze and cast swaying shadows. The room was warm and quiet. Only the ticking of a mechanical clock in the hallway disturbed the silence.

Nala Pasquier sat up in bed. She brushed her thick dark hair from her face, reached both arms into the air and yawned. She twisted her sleep shirt into place, displaying a picture of Beaker, the perpetually freaked-out Muppet, and Dr. Bunsen Honeydew, warning, *Stand Back. This might be dangerous.*

She glanced at the clock—6:35 a.m.—and lifted her phone from the nightstand.

*Good, no messages. And plenty of time before work.*

She could use the extra time for a workout, but also for mental stimulation. The conflicts at work had been building in the past few days, and she needed to reduce complexity, simplify and find insight. This morning, she would use the pod.

She padded barefoot to the adjacent workout room. The stair climber and weight bench were ordinary. The smooth white oval pod was not. Inside, it held a pool of warm saltwater; a cocoon of sorts. Other people might have a bathtub, but Nala had her float pod.

She had a theory about insight. To achieve a deep understanding required a shift in intellect. Ordinary consciousness was far too chaotic, overloading the senses. To obtain insight, she needed an environment that would allow her brain to function at a higher level. There were different ways of calming the senses, and Nala had studied them all. Meditation, yoga, peyote and more. She felt each had value, but none were as effective as her own homegrown approach.

Through practice, she had boiled the process down to two steps. First, stimulate your conscious brain with information, alternatives and problems to be solved. Once your mind was filled, then relax your body and eliminate sights, sounds and touch. Completely shut down all sensory input.

In a state of relaxation and sensory deprivation, the conscious mind drifts, allowing the subconscious to take over. In this dreamlike state, the subconscious processes the recent stimuli, still fresh within the brain's synapses. With careful attention and practice, her method could achieve incredible insight. She had done it on more than one occasion.

She touched the power button on the stair climber display and connected to her computer files. From the display, she could pull up reference material, email or anything else she might need. She stepped onto the pedals and began her workout. Her legs moved up and down, slowly at first but increasing in pace.

She began her mental stimulus by stepping through the work accomplished over the past week, completed tasks and those coming up. A review, mostly. She didn't stop on any one topic, but kept them flowing, like flipping playing cards in a deck.

Her legs moved rhythmically on the machine, and her heartbeat increased. Touching the computer display, she opened an electronic notebook and reacquainted her conscious mind with the details of each entry she'd made during the past week.

Her arms held on to handles that moved back and forth in synchronization with the motion of her legs. Her breathing became stronger, and small beads of sweat appeared on her forehead.

Nala shifted her focus to a specific problem in need of a solution. It was something she had been grappling with for days, something she could not yet understand. She asked herself questions, knowing consciously that she had no answers.

"The distance is impossible," she spoke aloud. "What did they do? At Fermilab? And how does the wave oscillation tie back to theory?" The questions went on, the thoughts continued, all very consciously.

Fifteen minutes later, her leg and arm muscles burned, her breathing forceful. The machine slowed and she stepped off. She stretched, allowing time to catch her breath.

When her heart rate calmed, she lifted the lid to the pod. It was like opening a peanut shell, splitting the pod in half. The interior glowed with violet light, her color choice, and the lower half was filled with clear water. A wisp of steam drifted across the surface.

She pulled her sleep shirt over her head, dropping it to the floor. Standing naked in front of the tub, she inserted two earplugs and stepped into the water.

It felt like nothing. Not warm, but not cool either. She lay down in the pod and stretched out fully, face up, with enough room surrounding her to ensure she did not touch the walls. She reached up and pulled the upper lid down, completely sealing herself inside, the violet light still glowing around her. With her muscles relaxed, she felt the high concentration of Epsom salt keeping her buoyant. Floating took no effort at all.

A minute later the violet light dimmed, and she was immersed in complete darkness. The pod was now devoid of sensory input. No light. No sound or smell. Not even the feeling of touch, as the skin-temperature water disappeared from her senses. She had achieved the state she needed, a brain filled with thoughts and senses calmed.

Nala closed her eyes; the darkness was the same regardless. It took a few minutes, but eventually every muscle relaxed and she was adrift not in water, but nothingness. The sounds were constrained to each breath and the thumps of her heart, but nothing more.

Her mind wandered. She didn't sleep, but it felt like a dream. Her body no longer existed, only her thoughts. She saw fleeting images in the darkness. A flash of light, a small boy's face, bubbles. Each image disappeared as quickly as it came. Without sensory input, the brain creates its own images.

*Hallucinations. They'll pass.*

Her heart rate elevated. A tumbling feeling made it impossible to determine up or down. She allowed herself to release, as if turning a page, and dropped into a deep meditative state.

Without effort, her intelligence blossomed; her ability to correlate and compare increased. Her conscious thoughts became objects floating in space. Lines of software, bits of data, equations and graphs, even conceptual ideas and assumptions.

*I am fully aware. Nothing can remain hidden.*

Reaching into an even deeper state, she envisioned a tunnel, a spiral path twisting away into the distance. She followed the tunnel as it tilted upward. A growing brightness led her forward. She was near her goal. As her mind reached out, bright light flooded from nowhere. Her physical body shuddered, causing her brain to snap back to consciousness. She opened her eyes wide and called out.

"Wah Xiang!"

Her voice triggered electronics in the pod, and the glow of violet light returned. Nala looked around. The pod was no longer a refuge of the mind; it was simply a pool of salty water.

"The Chinese," she whispered to herself. "They hacked me... that's how they knew... those bastards took my code and changed the fucking oscillation amplitude."

Her new knowledge was disturbing, and it made her angry. Still, her eyes shined with the full satisfaction of her ability to discover it. Her super power. When the insights came, they always surprised her. She trembled as a chill ran down her back.

Even more satisfying was the assurance that her method worked. Additional insight was there for the taking. Years ago, she had tried yoga with follow-on meditation. It had given mixed results, likely because it was too difficult to shut out sensory input. She had even once tried intense sex followed by a relaxing massage. It had worked to a degree, but verbalizing details of complex scientific topics was odd while bouncing on her partner's pelvis. She never saw him again.

Nala pushed on the pod lid and light poured in. Stepping out, she grabbed a towel, dabbed herself dry and looked in the mirror.

A smile spread across her face. "I have a feeling this is going to be a big day."

# 8 Chicago

An hour after leaving the White House, Daniel and Marie were seated in comfortable leather seats, climbing to thirty-five thousand feet on board a Gulfstream G280. The accommodations were better than anything Daniel had experienced in his career with the Navy. Most likely used by top brass out of Washington. *Thanks, Janine, you did well.*

The interior was arranged as four sets of seats, with a table between each pair. Marie sat across from Daniel, making herself heard above the piercing noise of the jet engines. "Honestly, it's been a fast ride at NASA. One job led to the next, and suddenly I'm working for the HEO admin. And today... wow. Starting off by being summoned to the White House? Well, that's a first."

Daniel looked over his new partner as she spoke. She wore stylish business clothes and little makeup and carried a slim briefcase. Her short brown hair flipped under when she pushed it behind one ear, but she wore no earrings. Marie looked understated and professional, her only jewelry being a gold ring on her middle finger.

"For your sake, I hope Ibarra doesn't make a habit of summoning you in the early-morning hours. He's a former astronaut, isn't he?"

"Shuttle. Three missions in the nineties. He transitioned to administration well. There are so many good people at NASA. Six months ago, I was training those guys." She nodded her head upward towards space. "Sergei and Jeremy, at least. I don't personally know Anton Golovkin, but they're all top-notch people."

"You train the Russians too?"

"Of course. Most of the ISS training is at Johnson Space Center. We have a lot of mockups there, plus the Neutral Buoyancy Tank for spacewalks. They train for the ISS arm operation in Montreal, and then there's advanced science training in Germany. And, of course, Soyuz training in Moscow. It's all around the world. They don't call it the International Space Station for nothing."

"Your pride shows." Her face lit up. Putting people at ease was one of Daniel's specialties. "What did you do before NASA?"

"In school. Colorado, Boulder. Space Operations Engineering."

"Huh." Daniel shrugged. "I had no idea a degree like that even existed."

"It's a small program. I was the first woman to complete it."

"Congratulations, then. It seems to have taken you where you wanted to go. You've accomplished a lot in a short time."

"I'm older than I look," she admonished. "Shall I put my glasses on? They add five years." Her black glasses rested on the table, the thin lenses making them appear to be more of a fashion accessory than an optical aid.

"Sorry," Daniel said. "I didn't mean to make you feel self-conscious. Bradley, too. He tends to grill people, but he's just being thorough."

"It's not a problem, you've both been very kind. The discussion of string theory was very helpful. I enjoyed it."

The conversation paused, and Marie turned it around. "How about your background? I'm sorry, I should know. But no one told me who would be at the meeting, so I didn't have time to research."

"No reason to apologize, it's just how the White House works. I'm in the Office of Science and Technology Policy, OSTP. We monitor programs and nudge them back in line when things go astray."

"And you're an investigator?"

"A science investigator. My degrees are in biology and astrophysics. I worked for the Navy for fourteen years. There's a lot of science in the military, more than people realize."

"Like?"

"Well, like nuclear physics. Every submarine is a mobile nuclear power plant. Radiation containment becomes pretty important when you've got a hundred sailors working right next to plutonium. These days, though, I see a lot more breakdowns in process than in technology. People cutting corners, unnecessary competition, that kind of thing."

"The job's not dull, is it?"

"We get our share of craziness. Last month, we had a guy out at Idaho National Lab who launched a few hundred weather balloons all at once. The winds carried them south to Salt Lake City and it turned out the balloons were underinflated, so they all started coming down. People panicked and flooded 911 with calls. Social media went crazy—the balloons were filled with neurotoxins, they said. A terrorist attack."

Daniel shook his head at the thought. "We helped him adjust his test protocols."

"Funny. Why do people always jump to conspiracy theories?"

Daniel started to make a political comment, but stopped. He smiled. "Some questions are probably best left unanswered. The world is a mysterious place."

Their plane climbed through the lower clouds over northern Virginia. Daniel glanced out the window to a sea of cotton puffs, stretching to the horizon. Farther above, a few streaks of white with gracefully curving tips contrasted against the dark blue. Tiny tendrils of frost formed around the edges of the window and produced an intricate microscopic pattern. If the world was mysterious, it was beautiful too.

"I suppose we're high enough that I can fire up my laptop," Daniel said. "Without a flight attendant, there's no way to know when we've passed through ten thousand feet."

Marie glanced out the window. "We have. But that's an old commercial flight rule. Even if it was still effective, it doesn't apply to military flights."

"They trained you on FAA regulations at NASA?"

Marie suppressed a laugh. "Not at NASA, no. But I'm a pilot."

Daniel's eyes widened. He had underestimated her, and he knew why—quantum physics. Lack of knowledge in one area was never a good indicator of broader accomplishments. "I'm impressed. NASA operations, fluent in Russian *and* you fly planes."

She nodded in acknowledgment. "You should taste my cooking."

"Good?"

"Terrible."

Daniel smiled. He switched the laptop on and connected to the onboard Wi-Fi. "We've got about an hour before we land. I don't see an email from Bradley yet. While we're waiting, can I fill in the physics holes for you?"

"I'd appreciate that. Dr. Bradley's briefing certainly got my attention. I'm used to talking about extraordinary things; we do it at NASA all the time. But particles that allow for extra dimensions of space? That just doesn't even seem of this world."

"Good old-fashioned quantum physics," Daniel responded. "The complexity of a galaxy on the head of a pin, with special rules that only apply at scales of the ultra-small. I completely agree, it doesn't seem of this world. I've been involved in this stuff several times in my career, and I'm still not sure I understand it. Not really. But I'll tell you what I know, and we'll both learn more when we get to Fermilab."

He tapped a few keys and then stopped and looked up. "I'm glad that Ibarra included you. We're going to need your experience once we dig into this, and I'm sure NASA will be well represented."

Marie settled into the comfortable leather seat like she was ready to pour a cup of coffee and read the Sunday paper.

Daniel had explained it before, and he knew where to start. "Quantum physics automatically sounds like a difficult subject, right? Like *rocket science*. It's one of those topics that makes people roll their eyes." So far, she wasn't rolling her eyes.

"The good news is that it's a lot easier to grasp today than twenty or thirty years ago. Our knowledge has increased dramatically since Max Planck and Albert Einstein proposed the quantum model back in the early 1900s. Today, the whole thing can be summarized in one diagram. I'll show you."

Daniel located a file and turned his computer toward Marie.

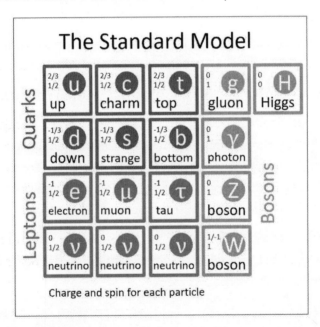

The Standard Model

Charge and spin for each particle

"That's it, the Standard Model. In this single diagram, you're looking at the underlying structure of our universe. It's a parts list, but it's also an architectural drawing. Everything you've ever touched or felt is here. The air you breathe, the ground you stand on, the sunlight that pours down, the stars in the night sky. All in those seventeen boxes. The story of our universe on a single page."

"You have a passion for this part of science." She held her hand over her heart.

"I have a passion for all discoveries." He paused. "If an alien landed next door and asked me, 'Does your species know anything? Or should I skip Earth and keep looking?' I would argue that humans are worthy. And I would point to two documents as proof. The Periodic Table of the Elements, and this diagram, the Standard Model. Together they demonstrate that humans have figured out what our universe is made of and that we understand its structure, its true nature. If the universe is intentional, the Standard Model is the artist's signature."

"A man with passion and a poet," she said.

"It's easy to be poetic. There's an elegance in this model. A symmetry of parts. We didn't make it that way, we simply discovered it."

"So, did God make it that way?" she asked with sincerity.

Daniel thought for a second and then provided his standard response. "When we discover evidence of intentional design, evidence for a creator, I'll consider it. Until then, I'll appreciate the elegance I see in the world as a natural consequence of being alive. Humans appreciate the beauty of the universe because we are part of it."

Marie nodded. "I like your answer. It's fair. I've heard of the Standard Model, but truthfully, I've never seen it. I guess I never had any need. So, what do the boxes represent?"

"Well, the six purple boxes at the top are quarks. These are the building blocks of matter, the Legos as Bradley described. When put together in the right combination, quarks make protons or neutrons. Quarks vary in size, electrical charge, and what they call 'spin.' These characteristics define the six types, or flavors, of the particle. As they were discovered, they were given odd names like *up*, *down*, *charm* and *strange*. Don't ask me who named them, I really don't know. But I can tell you that many of these quarks were discovered at Fermilab."

"Then we're heading to a pretty important place."

"We are." Daniel looked up at Marie and saw an adult who enjoyed learning. It was a good sign. He had encountered the opposite far too many times. Adults who had decided that high school or college was enough and gave their brain permission to be lazy for the rest of their lives. He continued with a renewed enthusiasm.

"The six green boxes at the bottom are also particles, the leptons, and they also have flavors. Six quarks and six leptons, grouped in four sets of three. It's the symmetry I mentioned. One of these lepton flavors is known to every school kid—the ordinary electron, which, of course, gives us electricity. Next to it on the chart is the electron neutrino, with its cousins, the muon and tau neutrinos. And while electrons are easy to detect because they have an electrical charge, neutrinos are almost impossible to detect because they have no charge at all. I'll tell you more about neutrinos in a minute."

"I've heard of these particles too, but it's interesting to see them organized in a diagram like this. And they're all real, right? Not just someone's speculation?"

Daniel laughed. "Real-world stuff. Each particle, each box on this diagram is a real and unique fragment of what the universe is made of. The people who discovered these particles can show you visible traces of them, lines shooting across a detector plate, that for a tiny fraction of a second represented that specific particle in all its glory."

"I bet they have photos hanging on the walls at Fermilab," Marie offered.

"You're probably right. Actually, I've never been there, so this will be new for both of us."

He pointed again to the diagram. "Finally, the orange boxes on the right are bosons, each representing a force, like the strong nuclear force that holds quarks together. The best-known boson is the photon. It carries the electromagnetic force, or light. And, of course, there's the famous Higgs boson. It's a bit different."

He looked up at Marie. "Remember the Force from Star Wars? The Higgs field is like the Force. It exists everywhere, and it's still pretty mysterious. It gives all the other particles their mass—at least, that's what physicists think it does. Like I warned, this stuff gets weird."

"Weird, maybe, but I like it," she said. "I like the symmetry and the simplicity. The diagram is very... inspiring."

"Well said," Daniel agreed. "It's not quite complete, though. It's missing gravity. Einstein described gravity as nothing more than a curvature of space, like a bowling ball on a mattress. He also theorized that massive collisions would produce gravity waves, like dropping a rock in a swimming pool. In 2016—"

"And now you're in my territory," Marie interrupted. "In 2016, scientists working in the LIGO project detected the first gravitational wave from two black holes colliding. It proved that gravitational waves exist."

"Precisely," Daniel said. "That was big news. It might not be long before we can add a new boson, the graviton, to this model."

"Quite impressive, Dr. Rice." Marie looked up at him, smiling. "You'd make a good instructor."

"Thanks. A fifth-grade classroom, that's where I'd end up."

"I was thinking more along the lines of college. Why fifth grade?"

"For me, it couldn't be any other age. Kids at that age are still inquisitive, not yet embarrassed to be smart, and are excited to learn. They latch on to science quickly. It's the right age to inspire them. Besides, I remember fifth-grade science class well. We grew pea plants and carefully studied their color and size variations to learn about genetics."

"That's too cool!" Marie exclaimed. "And this one class sparked your lifelong interest in science? You should find that teacher and tell her what a great job she did."

"I did. Mrs. Andrews, Emerson Elementary in Kirkland, Washington. I looked her up a few years ago. She was still teaching, so I dropped in on her class and thanked her personally." Daniel smiled, the memory still fresh.

"That's a good story, very sweet."

She put her hands together and turned the conversation once more. "But before my chance to catch up disappears, you said you were going to tell me about neutrinos, and I'm pretty sure Fermilab is involved."

Daniel was impressed; she had certainly been paying attention. "You're right, I did. Okay... neutrinos are probably the least understood part of the Standard Model. We *do* know that neutrinos are naturally produced... by the sun. They're flooding this airplane right now in massive numbers. They pass right through the atmosphere, this plane, our bodies, and the whole Earth without affecting much of anything. They seem to be completely harmless, some say useless, because no one knows why they exist. They don't do anything."

"That's interesting the way you express it," she said. "That they're useless. They take up three boxes on the diagram. Why would the universe have a particle that doesn't do anything?"

"Good question, and honestly, I don't have an answer." He paused for a moment. "I guess a physicist would say that neutrinos are a byproduct of decay. But that doesn't tell you much. We don't know much about them because they're so hard to detect. Enrico Fermi gave them their name way back in the 1930s, but they weren't actually discovered

50

until the 1960s, and the tau neutrino not until 2000. At Fermilab, by the way."

"Where else?"

Daniel noticed a flashing icon on his computer. "Hang on... it's an email from Bradley. He says there's no further contact with Soyuz. And I'm not sure what AMOS is, but he says they also have negative contact."

"AMOS is an Air Force tracking facility in Maui," Marie explained. "They use a telescope to scan an orbital vector. They can visually identify spacecraft from the ground."

"So, if Soyuz is still in orbit, Roscosmos and NASA can't find them."

Marie's lips tightened. "It's super weird that we're not spotting them. The transmissions indicate the capsule is still in orbit. Our ground controllers are good. It's not likely they would miss something."

Daniel heard her speak, but his real focus was directed back at the computer. "Bradley also sent an attachment. Background on the Diastasi program. There's a lot here, but this first part is interesting. The program isn't just Fermilab people. They also use a corporate partner, a company called Stetler."

*A corporation involved in a government science program.* He'd seen it before; the organizational complications, the higher personnel turnover, the control issues.

He looked out the window as the jet banked to the left. "At the very least, the scope of our investigation just doubled."

# 9  Illusions

Sergei hit the control panel with his fist, hard enough to draw blood from a knuckle.

"*Eto piz dets!*" he yelled. The Russian expletive caught the attention of his companions, even the American. After several hours of continuous transmission, they had waited patiently for any response. There had been none.

"It's Earth," Jeremy said. "It has to be."

Over time, their view out the window had changed. The wall of stars was still there, still separated from them. But they had learned that it could be *penetrated*. Twice now, they had passed directly through it and found yet more darkness on the other side. The wall was now behind them, still filled with a field of stars and the same thin blue ellipse.

Stranger still, as they rounded the other side, the blue ellipse increased in width, taking the shape of a disc. It was like looking at a Frisbee edge on, its disc shape revealed only when tilted. As the thin ellipse transformed into a disc, they could make out swirls of clouds and recognize landforms. The northern tip of Queensland, the sweep of Cape Cod, the Kamchatka Peninsula. Without a doubt, the familiar ground of Earth, but only as imagined in a nightmare.

Beyond its impossible shape, there was also the ubiquitous glow. It emanated from the land but also from the ocean, even the clouds. A deep orange-red that confused all the other colors of the Earth.

The discrepancy between his mind's view of what should be and the unreasonable reality out the window was making Sergei's head throb. "If this is Earth, where the hell is everyone?"

Anton took his turn looking out the window. "It's Earth. Even if our view has changed. Self-tests confirm our equipment is fine. We are transmitting, there is no question. The receivers are working, there is simply nothing to receive. No voice, no GPS, not even a carrier wave."

Sergei took a deep breath. It would do no good to allow frustrations to take over. "Our eyes tell us we are still in orbit. But the computer can't produce orbital vectors because there is no data. Our radios are operational, but we cannot raise anyone. Why?"

"They can't transmit?" Jeremy suggested.

Anton waved an arm at the window. "Something has happened down there and they're all dead."

"Then why no communication with GPS satellites? Or from ISS? More likely, something has happened to us, to Soyuz. But what?"

Each man sat motionless in his seat, offering no answers. After several minutes, Jeremy broke the silence.

"We have to keep trying. Alternate frequencies. Emergency and descent. Go to short-wave frequencies. We have to raise someone."

Sergei shrugged. "What choice do we have?" The pointless conversation was only consuming valuable oxygen, and a descent module separated from its service tanks had none to spare. He pressed his transmit button once more.

"*Moskva, Sayuz. Kak pashyevayesh... Moskva, Sayuz. Pozhaluysta otvet'te...* Hello, any station, please respond."

~~~~~~~~~~~~~~~~~~~~~~~~

From high above, Kwajalein Atoll is a narrow loop of sand lost in a vast expanse of ocean. The turquoise lagoon in its interior occasionally connects with the exterior blue, separating the atoll into a chain of individual islands, each dotted with palm trees, a few houses, roads and people.

Most of Kwajalein's inhabitants are crowded onto one sliver, Ebeye Island. The much larger main island belongs entirely to the United States Army. Its location in the middle of the Pacific is ideal for a variety of military purposes. During World War II, Kwajalein was bombed extensively, and rusting hulks of Japanese ships remain in the shallow waters. In the 1950s, the nearby atolls of Bikini and Enewetak were obliterated by hydrogen bomb explosions.

Modern Kwajalein is home to the Ronald Reagan Ballistic Missile Defense Site, a facility that launches EKVs, or exoatmospheric kill vehicles, that can destroy a nuclear weapon in space before it reaches its target. In theory, a missile launched from North Korea toward Hawaii would result in nothing more than a temporary flash in the sky.

Down on the ground, among the palm trees, the white-sand beach, the tropical sunset, the large white radar domes, the military aircraft, and the occasional EKV test launch, Master Sergeant Dino Vasquez hurried along the concrete path, head down and eyes fixed on a printout he clasped in his hands.

Without looking up, he pushed open the door to Space Operations, a building near the base of a hexagonal-paneled radar dome. His pace quickened across the old linoleum floor and past the 1960s-era metal desks. A banner on the wall displayed a picture of a satellite and the inscription, *Orbital Debris Tracking, Protecting Our Investments in Space*. Above one of the desks was a movie poster, Sandra Bullock floating in her underwear, the International Space Station being shredded by orbital debris behind her.

At this hour of the evening, there were only a few people still working in the Orbital Debris Program office. Most had already left for dinner at the mess hall or for a sunset beer at Franky's On The Beach. Vasquez headed for the only enclosed office in the building.

He stopped at a desk where a woman in civilian clothes typed at her computer. "Is the duty officer in?"

"Yeah. Major Katz. But he's leaving pretty soon. I wouldn't delay happy hour if I were you."

Vasquez knocked on the door and opened it without waiting for an answer. "Major, are you available?"

The man at the desk lifted his head. "Yes, Vasquez, just barely. What do you need?"

"Sir, I need your help. I think we need to alert JSC. I just got the latest debris trajectory report, and we're missing some objects."

"Missing? That's fantastic, Vasquez. Always good to be missing space debris. Good job, go get some dinner."

"No, sir, you don't understand. It includes some big stuff, not your ordinary bolt or astronaut's glove."

The major lowered his head again. "Outstanding, Vasquez. Great to hear. One more piece of junk that burned up in the atmosphere. Mark it in your shift log and we're done for the night."

Vasquez shifted his weight nervously. "No, sir, the report shows fourteen T3-sized objects that were on last week's report but are not showing up. Everything else is still on the report, more than five thousand tracked objects. But fourteen are missing. One is a decommissioned satellite, another a booster O-ring, and another is half of a solar panel. Big stuff, and they were all in stable NEO orbits. None were due to reenter for years."

The major set down his pen, looked up once more and stared at Vasquez as though he were an invading army.

"Well, Vasquez, that doesn't make much sense, does it? Your computer isn't working. I'd suggest you contact MIT Lincoln and let them know you want to compare datasets."

"I already did, sir. Talked to their operator and their duty officer. They ran the report and couldn't make any sense out it either. We're talking about big pieces of metal. Stuff that has been on every tracking report for the past five years. Thousands of orbits. And now they're just gone."

The major leaned forward in his chair and rested his elbows on the desk. "Vasquez, you're doing a fine job. I'm happy that you're so dedicated to the program. Very responsible. But what you're saying doesn't make any sense. Large objects in orbit, in stable orbits, don't just disappear."

Vasquez didn't flinch. "Well, these did."

~~~~~~~~~~~~~~~~~~~~~~~~

Nala Pasquier closed the blinds on her office window. With only the grounds of Fermilab on the other side, it didn't increase privacy, but it made her feel better. She returned to her desk and studied the computer screen. Displayed was a list of background processes, and she read each one. Some were clearly Windows services, a few provided support to her desktop apps, but many names were indecipherable and would need to be researched to discover their purpose.

"Shit," she muttered under her breath. "It's got to be here somewhere."

She opened an incognito browser tab and typed furiously. She mouthed more expletives as she worked and paused only to take another sip from the mug of tea on her desk. Arriving at the end of the list, she pushed the keyboard away, leaned back in her chair and stared at the ceiling.

"Who am I kidding?" she whispered, her eyes burning a hole in the ceiling tile. "No matter what I do, they're always watching." After a few seconds, her trance broke and she consciously scanned the ceiling, looking once again for the hidden security camera that she had never found.

She grabbed her phone and started an app. A window automatically popped up on the computer display over on her desk. The message on the computer was one that no one else would see, she hoped.

*Authorization required for download to external devices. Enter password.*

She typed. Progress bars displayed on both the computer and her phone.

"At least I'll have my own copy." She sent a nervous glance through the narrow window adjacent to her office door. The hallway was still empty. "Even if it is illegal."

# 10  Science

Marie watched out the car window as Illinois freeways and business parks gave way to suburbs and finally to cornfields. Daniel drove while the GPS provided navigation. He hadn't spoken more than a few words since they had left the airport. He gazed ahead, apparently lost in thought. Given the newness of their partnership, she thought it better not to interrupt.

In the distance, a tall A-shaped building rose above the trees just as they passed a sign directing visitors to Fermi National Laboratory. They passed under a large sculpture of steel arches and stopped at the curb in front of Wilson Hall. It looked more like two buildings, each leaning into the other. A glass atrium separated them, its edges curving hyperbolically toward the sky.

Marie looked up as they entered the cathedral-like interior. For people who studied the world of the very small, they certainly worked in a space that was very large. The opposing walls soared two hundred feet to a skylight at the top. If the intent was to impress, the architecture had certainly succeeded.

They stopped at the reception desk, signed in, and picked up visitor badges. A group of schoolchildren gathered nearby, their teacher herding them into as tight a circle as she could manage. Two boys with higher energy chased each other around the group like orbiting electrons.

Marie leaned toward Daniel. "Feels more like a public playground than a physics laboratory."

Daniel glanced at the kids as if he hadn't noticed, and smiled. A minute later, a young man approached the desk. "Welcome to Fermilab. I'm Josh, an intern in Dr. Park's team. Shall we go up?"

The elevator traversed the building's slanted exterior and deposited them on the fifteenth floor. They stepped out to a commanding view. A complex of buildings and parking lots transitioned to green prairie grass that stretched for several miles around the central core.

Superimposed on the land were three distinct rings. The smallest was just beyond the parking lot. In the distance was a larger ring, at least the size of horse racetrack. The third was so large it disappeared into the distant trees, its gentle curve only hinting at its full size. Each ring was marked by a mix of concrete paths, water ditches, electrical lines and other equipment, but the sum of the disparate features was indisputably circular.

"Beautiful," Marie mouthed.

"Yeah, it's a great view of the facility," Josh agreed. He pointed almost straight down. "That smaller circle is the Booster. The protons do about twenty thousand laps to build speed. The larger ring is the Main Injector, which accelerates them just under the speed of light." He smiled with pride. "It makes a vibration that you can feel in your bones. Sometimes I sit in the Main Injector while I'm eating my lunch."

He pointed to the broad curve of the largest circle. "The big one is the Tevatron. For twenty-eight years, it was the largest accelerator in the world. But it's no longer in use. Congress ended funding in 2011." The intern's words were tainted with disappointment, and Marie wanted to give him a sympathetic pat on the shoulder. There's nothing like having an enormous empty shell as a daily reminder of lost opportunity.

They continued down the hallway and stopped at the largest office on the floor. A gray-haired Asian man, casually dressed in a pullover sweater and wearing glasses, looked up from his work. He pushed away from his chair, his hand outstretched.

"Dr. Rice, Ms. Kendrick, so glad to meet you. You arrived very quickly. I was on the phone with Dr. Bradley less than one hour ago."

Marie recalled the briefing materials that Bradley had provided. Jae-ho Park was a Korean immigrant who had come to America as a college student. He was a key player on the teams that had discovered the bottom quark in 1977 and the top quark in 1995. Over the years, his renown had morphed to exalted status, and many considered him the father of experimental particle physics. Some of the staff called him Captain Quark, a play on his name and pop culture that Marie found irresistible.

Marie shook his hand, and Daniel did as well, far more vigorously. "Dr. Park, it's an honor," he said. "A pioneer in your field."

"Please, Dr. Rice. There is no need." Park seemed to be the personification of both humility and serenity, his Asian roots firmly shaping his personality. "Dr. Bradley explained to me the purpose of your visit. He also shared information about the most unfortunate accident with the Russian spacecraft."

He faced Daniel and Marie alternately as he spoke. "I spent much time on the phone with Dr. Bradley. I hear his concern, I understand it. But I'm afraid that your trip is wasted time."

Daniel lowered his eyebrows in doubt. "Wasted? Why?"

"There is simply no connection between the work we do at Fermilab and the disappearance of that spacecraft. There cannot be. We do amazing things here, which I will be happy to show to you, but our work is restricted to the boundaries of this facility—in fact, within just a few meters of the Diastasi test bench. We have no capacity to affect an object that is thousands of kilometers away."

Daniel shifted his stance. He seemed to be ready to say something, but only half-opened his mouth. His expression was remarkably the same as just hours before as they'd sat in Bradley's office and heard about the quantum dimensions of string theory. It was a look of skepticism, but carefully tempered by etiquette. Marie was beginning to recognize her new partner's style.

Daniel finally spoke. "I'm relieved to hear that, Dr. Park, and others will be as well." His body language showed strength, and his words seemed careful but compelling. "I'm sure you'll understand that we've been asked by the president's advisors to investigate and determine if there is any correlation. To do that, we'll need to review the Diastasi program, to whatever depth is required."

Park stretched his arms wide as if opening a kimono, or in his case, maybe a hanbok. "By all means, you are welcome to see what we do. You will find it quite incredible." He waved a hand in the air. "Please, do not mistake my dismissal as noncooperation. I am personally concerned for these astronauts. I was relieved to hear that transmissions from them were received, and I agree their situation sounds very unusual. But... I must repeat that we could not have affected this spacecraft."

Daniel gave a courtesy nod, but his skeptical expression remained. Park started down the hallway and motioned to them. "Please, come with me. I will show you myself. Let me explain our amazing capabilities, but also our system limitations."

They followed down the hallway and back to the elevator. Park tapped his badge to the elevator security pad, and they dropped to a basement level, several floors below the lobby. They stepped out into a concrete passageway lined with dozens of multicolored pipes, bundles of wires and electrical panels. The sight was entirely different from the public-facing Wilson Hall.

They turned a corner to a long concrete corridor with no apparent end. Enormous rectangles of layered metal plates stood bolted to the wall every few feet and disappeared down the corridor. A large pipe pierced the center of each rectangle, like an arrow puncturing a series of targets. Jumbles of wires and cables were attached to the walls and ceiling. If this was a planned scientific system, it was hard to distinguish from chaos.

"This is the linear accelerator, where it all starts," Park explained. "We insert source protons into the central tube, and the magnets you see along the wall accelerate them down this corridor. The proton beam exits at high speed and enters two additional accelerators, the Booster and the Main Injector. Once fully accelerated, the beam is directed to our neutrino test bench, which is where things get really interesting." He grinned and waved them forward.

They climbed stairs and walked down a smaller concrete passageway, sterile in comparison, with no equipment or wires. At the end was a doorway labeled *NuMI / NOvA* and beyond it a large workshop where the chaos of pipes and wires reappeared. Several pipes passed overhead, each labeled with something about their purpose, *150 GeV M'* or *8 GeV Recycler*, and some with more understandable words like *Waste Water* and *Nitrogen*.

They stopped in front of an elaborate machine, taller than a person and at least twenty feet long. It was a strange composition of hundreds of odd-looking parts, each performing some unknown function. Silver tubes connected at various points around its outside and one end opened in a curving shape like the inside of a trombone.

Marie laughed to herself. *A machine built by a mad scientist*, she thought. The only thing missing was Dr. Frankenstein waving his arms wildly and screaming into the sky, just as a lightning bolt split the air.

A set of parallel aluminum plates curved around its central opening. It looked like they might carry high-voltage electricity. She imagined Dr. Frankenstein throwing an old-fashioned switch on the wall, showering the opening with sparks. Or maybe not.

"This is the NuMI horn," Park explained. "It stands for 'neutrinos at the Main Injector.' We have many experiments that require high-energy neutrinos, and this is where they start. The proton beam I described to you earlier hits a graphite target—it looks like a stack of coins. The protons collide with the graphite atoms and tear them apart, like a billion tiny explosions. Out the other side comes a stream of neutrinos, also moving nearly the speed of light. We use the NuMI horn to focus the beam to the width of a pencil and send it on its way to the detectors."

Apparently the NuMI horn didn't require lightning to operate.

"We have two neutrino detectors, both very large. Down the hall is the three-hundred-ton detector, filled with a liquid scintillator—like water. We have a much larger detector, fourteen thousand tons, located in Ash River, Minnesota."

Marie glanced at Daniel wide-eyed, and Park noticed their surprise. "Yes, Minnesota. It is hard to imagine, but the neutrino beam travels from here to Minnesota in three milliseconds, passing through the Earth as if it were not even there."

"That's amazing," Marie said. "I just heard a similar description from Dr. Rice on the flight here. Apparently, neutrinos don't stop for anything."

"They don't even slow down," said Park. "Their interaction with solid rock is negligible. They have no electrical charge and almost no mass. The Earth is nearly transparent to them."

Park stepped over to a pipe exiting the elaborate machine. "So, you might ask how we can detect a particle that passes through everything. And the answer is, we detect them because we produce so many of them. If you send a trillion neutrinos into your detectors, occasionally one of them will hit an oxygen or hydrogen nucleus in a head-on collision. That is when we catch them. We see the results of that collision."

"And what do you do when you catch them?" Daniel asked.

"We find out what flavor they are. A neutrino oscillates naturally between its three flavors. It may start out as a tau neutrino, but by the time it arrives in Minnesota, it may have changed to an electron neutrino. Very strange, yes. One thing becomes another, like an apple becoming an orange while you weren't looking."

Daniel bent down and peered into the central opening of the NuMI horn. Marie hoped nothing was operating, or would start. The thought of a beam of high-speed particles blasting through a person's head was alarming. She touched his shoulder and pulled him back. "Don't do that!" Daniel seemed unconcerned.

Park rested a hand on the monstrous machine. "And now I'll tell you my secret." Daniel moved closer, and Marie wondered if the investigation was about to come to a grand conclusion.

"Neutrino oscillation has been a joy to study, but quite fascinating to control."

*That's it?* she thought. *You have control?* She wondered how anyone could expect to operate an advanced lab without control.

"Come with me." Park waved them forward and talked as they walked. "Like all quantum particles, neutrinos behave sometimes as a particle and sometimes as a wave. In the early twentieth century, physicists discovered that we can control this behavior. The simple act of observing a quantum wave collapses it to a particle. A very strange discovery that is not completely understood even today."

"The famous double-slit experiment," Daniel remarked.

"Indeed. In the past few years we have learned to control neutrino oscillation, to synchronize a trillion neutrinos into a coherent beam. It is very much like a laser, coherent light."

Daniel walked side by side with Park. "So, what do you do with a coherent beam of neutrinos?"

"As you shall see, Dr. Rice, amazing things."

Marie trailed behind. Park was certainly hinting that drama was around the corner. She was impressed with the equipment, but unclear about its purpose. *A neutrino laser? Are they making a weapon? How can this relate to Soyuz?*

They stopped at a closed door with a red sign. *Diastasi: Authorized Personnel Only*. Park touched his badge, and the door clicked open. "Diastasi," he said. "It is a Greek word. It means dimensions."

They entered a workshop with yet more pipes and wire bundles, but in this room, the pipes focused toward a large clear plexiglass box mounted on the far wall. Beneath the box, a young man with a thick beard looked up from his computer.

"Good morning, Thomas," Park said. "Could we power up for a test? I wish to show Dr. Rice and Ms. Kendrick what we can do."

"A demonstration!" remarked Thomas. "We can do that. Did our guests take the blue pill or the red pill?"

"Very funny." Marie laughed. She shook his hand and hoped she wasn't about to wake up to find that life was just a simulation. Given the explanation so far, exposing another side of reality seemed within the realm of possibility.

Park stood in the center of the small room and looked around. "In this lab, we change the limits of space. I do not mean space like *outer space*. I mean the physical, three-dimensional space that exists everywhere. You are familiar with string theory?"

Daniel nodded. "Mostly. Before we arrived, Marie and I talked about one of its more unusual side effects, that of extra dimensions of space."

"Quite correct," responded Park. "String theory describes ten dimensions of space, three at the macro level where we exist and seven at the quantum level where strings exist. These extra dimensions are just as real as the three dimensions that we perceive, but are much too small to see or feel. This presents a logical challenge—how do we imagine a dimension that we cannot see?"

Park stepped over to a shelf and picked up what looked like a plastic toy, cube-shaped, blue and translucent, with another cube visible inside it. "This plastic model is our best effort to represent a hypercube, or tesseract. It is a four-dimensional object, but within our three-dimensional world, you can only see part of it."

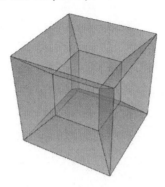

He turned the blue plastic cube in his hand, making the interior surfaces visible. "What I hold is just a shadow of its reality. If viewed from four-dimensional space, it is eight cubes, each perpendicular to the other. The leap in logic is how to imagine a cube being perpendicular to another cube."

Daniel responded, "I recall an animation on the Internet showing a tesseract, rotating to show how it looks in four dimensions."

"I have seen the animations as well," said Park. "I find them confusing, no better than this model." He held the blue cube up to his eye. "But what if we could change our viewpoint? What if we could expand a fourth dimension of space from its normal quantum size to several meters, a size that is much more relevant to us? What would we see?"

Marie was unclear whether this was a trick question. Thomas was smiling as though he knew the punch line that was coming.

"Yes, Dr. Rice, Ms. Kendrick. I propose that we move our viewpoint to a position outside our normal 3-D space. Would you like to see? Certainly, you must be curious?" Daniel's eyes darted around the room and then back to the cube. He certainly looked curious. Marie was too, but also wary.

Park replaced the cube on the shelf and stepped over to Marie. "Our demonstration will need your assistance. Ms. Kendrick, would you be our volunteer?"

Becoming a guinea pig for the mad scientist wasn't an appealing proposition. At this point, taking the red pill seemed to be where they were heading.

"Ms. Kendrick, I assure you that there is no danger and nothing for you to do. We will simply be taking a photograph of you. Live video, actually, with this web camera." Park picked up a small spherical camera mounted on a plastic stand. It reminded her of the GoPro camera she saw skateboarders use.

Not waiting for her answer, Park continued. Marie was the selected volunteer, whether she liked it or not. "This is an ordinary webcam. It transmits to the computer at Thomas's desk via Wi-Fi in this room. I'll turn it on." He flipped a switch on the base, and a few seconds later, a video window popped up on Thomas's computer. As Park pointed the camera at Marie, the view on Thomas's computer was that of the room, with Marie standing in the foreground.

Park smiled and held the webcam high. "We will now send this camera on an adventure. First, I will place it in our target space." He reached up, opened the top of the clear plexiglass box that was attached to the wall, and set the camera inside. The camera was now at eye level, pointing out through the side of the box. Its video feed still showed Marie standing in the middle of the room.

She glanced at Daniel, who was staring intently at the camera in the box and examining the setup in detail.

"We will now flood the target space with neutrinos whose oscillations are aligned along the direction of the pipe. We will then change their alignment so that they oscillate into a fourth dimension, a quantum dimension."

He turned to face them and used his right hand to designate another dimension, *out there somewhere.* "You must understand that for a neutrino to oscillate in another dimension is quite routine. To a neutrino, those extra dimensions are just as real as three dimensions are to us. In fact, it is precisely because neutrinos exist in extra dimensions that they have so little interaction with the matter we see around us. They spend a good portion of their time traveling in dimensions where matter simply does not exist."

Park paused and pointed to the box. "When we realign the oscillation, the contents of that box will be extended into a fourth dimension. The camera, the air, the space itself. The camera will still be within reach, but in a direction that you and I cannot see. From the camera's perspective, it will still be pointing back toward our three-dimensional space, yet will be outside of it."

Marie saw the smile growing on Daniel's face. He was definitely on board. Could this be real? Could they really expand space into an alternate dimension? Marie felt a nervousness within, like the anticipation of the first plunge on a roller coaster. They had crossed the boundary into the world of crazy.

"Do we have power now, Thomas?" asked Park.

"Clear to go," he answered. "The beam is at 137 GeV. Protons are moving nice and fast."

For the first time, Marie noticed a slight background hum. Maybe it had always been there, she wasn't sure. But she imagined it represented the sound of billions of protons rounding the curve of the Main Injector at nearly the speed of light. Thomas would simply open a magnetic doorway, and an immense amount of energy would suddenly blast through one of the overhead pipes and into this room. Even if the beam was only the width of a pencil, it was more than unsettling. Like standing behind a jet with the pilot about to press the start engines button.

"Please watch the camera," said Park, and he nodded to Thomas, who pressed a key on his keyboard.

Almost immediately, the background hum became a loud buzz that filled the room. The floor began to vibrate. If the mad scientist could be believed, trillions of neutrinos were moving at light speed, their oscillations in lockstep.

All eyes were on the plexiglass box. In a blink, a bright blue flash was followed by a loud pop, like a balloon bursting. Marie jumped at the pop and shielded her eyes from the flash in a natural reflex. As she adjusted from the brightness, she looked up.

The box was empty.

The camera had disappeared completely, a magic act straight from Las Vegas.

She gasped. "Oh my God." She looked at Daniel with a nervous laugh. Daniel stepped closer to the plexiglass box, searching. No trap doors, no mirrors. The camera had really disappeared. Park seemed perfectly calm, as if physical objects disappeared in laboratories every day. And in this lab, maybe they did.

"Now, please bring your attention to Thomas's computer. The camera is still operating, still transmitting through the Wi-Fi, but it is no longer in our three-dimensional space. It is about two meters away along a fourth dimension and been rotated slightly so that it continues to point at Ms. Kendrick."

Marie looked closely at the computer screen. The live video feed was still there, but the view didn't look the same. The room was still in view, and Marie saw herself in the foreground, but oddly different.

She stepped closer and the view became clearer and more frightening. Beyond her external clothing and skin, she could see her internal organs. It was as if an x-ray or MRI had been overlaid on her external body. She could see the folds of her brain within her skull. She

69

could see the large blood vessels and vertebrae in her neck, the bones in her shoulders.

"This is insane," she whispered, staring at the computer screen. "Stand beside me, Daniel."

Daniel moved into view. No longer just a man standing in a room, the image revealed everything an x-ray would, and more. His heart pumped inside his chest. His lungs expanded with each breath. The coins in his pants pocket were plainly visible, as were even the remains of the scone he'd had for breakfast in his stomach.

"It reveals everything—too much, in fact," said Marie holding her hands over her breasts, which did nothing to hide them from view. Every layer of clothing, skin, bones and organs were equally visible with complete clarity. She even noticed she could see right through herself and make out objects in the room behind her.

Daniel turned to Park, a large smile extending across his face. He shook his head as he struggled to find the words. "I've got at least a million questions for you."

# 11 Tesseract

Daniel put a hand on the empty plexiglass box, his face within inches of its surface. The room was still filled with the buzzing sound, as if the air itself was as agitated as he felt. His thoughts veered from one question to the next, his finger nervously tapping on the clear plastic while his natural skepticism was diluted by a strong dose of curiosity.

He turned to Park for answers. "How is this possible? A webcam that's outside our three-dimensional space, but is somehow still connected to Wi-Fi?"

"I understand your question, but there is no mystery," replied Park. "Electromagnetic waves require no medium to propagate—the Michelson-Morley experiments proved that long ago. Wi-Fi, like any electromagnetic wave, travels just as easily in a fourth dimension. When we positioned the webcam, we simply pointed it in the right direction, back toward 3-D space."

Daniel stood silent, absorbing this revelation. It made sense... sort of. But there was much more that was troubling. "So, the obvious question. Can you bring the webcam back?"

"Yes, of course!" Park motioned to the box. "In fact, we are consuming energy to hold it in its current *kata* offset. Once we remove the energy source, the camera will simply fall back to Kata Zero."

"Which means?" Marie asked.

Park pulled out a chair, sat and crossed his legs. For a man explaining the bizarre he looked remarkably comfortable.

"Each dimension of space has words to describe its directions. We say left, right, forward, backward, up and down. For a fourth dimension, we need new words, and for many years scientists have used *ana* and *kata* to describe these directions. They are Greek words that mean *up* and *down*. In this case, we have expanded in the *kata* direction by two meters." He spread his arms wide.

"So, you may ask, where did this space come from?" Park whispered the answer dramatically. "Nowhere!" He leaned back in his chair, smiling. "Minutes ago, this dimension was quantum-sized. Real, but far too small to place a camera in it. Now this same space is two meters wide, and we are holding it in place like a clown blowing up a balloon. At this point, we have two choices. If we simply withdraw the neutrino beam, the camera, along with the space itself, will fall back to Kata Zero, like releasing the air from the balloon. But if needed, we can temporarily lock this space by twisting the neutrino oscillation wave before reducing power—as if the clown has tied the end of the balloon. In either case, we can bring the camera back whenever we wish."

As Park talked, Daniel correlated each word with his objective. If Soyuz was in the same predicament, then just like the camera, it could be returned. But how? He probed further. "You say the camera would fall back to Kata Zero. Does that mean that gravity applies to a fourth dimension?"

"Yes," Park said. "Gravity warps space itself, and the *kata* direction is no different. We have measured, and the force of gravity still varies by the inverse square of distance. When Isaac Newton first proposed this relationship, he had no idea that it would apply in unseen dimensions. Sir Isaac would be proud, don't you think?"

Park reached over Thomas's shoulder and pointed to a diagram of the Standard Model that someone had taped to the wall. "Speaking in quantum terms, we have proven that both the photon and graviton travel in any dimension. This is a new discovery, and there are several physicists in this building that will earn a Nobel Prize. Once they are allowed to publish, of course."

Marie bit her lower lip. "While Daniel is figuring out the physics, my question is far more basic." She was now positioned out of the embarrassing view of the camera, but she stretched an arm just far enough for it to show up on Thomas's computer. The bizarre image still showed her skin, the ring on her finger, but also her muscles, veins and bones.

She shook her on-screen hand. "This is crazy. Why are we seeing our internal organs?"

"Ms. Kendrick," Park answered, "please accept my apologies for not preparing you in advance. I knew you would ask. Dr. Rice's questions were easy, but this one is harder."

He stepped over to a whiteboard and picked up a marking pen. "Why do we see inside our bodies? The question is fundamental to extra dimensions of space, and it takes some thought to fully comprehend the answer. The usual way to explain it is by analogy. Have you read or heard of the book *Flatland*? A book written in the late 1800s by a man named Abbott."

Marie shook her head, but Daniel nodded. "Many years ago. It was dated, but entertaining."

"I shall borrow from Abbott's analogy as many others have before me." He drew a circle on the whiteboard. "Imagine a two-dimensional world where flat creatures live like drawings on a piece of paper. Their bodies are simply circles on the paper, with the circle representing their skin."

He drew squiggly lines inside the circle. "Inside their bodies, they have a heart and a brain and bones. Their anatomy is not important. But as three-dimensional beings living outside of their paper world, we can see not only their skin, but inside their bodies." He pointed to the squiggly lines.

"Now just apply the same logic to the fourth dimension. The camera view is outside of our 3-D space, yet it is pointed back towards us. Seeing inside our bodies is perfectly normal. The camera sees our clothes, our skin and our internal organs, all at once."

Marie folded both arms across her and stayed out of view of the camera. Her internal organs looked well protected.

Daniel scratched his head. "The fiction becomes real. Okay, let me be a skeptic for a minute. What if you're wrong? What if you're misinterpreting what you're seeing, or perhaps this is just a video hoax and we're your latest con? Prove to me that the camera is in four-dimensional space. As a famous scientist once said, 'extraordinary claims require extraordinary evidence.'"

"And we are prepared to provide that evidence. Much of it comes from our test results, which will eventually be published. Additional evidence is in the live video you have just seen, though I must admit any Hollywood movie producer could do as well." Park laughed.

He picked up the blue plastic tesseract from the shelf. "But let me show you additional visual evidence that is far more difficult to fake because it provides a view no human has ever witnessed. Once you have seen it, you will agree it is quite convincing."

*A view no human has witnessed*, Daniel thought. *What's not to like about that?* "Dr. Park, you've got my attention."

Park turned the blue plastic block in his hand. "This is not a model at all. What I hold in my hand is literally a tesseract, a four-dimensional object. We made it in this laboratory."

"But all you have are three-dimensional tools. How?"

"Very slowly," Park said with a sly smile. "You have perhaps seen a 3-D printer? They are quite fascinating to watch as they build three-dimensional plastic parts, layer upon layer. You may have suspected that is where this model came from?"

Daniel nodded, and Park continued. "Yes, we have a three-dimensional printer. We programmed it to build a tesseract, put the printer into our target box and started it. We then sent the printer in the *kata* direction, stepping one millimeter at a time. As it built the plastic model, it moved further in the *kata* direction, and the result is this, an actual tesseract."

"No... really?" Daniel looked closely at the plastic cube in Park's hand. "But how can you be holding a four-dimensional object?"

"I'm holding the portion that appears in our three dimensions. There is more that we cannot see, but is just as real. I can even feel its weight." He bounced the cube slightly in his hand. "Think of the two-dimensional creature living on a flat page. If I placed a cube into his world, he would see it as a square. He could touch it and even grab its edge and carry it with him. But he would only be holding the portion that exists in his world. It is the same for this cube. I am a three-dimensional creature holding a four-dimensional object."

"I don't believe it," Daniel said, and he meant it.

"Then see for yourself." Park carried the tesseract to the target box, and the blue plastic appeared within the view on the computer screen. Daniel stared at the computer uncomprehendingly. Park's hand was in the frame, but it no longer held a cube within a cube. The screen showed a fundamentally different object, eight cubes tightly arranged in a way that Daniel couldn't quite grasp.

As Park rotated the tesseract in his hand, the object changed. One of the eight cubes impossibly popped out of the interior and then popped back in again. Daniel strained to make sense of an image that was not of his world. He looked at the plastic in Park's hand, then at the computer view, and back again. The two objects were certainly related, but only as an object is related to its shadow. Park held the shadow. The camera revealed reality.

"You should have seen the four-dimensional Rubik's cube we made," Thomas said, laughing. "Nobody wanted to play with it. Mentally stressful!"

Daniel only barely heard Thomas. His focus was on the tesseract. The stunning view was inexplicable, and his comprehension was lagging far behind. The face of the familiar world had removed its mask, and Daniel struggled to recognize what lay beneath.

Marie's lips were drawn, an expression grounded more in doubt than in awe. "Dr. Park, with all due respect, what makes you so certain that your program wasn't responsible for the Soyuz disappearance? Based on what we've seen, any reasonable person would come to the opposite conclusion."

Daniel heard her question and surfaced to the familiar three-dimensional world. "She's right, the evidence matches. If Soyuz was pushed into another dimension, it would explain the lack of radar contact. If our eyes can't see into the fourth dimension, neither can the radar."

Park placed the tesseract back on the shelf and sat down. His head bowed for a moment, and he looked up at his visitors. "You are correct, and I agree with you. I do. Perhaps there is a link." He paused for a moment, pondering his own question. "But you have only seen the effect of dimensional displacement. Please, let me explain our limitations."

His tone became serious. "First, we cannot point the neutrino beam just anywhere. We can only affect objects within the target space." He looked up at the still-empty box on the wall.

"Second, we cannot move living things. We tested it, once. Our targeted subject did not survive. We don't yet know why, but the technology appears to damage cell structure. No one would dare to experiment on a human being. The result would be disastrous." Daniel exchanged a look with Marie. It was an important revelation.

"And third, our ability to maintain coherency is currently limited to thirty meters. Beyond that, the alignment starts to break down, and the neutrinos return to their natural state of chaos. We are working on better alignment tools and software that will give us greater range, but this will require additional time and the utmost care. With greater range also come increased risks."

Park stood up and returned to the whiteboard. He wrote a large number two, and underlined it. "These factors will be sorted out in phase two of the Diastasi program. Until then, you have seen what we can do. No more. Moving a Soyuz capsule that is thousands of kilometers away is quite impossible."

"When does phase two start?" Daniel asked.

"Next year. Our corporate partner is just beginning to prepare."

"Stetler?" asked Daniel. He was glad the partner had been mentioned.

"You've been briefed, I see. The Stetler Corporation provides supplemental resources that are managed under a separate budget. I admit it is a back door, a way to gain team members without going back to Congress for more funding."

"And do these supplemental resources work here, at Fermilab?"

"Yes, right alongside government employees. They are physicists, operators and people from several other disciplines. Top-quality people. We are one team. We do not discriminate based on where people draw their paycheck. Thomas is, in fact, from Stetler." Thomas held up his security badge. It looked the same as Park's except that it was labeled Contractor in light blue.

Daniel paced. "We'll want to talk to them, including the management. Can you arrange that?"

"Yes, of course. We have a team meeting this afternoon. You could meet them all together if you wish. Feel free to ask them any questions. Some of them understand the technology better than I."

"No, I think I'd rather talk to them individually, first. But can you give me time if I need it?"

For the first time in their discussion, Park looked nervous. "I can do that."

"Are we good to power down, chief?" asked Thomas. Park nodded, and Thomas tapped a few keys. The buzz in the room slowly lowered in volume and pitch. A blue glow appeared in the clear target box, and with a very slight popping sound, the webcam reappeared exactly where it had started.

"Nice job," Marie said. "I can see the return trip is a bit less dramatic than the departure."

"It takes talent," Thomas grinned. "They should pay me a bonus when I stick the landing like that."

Daniel stared at the webcam, still wondering if the whole thing was an elaborate trick. The view on Thomas's computer had returned to normal, displaying the room, a close-up of Daniel's face and Marie in the background. Perhaps the magician would step out any minute and reveal his masterpiece of deception.

Park stood beside Daniel, whose eyes remained fixated on the newly materialized camera. "Dr. Rice, you seem unsure."

"Sorry," Daniel replied. "Maybe I'll warm up to this crazy idea. Something still doesn't feel right."

"You are skeptical, I understand," Park said. "I have an idea." He reached into a drawer and retrieved a black ring about ten inches in diameter. "One additional piece of evidence." His eyes sparkled as he held up the ring. "It is an ordinary O-ring, used for connecting pipes and other plumbing fixtures."

He gave the ring to Daniel, who turned it over in his hands. It was a simple circle made of rubber. Daniel shrugged.

Park picked up a triangular metal frame from the shelf, took the rubber ring and suspended it within the empty frame by attaching three metal arms on springs. The frame included a small plastic grip, and Park wound it up like a toy car. The springs on the frame tightened as he wound.

Park released the grip, gears turned, and a few seconds later, the three arms snapped into different positions, twisting the rubber ring into a double figure eight.

"A simple toy, yes?" asked Park. "Let's reset it and try again, only this time in a fourth dimension. Thomas?" As the buzzing sound returned to the room, Park flipped the arms back to their original positions, the rubber ring again perfectly circular within the frame. He wound up the grip and placed the device in the plexiglass box. The gears began turning, and the arms tightened on the rubber ring. "Once more, please, Thomas."

Anticipating, they each held hands over their ears. A bright blue flash, a loud pop, and the frame disappeared. Park allowed several seconds to pass in silence.

"I think we can bring it back now, Thomas." The buzzing sound lowered, and the frame flashed back into existence within the clear box. The disappearing act was just as impressive the second time around.

Park retrieved the frame, detached the now-twisted black ring, and handed it to Daniel. Marie stepped in close to see as Daniel's eyes grew wide.

"Holy..."

No longer a circle, and not even a figure eight, the ring had become an overlapping knot, like a pretzel. Daniel examined the rubber carefully.

"A trefoil knot, as it's called," Park said. "It's no trick. You'll find no cuts in the rubber, no splices. The rubber has simply passed over itself through the fourth dimension, creating the knot. One of our physicists, Nala Pasquier, thought of this little game. Ingenious, don't you think?"

# 12 Booster

The cylinder tumbled, creating glints of light in a sea of empty blackness. It slowly rotated end over end, twisting with each rotation, like an Olympic platform diver on his way to the water. On one side was a United States flag.

It was a spent booster rocket that at one time had propelled a research vehicle on its way to Mars. Its job complete, the booster had fallen into a long elliptical orbit around Earth, where it would remain, potentially for thousands of years. Over the eons, its orbit would decay through the slightest bit of friction with random molecules until its closest approach finally touched the highest reaches of Earth's atmosphere. Then, it would plunge to a fiery death.

But this particular booster would stay in orbit far longer than most others of its type, because its path had changed. Its orbit now passed through truly empty space. With the pull of Earth's gravity still fully in effect but friction near zero, its velocity would be maintained almost indefinitely. Contact with any molecules at all occurred only for the briefest moments as it passed through a thin plane where all mass existed. The plane of Kata Zero, containing the Earth, the sun and all the stars of the universe.

But even in this place seemingly devoid of a single quark or lepton, the booster was not completely alone. Nearby was another object, as black as space. A wedge, nearly invisible except for a single red light.

The wedge slowly pivoted as it surveyed the nearly empty space. Then, in an intense flash of blue light, it disappeared.

# 13 Magic

The likelihood of Fermilab staff eating lunch at a hotel restaurant seemed remote. Even so, Daniel requested a table in the back, far from anyone else. There was much to talk about before their plan for the afternoon kicked off.

Marie sat across from him, full of energy, her words spilling out in a stream of consciousness. "I feel like I've been watching a film crew making a movie. Like J.J. Abrams just said 'cut,' and the cast walked off the set. Was that even real? So, so weird."

"The tesseract." Daniel repeatedly shook his head. "You could tell it was beyond 3-D. As he rotated it, the changes in perspective… I'm not even sure what I was looking at, but it was mind-altering."

Marie nodded in agreement. "Even now I don't feel comfortable. The camera was so personally invasive. Truly fascinating to see your own brain, but at the same time, uncomfortable. Like sharing your medical records."

"Yeah, I wonder where they might take this technology. At the very least, it makes MRIs and x-rays obsolete. I suppose you could even position a remote-controlled scalpel in 4-D space and operate on a patient without ever cutting their skin. Tumor? No problem, just remove it from the inside-out. Routine stuff."

"Daniel, I've seen a lot of fascinating things in my career at NASA, but what we saw this morning was anything but routine."

Daniel's next question was for Marie, but also for himself. "Before we head over to Stetler, what do you think about the Diastasi connection to Soyuz?"

"There's a correlation, for sure."

"I agree, there's something there. Park says they have no ability to reach outside that room. But either he's not telling us something, or he doesn't know."

82

"It's the lack of radar tracking that's most convincing for me." Marie spoke confidently, the emotion she'd displayed earlier in the day now missing, or at least in check. "Think about it... those guys have literally told us they are alive, but no ground station can find them. Of course, if Soyuz were hiding in this bizarre quantum space..."

Daniel's thoughts were the same, but given the leap into the world of fantasy, it was good to hear it from Marie. "Ground radar would never see them." He held up a salt shaker, imagining it hovering in 4-D space above the table. "Park proved that radio signals can still get through—that's how the Wi-Fi camera worked."

"And why ground is receiving from Soyuz, but not vice versa. Our controllers have been trying to reach them for hours, but Soyuz doesn't acknowledge."

Daniel turned the salt shaker, and a few grains of salt spilled on the table. "Right. Just like the webcam, the antenna on Soyuz is pointed back towards 3-D space. But ground antennas have no ability to point to another dimension. Just like a Flatland person who can't lift his hand off the flat page, we can't point *kata*, either with hands or antennas."

Marie paused in thought. "Yeah, high-gain antennas are directional, like a searchlight beam. That might also explain why the transmissions from Soyuz are so broken." She touched his hand and rotated the salt shaker. "What if they're adrift in this other dimension and rotating? As they turn, they sometimes face toward 3-D space and the Earth, but at other times they're facing... well, who knows what?"

"Makes sense. Now we need to find out how this happened."

"And how we get them out of it," she said softly.

The task ahead was enormous and without any answers, yet. More importantly, this investigation was no longer a sideline activity commissioned primarily to satisfy Christine Shea's need for thoroughness. It was the critical path. "Time check. How long has it been now?"

Before Daniel could do the mental calculation, Marie answered his question. "Twelve hours since separation and reentry."

She became quiet and stared off into space. "I've sat in a Soyuz trainer. You're wedged in between the seat, the control panel and the parachute packs. There's not even enough room to stretch your arms. When they close the hatch, you almost immediately feel claustrophobic. After ten minutes, you have to force yourself not to panic. I can't imagine what it must be like for hours. Or days."

Daniel had a good imagination. Claustrophobia could be crippling. But there was also asphyxiation, hypercapnia, dehydration, hypothermia and explosive decompression. There were many ways to die in space, and he felt no need to speculate further on how this might end.

"The clock is ticking," he said. "Those guys are doing their job, let's do ours." He opened his laptop and pulled up the background documents Bradley had provided.

"Stetler is up next. It says here their contract goes back even before 2012, so they've been a player for a while. The company is run by Terry Stetler. And we already have an appointment with his CTO, Shawn Yost." He looked up at Marie. "Neither name rings a bell, and I know a lot of technology people. Not much online either."

He returned to skimming the documents. "There are sixteen engineers and scientists on Diastasi. Ten are government employees and six are Stetler contractors. Let's focus on those six. I want to find out what they know."

Marie nodded. "How do you want to do this? Work together? Split up? I'm just being conscious of our need to move quickly."

Daniel thought for a moment. "Let me ask you this. Do you see any evidence that Park is lying to us?"

"No, not really," she answered. "Nothing obvious, at least. He didn't avoid any of our questions, and there weren't any locked rooms that we didn't see. I thought he was open—proud, even. But I was a little surprised that he was so adamant that they had nothing to do with Soyuz. The link is pretty clear to you and me."

"That's exactly it," said Daniel. "Towards the end, he agreed there might be a link. It suggests he may not know what's going on."

"Possible," she agreed. "But he's right there at Fermilab. He sees what everyone is doing, doesn't he? How does someone alter the equipment or boost the energy level without him knowing about it?"

Daniel shook his head. "I don't know. Maybe it's not Fermilab at all. Maybe it's coming from somewhere else. But that's a pretty short list. If you need neutrinos, it's either Fermilab or CERN. I suppose we could get someone out to the LHC in Geneva." He heaved a sigh. "What we really need is more information. We meet with Yost in thirty minutes. Let's see where we stand after that and sync with Washington on next steps."

Their food arrived and they ate in silence. Daniel thought about how a police detective would view the case. Motive would certainly come into play. Even if someone had the capability, who would send a Soyuz spacecraft and three astronauts into oblivion? Terrorists? A scientist with a grudge or under extortion? There were possibilities, but no definitive answer.

The waitress cleared her plate, and Marie pulled out her phone to check messages. "Well, this is interesting."

"What have you got?"

"It's from Augustin Ibarra. He says they received a report from an Army orbital debris tracking station at Kwajalein Atoll. The report says that several big pieces of space debris are missing."

"Missing? Like, lost?" Daniel asked.

"That's what it says. They track a long list of space junk. Some things are big, decommissioned satellites and stuff like that. Others are small, like a bolt that drifted away during an ISS repair EVA. Because of the high velocities involved, all of them are hazardous to human spaceflight." She set her phone down and looked up. "You saw the movie *Gravity*, didn't you?"

Daniel nodded.

"Well, the guys who track this stuff know every detail. Orbital vectors, when each object will hit the atmosphere, everything. And they're saying that fourteen objects are missing. They didn't burn up, they're just gone."

"That's scary."

She waved a hand. "No, not scary. It could be confirmation, Daniel. Soyuz may not be by itself after all."

He paused, silently thinking. "Do we know when this junk went missing?"

"They don't know for sure. They update their tracking data once a week, and the update was just this morning. So, it could have been anytime in the past week."

Daniel laid out a timeline in his mind. Cause and effect. A logical progression of events. "So, this junk potentially went missing before Soyuz, right?"

"That's possible," she answered.

Daniel leaned his chin on a hand. "Huh. We seem to have a magician on our hands. Somebody that can make things disappear."

# 14 Corporations

The Fermilab corporate office building was stunning in its modern architecture. Made almost entirely of glass, the building was long and narrow, lifted above the ground on stilts, with knife-edged points on either end. Oddly dangerous in appearance, one end seemed to be skewering a rectangular blue building through its midsection.

Daniel opened the door for Marie, beneath a sign that read, *Office Technical and Education Building*. For such an amazing design, the building bore a remarkably mangled name. *Particle physicists*, Daniel laughed to himself. *How could such smart people be so terrible at naming things?* He expected the conference rooms to be named Up, Down, Charm and maybe even Strange.

They climbed a grand staircase along the glass wall, a view of the Tevatron ring disappearing in the distance. Passing through a second glass door, they entered the corporate side of Fermilab. The reception area was immaculate, every molecule neatly in its proper place. Frosted glass, a visitor's log and a jar of jelly beans capped the reception desk. Backlit brushed aluminum letters formed the words *Stetler Corporation*. As they entered, a woman with luxurious hair straight from a shampoo commercial looked up and provided a wide, corporate smile.

"Welcome to Stetler, how may I help you?" she asked in a pitch-perfect voice.

"Daniel Rice and Marie Kendrick. We have an appointment with Shawn Yost."

"Mr. Rice, Ms. Kendrick, would you mind signing in? Is there anything I can get you? Soft drink? Coffee? Water?"

"No, thanks, we just came from lunch," Daniel responded as he registered in the log.

They took seats, Marie expertly using only the front edge of a backless chair and Daniel worried he might inadvertently lean back and fall over. On one wall hung an abstract painting with circles and lines and things that looked like flashes of light. *Particles smashing into each other?* he wondered.

Five minutes later, Daniel was just about to ask again when a woman in a matching blue skirt and blazer walked in, her blond hair perfectly styled and her hand already extended.

"I'm so sorry to keep you waiting, Mr. Rice," she said and took his hand in a gentle but businesslike handshake. "Joni Thorson, Director of Government Relations. So glad to meet you!"

She turned to Marie. "Ms. Kendrick? Joni Thorson. So glad you could pay us a visit." Daniel recognized the type. Warm and bubbly, gracious and mannered, and one hundred percent fake.

"Did you just fly in?" she asked.

"Earlier today," he explained. "We spent the morning with Dr. Park over at the lab."

"Isn't he the loveliest man?" Joni continued gently touching Daniel on the arm. "I've heard one of his lectures on the work they do. I was so impressed! He is just remarkable. Well, let me take you to the conference room—it's right down the hall. Can I get you anything? Soft drink? Coffee? Water?"

"No, thanks," Marie said, glancing at Daniel out of the corner of her eye. "We just came from lunch."

They walked through another glass door and down a hallway decorated with modern artwork. They passed several offices, each shared by several studious-looking people transfixed by their computer screens. Near the end, they turned into a large conference room with windows looking out over the Fermilab complex.

"Please make yourselves comfortable. Shawn will be joining us in just a minute." They each found a seat along the massive mahogany table, the bulk of the chairs remaining empty. "Did you get a tour of Fermilab, or perhaps you've been before? Isn't it an amazing place?"

Daniel took the lead. "We did. But our purpose today is very specific, Ms. Thorson. And time-critical. We are here from the Office of the National Science Advisor to discuss an urgent national security issue."

"Oh, yes, I know," she said with emphasis, as if she had overheard a juicy piece of office gossip. "It's that terrible tragedy with the astronauts. It's all over the news. Those poor men, I feel so bad for them and their families. They said they probably crashed into the ocean. And please, call me Joni. We're very informal here."

Daniel would have flashed his badge at this point, if he had one. "Joni, thanks for your concern. Would you mind bringing in Mr. Yost? We have a number of questions we'd like to ask him."

"I'm so sorry, I know you're busy," she said while standing up. "Let me just check to find out what might be keeping him. Stay right here." She left the room, and Daniel turned to Marie, smiling, his eyes rolling up to the ceiling.

"She's their smooth talker," Marie said. "Government relations and all that. Her shtick might even work on the guys who sign contracts."

"She reminds me of my sister," Daniel laughed. "She does fundraisers for a Denver arts organization. It's the same personality."

"Nice office, though," Marie said, looking out the window. "It beats working on E Street in D.C."

"Or in *La Bastille*," Daniel agreed.

They waited impatiently for several more minutes. Finally, the door opened and Joni ushered in a man in gray slacks, a white shirt with no tie, and a gray suit coat. He looked to be in his early fifties, with a thick head of graying hair that perfectly matched his suit.

"Mr. Rice, Ms. Kendrick," Yost said, extending his hand. "Sorry to keep you waiting, I was on an overseas call. Shawn Yost, Chief Technical

Officer at Stetler." He shook their hands and stood at the head of the table, even though there were many chairs to choose from. Joni took a seat opposite Daniel and Marie.

"Is there anything we can get you? Soft drink? Coffee? Water?"

Daniel spoke up this time. "No, we… no, thanks. Nothing for now."

"Well, then, let's get right to it." Yost took the chair at the head of the table. "I understand you're investigating the Soyuz accident that we've been hearing about on the news. Such a tragedy, we were very sorry to hear about it. You're from NASA, Ms. Kendrick? Did you know the astronauts?"

"Yes, I know them," Marie said. Daniel noticed her deft use of the present tense.

Yost crossed his arms. "I know they're still holding out hope that the capsule came down somewhere, but I can't imagine what might have—"

Daniel cut him off and played his hand. "Mr. Yost, we're here from the Office of the National Science Advisor. I have specific authorization from the president himself to leverage any government agency or resource. I say this to make sure you're aware of the importance of our discussion over the next few minutes. Our objective is to determine if the Diastasi program has any connection to the disappearance of the Soyuz spacecraft. We will need your cooperation."

Yost hesitated for a split second, but he maintained a smooth smile. Daniel noticed a slight flush. The first few seconds in any interview were critical, and Daniel had his part honed to perfection.

"Mr. Rice, I can assure you that Stetler Corporation maintains the highest possible level of security. It's our top priority. In fact, Stetler provides overall security to Fermilab as part of our contract."

"Then I'm sure you'll be very cooperative in our investigation. First, we'll need access to your program documents. Do you have a document store?"

"I'm afraid all program documents are classified, Mr. Rice. As a government contractor, we can only respond to a certified request for specific documents."

Daniel responded clearly. "I'll need full access. Today."

Yost laughed. "Sorry, I don't mean to make light of your request, but it's not something we can do. Document requests from any outside agency are handled by our records department. The time frame would be more like two to three weeks, per document."

Daniel ignored the deflection and continued directly. "Mr. Yost, how many of the team members are based in this office?"

"For Diastasi? All six work here at OTE."

"Very good, I'll need to speak to each of them individually. Today, please. It won't take long, fifteen minutes each."

"Now, I'll have to stop you there, Mr. Rice." Yost held his palm out as if stopping traffic. "Our employees are very busy people. They have project deadlines that are set by Fermilab. I cannot allow our schedule to be interrupted or our contract jeopardized. I will be happy to answer all your questions, and I can provide background checks on each employee."

The line between self-importance and obstruction was narrow and Daniel didn't have the time or patience for either. There were three ways to get past barriers: straight through, by deconstructing the logic presented by the opponent; going around by ignoring the barrier; or tunneling under by constructing a path your opponent didn't see coming. Daniel chose the tunneling option.

"One minute, please." Daniel pulled out his phone and touched a contact he had recently stored. He placed the phone on the table and set it to speaker.

The voice was loud and clear. "Hello, Park here."

Daniel leaned forward. "Hello, Dr. Park, this is Daniel Rice. I'm over at Stetler Corporation right now and we need your help. First, we're going to want to look at program documentation, both government and Stetler documents."

"No problem," Park responded. "We have everything you'll need over at Wilson Hall."

"That's great. Thanks. And, Dr. Park, we're coming up a little short on available time for the Stetler team members. They are of course all very busy doing work for you. This morning, you mentioned that you had a full team meeting coming up this afternoon?"

"Yes, in about an hour. Did you wish to attend?"

"You did offer to give me some time. But instead of my attendance, perhaps you could cut the meeting short by fifteen minutes, and I'll talk to the team members over here. Would that work?"

"Yes, Dr. Rice, that would be fine."

"Thanks so much, Dr. Park. I appreciate your help on this."

Daniel hung up and looked squarely at Yost. "Your employees now have extra time."

Yost turned to the window for a few seconds and then back to Daniel. "My apologies, *Doctor* Rice. Your investigation is clearly vital, and we will, of course, do our best to help. Joni, can you let the team know that we will need a few minutes of their time this afternoon?"

Daniel pressed. "Just have them come into this conference room one at a time, please. I promise we'll get them back to work as quickly as we can. I also want to speak with your head of security. Who would that be?"

"Yes... um... that's Bill McLellan."

"And is he here in this office?"

"Either here or somewhere on the laboratory grounds."

"Please ask him to make some time this afternoon to meet with us. Thirty or forty minutes should do."

"Anyone else?" Yost's overtly courteous behavior had disappeared.

"No," said Daniel, "that will be enough for today. The president and his national science advisor thank you for your help."

A blank look on his face, Yost shook their hands and left the room along with Joni.

When the door closed, Marie turned to Daniel, her eyes wide. "Daniel Rice, I'm impressed. You seemed so unassuming. But when you're ready to rock and roll, you just take command, don't you?"

Daniel grinned and looked out the window. "Did you notice his response to my suggestion of a connection to Soyuz? He defended his employees, offered to show us their background checks and defended the corporation's security. He even offered up the fact that Stetler provides overall security to Fermilab, which was interesting to learn. But he never once denied that the technology could be the cause. And he's their chief technical officer. That's a hundred and eighty degrees from Park's response. Park insisted it couldn't happen, that they didn't even possess the capability. Yost never mentioned it."

"You're right," she answered. "I wonder what his employees will say about that."

Daniel nodded. "Let's ask them."

~~~~~~~~~~~~~~~~~~~~~~~~

They split up for the afternoon. Marie returned to Wilson Hall and discovered that documentation was handled by a single clerk on the tenth floor. She stopped first at Park's office, reasoning that the five extra minutes spent in introductions would likely save hours. There's nothing like the top boss standing in your cubicle to ensure your priorities are straight.

Minutes later she had a desk, a computer and access to a list of file folders that the clerk thought might be of use. He even dropped a stack of paper on the desk—program test results that were not stored electronically.

She dug into a folder marked *Diastasi Design* and quickly located detailed program objectives, as well as the test bench system design. A lot of it was deep in the weeds, but she noticed that several documents called for a one-meter cubicle target box and spelled out a limit of 150 GeV on the particle beam energy level. She didn't know whether that was low or high, but at least it was a limit. There was nothing that suggested anyone had been working to increase the test capabilities.

As she reviewed, she noticed several key names coming up repeatedly. Park wasn't one of them, but perhaps that made sense. The director could hardly be expected to create design documentation or build a test bench. But three other names stood out: two physicists, Jan Spiegel and Nala Pasquier, and a mechanical engineer, Donovan Rohrs. Interviews with each would be useful.

Spiegel was in a meeting. Pasquier was a Stetler employee, and Daniel would pick that one up. Rohrs was located just down the hall.

He was writing on the whiteboard when she stepped into his office. "Mr. Rohrs? Do you have a minute?"

A wiry man with a bony face, he wore oversized pants that looked like they might slip off any minute, held up only by a belt cinched tightly above his waist. He peered over his thick glasses, remaining stone silent.

"I'm Marie Kendrick. Here on a special project. Dr. Park mentioned you might be able to help me." The name drop received some attention. The man blinked hard and set his marker down. His head still seemed miles away, solving some complex problem.

"Sorry to interrupt your work." She flashed a big smile. It might help.

"Marie," he said, his head in a cloud. "I don't know anyone named Marie."

She did a double take. "Sorry, can we start again? *I'm* Marie. I have some questions about Diastasi."

He pointed to the whiteboard. "This is Diastasi."

Simple conversational skills seemed to elude Rohrs, so she stepped into the office and closed the door. The whiteboard had a drawing of boxes and connecting lines, with notations scratched all over. It was a mess, but perhaps it made sense to him. "I've seen that you were the primary engineer in establishing the Diastasi test bench down in the lab."

He stared at her.

*Awkward, but maybe not hopeless.* "Are you perhaps designing the next phase? An expanded capability?"

He pointed again to the whiteboard. "This is Diastasi, phase two." He looked at her visitor's badge. "You're not supposed to be here."

"I can assure you, Mr. Rohrs, I have the full backing of Director Park to be here. That's how I learned about your work. Shall we talk to him?"

He said nothing and continued staring at her badge. She had already seen that every element of the current design had passed through Rohrs, even if that seemed farfetched now that she had met the man himself. But if phase two existed solely on his whiteboard, Fermilab might be off the hook.

"Mr. Rohrs, has any portion of phase two been implemented? Is there a phase two test bench somewhere at Fermilab? Anything like that?"

He tapped on one of the boxes in the drawing. "Phase two requires a fourteen gigavolt step-up coil inserted between the main injector and the graphite target loop. And three-millimeter lead shielding in the NuMI horn. And—"

"So, I'll take that as a no?"

Rohrs picked up the marker and returned to his work. "No one builds until the design is finished."

"And when will that be?"

He paused for what seemed like forever. "Six months."

It was like pulling teeth, but at least they were out. Marie thanked him, exited the office and took a deep breath as she walked down the hall.

*And I thought NASA engineers were strange.*

~~~~~~~~~~~~~~~~~~~~~~~~

Daniel watched the conference room door close and returned to his notepad. Over the past hour, he had talked with five people: two physicists, two project managers, and Thomas, the systems operator who had performed the morning demonstration. None had provided any further insight. In fact, each seemed to corroborate the statements Yost had made earlier. Deadlines and security were both tightly controlled.

When Daniel asked them direct questions about the technology, it was hard not to notice the similarity in their answers, as if they had been coached in advance about what to say to the government investigator. If needed, Daniel could easily escalate. An FBI agent reading Miranda rights created a different dynamic in the conversation. But bringing in the FBI could take time, and every hour counted. Uncovering the right piece of information might still save the lives of the three men literally lost in space.

Daniel sat alone in the conference room, reviewing his notes. The door opened and Joni's head popped in. "I have another team member, if you're ready."

"All set," Daniel replied. "Who do we have?"

The door opened wider and a woman walked through. She turned back to Joni, said thanks and closed the door behind her. She was attractive, late thirties or early forties, with dark skin and hair.

She displayed an internal confidence as she walked towards him. "Hi. Nala Pasquier. I'm a particle physicist here at Fermilab-slash-Stetler."

She was well-dressed in a patterned skirt and a loose white blouse with demi-length sleeves. She wore several multicolored bangle bracelets on each wrist. There were no stereotypical white lab coats for the scientists at Stetler; they each dressed as they wished.

Daniel stood up. "Dr. Pasquier, I'm pleased to meet you, and I do appreciate your help."

She stood close to Daniel as she shook his hand. "Nala, please. I don't do formality very well. Is that a government thing? Some of the Fermilab people do that too."

"You're probably right, we do get overly formal. In my case, it's the influence of the White House." Daniel offered the chair at the head of the table, and Nala took it.

"Is that where you work?" she asked. "The White House? Do you get to hang with the president?"

Daniel smiled. "I've met him a couple of times, but I can't say we're best buddies. My office is actually next door, and my view is a parking lot. Less glamorous than you'd think."

"But you're a scientist, right? You work for the president's science advisor, and before that you worked for the Navy? Sorry, I googled you a few minutes before I came in."

Daniel shifted in his chair. "That's right, the Office of Naval Research. Now I conduct special investigations for the president's science advisor, generally to keep scientific programs in line with their objectives. And you are a particle physicist. Have you been at Fermilab long?"

"Nice switch," she said with a slight nod. "You *are* supposed to be grilling me."

"Not how I would put it, Nala. But, yes, I have some questions for you about the work you do here."

She stiffened slightly in her chair. "I've been here for three years, working on various neutrino test bench systems and oscillation control software. Before that I was on contract to Argonne to develop a prototype for an advanced neutrino detector. And before that I was a grad student at U of Chicago, working on my thesis, 'Temporal Density Variations in a Normalized Higgs Field.' I'm a US citizen, I have a TS/SCI security clearance, and I live in Aurora, Illinois. I'm Haitian-French, and I always vote Democrat. Anything else you need to know?"

She exuded attitude, and Daniel had to suppress a smile.

"I have no doubt you salute the flag outside the building each morning. But right now, I'm less concerned about security and more interested in the project work. I'll be direct, too, and we'll get along just fine."

Having earlier acquiesced to the continual offers of refreshments, Daniel took a sip of water. "Nala, I've seen what you do here. The results are nothing short of mind-blowing. But my question is about capability." He leaned forward and looked at her squarely in the eyes. "Are you aware of any capacity to affect the position of an object that is outside of the testing room? Specifically, an object that might be hundreds of kilometers away, even an object in orbit around the Earth?"

Nala sat nearly motionless except for the hard squint in her eyes. "Who are you again?"

It was the most interesting response of the day. "Dr. Daniel Rice, from the Office of Science and Technology Policy."

"Not from the FBI or CIA or military police or anything like that?"

"No, I'm a scientist asking a question about the science that is being conducted here."

She waited a few seconds. "No, sir. Nothing like that can be done here. We don't have that capability."

Daniel waited patiently. "That's all?"

Nala just nodded.

He pushed on, wondering where the conversation might go. "Okay, I appreciate your honesty, Nala. Could you tell me about Stetler Corporation?"

She looked down and played with her bracelet as she talked. "Like what? The company story? It's pretty boring."

"No, like what kind of an employer are they? What kind of leadership? Their relationship with the Fermilab government scientists, that kind of thing."

"Well, Stetler is like any contractor. They pay better than an equivalent government job, and they provide better office space. But there are drawbacks too."

"Like?"

"Well, for one, you end up with two bosses, the company and the client. The client asks for something and management tells you to do something else. You're stuck in the middle. Stuff like that."

"Give me an example. Anything recent?"

"Yeah, happens all the time. You deal with classified information, right?"

"A little, mostly in my past with the Navy. There aren't too many scientific programs that are classified. This one is a rarity."

"Exactly! It's bullshit if you ask me." She nearly rose out of her chair. "Sorry, I don't mean to be rude. I love my work. This is the most amazing program I've ever worked on, and this whole team is going to be famous someday. But this classification crap just gets in our way and slows us down."

She waved her arms in the air. "I can't talk to anybody. I have colleagues from Argonne and U Chicago that I'd love to use as sounding boards. But I can't. I'm not allowed to talk to any of them. It's *all* classified." She stretched out the word, in obvious contempt. "The Fermilab bosses aren't so bad about it, but Stetler management is … well, let's just say they take it very seriously." She looked over her shoulder as if she expected to find someone else in the room.

"Are there lots of secrets here?" Daniel asked.

"Secrets?" Her face twisted in mock horror and she leaned in close to Daniel. "We're masters at keeping secrets. I'm uncovering the fundamental architecture of the universe, but all my mom knows is that I play with fancy magnets."

# 15 Leaders

Terry Stetler leaned back in a tall leather chair at the narrow end of an office shaped like a thin slice of pie. The long walls of glass gave him views in two directions. If he tired of the prairie grass on one side, he could swivel his chair ever so slightly and look out across the intricate network of buildings of Fermi National Laboratory—the place where, as the glossy brochure in his reception explained, scientists glimpsed the true nature of the universe.

Stetler was not one of those scientists. He was a businessman who pursued the profitable side of science, otherwise known as technology. He employed many scientists, but did not speak their language or understand their joy in discovery. That's not to say that he found no joy in their discoveries; he did. As long as there was profit. The revenue didn't have to come tomorrow or next week. He was a patient man, but he saw no reason to pursue a line of inquiry purely out of curiosity.

He had learned early in his career to attach himself to the scientists and engineers of the world. They would work practically for free if you gave them a good project and a fast computer. Just turn them loose, reward them when they struck gold, and occasionally thin the ranks by eliminating the B-level people. It was a simple formula that had served him well. Stetler owned patents on technologies that produced millions in annual revenue, without so much as a dime spent on production.

Stetler might have been satisfied with this plan for the rest of his career, but three years ago, he had gotten lucky. Very lucky. With his team already providing testing support to Fermilab, a new program had kicked off, Diastasi. Several of his key staff members were perfect for the job, and he had quickly negotiated a contract extension. Suddenly he was on the inside of cutting-edge science that would spin off many profitable technologies.

But like all paths to riches, the road had its bumps. At the end of the first year, his scientists were still in basic research, and monetization seemed years away. He'd decided a faster path was prudent. That decision was now two years in the past, and he felt comfortable with the changes he had made, even if the stakes had increased.

Stetler lowered the shade on one window to block the late-afternoon sun and swiveled to face his chief technical officer, Shawn Yost. Yost squirmed in his chair as Stetler's gaze fell upon him.

"You're worried? About what?" Stetler queried.

"About everything!" Yost was animated. "The engineers, for one. They know too much. A single person could blow this whole thing sky-high."

"Relax, Shawn," answered Stetler. "Your paranoia controls you. How can you have a serious project without knowledgeable scientists and engineers? Yes, there is risk, but there is also control." Yost was a good soldier, and like a border collie, his herding instincts were strong. His skills were sufficient to be in charge of a technical team, but his capacity for strategic thinking was limited, more along the lines of a golden retriever.

Stetler spoke carefully to ensure maximum comprehension. "It's really quite simple, Shawn. You don't control engineers by withholding vital project information, you control them by reminding them who's in charge. And that is you, Shawn."

Stetler lifted both eyebrows, hoping to see a light come on. "Let the engineers do their jobs. If anyone becomes uncertain about their objective, simply pull out their employment agreement. Confronted with a nondisclosure and a five-year noncompete clause, people become quite cooperative."

Yost's face tightened like a bulldog's. "The goddamned employees are just half of it. The worst part is this classification crap. It's holding us back. Hell, we should have a dozen profitable industries employing ten thousand people by now. But, no, in their infinite wisdom, the goddamned government says we're not ready. Keep studying, they say. Keep everything strictly classified. Fucking morons."

Stetler carefully folded his hands. "Eloquent as always, Shawn. But remember, classification is a two-way street. No other competitor has the slightest idea what is happening here. We're on the ground floor of a great opportunity, and with the help of our new partner, we're years ahead of the competition. We'll be fully monetized before they even figure out what a neutrino is."

"Trust me," replied Yost, "they know what neutrinos are."

"Well, they don't know what to do with them, do they?" Stetler snapped. "For now, classification is to our advantage, and we have support in Washington. Cummings will keep the competition on a leash for at least another year. By then, we'll have several patents, and the good senator will be comfortably reelected."

"You sure about that? What about this government prick?" Yost snarled. "Doctor fucking Rice. Arrogant ass. He walks in like he owns the place. Ordering people around. Asking questions."

"Yes." Stetler paused in thought. "Rice could be a challenge. But every challenge has a solution. The time Rice spent with our employees today was necessary, but well controlled. Thank you, Shawn."

Stetler swiveled, gazing out the window to the Fermilab grounds. "Going forward, however, we'll need a more complete security plan, with both tactical and strategic components. McLellan can fill the tactical role. Tell him to tail Rice and make sure he has no further contact with any employee. McLellan has the full authority of the Department of Energy to enforce security throughout Fermilab." He turned back to Yost. "Make sure he uses it."

"We could do a hell of a lot more than that," Yost barked. "The man's a beast and he doesn't have to play by police rules. When he's wearing that badge, he's untouchable."

Stetler smiled. "So right. There are advantages of being a full-service contractor. But, Shawn, let's not get overly dramatic. I think we want to focus on keeping people's mouths shut. At least for now."

Stetler swiveled back to the window. "And then there's the strategic component—redirecting Dr. Rice. There is the obvious path—new orders from his superiors. The senator may be able to help there. But we need more than just a top-down approach, and the senator will need support." He touched fingertips to his forehead. "What we need for Dr. Rice is an offering. Something that will be of value to him, something very real, but that takes him in a different direction."

# 16 Influence

There are more than twelve thousand registered lobbyists in the United States. To register is to publicly pledge to follow the rules as defined by US law. By some estimates there are ten times as many *un*registered lobbyists who abide by no rules at all.

William S. Conrad was an unregistered lobbyist. Conrad had a long history of successfully arguing for his clients, and convincing members of Congress to do exactly as requested. Large donations helped.

Conrad sat alone at a table in the Senate dining room, a feat no ordinary citizen could have accomplished. His finely tailored suit, Rolex watch and perfect haircut made a clear statement to anyone around that he was a player. Conrad stared intently at his phone, catching up on messages, but looked up as the elderly man approached the table. He stood quickly. "Senator, it's great to see you again. You're looking sharp as ever." Conrad shook hands with Senator John J. Cummings, the senior senator from Oklahoma, and offered him the open seat at the table.

As Cummings sat down, a waiter arrived, picked up his napkin and handed it to him. "Good evening, Senator. The usual?"

"Make sure it's Old Fitz bourbon, Vincente," the old man croaked.

"Twenty-year reserve, yes, sir," the waiter responded.

Cummings waved the waiter away and turned his attention to Conrad. "I read about you in the *Post* the other day."

"Don't believe everything you hear in those rags, Senator," Conrad replied with a smile. "I haven't killed any kittens or puppies since, oh, at least July."

"No, Conrad, I'm quite sure that animals are not your thing. But alone in an Arlington restaurant with the wife of one of your clients? Hell,

I'm sure she's a fine piece of ass, but you might want to watch where you're poking around."

"I can assure you, Senator, it was just business. The reality is I work too hard." Conrad's smile was as genuine as he could make it.

"Yeah, I can guess what type of business," the senator chuckled. "But I like you, son. You've done well for yourself, you show a lot of enthusiasm, and your clients have been loyal contributors to my reelection campaign. Very loyal, and I appreciate that. All we got to do is just keep the ball rolling and we'll be able to continue our fine work for the people of Oklahoma."

"Glad to hear we've been useful, Senator. Just doing my part. I can assure you that my clients also appreciate your hard work on the Hill on their behalf. Just last night I got a call from one of them, the Stetler Corporation?"

"Stetler? That bastard from Alabama? He just wants everything nice and quiet so he can F his competition." Cummings lowered his voice for the single letter. "Yeah, yeah, I know. Stetler's on my list, and don't worry, it's the good one. He's lucky he's Crimson Tide, I can just barely tolerate that excrement. If he was a Longhorn, why I'd probably have to take him out and shove a shotgun up his ass."

Conrad smiled. "Senator, I do enjoy our conversations precisely because you lay things out so clearly."

The waiter set a cocktail glass next to the senator, who made no motion of acknowledgment. "So, what does he want from me today?"

"Mr. Stetler is a very satisfied client. He simply wants to confirm your continued support for their work. And he believes it's in everyone's best interest that the Diastasi program remains classified. I'm sure you'll agree. He also asked me to let you know that he is making an additional donation to your reelection fund. I believe your treasurer will see the funds deposited today."

"That's excellent. Very good. Yeah, don't worry. I'll make sure the committee gives him room to work. God bless free enterprise."

"Oh, and, Senator, there was one other thing. Apparently, the White House has sent someone out to Stetler's offices. A science investigator. Junior-level person, but he's causing a disruption. Some crazy idea that their program caused that Soyuz capsule to crash."

The senator took a long drink from his glass. "The hell you say?"

# 17 Analysis

Marie set her glasses on the table and rubbed her tired eyes. She took another sip of water and looked at her watch. Nearly 9 p.m. here, and an hour later back on the East Coast. It had been a long day that had started at the White House and never let up. A private jet, a particle physics lab, a peek into the bizarre world of string dimensions, and an investigation that was still unresolved. She felt the stress building in her body.

Her associates, *her friends*, were still missing. She quickly calculated in her head—twenty hours since separation from the service module and its life support system. *They're still okay*, she told herself. *The emergency oxygen bottles will keep them going another twenty.* There were many variables in oxygen consumption, and she could list each one of them. In the end, it was only an estimate.

More troubling was the wide gulf between what they'd learned so far and where they needed to be. She couldn't yet visualize how this ended happily, but having Daniel as a partner gave her hope.

He sat across the table, his dinner plate pushed to one side and his laptop open. The tight lips, the creases in his forehead and the intensity in his eyes were the outward signs she'd seen in him all day. His focus seemed absolute; his determination was unshakable. She had watched him at the lab demonstration and at Stetler. He noticed details and he asked the right questions. She was thankful for those qualities.

She took a deep breath and turned her attention to their work. She picked up her phone, flipped open a plastic stand and set the phone upright on the table. She pulled a small black plastic tube from her accessory case and unrolled it on the table, creating a paper-thin rectangle with a keyboard drawn on its surface. A small blue light near the top indicated the keyboard had connected.

"Your news or mine?" she asked.

Daniel looked up from his laptop, Stone Age by comparison. "Let's review yours first," he answered.

"I found some documentation for Diastasi that indicates their phase two work may already be underway, despite what Park told us. And I talked to a few of the Diastasi people in Wilson Hall about it. One guy had a whiteboard full of design sketches. When I tried to pin him down, he said that no one builds anything until design is complete. That matches their project documents—they have a formal signoff procedure to move from design to construction. It seems doubtful they have anything running, beyond what we saw in the lab."

She touched the screen. "I also got two emails from Augustin Ibarra. One says there's a theory, maybe just a conspiracy theory, that the Russians are lying and they faked the technical evidence. Apparently, this is all over the news right now. There are some media personalities promoting this idea, blaming the president for complicity. I think Ibarra is just keeping us informed. I wouldn't worry too much about that one."

"Speculation is easy," Daniel said. "It's harder when evidence is required. I agree, I think we can ignore conspiracies."

Marie continued, "The second email is the one to review. You have a copy too. It's a text transcript of the audio from Soyuz. They pieced it together from several repeated transmissions."

Daniel found the email from Ibarra on his laptop and read out loud.

"...tried correcting for descent anomaly without success. All thrusters are working, but altitude is no longer...

"...our orbital height above the disc varies between seventy and one hundred forty kilometers. The disc is hard to describe, but shows land and ocean without any...

"...position data sent via S-band message, please review and respond on 922.763 ...

*"We will continue to transmit with ten-minute breaks. So far, we are unable to receive your transmissions. We have checked our equipment...*

*"...but we make this assumption because we see the fire, has Earth been destroyed?"*

He looked up into empty space over the table. "A disc, with land and ocean. And he can measure their height above this disc. He doesn't seem to be describing Earth. But then he says there's a fire and asks specifically if Earth has been destroyed. So, he must believe he's orbiting Earth. It's confusing."

Marie thought again of her friends wedged into the small Soyuz capsule. "Sergei Koslov is a highly-experienced cosmonaut. I can assure you he's reporting precisely what he sees."

Daniel nodded in agreement. "The rest of the communication is perfectly reasonable, so he's still got his wits about him. It's not like he's suffering from hypoxia or hallucinating. I agree, I think we have to assume it's an accurate description of what's outside the window."

Daniel paused in thought and Marie didn't interrupt. She could tell he was searching for meaning in the confusing transmission. He was methodical in his approach, collecting and studying before saying anything.

After a minute, his thoughts became words. "Let's assume... that Soyuz is in the same position the web camera was in earlier today. It's offset into another direction, a *kata* direction. The astronauts' eyes would have the same view as the web camera. They would be looking back at our three-dimensional space, from a fourth dimension. What would they see? Wouldn't they be able to see inside three-dimensional objects like the Earth, just as the web camera could see inside our bodies?"

Marie nodded. "Yeah, I see what you mean. From their space, they would see the land and the oceans, but also the underlying rocks...

110

and Earth's molten interior." She shook her head in disbelief even as she convinced herself of the truth.

"Exactly." Daniel was confident. "That's the fire that he described. Sergei sees the glowing magma inside the Earth and he thinks the planet is on fire."

It felt like a piece of the puzzle had fallen into place. "It makes sense," she whispered. "Hard to believe, but then we both saw the same thing today with our own eyes."

Daniel shrugged. "But it doesn't explain the disc. If you're looking at Earth, why describe it as a disc? He said it twice, it seemed intentional."

Marie had to admit that no astronaut would describe the Earth in this way. "We should show this transcript to Park. He might shed some light. And it might put a crack in his steadfast refusal that his program had anything to do with the Soyuz disappearance."

"Agreed, the sooner the better."

Daniel picked up his phone and dialed. There was no answer, and Daniel left a message to call back as soon as possible. "Maybe the Fermilab main number?" He dialed again and looked up at Marie. "Recording. Of course, the office staff has left for the day."

"How about Fermilab security?" Marie offered. "They might be able to reach him at home."

Daniel searched for a number for security. It took a few minutes, but he finally located it and dialed. He shook his head and put the phone on speaker for Marie to hear. A recording from Stetler Corporation played, suggesting the caller dial 911 after hours.

Daniel hung up. "That's what they told us earlier today. Stetler runs their security too. Sign of the times, I guess. The government uses private contractors for just about everything."

"NASA too," she said. "More than half the work is now handled by corporations. Each of them claims higher efficiency. That's debatable. But even if they are more efficient, we're left trying to coordinate among a dozen different entities. For us, it's a mess."

"I'll send him a text. Probably the best we can do for now." Daniel typed a short note and looked up when he had finished. "Let's switch gears and talk about my news."

"You said you got another email?" Marie asked.

"Yeah, anonymously. It's from somebody at Stetler, and it's pretty interesting. Here, take a look." He turned the laptop around so that Marie could read the email.

| | |
|---|---|
| *To:* | *Daniel Rice* |
| *From:* | *trp_1237@gmail.com* |
| *Subject:* | *Kairos* |

*A colleague told me you were in our office today and gave me your email address. No one wants to say anything because security at Stetler is so tight.*
*There's a CERN team called Kairos that you need to know about. It's more of a skunk-works project, off budget, and run by a French guy named Laurent. Nobody is sure of his first name. Last year, some people from his team were asking questions and it was clear that they were pursuing the same thing we are at Fermilab. We could tell they were fishing and we didn't give them anything. We had also heard they had a security breach just a month ago. It's fairly common. Swiss security isn't as good and this French team's work is sloppy. Anyway, I thought you'd want to know. Sorry for the secrecy.*

Marie wanted to be clear she understood its meaning. "CERN runs the Large Hadron Collider, right? The one in Geneva."

"Right," said Daniel. "Where the work on quantum dimensions started. So, what do you think?"

"About the email?" she answered. "It's provocative. Someone is offering a tip but disparaging the competition at the same time."

"It's not much to go on, but we're not getting very far here either. And the clock is still ticking."

Marie took a deep breath. "Have you responded?"

"Yeah, I suggested we meet privately. But nothing back yet."

"Can we enlist someone at CERN to help us?"

"I've already sent a request and Bradley is following up. But he also suggested we might need to go to Geneva."

Marie thought about the long flight. By the time they got there, it might be too late. It was true, they weren't making much progress at Fermilab, and this was the first tip they'd had. Neither alternative was encouraging and she felt weary and helpless.

Daniel looked equally deflated. "We're a long way from a solution, but there are a few steps we can take. I'll call the White House and ask Shea to bring in the FBI. A science investigator asking questions is one thing, but law enforcement could make a difference. And I'll keep trying to reach Park."

An unpleasant feeling writhed inside Marie's stomach. She wished she could do more.

# 18  Conspiracy

Terry Stetler lowered the blind on each of his office windows. At night, the windows transformed into one-way mirrors. People outside could see into the brightly lit office, but the only thing Stetler could see was his own reflection. The effect made him feel self-conscious.

He picked up his phone and dialed into a secure conferencing system. He waited through a wordy recording from a faceless British female, entered the conference number and password and was connected into the call. His counterpart in Beijing was already on the line.

"Good evening, Terry," he said in accented but otherwise perfect English.

"Good morning to you, Jie Ping," Stetler replied. *"Nǐ hǎo ma?"*

"I am doing well, Terry. And how are you?"

"Fine, just fine. Tell me something good, Jie Ping. I need it to finish my day."

"Most welcome news, Terry. Our talented team has completed their level three tests on the oscillator alignment, with only minor adjustments to the control software. Our work is ahead of schedule."

"That's always good to hear, Jie Ping. Let me ask you, have there been any hiccups in the system testing? Anything out of the ordinary, perhaps?"

"No, Terry, the system is performing as planned, with all testing completed on schedule. Our team has produced exceptional results."

"Jie Ping, what range are we at now?"

"An excellent range now, Terry. Our team has produced dimensional expansion of more than one hundred meters and is now able to target at two hundred meters."

"And when will we achieve kilometer range?"

"Exactly on schedule, Terry. I believe that range is planned for March of next year."

"Jie Ping, please excuse me for being blunt, but you wouldn't know about a missing spacecraft, would you?"

"Ah, Terry, you are referring to the unfortunate Soyuz accident. We have heard about it on the news programs. Very sad indeed. But then, when relying on Russian technology, the world must accept high risks."

"Yeah, I'm sure you're right, Jie Ping. And I have no doubt that Chinese technology will resolve that."

"Chinese orbital flights are increasing in number and duration. I am confident that Soyuz will be retired soon and the world will no longer suffer unfortunate deaths."

"Jie Ping, listen carefully, because what I'm saying is important. If my government decides that the technology we are developing is dangerous to space transportation, they will not only kill the Diastasi project, they might even shut down your accelerator. The stealth missiles they have these days can make it look like an industrial accident. Do you understand?"

"Terry, your statement makes no sense. How could the technology be dangerous? Our range is still very limited, and ground-based only. Our goal is the same as yours, to develop sufficiently to open market opportunities. This is strictly a business venture."

Terry Stetler sighed. There wasn't much hope in having any meaningful discussion. The cultural differences and the limited level of trust between them prevented his words from having any real impact. It was more of a dance between partners, a dance that could change to sparring at any time.

Their discussion touched on many other topics, and at the appointed end time, the conference call concluded. Both parties disconnected, and both returned to their work with no changes in motivation or method. For Stetler, it was an affirmation. When working with the Chinese, you could lay out a plan and a schedule, but you gave away control the moment you brought them into the project.

On schedule, Shawn Yost knocked on the door.

"You ready to talk?" he asked, peering in.

"Yes, Shawn, come in. I just got off the phone with Jie Ping. Squirrely as usual."

"Did they do the Soyuz thing?"

"Of course, he says no. They are not able. Range limitations."

"He's lying."

"Possibly. But I can't quite figure out the motivation. If Wah Xiang is responsible for a major international incident, Jie Ping of all people would know the consequences. He wouldn't withstand the scrutiny, even from Chinese leadership, much less the rest of the world. It would be the end of him."

"This whole fucking thing is going to blow up in our faces. Cut them off now, just get rid of those Chinese bastards," Yost snarled.

"If only we could," Stetler replied. "I don't trust him for a second. But accelerators are not exactly stocked at Walmart."

# 19  Motivation

Daniel plugged in his electronics and plopped onto the bed to give his body a recharge. He made two phone calls, one to Christine Shea and the other to Spencer Bradley, and left two messages. He provided a status update along with his judgment that the Diastasi technology, if not the team, was in some way involved in the Soyuz disappearance. He knew a duty officer at the White House would review Shea's message and decide how to handle it. The response might be nothing, or it might entail a return call at any time during the night.

He was tired, but felt he should use the alone time to process the events of the day. A hot shower would be the best place to think. He started the water and let the bathroom fill with steam. Stripping down to bare skin, he stepped in.

The hot water felt good and brought him to a relaxed state of mind. He let the water pour over his head. The unimportant distractions were cleansed away, leaving only essential elements.

*Ignore the spoken words and focus on motivation*, he thought. *Who is motivated to obfuscate? Have I asked the right questions to reveal the truth? Even if I have, would they tell me?*

The physical universe was always faithful. Run the right test and it responded with reality every time. But people were different. They could choose to disguise reality.

Daniel remained deep in thought, and time passed without notice. His skin hot, he finally turned off the water and wrapped himself in a towel. His decision to bring in the FBI was the right one. If nothing else, they would provide more gravitas and back up his authority. But he was less sure about the CERN tip. Perhaps Bradley would find the right investigator already in Geneva and save valuable time.

He heard his phone, the ringtone indicating the caller was not in his contacts list. He looked at his watch on the counter—nearly 11 p.m.

*It's not Park or Shea. Who else would be calling at this hour?* He stepped into the bedroom and picked up the phone.

"Rice here."

A woman's voice was on the other end. "Daniel Rice?"

"Yes."

There was a pause. "It's Nala Pasquier. You talked with me today?"

*Huh, that's unusual.* He had given his phone number to each of the people he'd interviewed. Standard procedure. But he hadn't really expected anything to come of it.

"Yes, Nala. Did you think of something else?"

"No, not really." Her voice was weak. She sounded nervous. "But I want to ask you a few questions. Can we meet?"

"I'd be happy to answer as best I can."

"But not on the phone."

"Okay, should we set a time?"

There was a hesitation. "No... not... I need to talk to you right now."

"I see, okay. You say we need to meet right now, and you have questions. But is there anything else you're going to tell me?"

The line was quiet for a moment. "Maybe. It depends. Can you meet me at the King Street Tavern? It's in Aurora."

Daniel paused and tapped his lip. It might be nothing. Then again, it could be everything. "Okay, I'll be there. Give me about fifteen minutes. Will that work?"

"I'll be waiting."

The phone went silent, and Daniel stood in the room with the towel wrapped around his waist, his curiosity spiking.

# 20 Collaboration

Nala Pasquier sat alone in a booth and took a sip from her drink. The bar was dark and mostly empty. Two men on barstools were engaged in a heated political discussion, the logic of their argument blurred by alcohol. At another table, a couple leaned in close for a more private conversation.

Nala looked at her watch, nearly midnight. *What the hell am I doing here? Is he even coming?*

The bar door opened and Daniel walked in. She made eye contact and tracked him as he walked to the table.

"Have a seat," she said. "They make a kickass margarita here, if you like tequila."

"I'm sure they do, but I'll pass this time," he said.

"Oh, come on, don't make me drink alone."

Daniel sat down across from her. "Are we talking or socializing?"

*Or baring everything.* She looked down and fidgeted with the napkin on the table. After tonight, she'd need more than just a drink. Therapy, most likely.

A waitress arrived at the table. "I'll have a draft beer, a lager if you have one," he said.

Maybe it was a symbolic gesture; regardless, she appreciated it. Nala studied him. The government investigator, the outsider. Another authority figure but without the uniform? Or Search and Rescue? She liked what she saw. He certainly looked like a genuine hero type. A strong face but gentle eyes, no overly fashionable whisker stubble, just clean-cut. Soft brownish hair with a little gray and enough length to allow it to blow in the wind. She imagined him driving in a convertible, on a curving road by the ocean, and letting his hair fly.

But always the doubter, particularly with men, she waited for people to prove their authenticity. He still wore the same business suit he'd had on earlier in the day, minus the tie. It seemed corporate, and she had little trust in corporations.

"Who are you, Daniel Rice?" Her eyes never left his.

"You asked me that earlier today," he answered. "We seem to be covering the same ground."

"Right you are. Let me adjust, then. How much authority do you have?"

"Within the law? All I need. I told you, I was sent here by the president's national security advisor. That's the president of the United States, in case I wasn't clear."

"Yeah, I got that. The big guy who lives in the White House." She looked down at her drink on the table and thought about how to approach the delicate discussion ahead.

"I need someone who can fix things. Things that are broken. Can you?"

"You're being vague again, Nala, just like this afternoon. I'm a representative of the United States government. I have the full backing of the executive branch. If I need the FBI, I make a phone call. If I need intelligence, the NSA will provide it. Hell, if I need Smokey Bear, the Forest Service will have him on the next plane."

She smiled. *I like this guy.* Her thoughts quickly snapped back to reality. *Don't kid yourself, he knows exactly what he's doing, and I'm on trial.* Her job was on the line, and maybe more.

Daniel waited as the waitress set a beer on the table and returned to the political discussion at the bar.

"Nala, this isn't a game," he said. "You clearly have something to tell me or we wouldn't be here. If you're concerned about disclosing information, I'm sure I can help. But I can't do anything if you don't tell me."

She looked down at her drink, dipped a finger in the ice and stirred it around. "Yeah, you're right, Mr. Government Man. I can be a bit paranoid at times. It's hard not to be in this environment. Overbearing security everywhere you turn, corporate execs breathing down your neck, tech guys inspecting your computer files and going through your email. They treat us like we're all spies, guilty until proven innocent."

"Do they have reason to worry about you?"

"Meaning?"

"Are you, by chance, breaking the rules?"

Nala felt her blood pressure spike. "Me? You think I'm the one? I'm the best they've got. I'm the one who figures out how to make this stuff work. Jesus, of all the fucked-up people in this company, I'm the *only* one you should trust."

Daniel remained motionless, as if waiting for a danger to pass. "I'm glad to hear that. But I need unshaded truth, and you're hinting that you have additional information. Let's set some ground rules, shall we? You provide nothing but the truth, and I will follow up on everything you tell me. Fair?"

She took a deep breath and returned to stirring the ice in her drink.

"You want things fixed?" he asked.

"Look, I know you're just doing your job." She shook her ice-stirring finger at him. "But just make sure you figure out who the bad guys are, and you might think about doing that pretty quick before we all get burned."

"Good, we're in agreement, then." His tone softened, sounding more like a friend than an investigator. "Are you concerned about your employment?"

"What do you think? They could fire me in a second. Hell, they could accuse me of all kinds of security violations and ruin my career." She recognized her own sharp tone and immediately regretted her words. *Stop being so confrontational. He might be the best shot you've got.*

She relaxed as best she could. Telling the truth would be hard, but she had to start somewhere. "Look, this is groundbreaking science, it's incredible stuff. I'm on a dream project and I don't want to lose it."

"So, it's Yost? Or Stetler? What are they doing?"

She shook her head. "Those guys are just the start. It's more. Way more."

"Well, then, where shall we start?"

She looked down at her drink and took a deep breath. "First, I need to explain some things about the science."

"I think I know a fair amount," Daniel said with conviction.

"You know only what Park and Yost told you. You never talked to Jan Spiegel, did you? I know you didn't. I asked him and he said he never spoke with you."

She picked up her drink, thought better of it, and set the glass down to one side. *Enough alcohol, it never helps.* Daniel waited patiently, his brown eyes locked on her.

"Let's start with Spiegel," she began. "A very bright guy, bordering on genius. A Dutch physicist who was at CERN in 2012 when they found the Higgs boson and string dimensions. He's got this whole thing figured out. He's been working on a model for dimensional expansion and compression. And *that's* what you need to know that Park never told you."

"What, a model?"

"No, compression. Remember that. Expansion of a quantum dimension is one thing. You've already seen that with Park's little demo. But it's the compression that's the crown jewel. Spiegel has figured out a mathematical model, and we're testing it in the real world. He's got an equation—we call it the Spiegel formula for dimensional compression, or collapse, or whatever word you want to use. Here, I'll write it for you."

She took a pen from her purse, pulled the napkin from under her drink, slightly damp, but a workable drawing space, and wrote from memory.

$$\tau = \frac{1}{1 + e^{\sqrt{q}(d-m)}}$$

"It may look hard, but it's really not. It's a mathematical relationship between compression and expansion. On the left side, the Greek symbol tau represents compression. On the right, the letter $d$ is the expansion factor for a quantum dimension. The rest are coefficients that we've determined from lab tests."

She turned the napkin around so that Daniel could see it. "You're looking at a very famous equation, you just don't know it yet. This will be taught in all future college physics courses. It will be as famous as $E = mc^2$. No kidding."

Explaining the physics brought her intellect into the conversation. Her anxiety disappeared and her self-confidence returned.

"Very simply, this equation is telling you that if you expand a quantum dimension to a macro size, another dimension *must* compress. Two different dimensions, inversely related. No one really knows why. It's like space can't help itself, like the universe is a balloon. You squeeze in one direction and the balloon expands in another."

She squeezed an imaginary balloon, looking to see if the light had turned on for Daniel. *Not there yet.*

124

"What you saw today was the expansion. Thomas sent a webcam a few meters *kata*. To do that, he *expanded* a quantum dimension. Right? But you didn't see the compression, not unless you measured carefully. And that's what you missed. Dimensional *compression*. It's a big deal. The crown jewel."

"Certainly sounds like a big deal. The Nobel Prize work that Park mentioned?"

"Yeah, Spiegel will get the prize. I just did his validation testing. But I'll be there cheering for him when he receives it."

"Okay. Compression. What does it mean, in practical terms?"

"Well, just do the math. If I expand in the *kata* direction of one or two meters, I'm taking a quantum-sized dimension that is normally only a few picometers and expanding it by a million times. The Spiegel formula tells you that another dimension, say the up-down direction, must compress. And the formula tells you how much. Here, I'll graph it for you. It's easier to see."

She took his napkin and drew a simple curve.

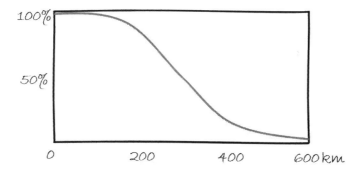

"This is the same equation, graphically. Imagine a ruler that sits under the blue line. It shrinks as you move left to right. At a few meters of expansion, like we're doing at Fermilab, we're at the top left edge of this curve. Virtually no compression, the ruler hasn't shrunk at all. But expand *kata* to three hundred kilometers? Well, then things get interesting. The ruler shrinks to about half its original length."

Daniel stopped her. "I'm not sure I understand. What shrinks?"

"The ruler." She showed him the imaginary ruler in her hands. "A physical object, any object. Space itself shrinks. Just like a squished balloon."

His face contorted. "Space shrinks? The whole world, everywhere?"

"No, not everywhere. It depends on your perspective—this is a relativistic effect. Remember Park's demo? The space inside that plexiglass box was affected. But only that space, nothing outside. From the webcam's perspective, space really did compress. You didn't notice it because the effect was way too small, the upper left part of the curve." Daniel studied the graph on the napkin and still seemed puzzled.

*Cut to the chase. He'll get it.*

"Carry the math a step further. If I expand to six hundred kilometers, the ruler compresses to one percent its original size. Go to a thousand kilometers, and now that ruler has shrunk by a hundred thousand, times. Think about that. Point your equipment in a direction and you can compress space by a factor of a hundred thousand. A planet, say Mars, that was fifty million kilometers away is now only five hundred kilometers away. At that distance, I could hop on a jet, do a tour of Valles Marineris and be back by lunch. A star that was ten light years away is suddenly sitting out at the orbit of Jupiter."

Daniel tensed, his eyebrows pinching together. "Are you telling me this technology is a transportation device?"

"Well, theoretically. It makes distance almost irrelevant. With the right directional control, I could get so close to Mars I could literally step out onto the planet's surface. Of course, Mars itself would look different because of the compression. So, I'd be stepping out on a flattened disc."

126

Daniel froze, his lips tightened.

"What?" she asked, noticing the reaction.

"Your description. A flattened disc. I heard the same thing earlier today, a message from one of the astronauts. And now it makes sense. From his perspective, the Earth has been compressed from a sphere into a disc."

"Yeah," she said. "I know."

Daniel looked up, surprised. "You know? What do you mean you know?"

"You're right. Those astronauts are not in 3-D space."

Daniel's face reddened and his voice intensified. "You knew this but you said nothing? You do understand they may die?" His emotion hit her like a punch in the gut. He was right to be angry, and she felt sick.

"Sorry. Really, I'm sorry. I... I didn't know for sure. When I heard the news about the missing spacecraft, I thought it might be possible. When you came to the Stetler office and started asking questions, well... I thought you had already figured it out. I mean, why else would you be asking these pointed questions about Diastasi affecting orbiting spacecraft?"

She lowered her head. "I should have said something earlier. I've been feeling guilty for hours."

Daniel held a fist up to his lips and didn't say anything for nearly a minute. His face was austere and her anxiety returned, not knowing where this might go.

"Nala," he started slowly, "I'm bringing in the FBI tomorrow. It's possible you could be charged for withholding relevant information."

She held her head in her hands and pushed her hair back. "Daniel, it's not me. I'm trying to help. I'm sorry I didn't tell you this earlier, but Jesus Christ, we were sitting in the Stetler office with Yost

127

one step away. Yost *warned* us to stick to the basic facts and not to speculate about potential capabilities. For all I know they had that conference room wired for sound. What was I supposed to do?"

"You could have told me more than you did."

"Yes, I could have, and I'm trying to tell you now." Her words hung in the air and Daniel remained silent. "You're accusing me, but there's so much you don't know."

"What else do I need to know?"

Nala looked up in the air and took a deep breath. *This is where it really gets tricky.* "I'm sorry," she said carefully. "You won't be able to save them."

"The astronauts? Why not?" Daniel demanded.

"The technology... it's not really a transportation device, at least not for people. We can move things. Cameras, electronics, plastic. No problem. But when we try to move anything alive... the results aren't good."

"So, you've attempted this?"

Nala winced. "Once. A test. We sent a rat. When we brought it back, it was... a mess. The bones and hair were still there, but most of its flesh had dissolved into a bloody goo. We had a full necropsy done and the lab guys said they'd never seen anything like it. The rat's cells were physically deformed, the cell walls were broken. Every one."

"And you think it was the transfer from another dimension?"

She nodded. "We thought it might be an asymmetric effect—the expansion didn't kill it, but the collapse back to 3-D did. Anything that goes into 4-D space has to be precisely realigned on return, to cancel out any *kata* rotation. If we're off by a few nanometers... well, that's okay for a camera, but it's disaster for living things. When you told me that the astronauts had communicated from *kata* space, that confirmed it. The expansion didn't kill them."

Nala looked up at Daniel and tears formed in her eyes. "But no one can ever bring them back."

A new reality had begun. Her job was certainly in jeopardy. She might even be charged as a criminal. But a weight had been lifted.

*The secrecy ends now.*

# 21  Surveillance

The black SUV was parked in an empty alley behind a row of commercial buildings. The nearest streetlight was a half block away, but it provided enough illumination to expose the word *Security* written on the side of the car. Inside, a large man held his mobile phone to his ear.

"I know it's late, but you wanted me to call you if anything happened."

On the other end of the line a tired voice. "Yeah. Yeah. What's going on?"

"He's in a bar talking to that woman, Pasquier."

"At this time of night? Shit. What are they talking about?"

"I don't know. I'm not that close. He might be hitting on her. But she looks upset, like maybe she's pouring out her life story."

"Shit... Put an end to it."

"You want me to take her in?"

"Tell that bitch to report to me ASAP. Tell her she's in breach of her employment agreement. Hell, drag her into your car, whatever you need to do, but put an end to it."

"Will do."

There was a pause. "Do you have the file on her?"

"Yeah, a dossier on every employee, just like you asked."

"Give it to him. I'm heading to the office now."

The large man hung up and the car was quiet. He thought about his next steps. Not being on property, he was currently outside of the boundaries of his authority, and with plenty of witnesses. This would need to be handled carefully.

# 22  Connections

Daniel's mind raced. Park's demonstration, the communications from space, and now corroboration from a physicist who was in a position to know. There was an unmistakable link between Soyuz's disappearance and the Diastasi technology. Yet no motive and no one to hold responsible.

He glanced at Nala. She had provided a breakthrough, but his relief was accompanied by the sinking feeling that she might be right. The astronauts might never return, at least not alive.

In the jumble of thoughts, one stood out. *Correct this out-of-control program, or shut it down.*

His experience would lead him to the right decisions regarding the science, even as bizarre as things had become. But he was less sure about the fate of the players. The FBI would be required. He had to make the call tonight.

For now, his focus remained steadfast on his objective. Find a way to return three astronauts to safety. His best option sat across the table from him.

"Nala, let's keep it very simple. I have just two questions. First, how do we bring Soyuz back?"

She looked up, her expression weary. "I'm trying to tell you. I don't know how to get Soyuz back because I don't know where it is."

Daniel pressed. "Of course, you do. You said it yourself. They've been moved into a quantum dimension. They're *offset* in the *kata* direction, as people here like to say."

"Yes, Daniel, yes... of course, that's where they are." Her voice was tinged with frustration. "But it's too general. To bring anything back from a *kata* position, I'd need much more. Precise coordinates for the 3-D space that was expanded, and just as precisely, how far in the *kata* direction it was taken. But more than just location, I'd need controlling software that could reach to that space, flooding it with a coherent neutrino stream, and collapsing their offset back to Kata Zero. I don't have any of that data, or that software, or the lab equipment to do it." She held her head high, but her eyes were heavy.

"Who does, then? Because if we don't figure this out soon, there are going to be three dead men in that spacecraft, and the stakes go up pretty dramatically."

"Jesus, you know how to hit the guilt button. I'm sorry. I'm sorry. How many times should I repeat this?"

He genuinely felt empathy for her, but her answers still felt vague and perhaps self-serving. "Look, I know you're sorry for not speaking up earlier, and I see that you're helping now. Let's get past that, okay? Let's focus on returning these astronauts safely. How do we do that?"

"I don't know. I don't think you can. Their bodies won't survive it."

Daniel shook his head and kept his voice low. "I'm not willing to give up just because you had one disastrous test on a lab rat. You said yourself you don't understand what's going on. Maybe there's a solution."

She looked down and nodded slightly. "Yes, maybe."

"And will you help us try to find that solution?"

"Of course."

Daniel held a hand to his face and rubbed at nothing in particular. She looked sincere. The touches of guilt and insolence were good, too—common traits of informants. She clearly knew how the technology worked and had identified the dangers. But she probably knew more than she was saying. "My second question. Who did this?"

She hesitated. "I can tell you my suspicions, but I don't know for sure."

"Okay, let's start there. Was it this Kairos team in Geneva?"

"Kairos? Who told you that?" She looked genuinely perplexed.

"I received an email."

"Kairos is a CERN team. But what do they have to do with this?"

"You don't know?"

"I know *of* them. We had some contact with them last year. They were asking a bunch of questions about the technology. But we haven't had any interaction since then."

"But could they be responsible for Soyuz?"

She looked down at the table and shook her head. "No, no. Forget about Kairos and CERN. I don't know what they're doing, but they're not the problem. Focus on Stetler." Her hesitation disappeared and the words poured out. "It started last year. An argument about the pace of the program. Fermilab, Park specifically, wanted to go slow. He put together a multiyear plan. Start with small distances, small *kata* offsets, and work up to larger offsets. But Stetler wanted to go faster, go bigger."

"Why?"

"Profit. It's always money, and this technology could be big. Last year, we created a presentation that highlighted potential applications. A Mars base that could be transported to the surface of the planet simply by compressing space and making a small step. Just build the whole thing on Earth, zap it with coherent neutrinos, and it's suddenly on Mars."

"A Star Trek transporter," Daniel said.

"Yeah, at least for equipment. Remember, no people. But that was just one idea. There was another plan to clean up space junk by targeting old rocket boosters and offsetting them in a *kata* direction. A cheap way to eliminate hazards to space flight. Good stuff with lots of potential."

Daniel made the connection immediately. *The report from Kwajalein. Space hardware that had simply disappeared.* A puzzle piece fell into place. It was a plausible explanation for the cause, and evidence that Nala was telling the truth. She had no way of knowing about that report, but she had just confirmed it. A tipping point. *Put away the threats.*

"That's very helpful, Nala. So, what happened with the conflict?"

She shrugged. "Fermilab won. Of course they did, it's their program. Since then, Park's go-slow plan has been our guide. My work for the past year has focused on the control software for the NIC. That's the Neutrino Induction Coil. It's what aligns the neutrino oscillation. The software controls the neutrino oscillation amplitude, which controls the size of the space expansion. Bigger amplitude, larger expansion."

"Who took it?" Daniel guessed. Nala looked puzzled, so he repeated, "I know where you're going with this. Who took the technology?"

She answered slowly. "Nobody actually took it. It was handed to them. Well, most of it. There's another player. A company in China, called Wah Xiang. They manage The Higgs Factory."

"The accelerator the Chinese are building?"

"Yeah, we thought that too. It's finished. Ahead of schedule and apparently already online. Wah Xiang is handling their operations. Fermilab wasn't willing to go big, so Terry Stetler made a deal with Wah Xiang."

Her composure had returned and her voice was steady. "I have no idea what they're doing over there, but I do know one thing. I'm sure I've been hacked."

"You? By the Chinese?"

"Yeah. The control software that I wrote is protected. It's locked and version-controlled through our secured server. There are only two people with the authority to unlock the source code—Director Jae-ho Park and me. Not even Yost or Stetler can get to it. It's mission-critical software that ensures both the accuracy of our tests and our safety. You don't want to be messing with that software unless you know what you're doing."

"And you think the Chinese company stole this software?"

"Yeah, I do. A couple of months ago, I noticed a background process slowing down my computer. At the time, I thought it was more spyware. Stetler puts this crap on our machines to keep tabs on us. But just yesterday, I was thinking about it and I put two and two together. They hacked me. The Chinese, Wah Xiang. I think they took the source code and are messing with the oscillation amplitudes. Really dangerous stuff."

Daniel was, at first, elated. A second tip, and this time not anonymous. It could explain both the Soyuz disappearance and why Park had been so forceful in his defense of Fermilab. If she was right, the Diastasi program had nothing to do with Soyuz, and Park had been truthful.

His satisfaction didn't last long. If another player, located in an uncooperative, even hostile country, held the key to bringing the astronauts home, then hope for their safe return was a fantasy. He thought of the diplomatic complexities, the difficulty of getting cooperation when agreeing to cooperate also meant admitting guilt. Even when relations were good, China's belligerence was well known. If they were accused of espionage, theft, destruction of property and jeopardizing the lives of astronauts, their response would almost certainly be denial. To get Chinese cooperation would take time. Time they didn't have.

Nala's dark eyes lifted from the table and locked onto his. "Daniel, it's bigger than Soyuz."

"What? There's more?"

"I'll do all I can to help you. But, honestly, the problem is bigger. Think about it. Wah Xiang didn't intentionally target Soyuz. It would be an act of war. What's in it for them? It's far more likely that Soyuz was a mistake. The Chinese don't know what they're doing. They've got my software and they're tinkering with it to expand to distances we've never tried. Do you see? Soyuz is a royal fuck-up."

"So, they've got technology they can't control," Daniel said.

"Worse," she said. "They've got massively dangerous technology that they can't control. You have to fully understand what it means to compress space. There are stars out there, black holes, you name it— there's dangerous stuff. If you're ramping up the oscillation amplitude, you'd better know what you're pointing at. You don't want a white-hot nuclear furnace coming anywhere near you."

Nala looked across the bar, and Daniel turned to see what caught her attention. A large man in uniform was heading straight for their table. The badge and holstered gun made his intentions clear. At least six feet tall and built like a climbing rock, he had an intense stare—directed at Nala.

"Ms. Pasquier?"

"Go away," she said curtly. "You have no business here." She looked in the opposite direction.

"You know who I am, then." He carried a white envelope in one hand and rested the other on the top of his holster. The size of his arm alone was intimidating.

"Mr. Rice, Chief McLellan, Fermilab security." He tipped his head, briefly acknowledging Daniel's presence and returned his burning stare toward Nala.

"Ms. Pasquier, you need to come with me. We have some questions."

136

Nala looked up toward the gruff voice. "You can ask me right here."

"Noooo," McLellan said with a light chuckle. "This is official Fermilab business, we don't work in bars. We'll need to go over to the security office."

"And where is that?" asked Daniel.

"OTE Building. You can stay here, Mr. Rice."

"I think I'll stay here, along with Mr. Rice," Nala said, looking at Daniel. The men on the barstools stopped their conversation and turned around to watch the confrontation.

McLellan moved closer to the table and lowered his voice. "Ms. Pasquier, this is not an invitation for you to accept or decline. You are employed by Stetler Corporation, and the employment agreement, which you signed, is very explicit. You are required to obey all laws of the United States and the state of Illinois, including directives related to disclosure of classified information. We have reason to believe you may have violated one or more of those laws or directives. Your employment agreement specifically says that you agree to cooperate in any investigation and that you will voluntarily submit to any government authority. And right now, that's me."

Nala remained motionless as the man moved closer. "I can have you arrested and you can spend the night in jail, or you can accompany me to the security office and we'll do this right now. But one way or another, you will be answering our questions. Am I clear on this?"

Daniel stood, McLellan still towering above him. "Chief, that's a load of crap and you know it. Her rights as a citizen can't be signed away in an employment agreement. She's been talking to me alone, I'm a federal investigator and I have full clearance."

McLellan pivoted. "This doesn't concern you, Mr. Rice. Your job and your clearance level don't matter in the least. You have a complaint?

File it at the office in the morning. This is a policy enforcement matter and I suggest you stay out of it."

Daniel's face hardened. He held up his hand and was about to speak, when Nala interrupted. "It's okay, I'll go with him. You don't need to get involved. I'll clear this up and contact you when I'm done."

Daniel leaned over the table toward her. "Nala, you don't have to do that. He has no authority over you, and you're not on Fermilab property."

She stood and McLellan took a step back. Nala positioned herself between the two men and faced Daniel. Her eyes were tired, but she managed a half-smile at the corner of her mouth. "Look... Dr. Rice... Daniel." She touched him on the shoulder. "Thank you. I appreciate your concern. But this has been coming for a long time. I might as well get it over with. It's only a job."

Daniel appraised his options. She seemed resolved to deal with the conflict. He felt bad that he had been rough on her earlier, but that could change. It would change. With a few phone calls, he could bring in a squad of White House lawyers that would put McLellan in his place. But at this very moment, her best move might be cooperation. Challenging law enforcement, even a corporate cop, was tricky business. Within the legal system, he would have more leverage.

"I'll go with you," Daniel stated.

"You won't." McLellan was firm and intimidating. "As I said, this is a company matter."

"I'll be fine," she mouthed.

Daniel took a deep breath. "Remember, you're not obligated to answer any questions. You have rights that transcend your employment. Tomorrow morning, I can bring government attorneys to help protect you."

Nala nodded, looking down.

138

Daniel glanced at the huge man and back to Nala. "Drive your own car and keep your phone by your side. You're not being arrested, and no one can take anything away from you. Call me if you need help of any kind, I don't care how late."

She reached forward and held Daniel by both arms. "Thanks. You're a good man, Daniel Rice." She gave a small laugh, an expression of pure fatalism. "You've got my number, give me a call tomorrow. I may have lots of free time." She leaned in and whispered, "Unemployment does that."

She turned to McLellan and pulled her car keys out of her purse. She jingled the keys in front of him and raised her eyebrows in question.

"That's fine," McLellan said. "Stay close and follow me. And, Mr. Rice, this is for you."

He handed over the white envelope. "What is it?" Daniel asked.

"I was asked to give it to you, that's all I know."

Nala looked at the envelope and at Daniel, and then turned to follow McLellan. As the bar door closed, Daniel reached for the car key in his pocket.

# 23  Chinese

China has a larger number of journalists in prison than any other country in the world. More than Iran, Saudi Arabia, Cuba, North Korea and Russia combined. Its censorship and control of the Internet doesn't just apply to web page authors; it extends even to users. Simply pressing a "Sign the Petition" button, which in most parts of the world is recognized as nothing more than marketing click-bait, can land a person in prison.

The same level of control and censorship prevails in China's scientific community. Researchers around the world commonly use the Internet as a tool to collect information or cross-reference their work against similar studies, but in China, researchers never know which sites have been filtered from their view, potentially skewing their results.

The system used by China is the antithesis of scientific discovery. Instead of coming to evidence-based conclusions, Chinese researchers are far more likely to be influenced by the opinion of a member of the Central Committee. This structure commonly produces what is referred to as the *argument from authority*, an arrogance unequivocally dismissed by scientists elsewhere in the world.

~~~~~~~~~~~~~~~~~~~~~~~~~

The office building on the edge of Yanshan University in Qinhuangdao was new, a twenty-story structure built to provide office space for a long list of Chinese and international companies working at The Higgs Factory. In fact, most everything around the city of Qinhuangdao was new. "The Factory," as it was called, was China's recent entry into the world of particle physics. The enormous accelerator ring covered more than one hundred square miles across the countryside, and an entirely new city had sprung up out of rice paddies and former industrial sites. The main accelerator was nearly twice the size of the Large Hadron Collider in Geneva and was now regarded as the largest machine ever built by humans.

Lao Yan sat at a circular table on the top floor of the office building. His was a modest office, particularly for a man so trusted by the Central Committee. He stroked his short white beard and shifted his position to ease some discomfort in his lower back. Across the table, Zhu Jie Ping, a much younger man, sat upright, almost at attention. A year earlier, Zhu had been named the CEO of the Wah Xiang Corporation. If Lao's tutelage of his protégé was successful, Zhu would eventually move to a higher position, possibly even becoming Lao's replacement. If not, Lao would remove him altogether. The Central Committee was watching.

"Jie Ping," Lao said. "We have a long history together and you have done well over the years."

"Thank you," Zhu replied. "Your counsel continues to be my guide."

"Then you must take care to listen to my counsel today." Lao leaned forward in his chair. "In your hands lies a great opportunity. New technology, an entirely new science. You have done well in acquiring it from the Americans. They are naïve and have no sense of how to lead. China will advance this technology and create a bright future for all citizens of the world. The Americans will watch our bright path, and they will wonder what happened to their own. Their lawyers will shake legal documents in the air, as though pieces of paper grant privilege over others. And as the lawyers argue, China will grasp the opportunity and move forward for the benefit of all."

"I am proud for my country," responded Zhu. "I am honored to take a leading role."

"Jie Ping. You have done well in all that I mention. But you have also created a great trouble for us. The technology has certainly been responsible for the Russian spacecraft incident."

"Well, I—"

"Be truthful, Jie Ping. Just as the unfortunate death of our colleague last month was your responsibility, you must also carry the

141

weight of mistakes made by your team members regarding Soyuz." Zhu shifted in his seat, his eyes downcast. "Jie Ping, China takes what it needs. China will lead the world, but China does not kill."

"I understand," Zhu finally said and bowed his head.

"You must correct your path before there are more deaths," Lao told him. "Do this now."

Lao rose from his chair. Zhu stood and bowed once more.

~~~~~~~~~~~~~~~~~~~~~~~~~

Zhu marched down a long corridor in The Higgs Factory main building. *Incompetence*, he fumed. *We have the most powerful accelerator in the world, and the American control software, yet this team cannot complete even the simplest of steps toward our goal.*

He recalled the demonstration a month before, with several Central Committee members in attendance. They had already proven the ability to transport electronics, weapons, even an armored tank from one place to another. The day before, they had transported a military jet more than five hundred kilometers in the blink of an eye.

But for this demonstration, they would step to a new level. China would be the first country to create a human transporter, a device that would revolutionize travel—on Earth, but also to the stars.

They had selected their colleague, Chen Yong Tao, to be the world's first Katanaut. Chen was to be transported to a 4-D position hovering over Tiananmen Square, confirm his arrival by taking a photograph, and then be returned to the laboratory for the celebration.

On the day of the demonstration, Chen arrived in a flight suit, the flag of China emblazoned across his chest. There was, of course, no need for the suit, but it provided an excellent photo opportunity with the Central Committee members.

His departure was flawless. The return, however, was catastrophic. The pulpy mass spreading across the floor of the laboratory was not recognizably human. Red blood mixed with other fluids, white and yellow. The liquid slop was only slightly held together by rubbery bones and a few lingering patches of flesh. They wouldn't have believed it was Chen, except for the Chinese flag perfectly intact on his flight suit, and an intriguing photograph recorded in his camera.

Zhu remembered the day well, and the humiliation. It angered him, but at the same time it increased his determination. They would succeed, even if he had to fix the software himself.

He opened a door marked in both Chinese and English, "担保 Secured." A guard checked his face and badge and nodded as he passed. Zhu was agitated, his rage increasing as he made his way up a gangway and under a maze of pipes. He abruptly opened another door and walked into a room filled with computers, a worker in front of each.

Zhu felt the heat rise into his face and he spoke loudly, almost yelling. "Supervisor!"

A young man vaulted to the front of the room. He bowed to Zhu and held his hands at his side in attention. "Yes, CEO," he said. "How can I help?"

"The incompetency of this group will end today," Zhu commanded loudly for all to hear. "The software will be revised. The Russian spacecraft will be returned to its original position. Your failure must be corrected immediately!"

"Yes, CEO," said the supervisor, his eyes darting around the room. "At once."

The command had been relayed, the hierarchy firmly maintained. Zhu expected that his demand would become the team's entire focus, but he also understood their chance of success. They had already tried twice. The first had been a blunt attempt to exactly reverse the equipment settings from when the Soyuz spacecraft had been mistakenly caught in their neutrino beam. Naturally, their attempt had returned only empty space. Being a spacecraft in motion, Soyuz had moved on.

In their second attempt, they had dramatically widened the beam, casting trillions of coherent neutrinos over a large sector of space with the hope of collapsing whatever 4-D space had been created. They had repeated this blast of particles every ten minutes for more than an hour, as if casting a fisherman's net in hopes of snagging a swimming carp. They managed only to retrieve a single decommissioned satellite, which had quickly burned up on reentry.

There were other alternatives, but they would require additional software changes and higher power from the accelerator. Zhu knew the accelerator would produce the required beam, but he was much less confident in the software that controlled it. A single miscalculation, an errant line of untested code, and the beam could easily pick up much more than just a wandering fish.

*We may catch the carp,* he thought. *Or just as easily destroy the boat, or the village.*

# 24 Message

Inside the cramped Soyuz descent module, the electric heaters were off. The colored lights across the control panel had gone dark. Smells of human sweat filled the cold air, and microbeads of condensation covered every metal surface. The silence in the cabin echoed death.

Sergei's eyes fluttered open. The display directly in front of him still showed some activity, about as much as Sergei himself showed. Cabin pressure normal, oxygen at twelve percent and descending. Sergei glanced to his right and saw that Jeremy's eyes were closed. Humans lose consciousness when oxygen gets below ten percent and die below five. But lack of oxygen was not what worried Sergei.

The next line down showed carbon dioxide at four percent and climbing. The scrubbers were saturated, and the simple act of exhaling now created a toxic environment. At this level, their blood was already acidic and its hemoglobin less able to absorb oxygen. Soon, it wouldn't really matter how much oxygen remained. Each breath would become poisonous.

*Not much longer*, he thought. *A headache and we'll just go to sleep.*

There was an alternative that didn't require waiting for death. Flip a few switches to override the security lock and he could simply open the hatch to the vacuum of space. Quick, but not a good way to go, and Sergei had already decided he would fight if anyone panicked and reached for the hatch release. They would tough it out to the end, whenever that was.

He reached out and pressed a button on the radio panel. A green light appeared, confirming it was still operational. They had transmitted for hours, reporting their position and status, as best they knew them. But without a single response, he had eventually stopped to save power, leaving the radio in a passive receive mode.

It took willpower to look out the window, but he did once more. The view confirmed his fears: something was desperately wrong. The object below them barely resembled the Earth he knew.

The flatness was jarring. Even the towering cumulonimbus clouds of the tropics seemed to lack their normal height. The disc itself constantly changed in shape, shrinking in width each time they approached. They regularly penetrated the wall of stars, rounding the edge of the blue ellipse, providing a familiar feel of orbiting. Sergei could swear that for a split second, he felt atmospheric turbulence at the exact moment they passed through to the other side.

The disc was now near its full width, and he recognized the coastline of Ireland appearing beneath the clouds. But instead of lush green landscape, it glowed a reddish-orange. It was like peering into a pottery kiln. Everything glowed, even the ocean. The whole world seemed to burn, but without flames. Sergei couldn't imagine how any life on Earth could withstand it. If he and his comrades were the sole survivors, it would be a temporary victory. Without rescuers, there would be no rescue.

They had ended any pretense of a quick solution, or any solution at all. The dark humor had started around hour twelve. Jokes about astronaut bladder control and puking in microgravity had morphed into humor about pilots at the gates of heaven. But as the hours had passed with no radio contact and no means of affecting their situation, the conversation had faded.

A loud buzzing sound burst from the speaker, shattering the silence of the cabin. Sergei's adrenaline spiked. Anton awoke, confused. Jeremy pushed from his seat, hitting his head.

It was not static. The buzzing was more like an electronic feedback, or the vibration of a stringed instrument, a cello, perhaps. Sergei was electrified. *Anything different is good.*

He turned the volume up higher. The tone changed, the buzzing sound alternating between lower and higher frequencies. There were a few gaps of silence and followed by more buzzing. After another brief silence, two distinctive words formed from the buzzing sound, words that the astronauts knew well.

"*Kak pashyevayesh*" buzzed from the speaker.

The three men looked at each other, confused. Sergei keyed his microphone.

"*Sayuz zdyehs, pozhaluysta otvechat.* Soyuz here, please respond."

He waited and then repeated his transmission. The cabin was silent, each man frozen in place.

"Let me try," said Jeremy. He repeated the same transmission, and they waited.

"They're not hearing us," Anton said, with desperation in his voice. He looked over at Jeremy. "Russian controllers, do you think?"

"Not likely," Jeremy said. "*Kak pashyevayesh.* Why would they ask how we're doing? It must be someone else. Someone who found the frequency? Sergei, check the source identifier."

Sergei flipped a switch, and a few seconds later, the main display returned to life. He touched it and Russian text appeared. "Source of last transmission is blank, no identifier. Maybe an amateur radio operator? But even that should give a source identifier of *Unknown*. This is just blank."

On its own the display updated, a yellow rectangle appearing near the top along with the Russian word *Soobshcheniye*.

Sergei's face contorted in disbelief. "We have a message?"

He could hardly trust his eyes. The yellow rectangle was a gift. Hope for continued life. They were not alone. His fingers fumbled, but he

147

eventually picked the right buttons and opened the message window. The three men leaned close to the screen.

```
Message received 07:49:15 UTC
Source Relay     S-Band
Frequency        922.763
Source ID        ---
Subject          ---
Length           13K
Body:

review and respond 922.763
```

"Review and respond on 922.763. Review what?"

"It looks Arabic," Anton said. "Could it be from an Arabic speaker? Egypt? Saudi Arabia? Do they have any space communication capability?"

"Not sure," Jeremy answered. "But I think we ought to do what it says and respond."

Sergei couldn't agree more. If the message represented a lifeboat, he was ready to jump in. He switched to the frequency and started transmitting, though he was not sure what to say, and in which language.

"*Sayuz zdyehs, otvet.* Soyuz here, responding on 922.763." He repeated his transmission several times, then listened. The radio was silent.

"Anyone know anything in Arabic?" His companions shook their heads.

*"Allahu akbar?"* offered Jeremy. Sergei shrugged. Though it made no sense, he transmitted the Arabic words, just in case. He waited, but was met only by silence.

Desperation consumed him, a drowning man in reach of a lifeline but unable to grasp it. *"Blyad!"* he pleaded to the radio. "I'm not asking for much. Just a response... something... anything!"

# 25 Confrontation

Nala drove through the streets of Aurora, following the black SUV back to Fermilab. Her doubts were growing about this plan. The man in the SUV was the security chief for Fermilab, that much was legitimate. But as a contractor, he reported not to the government, but to the executives at Stetler. It made her nervous, as if the government had already washed their hands of anything that might happen next.

Daniel had been right about taking her own car. She knew she didn't want to be sitting next to McLellan right now. He hadn't made a fuss about her driving separately, just as long as she stayed behind him. She thought about making a hard turn and hitting the gas. Of course, he would turn around and be on her tail within a few seconds, and after that, things could get ugly.

*Better to get this over with*, she thought.

The two cars passed through the Fermilab gate and stopped at the entrance of the OTE building. As she stepped out into the lighted parking lot, she yelled to McLellan, "This is stupid. Who's going to be here at this time of night anyway?"

"Mr. Yost is here," McLellan replied. "I talked to him myself. He'll have some questions for you." He motioned for her to follow.

McLellan pressed his security ID against the door's touchpad, and she followed into the main lobby, dark and deserted after hours. Alone with a man twice her size who had already threatened her once tonight, Nala discreetly reached into her purse and transferred a small can of pepper spray she kept for emergencies into a pocket.

They climbed the staircase to the second floor, but instead of entering the security office, they turned down the hall, toward the Stetler offices. Clearly, this was going to be Yost's interrogation. *McLellan is just a flunky rent-a-cop, serving his master.*

They entered the lobby, dark except for accent lighting around the reception desk. As they passed her workspace, she thought about any personal belongings that might be in her desk. A Christmas card from a friend, a romance novel she read at lunch. Maybe more; she couldn't exactly remember. *They've probably already looked, anyway.*

McLellan opened the door to Yost's office, and she walked in behind him. Yost sat at his desk in jeans and a t-shirt.

"Shawn!" she shouted as if they were best friends. "Working late tonight? I bet you're getting a lot done. Really good stuff for our partners at Fermilab." She sat in a guest chair, and McLellan leaned against the window, crossing his arms.

"Cheerful to the end," Yost replied. "Your sparkling personality won't help you this time."

"Never hurts to be positive." She flashed her teeth. "Or cheeky."

He lifted a printed sheet from his desk and looked it over. "It's a shame you ignored my instructions and disregarded our security protocols. I have information here that you've been providing details of classified information to persons outside of the program. A clear violation of your security clearance."

Nala adjusted her stare to match her opinion of Yost. "Prove it."

Yost ignored the challenge and slapped the paper. "As if that weren't enough, according to our email admin, you've been doing personal business on company time. Another violation of company policy. The juicy photos you send to people—really, Nala."

She slid to the edge of the chair. "You are a piece of work, Shawn, a real slime bag. I bet you enjoyed looking through my email."

"I don't know. It might be you who has the morality problem." He opened his desk drawer and withdrew a photograph. Nala and another woman were dressed as biker chicks with head bandanas, assorted piercings and fake tattoos.

"You piece of shit, that's personal property." She lunged for the photo, but Yost pulled it back and McLellan started forward to restrain her. "No longer," Yost said and put the picture away in his desk drawer. "Your employment agreement notes that all materials within Stetler offices belong to the company." McLellan stood next to her. His bulk was threatening and he stared straight down at her.

Nala rose from the chair and glared at McLellan, who was still more than a foot above her. "Back off. And stop looking down my top, pervert." She stood her ground until McLellan stepped back to the window and refolded his arms.

Standing tall, she turned to Yost and unleashed. "I've had all I'm going to take from you. I've had enough of this constant intimidation and harassment. Enough of your so-called security. Convenient for hiding your corrupt business practices, isn't it, Shawn? I am sick and tired of every detail of my personal life available for your inspection. Jesus Christ, I can't even dress up for Halloween. What did you think you were going to do with that picture, extortion? What is wrong with you people?"

Yost's body language remained businesslike, but the smirk on his face betrayed a sickness within. "Nala, your employment is terminated, effective immediately. Human Resources will be sending a letter to this effect with additional information closing out payroll and benefits. And we'll need your badge." He held out his hand.

She hesitated and McLellan stepped forward. "Or we can search you for it." She reached into her purse and laid the badge on the table.

Yost put the badge in his drawer and held out a single piece of paper. "We will also be forwarding the information in this letter to the director of Fermilab and to the Department of Energy. They will decide how to handle the disclosure of classified information."

Nala took the letter. She thought about tearing it up, but decided it might be useful to the lawyers that Daniel had promised. "The government will be on my side. You know there's a federal investigation coming your way. They're going to take you apart." She hoped her statement was true.

Yost grinned as if he owned the world. "Nala, it doesn't work that way. Don't count on Rice or anyone else from the government to help you. We didn't classify the program, the government did, and they aggressively prosecute leaks. It doesn't matter why the program was classified or what information was leaked. Hell, it doesn't even matter who it was leaked to. For people at your level, the government always prosecutes. It's a way to maintain power."

Hearing his words produced a sick feeling deep inside. She had no way of knowing if what he said was true, but it sounded like it might be.

"I should also warn you," Yost continued, "that any disclosure of Stetler proprietary information, such as authorized company plans to make use of Diastasi technology, or any libelous statements you make against Stetler Corporation, will most definitely result in an expensive lawsuit against you. And I want to make sure you understand… we never lose."

Nala thought about the work that she had done over the past year. The science was groundbreaking. The team had accomplished so much and she had been a major contributor. Yet here she was, standing in front of a corporate suit who couldn't see past the edge of his desk.

"You don't have a fucking clue what this is about, do you, Shawn? This program, this science, the discoveries we've made. Dozens of smart people are exploring the deepest recesses of the natural world, uncovering fundamental truths about the structure of the universe. And all you and Terry Stetler can think about is how to make money from it."

"You didn't seem to mind taking a paycheck."

"Never mind." She looked to the floor and shook her head. "The intellectual capacity just isn't there. I'd have better success explaining it to a dog."

153

She turned to leave, and McLellan blocked her exit. She looked up at the huge man and back at Yost. "Is your jerkwad goon going to rough me up?"

McLellan put his hands on his hips, which made him look even bigger. "You have a nasty mouth, little girl. Learn to control it or you might get hurt."

Yost motioned to McLellan. "Make sure she leaves the property."

Nala stepped past him and started down the hallway. McLellan was agitated as she walked past him. "You sure you want to let her go? I can get the sheriff's department to put her in a cell."

Nala never heard Yost's response; she was already halfway to the stairs. She took the stairs two at a time, hearing McLellan somewhere behind her. *Don't look back, just get to the car and get out of here*, she thought. But she kept a hand on the pepper spray in her pocket, just in case.

# 26 Distress

The oxygen and carbon dioxide numbers on the Soyuz display panel were still moving in the wrong direction. Sergei hadn't expected anything different.

His thoughts wandered to topics both deep and simple. The brevity of life. Last summer at the lake house. The last time he spoke to his father. The permanence of death.

The display updated. Oxygen ticked a percentage point lower and carbon dioxide ticked higher. He wondered if a supernatural being might have the grace to materialize and cause the numbers to reverse course. Now would be a very good time to intervene.

*God*, he thought, *what a useless concept.*

Common wisdom among the faithful is that people who lack faith begin to question their choice when facing imminent death. Sergei was proving them wrong. *All-knowing, all-powerful, and benevolent? Then where is he?* Of the three characteristics commonly assigned to gods, at least one was clearly mistaken.

Sergei glanced at Jeremy sitting next to him, motionless. He could make out a rhythmic tremble over the carotid artery. A pulse was a good thing to have. He couldn't see Anton and didn't have the energy to reach around and touch him. Perhaps Anton had been the first to go.

There was little to do but wait. It had been more than thirty minutes since the buzzing sound had burst from their radio, followed by the cryptic text message. They had responded, just as the message had asked. Multiple times. He was reasonably sure the radio was still working, but entirely frustrated that it remained silent.

He pulled his extension rod from its holster, a simple tool designed to press buttons on the panel while strapped into the seat, or in Sergei's case, when the body was too weak to move. *One more radio check*, he thought.

He reached out with the rod but was interrupted by a flash of blue and a loud pop that shattered the silence of the cabin. Sergei jerked reflexively. Jeremy opened his eyes.

Hovering in the air, three feet in front of them, a shiny metal oval hung motionless. It resembled a silver serving tray, but split down the middle with a curving line like an Asian yin-yang symbol. To the left of the curve were two lights, one green and one yellow, and a silver panel. To the right was a circular hole.

Sergei's mouth hung open. "What the hell?" He dropped the rod and reached out with his hand, trying to touch the oval, which floated just out of reach. His brain was fuzzy, his body tired, and his arm moved slowly, but the thing floating in front of him seemed to beckon. *Am I dying? Is this part of dying?*

Confusion overwhelmed him. He wasn't sure if what he saw was even real. But if it was a figment, Jeremy saw it too, his arm also reaching out.

A piercing whistle burst forth, its shrill pitch escalating and then ending with a loud pop. The yellow light flashed, shockingly bright and instantly illuminating the cabin as if the sun itself had exploded into their small space.

The light was intense enough to blind, but they didn't flinch. Their eyelids didn't even close. Locked open, their eyes stared straight ahead, their faces frozen in an expression of surprise, their arms motionless, still reaching out to the floating device.

~~~~~~~~~~~~~~~~~~~~~~~~~~

Nothing in the cabin moved. The extension rod hung immobile in midair. A drop of sweat. A small thread. A speck of dust. All the things that drift naturally in a weightless environment were now fixed in place. Even the molecules of oxygen, nitrogen and carbon dioxide that were, a moment before, being sucked into Sergei's mouth were now motionless, as if momentum itself had been erased.

156

An eternity passed. Or maybe it was a second.

The yellow light on the device blinked off. Its green light turned on, projecting a narrow beam like a laser pointer. The silver panel opened and a slender metallic projection extended. As it grew in length, the metal narrowed in width, becoming a sharp needle at the tip.

Without sound, the oval pivoted. The green laser beam swept across the cabin and stopped directly in the center of Sergei's forehead, imprinting a green dot on his skin. The device moved closer, the long needle poised.

It stopped directly in front of Sergei's face, and the needle extended still further, piercing Sergei's forehead. There was no cry. He made no motion, and his expression remained unchanged.

The needle retracted from his forehead. A drop of blood released from its end and drifted weightlessly in front of Sergei's face, the only other bit of mass still in motion.

The needle retracted back into the device. A moment later, the slender projection reappeared, extending outward. The oval turned, and the green dot came to rest on Jeremy's forehead.

The process repeated with Jeremy and then Anton. When it was complete, the device returned to the center of the cabin. A spot of blood stood out on each man's forehead, but otherwise their bodies remained frozen in their seats.

The yellow light blinked on once more, and along with it, the piercing high pitch resumed. A second intense flash filled the cabin, and when the brightness dissipated, all three men had vanished.

# 27  Shards

Daniel opened the door of his hotel room and dropped McLellan's envelope on the bed. With bleary eyes, he read the clock on the nightstand: 2:30 a.m. The need for sleep was strong, but other concerns kept him moving.

His doubts about a successful outcome had grown, with Soyuz now past the twenty-five-hour mark. On the plus side, the sand in the hourglass hadn't run out yet, and he had finally learned who was to blame. On the minus side, the culprits were likely ten thousand miles away in China, and he still had no solution that kept the astronauts alive. If Nala was right, a solution was not even possible.

But what about Wah Xiang? Was this Chinese company really responsible for Soyuz? The Kwajalein report was a perfect match to Nala's disclosure of a plan to target orbital debris. But didn't that point the finger at Stetler? On the other hand, he had found no evidence that Fermilab had long-range capability, and Nala believed the Chinese did. She also knew how the control software worked—she had written it—and she believed her computer had been hacked. He would need to call in the electronic forensics team for that part of the investigation.

Yes, the Chinese were the likely culprits, but the bulk of the accusations were coming from just one person, an uncomfortable fact. He thought of the new accelerator, The Higgs Factory. According to Nala, it was already online and caught up with Fermilab on control of quantum dimensions—and perhaps well beyond? Certainly, the CIA or NSA could at least confirm whether the Chinese accelerator was running. Shea would know, or she could easily find out.

And then there was the need to shake loose additional information from Fermilab or Stetler employees. Whatever Nala knew, others did too. It was a job best suited to the FBI, and the same person could get that rolling.

He picked up his phone and placed a call to the president's national security advisor, Christine Shea. As had been the case with all of his calls to her, a White House staffer answered and took a message. He left enough detail to feel confident that she would get the big picture. Someone—the State Department, perhaps—would need to begin a diplomatic effort with China.

*To do what? Get them to admit they took out a Russian spacecraft and killed three astronauts? Yeah, sure. That'll happen.*

Shea might pursue the diplomatic route, or she might advise the president on stronger options, joint US-Russia options, even military options.

*Let the politicians do what they do.*

The rest of his message to Shea was more straightforward. Bring in the FBI, just as soon as they could get to Fermilab. But as much value as the FBI would bring to the investigation, they were not scientists. To bring Soyuz home would take more than a badge; it would require detailed knowledge of quantum dimensions, access to coherent neutrinos and the software to control it all. Daniel had a pretty good idea who held that key.

He found Nala in his phone's contacts list.

The charges against her were serious, but manageable within the Justice Department. Rules were unevenly enforced. Occasionally, leakers went to prison, but there were just as many cases where the government took no action at all. High-level members of any administration often intentionally leaked classified information. It was a political game, even the decisions about what was classified and what was not. Besides, the president was on their side.

He wanted to tell all of this to Nala. She had looked anxious leaving the bar, and with good reason. His decision to follow them had been easy. He had been concerned for her immediate safety, but he also felt uncomfortable letting her out of his sight. She was the key to delivering Soyuz, and without her, the investigation was going nowhere. He hadn't bothered to hide—on public streets, it didn't really matter if McLellan saw him. But as their cars had reached the property, Daniel had noticed the security gate and the night watchman. Without the right credentials, it would be difficult to gain access at night. He'd pulled to the curb and watched from a distance. Perhaps it was irrational to think McLellan might do her physical harm. He had watched their cars disappear behind trees and reluctantly returned to the hotel.

There was still much to discuss with Nala. For now, Daniel kept it simple. *Checking to see if you're okay*, he typed.

He noticed a message from Spencer Bradley. A resource in Geneva had been assigned to investigate the CERN Kairos team. Even though Nala had discounted the tip as worthless, Daniel knew better. An incomplete investigation could miss a single detail that might become the turning point. Given that it was already midmorning in Geneva, perhaps they would hear back soon.

Marie was next on his mental list. A ridiculous time of night to call, but she would need—and want—to be briefed. She picked up on the first ring.

"You awake?" he asked.

"Yeah." She sounded tired. "Still thinking about all this. There's no way I can sleep."

"Can you come down to my room? You'll want to hear this."

"Sure, just a sec."

He heard some fumbling and she hung up. A minute later, there was a knock on the door and Daniel hopped up. She was adjusting a sweater and brushing her hair back when he opened the door.

"What's up? You got something?"

"Sorry, it's really late. But I figured you might be awake."

160

She walked in and took a seat on the small sofa. Her eyes looked bloodshot and her makeup was washed away. "Don't worry about it. I've been feeling pretty useless since we left the Stetler office. Anything you've got is better than just sitting there."

"I just got back from a bar. I met one of the Stetler employees, a physicist, Nala Pasquier. She called me… and she had a lot to say."

Marie looked surprised about the development. Daniel described the initial call, their meeting and much of what Nala had told him. He reached into his pocket and offered the cocktail napkin with the equation scrawled across it. She held it in both hands, as if assessing the authenticity of an ancient artifact.

"The Chinese? They did all of this?" she asked.

"That's what she says." Daniel sat on the edge of the bed and rubbed both tired eyes. "The equation on that napkin seems to represent a prize of high value, not only to Stetler but to the Chinese. The Diastasi program is not just a scientific discovery; it could open a whole new branch of profitable technologies… and potentially weapons, too."

"So, Nala confirmed our thinking that Soyuz is stuck in this… *kata* space. But she didn't tell you how to get them back?"

Daniel didn't hold back. "She doesn't think it's possible. She says the return trip to normal space is deadly. They don't know exactly why, but they have some experiment evidence. I'm sorry."

Marie nodded her head slowly as she absorbed the difficult news. She didn't debate the information, but she asked several more questions, and Daniel filled her in as best he could. Together, they agreed there were possibilities, however slight, which was better than idling at a dead end.

If there was any hope of a return for the astronauts, they would first have to locate the capsule. But just as no human hand could point in the *kata* direction, no radar antenna could either. If you didn't know precisely where Soyuz was located, zapping a random parcel of space with neutrinos was a hopeless exercise, like target shooting wearing a blindfold.

As Nala had described, they would need accuracy. A way to determine both position and velocity. "If only we had radar in *kata* space," Daniel offered.

Marie perked up at the suggestion. "Could we?"

Portable radar. Did such a thing exist? And could it be zapped into this bizarre extra dimension, just like the cameras? He didn't know, but Nala might.

Sometimes, the universe was in sync. Daniel's phone rang, identifying Nala as the caller. He felt a spike of adrenaline and picked up. "Are you okay?"

The voice on the other end was tired. "Yeah, I'm fine, thanks. It was a major blowup. I'm emotionally drained... and jobless... but actually feeling pretty relieved that it's over. Driving home now."

Daniel let out his breath and mouthed to Marie, "It's Nala." He returned his attention to the woman on the phone—no longer just an informant, but a collaborator. "I'm sorry you lost your job. I shouldn't have let McLellan take you out of that bar. He had no authority to do that."

"Thoughtful of you, but not logical. Never talk back to a cop with a gun. Especially for a black woman, that strategy doesn't turn out well. It wouldn't have made a difference anyway—they would have fired me in the morning. Good riddance. I'm glad to be gone from that company."

Daniel didn't switch the phone to speaker, but he moved closer to Marie to allow her to listen. "What did they tell you, specifically? Was it Yost, or Stetler?"

"It was Yost. He threatened to sue me and said the government would prosecute me for leaking classified information. He said it didn't

162

matter who I was talking with, he says the government always prosecutes."

"They don't, Nala. He's wrong. Prosecutions for disclosing classified information are not cut and dried. You've done a service to your country, and that makes a huge difference. I can help protect you."

There was a long pause on the line, and Daniel thought he might have lost the connection. But he heard a sigh. "I appreciate your help, Daniel. You've been lovely. Well, hard on me, and then lovely. What is it with you? Are you like two different people? Mr. Interrogator and then Sweet Talkin' Dan?"

"You see right through me." And she had. "My apologies, it's part of the method."

"The *method*? It figures. So, which one is the real you?"

"Neither, I guess." He didn't mind the personal question, but there was work to do. "Nala, I have an idea. I think I know how to locate Soyuz, and I want your response."

"Does your brain ever rest, Scientist? Okay, just got home. Three a.m., but I'll give you whatever attention I have left."

For the time of night, Daniel was surprised that his brain was still working at all. "You said we needed an exact location of Soyuz before we could move them back to our space, right?"

"Right, before we can return them to Kata Zero."

"What if we could put a radar unit into *kata* space? Then it would be able to point in the *ana* or *kata* directions, wouldn't it?"

"Yeah, it would," she answered. "But isn't a radar antenna a big piece of hardware? Like house-sized?"

Daniel thought about it. "Some are. But I think the military uses fairly compact radar units in antiaircraft missiles. I'm not sure of their range, but if we could get one up into 4-D space, we could point in every direction and we might hit something."

"Yeah…" She paused. "Good thinking, but it all depends on how big it is. What you saw at Fermilab is all we've got. A target box about a meter on each side. If it doesn't fit inside that box, we can't send it."

"Is there any way to enlarge the box to, say, room size?"

"Maybe… sure. But that would take time. Even if we scrambled the whole team, we'd need a few days to get the equipment running."

"Okay, thanks. I know I'm reaching. Just not willing to give up yet."

"I didn't mean to burst your bubble. It really is a good idea, sending radar out there. Just complex to set up."

She was right, of course. They were still a long way from a solution. "Do you think this Chinese company has anything like this already set up?"

"Realistically? No. Look, Wah Xiang got into this mess because they don't know what they're doing. How do you leverage incompetence? And how do you solve the problem of returning people? We just haven't studied this enough."

Daniel physically deflated. "Nala, thanks. I'll let you go. You've done a great job and helped us more than you know. Get some sleep."

"You, too," she said. "And thanks for caring. I meant what I said at the bar, you're a good man."

Daniel hung up. He sat on the edge of the bed, his head resting on his hands. There was still hope, he wouldn't give up on that. But the list of prerequisites to success was long. Unfortunately, the clock was still ticking.

Marie leaned forward. "She sounds like she knows what she's doing. And she's clearly identifying the Chinese company as the problem."

Daniel nodded. "She has. I've already asked Shea to get a diplomatic process started. Or a military one—their call."

He picked up the white envelope that had been sitting on his bed unopened. He reached in and pulled out a thick stack of papers, photo copies of various documents. "Their security guy gave me this." He read the first page.

**Fermilab Security Internal Investigation. Subject: Nala Pasquier**
Over the past two months, subject has repeatedly accessed secured files with transfers to an unknown external device. She has made multiple calls to a number in China that has been traced to a Central Committee staff office.

The page continued with a long list of dated entries.

...

| | |
|---|---|
| 8.24.21 7:16 PM | Mobile call placed to 86 10 626 4371, Beijing, China, 13 minutes |
| 8.27.21 8:39 AM | Incognito browser initiated |
| 8.27.21 8:40 AM | External file transfer from secured folder: Diastasi\NIC\archive |
| 9.12.21 7:01 PM | Mobile call placed to 86 10 626 4371, Beijing, China, 19 minutes |
| 9.13.21 9:50 AM | Incognito browser initiated |
| 9.13.21 9:52 AM | External file transfer from secured folder: Diastasi\NIC\source |

Daniel passed the page to Marie and examined the others. Each provided phone record details or listings of files held within folders.

He dropped the pile of papers on the bed and looked up. He thought of the phone call, the bar, and his whole experience with the woman who for the past several hours had single-handedly guided his investigation away from herself and toward Stetler.

165

*No way. This can't be true… can it?*

# 28  Reality

The top of the atmosphere is not any specific place. Air thins gradually with height. But eighty kilometers up is as good as any to call the top. It's a height where the light and warmth below dissolve into the cold space above.

At the top of the atmosphere, the brilliant sun peeked above the gently curving horizon. To the west, long shadows spread across the ground and eventually blended into dark side of the planet. In the foreground, an expanse of mountainous land was topped by scattered clouds tinted orange by the early-morning light.

Out of the darkness from the west, a brilliant blue light exploded across the sky. A low boom rumbled through the thin air, and a burning object moving at high speed blazed a searing orange trail in the early-morning twilight. It left behind a long white contrail of smoke that lingered in the air and pointed the direction of the object's path, descending eastward.

The Soyuz capsule bounced wildly as the buffeting of the atmosphere increased. Its design provided for descent path control; a slight rotation counterclockwise, and lift increased, flattening the descent. A rotation clockwise, and lift decreased, and the descent angle steepened. But this capsule exhibited no hint of control. It spun around in circles, leaning left, then right, rising and then falling in a wildly erratic path.

The contrail abruptly came to an end, the spacecraft's speed having been reduced below the point where atmospheric friction melts metal. Still at supersonic speed, it hurtled above the high peaks of western Wyoming, the mountain ranges graced with fresh snow colored pink in the twilight.

At twelve kilometers above the surface, an exploding bolt automatically fired near the top of the capsule, blowing off a metal ring and releasing a drogue parachute. The chute stabilized the capsule, stopped it from spinning and further slowed its speed. A few seconds later, another small explosion and the huge main chute deployed, blossoming into its full size and ending the plunge. The heat shield that had protected the capsule through the fiery descent blew away from the bottom, exposing six small rockets.

The enormous parachute dwarfed the small capsule, now swaying gently below it. The dazzling orange-and-white cloth stood out against a bright blue sky. The capsule drifted past a towering volcanic monolith, crossing an imaginary line into South Dakota. Here, the mountains became forested hills, and beyond, a broad expanse of prairie stretched out into the distance.

As the capsule crossed a ridge, it descended into a broad valley, colored brown but bisected by a meandering creek and the light green of elm trees along its banks. In this vicinity, there were no towns or roads and few signs of civilization. Just the beauty of the undisturbed surface of the planet Earth.

The enormous orange-and-white parachute could be seen for many miles around, and even in an area with sparse population, it was no ordinary sight and would be noticed by many. Somewhere, a phone call to 911 was already being made, telling the operator that a military plane must have crashed and the pilot ejected.

The capsule continued its gentle descent to the valley floor. As it came within twenty feet of the ground, six retro-rockets fired, creating a blast of white smoke and dust. The capsule hit the ground, and the lines to the parachute went slack. Several startled birds flew off towards the creek. A squirrel on a nearby rock scurried into the shadows. The cloud of dust began to clear just as the parachute itself folded into the surrounding grass.

With the rockets shut off and the dust cloud dispersed, the area returned to its prior state of calm. The rising sun, still low in the east, poured its light across the land, and the various inhabitants of the planet Earth soaked up its warmth.

Alone in a valley in the Black Hills of South Dakota, the Russian Soyuz spacecraft had completed its journey home.

# 29 Dakota

*The couch was comfortable, but the cat's claws were not. Daniel peered over the edge to see Darwin reaching up from the floor below. "What's up, buddy? Hungry?" The cat jerked his chin to the right.*

*At the far end of the couch, Janine was absorbed in a magazine, her legs curled under her and a blanket wrapped around her shoulders. She took a sip from a drink that bubbled like a witch's brew.*

*He was surprised to see her. "Janine! I forgot to say thanks for watching Darwin. He seems pretty happy." Daniel watched the frothy liquid flow over the top of her glass, and was thankful that it was evaporating before hitting anything.* Probably liquid nitrogen, *he thought.*

*"My pleasure." Janine put the magazine down. "Boring read, actually." She pulled the blanket off to expose bare breasts and smiled sweetly. "Want to do something fun?"*

*Daniel wanted to answer. He tried to form the words, but his mouth didn't seem to be working. She stared at him, her fingers drumming on her thigh. Darwin meowed loudly.*

*"He's right, you know. It's your bones, Daniel. They're showing. You should look into that."*

*Daniel noticed that he was naked too. His skin was transparent and he could see the bones inside his arms. He looked down at his legs. A bone from his right thigh protruded into midair. His heart pounded. He looked at Janine and could just make out her skull under the skin of her forehead. None of it was right, but he wasn't sure why.*

*He could hear a phone ringing and looked around trying to find it. The ringing became louder.*

Daniel's eyes opened and he sat up straight. His heart pounded. Consciousness, but with a lingering feeling of a bizarre and unnatural world of the subconscious. He grabbed the phone, an incoming call from Christine Shea. "Morning, Ms. Shea, Daniel Rice here."

The clock on the nightstand read 7:04. *Damn, I should have been up by now.* With only a few hours of sleep, Daniel's brain was still fuzzy and the dream remained fresh.

Shea broke through the cobwebs. "Soyuz is down. In South Dakota. I need you there as soon as possible."

"Down? Landed?" He sounded hoarse.

"Yes, landed. All in one piece. But something went wrong, that's why I need you there."

"Are they okay?" he asked, finally thinking straight.

"Probably not." Shea's voice was firm. "The capsule is empty."

~~~~~~~~~~~~~~~~~~~~~~~~

Daniel stood at the doorway to Marie's hotel room, feeling uncomfortable that he had so little to tell her.

"Empty? How could it be empty? Did they get out?" Her eyes filled with tears, her expression a mix of surprise and anguish.

"That's all I know right now. It's their capsule, they're just not in it. We need to get out there ASAP."

Marie turned and ran back into the room, pulling a jacket off the bed and reaching for her packed suitcase. "Ready," she said. A tear rolled down one cheek and she quickly brushed it aside. "Keep talking. Tell me what you know."

Daniel picked up his bag and they hurried to the elevator. "A normal landing, about an hour ago. It came down in South Dakota, just north of Rapid City."

"Normal. The parachute deployed? Soft-landing rockets fired?"

They exited the elevator and ran through the lobby. "Yeah, a normal Soyuz landing, just not in Kazakhstan."

"Why South Dakota, then?" she yelled as they hurried across the parking lot.

"Nobody knows. It might be random. Soyuz must have dislodged itself from 4-D space somehow and returned to where it started, in the atmosphere on reentry."

They threw their bags in the backseat of the car and climbed in front. Daniel squealed the tires as they sped out of the parking lot and headed toward the freeway.

Now in the relative quiet of the car, her volume lowered. "Was the hatch open or closed when it landed?"

Daniel's eyes left the road for a moment and he looked over at Marie. "What are you suggesting? They climbed out?" An open hatch might imply the astronauts had found some other shelter, though what, he couldn't imagine. More likely, an open hatch meant their bodies were still somewhere in space.

"An open hatch means egress." She held her hand to her mouth. "I need to know how it ended."

Daniel returned his attention to the road. "I only talked to Shea. I didn't ask, and she didn't say. Sorry." He was just as worried as Marie. The situation certainly didn't look good. Of course, these were men he'd never met, whereas for Marie they were colleagues, even friends. He understood how she must feel.

"There's a plane waiting for us at DuPage Airport, and we'll be in South Dakota in less than two hours. We'll know soon."

Marie nodded and Daniel pushed the pedal to the floor as he sped on to the interstate.

As they drove, he thought about the Fermilab experiment that had moved a rat through quantum dimensions. Nala had described the rat's body as liquefied. He wondered how well the recovery team had searched the Soyuz cabin for remains.

# 30  Lost

The military transport Gulfstream C-20H reached cruising altitude and leveled off, the roar of the engines diminishing slightly. Daniel and Marie sat in a forward area of the plane that was allocated for passengers. Two men in Air Force uniforms with lots of gold braid on their shoulders sat a few rows back, and a woman in civilian clothes sat across the aisle, absorbed in her own work. A large pallet of equipment hidden beneath multiple layers of plastic shrink wrap was strapped to the floor behind the rows of seats.

Daniel reviewed the stack of papers once more. Phone records and computer network logs. They all looked legit, and damning. "They're basically saying Nala has been spying for the Chinese."

Marie shook her head. "Don't they always?"

"So, you don't buy it?" Daniel asked.

"Not for a second." Marie kept her voice low and their conversation private, but her passion was obvious. "She called you. She spent hours providing relevant information. She brought up the reference to a disc-shaped planet, and she explained why space junk is going missing without you ever mentioning the Kwajalein report."

Marie's intensity increased to a level that Daniel had not yet seen in her. "On top of all that, if Stetler is involved with the Chinese, as she says, they have every reason to try to discredit her."

Daniel was puzzled by her defense of Nala and felt the need for objectivity. "Do they have reasons to discredit her? Yes... of course they do. But what if the truth is just the opposite? What if she really is feeding information to the Chinese? She would have every motivation to point the finger at someone else. And these documents appear to be valid. The phone records, for example."

Marie shook her head vigorously in disagreement. "Yes, it's possible she's a deceptive, out-of-control employee. But let me approach

174

this question slightly differently... as a woman. There's a long history in both business and government of women being discredited by men who are their superiors. Discredited when they bring up sexual harassment, discredited when they challenge an entrenched idea, and discredited when they expose fraud, or bias, or anything that shouldn't be happening in the workplace. I'm sorry, but that's just reality and it's been going on forever."

She waved her hand through the air as she made her point. "The opposite, a woman lying and her male superiors completely innocent, is almost never true. Except maybe in Hollywood. I've seen the system in action—most women have—and I'd bet a large sum of money that Nala was telling you the truth."

Daniel tapped nervously on the armrest as he absorbed her argument—and her passion. She was almost certainly right, but this was a serious charge of espionage, and completely out of the realm of scientific oversight. He had reached the limit of his authority, and probably his skills too.

If it was a case of character assassination, he knew why. "Marie, you're right. There's plenty of evidence supporting her, and one glaring flaw with this packet of evidence against her."

"What's that?"

"Why did they give it to me?"

Marie remained silent, which seemed to solidify her point. There was little reason for Stetler to involve Daniel in a case against their employee—except to discredit her.

After a minute, Daniel finally spoke. "We're going to need help. Last night I made a call to Shea. She'll send the FBI into Fermilab and Stetler, probably today. Those guys will have to sort it all out in our absence."

Marie nodded. "That's the right plan. Don't expect the FBI to understand the science going on there, but they'll have a better shot at figuring out if anyone is lying. Our job has shifted, at least temporarily, to South Dakota."

Daniel leaned back in his seat and looked out the window. He thought about his encounter last night at the bar, Nala's explanation of spatial compression, and her certainty of Chinese involvement. She had provided so many details. Her concerns were real, or at least they felt real. He only wished he had more evidence, beyond her word.

The drone of the airplane's engines was hypnotizing and the lack of sleep became impossible to ignore. He closed his eyes.

~~~~~~~~~~~~~~~~~~~~~~~~~~

Marie tucked the blanket in behind Daniel's shoulder. His head rested against the window shade, now closed. For nearly an hour, she had scoured her brain for every detail of Soyuz operations and systems that might result in an intentional egress, either in space or during reentry. She could think of at least a dozen scenarios, but most of them resulted in a quick death to the occupants. It was a discouraging exercise.

The plane's engines throttled back and the nose dipped. Daniel's eyes opened and he sat up in his seat.

Marie held out a granola bar. "Hungry?"

"Yeah, thanks," he said, taking the snack. His voice was scratchy. "Guess I was out for a while."

"You're lucky," she answered. "I can't sleep on planes. You just closed your eyes and were gone. But you were up late last night."

Daniel blinked and rubbed his finger through the corner of his eye. "So, I'm allowed the downtime?"

"You bet. Part of being a human." The pace had been relentless and it wasn't showing any signs of letting up. She could tell it was wearing on him. It was wearing on her too, and she regretted being so

176

vocal in their argument about Nala's credibility. She appreciated that, in the end, Daniel had agreed. He had adapted his viewpoint in the face of new information. She couldn't say that of most people.

A few minutes later, the plane touched down at Ellsworth Air Force Base on the outskirts of Rapid City, South Dakota. It taxied to a low-slung building in desperate need of a coat of paint. They gathered their bags and stepped out onto the plane's built-in stairway. A gusty wind blew across the tarmac, picking up dust and tossing scraps of paper past the stairs.

A man in uniform met them at the bottom. "Dr. Rice? Ms. Kendrick? I'm Staff Sergeant M.T. Peabody. Aide to Colonel McGinn."

Daniel practically yelled and still the wind drowned him out. "Sergeant Peabody, nice to meet you. Where do we go from here?"

A bit of something hit Marie in the eye. "Someplace calmer," she yelled.

Peabody shrugged with a grin on his face. "Yeah, it really blows this time of year. Well, year-round, really." When he didn't seem to be moving, Daniel pointed to the dilapidated building behind him and Peabody swiveled. "Yeah, sorry, right this way, folks."

They followed him into a low-ceilinged waiting room with furnishings straight out of the sixties. Peabody looked behind him as he walked. "First time at Ellsworth?"

"Yes," said Daniel for both of them. "Is Colonel McGinn in charge of the Soyuz recovery?"

"Yes, sir," Peabody replied. "He's over at the hangar right now. They brought the capsule in a couple of hours ago. I've never seen a Russian spaceship before."

They exited to the street side and back into the wind. A car was parked only steps away, and Marie was thankful to climb into the backseat. The terminal might not be modern, but taking military flights certainly avoided congestion on the ground. Daniel climbed into the front and pulled out his phone. "Text from Bradley," he said over his shoulder. Marie nodded and Daniel typed.

Peabody gunned the car's engine and sped away from the curb. "Home of the B-1B," he said to Daniel.

Daniel looked up from his phone. "The bomber?"

"Yes, sir, the Lancer," Peabody confirmed. "And a few F-16s." Peabody pointed to a parked aircraft painted in camouflage. "That's an F-16 over there."

"I see." Daniel returned to his keyboard.

"I flew in the backseat once," Peabody announced with a huge grin. Daniel looked up again, a pained expression on his face.

Marie reached up and touched his shoulder. "I got this," she mouthed. She leaned forward just a few inches behind Peabody's ear. "You flew in the backseat? What an experience."

"Lieutenant Conner put that baby on its tail. We shot straight up. Ten thousand feet in five seconds."

"What a thrill, I've never done that," Marie engaged him enthusiastically. Daniel smiled and returned his focus to the phone. The drive across the air base was only a few minutes, but Peabody pointed out every barrack, mess hall and activity center. Marie played the part of the perfect guest.

"You never have to leave the base," Peabody said. "Unless you want to go to the reservation for gambling."

"Alas, probably not this trip," Marie lamented, almost believably. Her enthusiasm was not entirely a façade. She did enjoy talkative people and believed in her heart that they should be encouraged. Otherwise, society is left only with smartphone zombies wandering aimlessly through shopping centers. She had that tendency herself.

They pulled up in front of a large building with two enormous doors, both shut. "You can leave your bags in the car," Peabody told them. They walked to a more human-sized door near the corner of the building and entered a hangar that could have easily held a 747, maybe two. The ceiling far above echoed their steps and the sounds of people working. The enormous concrete floor was empty except for the small capsule resting in the center, a flurry of men and women on it, around it, and inside it.

Peabody got the attention of McGinn, who turned to greet them. "Colonel Steven McGinn," he said, shaking their hands. A tall, thin man with a full head of gray hair and glasses, he was dressed in tan military fatigues, a silver eagle on each lapel.

"You're from the White House?" He looked at Daniel, who nodded. "And NASA, is that correct?" Marie did the same. "I just talked to Spencer Bradley on the phone. He briefed me on what you're doing, so the three of us can speak freely."

Marie turned her gaze to the Soyuz capsule behind McGinn. An aluminum scaffold stood to one side, allowing people to easily climb to the top of the spacecraft. A man crouched on the scaffolding and handed a tool to a woman inside, whose head was visible through the open hatchway. Marie had been in so many training mockups, it was hard to believe this was the real thing.

"Ma'am, we collected a few personal items from the cabin, including a photo of Jeremy Taylor's family. What do you want us to do with them?"

*Jeremy's family*—that hit home. This capsule was very real, and so was the loss of three men. "I'll take care of it," she answered. "Did you pull the flight recorders?"

"Yes, ma'am. Flight data and voice. Both were intact. Our guy Pixie is rigging some electronics right now. We're not exactly prepared to handle Russian technology here, but your bosses at the White House

179

asked me to tap into those boxes, if we could. They want to know what's there before we return this equipment to the Russians."

"Good plan," Marie replied. "I want to know what's on those recorders too."

"Crazy question, I'm sure," Daniel started, "but is there any chance they climbed out by themselves before anyone got to the landing site?"

The colonel spoke in slow drawl. "No, sir. That hatch was closed and locked. We had to trigger the ground release switch from outside to open it. Took a while to find it, but we did. The recovery team said it smelled pretty bad in there." He looked over at the capsule. "No, sir, before we got there, that hatch was never opened. How those guys got out? Well... that's anybody's guess."

"And, your search inside? Any...?" He didn't finish the question.

"If you're asking about remains, there are none. No fire, no explosion, no windows blown out, no other points of exit. An ordinary Soyuz capsule returned from space, minus the occupants."

Marie stared silently at the capsule. She took a step forward, stopped and looked up at McGinn. "Do you mind?"

"No, ma'am. Feel free to get up close. We're almost done here anyway."

Marie stepped to the capsule and peered in its small round window. Inside, a light hung from a wire and a woman was unscrewing a box mounted behind one of the seats. Marie put one hand on the capsule's cold metal surface and closed her eyes.

She thought of her colleague and friend, Sergei Koslov. A man full of life, with infectious enthusiasm. She thought of the backyard barbeque in Houston. Sergei, the center of attention, a smile always on his face. The bottle of vodka he had brought to celebrate the completion of

Marie's training class. Her promise to kiss him when he returned from space. She felt a lump in her throat.

Still more difficult were her thoughts of Jeremy Taylor. His lovely wife and their shy five-year-old daughter at the same barbeque. Jeremy laughing at Sergei's terrible jokes, and Marie's threat to add one more exam before she signed off on their training. Jeremy's little girl giggling when her father snatched her into the air.

Tears welled in her eyes. She blinked hard and a drop fell on the metal surface. She took a deep breath, kept her face hidden from view and wiped away the moisture from her cheeks. She looked over her shoulder. Daniel was speaking with Colonel McGinn. Her brief moment of reflection was enough. There was a job to do.

As she rejoined them, Daniel was in the middle of an explanation. "Given what we saw at Fermilab, we think there's a relationship."

"That's a hell of a story." Colonel McGinn's gaze fell upon the capsule and back to Daniel. "Pushed into another dimension? And the technology that can do this, you've seen it yourself?"

"Up close and personal." Daniel raised his eyebrows. "But I have to say, describing it to you makes it sound pretty crazy. I wouldn't fault you if you didn't believe me."

"That's just it, I think I do believe you," McGinn said. "Dr. Rice, you're not the first. Dr. Bradley rattled off something similar."

"I hope his version is better, because we're coming up short." Daniel pointed behind him toward the capsule. "We have the hardware back, but it's still missing a few critical items that should have been inside."

McGinn nodded and looked at Daniel and then Marie with a grimace on his face. "Dr. Rice, Ms. Kendrick, missing astronauts may be only half of this story." He took off his cap and scratched the back of his head. "That capsule? It isn't just missing three men. It came back with an extra piece of hardware, and I highly doubt it's anything you'll find on a Soyuz parts list."

# 31 Found

Daniel followed Colonel McGinn as they climbed the steep metal stairs at the side of the hangar, Marie not far behind him. The view across the vast space was impressively empty. A sea of concrete surrounded the tiny Soyuz capsule near its center. He wondered if 4-D space was just as empty.

McGinn unlocked the door and flipped on a light that revealed a small office. "I'd offer you a shot of whiskey if I had it," he said as he reached into a cabinet. "Might help to make any sense out of this thing." He pulled out a small cardboard box that made a reverberating clunk when he set it on a table in the center of the room. "I suppose NASA will find some fancier container for it, but we used what we had. Go ahead, take a look."

Marie motioned to Daniel to do the honors. He opened the top of the box and peered inside. Wrapped in a towel, the object in the box took two hands to lift it out. "Not some ancient stone tablet, is it?"

He laid the object on the table and unwrapped the towel, revealing a highly polished silver metal plate, about an inch thick. It was teardrop-shaped, with smooth, elegant curves that ended in a point. But not quite a teardrop; its shape was asymmetric, with one side convex and the other mostly concave.

"Interesting." Daniel slid the heavy metal object around in a circle. Its polished surface gleamed from the overhead light. Every edge was rounded and buffed to jewelry perfection. "A shape like the number six or nine."

Marie pulled her chair in for a closer look. "More like half of a Chinese yin-yang symbol." Daniel nodded; she had a point. The drop shape at one end could nicely fit into the negative space at the other end. It seemed like a piece was missing.

"What is it?" Daniel looked up at McGinn.

He shook his head. "We haven't the slightest idea. But you're right, Ms. Kendrick, this is only half of a whole. Its matching partner is still in Soyuz. We haven't been able to take it out."

"And the two pieces fit together?" Marie asked. "Is it really a yin-yang thing?"

"Pretty much." McGinn held his hands together, with one hand pointed opposite the other. "Put together, they make an oval shape. That's the way we found it, an oval resting on the Soyuz control panel. They easily pull apart, they're magnetic." He reached into the cabinet again and pulled out a small nail. "Try this."

Daniel held the nail near the edge of the object. When he released it, the nail snapped to the metal. "Okay, definitely magnetic. But why can't you take the other half out?"

"It won't budge," McGinn answered. "The thing is sitting on top of the control panel, practically glued in place. You can put your full weight against it, but it doesn't move. We can't see any bolts or other attachment points, but somehow it's locked in place."

Daniel pointed to a circular hole in the center of the teardrop. "What's this opening?" He peered into the hole. "There's nothing in there."

"I was hoping you'd tell me," McGinn answered. "As far as we can see, it's just a hole. You can shine a light in there, it's just more of the same smooth metal. The matching plate back in Soyuz is different. No hole, but maybe some lights—like LEDs. And something drawn on it. Nobody's figured either one out yet, but then we're not experts. We service B1-Bs out here, not Russian spacecraft."

Daniel rotated the heavy plate and inspected the metal closely. McGinn touched the pointed end. "Try standing it up on that. And I should warn you, this is where that shot of whiskey might come in handy."

Daniel looked quizzically at McGinn. He lifted the object and set its weight on the curved tip. "It'll just fall over."

McGinn laughed. "The hell it will."

Daniel wondered if he had really understood what McGinn wanted him to do. The thing was a plate of metal. He felt its weight in his hands as it rested on its narrow point, obviously top-heavy and unstable. It wouldn't stand on its point any more than a kitchen carving knife would.

McGinn waved his hand. "Try it. Just let go."

Daniel shrugged. He let go and squeezed one eye shut, ready for the loud bang when the object's full weight smacked the table. But nothing happened. The object balanced on its tip and even straightened slightly, its heavy rounded top suspended above its narrow tip. It looked very much like the number nine, delicately balanced on its stem. The tip's curvature alone should have caused it to roll to one side, but the object stood firmly in place.

"Push it," suggested McGinn. His expression was nothing but serious.

"Really?" Daniel held out a finger and gave a gentle push on one side. The inverted teardrop leaned as he pushed, and when he let go, it righted itself again. "That's not possible, the weight's all in the top. How's it staying upright?"

Marie put her hand on the object and pushed it all the way over until its side touched the table, then let go. Again, the object quickly righted itself, standing back on its point. "Weird."

Daniel picked it up off the table and shifted the object between his hands. It felt like any ordinary metal plate, about ten pounds in weight. He set it back on the table, this time with the rounded end on the table like a number six. The object rolled to one side and lifted up, back onto its point.

Daniel rubbed his lower lip. "I've seen kids' toys that have hidden weights in their base so they'll always stay upright. Like a punching bag or a free-standing basketball hoop. But this thing feels different. Maybe a little lopsided. Kind of like…" A shiver ran down Daniel's body.

*Like Park's tesseract.*

He lifted the object in both hands, tilting it one way and the other, imagining what else might be attached that he could not see, and could not even touch. It was an unnatural feeling and highly disorienting. There was something otherworldly about this object.

McGinn shook his head. "We couldn't figure it out either. And just in case you're wondering, it seems safe to handle. It's not lead, and we checked for radioactivity. It appears to be chrome or titanium. Maybe silver."

Daniel laid the object flat on the table, where it stayed put with no tendency to dance on its point. "It's none of those. There are only three metals that are magnetic—iron, nickel and cobalt. So, it's one of those three, or an alloy. It's most likely cobalt, which is silver in color."

Daniel continued to stare at the strange object on the table. "So, this yin thing was found in an empty Soyuz capsule. How did it get there?" He looked at Marie and Colonel McGinn, both with blank expressions. He didn't blame them; he had no answer either.

Marie had been mostly quiet, observing Daniel as he interacted with the object. But the question seemed to trigger an idea. "That's why I asked about the hatch earlier. Like the colonel explained, Soyuz hatches can be opened from the inside or outside—once a ground release is triggered. But let's be clear. You can only *close* a Soyuz hatch from the inside."

Marie's point sunk in. McGinn's recovery team had found the hatch in the closed position but no one inside that could have closed it. It made no sense. Daniel tossed out one idea, even though he doubted it himself. "Maybe this thing is a device that was able to close the hatch?

The astronauts climbed out, someone put this device inside and sent Soyuz home?"

Marie looked puzzled. "Who, the Chinese?"

McGinn shook his head. "Look at this thing." He placed it back on its point, and the balancing trick continued to amaze. "If that was manufactured by the Chinese, I want some stock."

"Well, it is a yin-yang thing. That's Chinese, isn't it?" She shrugged. "Sorry, that sounds dumber now that I've said it."

They all stared at the shiny teardrop, each remaining silent. Daniel glanced at McGinn. The events of the last twenty-four hours told him that anything was possible. "There are other explanations. Not only for how this thing was manufactured, but also for how the astronauts got out." He looked over at Marie. "We've seen a few things lately that have similarities." She nodded. He didn't elaborate; it wasn't necessary. He could see the gears turning in her head.

McGinn stood up and pulled out a phone. "Sit tight, let me check on those flight recorders. If we can find out what was going on in the capsule, it might help." He stepped out onto the top of the stairway and closed the door. Daniel pushed the object again, as if its impossible behavior might have changed while they were talking. It hadn't.

He rested his elbows on the table, his eyes just inches from the object. He glanced over at Marie. "What do you make of it?"

She had only touched it once and seemed to be keeping her distance now. "It came from *kata* space. That's what you're thinking too, right? This thing jumped inside Soyuz, and no one ever opened the hatch."

"And the astronauts jumped out."

"Right." She sighed. "But I'm not sure if that's good or bad."

Daniel thought for a moment and continued his close-up gaze of the object. "Nala told me last night that they couldn't return living things

187

from 4-D space. That living cells are damaged in the process. This sure feels like someone else understands that limitation. Soyuz is back, this thing came with it, but those guys didn't come along for the ride."

Marie's lips tightened and she visibly shivered. "They could be anywhere."

He agreed with her assessment. Missing astronauts could be good or bad. "I was also thinking about why this thing stands on its point."

"Yeah, me too. What do you think?"

"There's more to this thing," Daniel said. "A part of it we can't see, just like the tesseract Park showed us. I think it might be a four-dimensional object."

"With extra mass on the bottom?"

"Yeah. Something we can't see is keeping it stable on its point."

McGinn opened the door. "News flash, we've got something off the flight recorders. Follow me." Daniel wrapped the yin object in the towel, placed it back in the box and returned it to the cabinet. Not the most secure of storage places, but at least the office was locked. It would do, for now. "Where to?" he asked.

McGinn led the way down the stairs into the hangar. "The electronics shop, it's right next door." They exited to gusty winds and immediately entered a smaller building only a few feet away.

They walked through a workshop, filled with shelves of equipment and several waist-high wooden tables. Each workbench was covered with avionics components, their cut wires dangling in the air. Alone at one workbench, a young man in uniform was wrestling a large electronics cable into a socket. He looked up as they approached.

McGinn slapped him on the shoulder. "Pixie, meet our science team, Dr. Rice and Ms. Kendrick."

His name tag read Senior Airman Elwood Tinker, and he set the cable down to reach out his hand. "Call me Pixie, everyone else does." On the workbench in front of him were two orange metal cylinders with Russian writing on the side. "Some good stuff here." He pointed to the cables running from the cylinders to another electronics box. "Russian-style data ports, but I got everything linked up."

"What'd you find?" McGinn asked.

"Voice and data. Both are… good. What do you want first?"

"How about the voice?" Marie answered.

Pixie nodded and reached for a keyboard. He typed a few keys and a list displayed on a screen next to the electronics. "It's mostly radio communications." He touched an item on the list, and a window popped up displaying an audio graph. He touched it and a recording played. The voice coming from the speaker was sharp and clear.

"*Moskva, Sayuz. Peredachu na 922.763. Otvechat…* Houston, Soyuz. Transmitting on emergency frequency 927.0. Respond."

"Sergei!" Marie smiled.

Pixie looked over his shoulder and smiled back. "There's several more like that, ma'am, in English and Russian." He turned back to the display. "But let me show you this one. It's different." He touched the display and another audio graph displayed, its waveform looking nothing like the previous one. He touched it and a strange sound came from the speaker—a buzzing sound, or more like a vibration that varied in pitch.

Daniel listened carefully. "Sounds like a violin. Or maybe one of those Vietnamese dan bau instruments. You know, where the performer can produce a vibrato."

A few more seconds passed. "So, what is it?" Marie asked.

Tinker held his finger in the air. "Wait for it, ma'am." The vibrational sound continued, then a silence, followed by two words.

*"Kak pashyevayesh,"* buzzed from the speaker.

Marie tilted her ear closer to the speaker. "Russian, but clearly not a person's voice. Like it was computer-generated."

"Yes, ma'am."

"Can you match the audio with the source metadata?"

Pixie grinned. "My thought exactly. I checked—the source was not Roscosmos, or any other ground station. The source ID was blank."

Marie paused. "Okay, that's strange. An unidentified source, but issuing a common Russian greeting."

"Sorry, I don't know any Russian," Daniel said. *"Kak, pash-*whatever. What does it mean?"

Marie spoke, but from the expression on Pixie's face, he had the answer too. "Any first-year student of Russian knows this one. *Kak pashyevayesh.* It's just a greeting. It means 'how are you?'"

Daniel held one hand up. "So, let me get this straight. We've got a transmission to Soyuz from an unknown source... while they're stuck in 4-D space... and this clandestine voice is only saying 'how are you?' What sense does that make?"

Pixie nodded rapidly. "I've got a theory, but first let me show what I found in their data recorder." He typed a few keys and a new window popped up, displaying a text message.

```
Message received 07:49:15 UTC
Source Relay    S-Band
Frequency       922.763
Source ID       ---
Subject         ---
Length          13K
Body:

review and respond 922.763
```

Pixie pointed to the screen. "They received this message about an hour before reentry and about five minutes *after* that audio I just played. See here? The source ID is blank again."

He turned around to face McGinn. "Sir, the radio transmission and this message. They had to come from the same source. And that script? It's not Arabic. It's not Farsi either. Or Bengali, or Punjabi. I checked." Pixie licked his lips. "Sir, I know it sounds crazy, but I don't think it's from this planet."

McGinn moved close to the display and stared at the message text. Daniel and Marie did the same. Daniel pointed to the screen. "But the first line of the message is in English. 'Review and respond.'"

"Yes, sir. But the rest isn't."

Marie leaned her elbows on the workbench. "Well, it's not Russian, that's for sure. Are you a linguist, Pixie? How do you know it's not one of those other languages?"

"Internet, ma'am."

Marie looked skeptical. "You think the source is alien? Just like the yin-yang object back in the hangar?"

Pixie nodded his head vigorously. McGinn remained silent, folding his arms and taking a deep breath. Pixie appealed. "Sir, I'm no language expert, but it's not hard to look these things up. I've checked—"

McGinn stopped him. "Relax, Pixie, you sold me." McGinn jerked his head toward the hangar. "That thing upstairs didn't come from around here either. And these characters look a lot like what's displayed on that thing still stuck in Soyuz."

"Wait a second," Daniel interjected. "Let's think about this. Look, Airman Tinker, er, Pixie, I'm not saying you're wrong, hell... you might be right." Daniel blinked hard. "But we'd all be wise to look at the more ordinary explanations. Marie, what if the Chinese sent this message? Would we know it came from them?"

Marie thought for a second. "Yeah, we would. Incoming data communications are filtered. China's not an ISS partner; they're considered a foe in the military sense of the word. Any text from a Chinese source would end up in a virus quarantine folder."

"And did it?"

Pixie shook his head. "No, sir. I pulled it from their routine inbox."

"Okay." Daniel nodded. "But maybe it originated from some other location. The ID is blank, so it sounds like the system couldn't identify the source."

"That's right," Marie answered.

"What if this script is some other form of Punjabi? I'm pretty sure there are lots of dialects in India." He looked at Pixie. "And maybe a language expert could explain why it doesn't match what you saw on the Internet." Pixie nodded in agreement, and Daniel returned to Marie. "If the message came from India, would we know it?"

She shrugged slightly. "Well... I doubt the security software has been written to cover every possibility. I don't know about India, or Iran.

192

There might be a ground station that would show up with a blank source ID."

Daniel leaned on the workbench, rubbing his forehead. *Focus. Examine the evidence. Apply Occam's razor and separate fact from fantasy.* This Chinese company, Wah Xiang, was the prime suspect. If they had the technology to push a spacecraft into a fourth dimension, they could easily have discovered the means to bring it back. They might be farther along than anyone thought.

He turned back to the message still displayed on the screen. The unknown script, three lines, three repetitions of the same thing, whatever it meant. Repetition. Why repetition? He stared intensely and paused on the third character. He looked up as the meaning hit him.

"Holy hell, I think I can read it."

# 32 Yin

Daniel paced the floor of the electronics shop. Marie reached an arm out to him. She could see the strain on his face. She was either watching a genius ready to unveil the meaning of life, or a person about to have a nervous breakdown.

Daniel touched her outstretched hand. "Just a second," he said without looking up, and continued pacing. He muttered under his breath a few times and stopped to mouth words to empty space. His portrayal of Sherlock Holmes, or a demented soul, was nearly perfect.

"You think you can read it?" she asked softly.

Daniel nodded. He stopped his pacing and stared right through Marie. He held three fingers to his lips, obviously still deep in thought.

"What?" Marie demanded.

Daniel took a deep breath. "Let's start with the text message. Consider two options, one ordinary and one fantastic. The first option is that the message came from the Chinese, or from India, or some other ground station that we haven't figured out yet. The second option"—he shrugged, holding his palms to the sky—"is the Pixie theory that this message has an extraterrestrial source." He pointed at Pixie, who still sat at the workbench. "By the way, if you're right, we'll name it after you."

He started pacing again. "Actually, I can see arguments in favor of both. On the one hand, at least we know the Chinese exist. Being real is always a good start. And we believe they have a new particle accelerator that gives them the opportunity to reach into 4-D space, a clear requirement in order to communicate with Soyuz. That probably rules out India; they don't have the technology. The Chinese also have the motive for a rescue. They may have blundered into this situation, and it's in their interest to find their way back out."

He stopped in midstride and held a finger in the air. "On the other hand, it's hard to understand why a Chinese-sourced message contains Punjabi, or any other written language beyond English, Russian or Chinese. But there's the script—and yes, I think I can read it." He pressed his brow together and turned to Marie. "The English line, 'review and respond.' It's standard phraseology in space communications, am I right?"

She nodded. "Sure. It's common for any NASA or Roscosmos flight. Basically, it means 'I'm sending you something and I won't take action until you respond.'"

"Very likely transmitted by Sergei himself at some point, allowing anyone on the radio frequency to intercept it. Anyone with access to *kata* space, that is. But this line makes little sense if the source is Chinese. What are they asking for? Review what? Why not just fix the problem and bring Soyuz home?"

Marie had asked herself the same thing. A message from the Chinese to Soyuz didn't seem to have much purpose. It would be an admission of responsibility. If they were going that far, why didn't they just contact Roscosmos and fess up?

Daniel continued. "It also doesn't make much sense if the source is little green men. Again, there's nothing to review. But the phrase itself is used to solicit a response, and you could say that's all the little green men were asking for. Give us a microphone click, respond to our message, and we'll take action."

Daniel stopped. It wasn't clear if he was done analyzing, so Marie didn't respond. She didn't really have a response to give. There were a lot of hypotheticals floating around the room and she wanted to see where they landed.

He finally broke the silence. "Yeah... strange stuff to be talking about. That's why I'm still leaning Chinese. It's the simplest explanation, Occam's razor being the guiding methodology. One other question, and then we'll get to the script." He pointed to the orange cylinders on the workbench. "Over the past twenty-four hours, we've heard snippets of the communications from Soyuz, probably including this Russian greeting, *kak pashyevayesh*. You're our Russian expert, Marie, do you recall hearing it? Maybe Sergei said it at some point?"

"Yeah, I think he did," Marie said.

Daniel moved closer to the screen, still displaying the cryptic message. "Look closely at the script. One phrase, repeated three times. There are eleven distinct characters. If we're reading left to right, the first character is the same as the third character. Does that sound familiar? Like any other phrase we've heard recently?"

The point laid out so clearly, Marie immediately saw the answer. "*Kak*. The first three letters are *kak*."

Daniel pointed a finger at Marie and smiled. "The prize goes to my brilliant associate. *Kak*, indeed. Now, look at the rest of it. If the first part is *kak*, then the character that looks like a *3* is a vowel-sound, like an *a*. That character is repeated twice more. The sixth character is the same as the last character, the one that looks like an *n* with a dot over it? Substitute the phonetic sound, *sh*. And look at the seventh character, the one that looks kind of like a lowercase *j*? It's the same as the tenth character. Substitute the sound, *ye*."

Daniel smiled. "It's a puzzle. Like that old TV show, you know, the one where Vanna White reveals each letter in a phrase? I may not be able to see every letter, but I have enough to be confident the phrase is *kak pashyevayesh*. Someone was speaking to Soyuz by echoing a radio greeting in both the audio we just heard and in written text. And not once, but three times. It certainly gets your attention."

Once explained, Marie could see the word as plain as day. Repeated three times in a text message to Soyuz, and vocalized in the buzzing sound. Why? There didn't seem to be any point. "You've got the answer, Daniel. But why does anyone send a message to *review and respond* and then key on a Russian phrase that has no relevance?"

Daniel didn't respond. He looked up in the air and slowly started pacing again. He shook his head. "I don't know. It makes little sense in either scenario." He continued pacing, clearly not letting the question go.

While Daniel pondered, there was another nagging thought in the back of Marie's head. A key item on the checklist for any flight that ended in disaster.

*What were the last words of the flight crew?*

She did her best to keep her emotions in check. "Pixie, we need to locate the end of the voice record. Can you do that?"

Pixie nodded and returned to his keyboard. He searched through several folders and finally pointed to the screen. "Got it, the last two minutes. Their system uses an active mic that shuts off when there's silence, but you'll hear a click to indicate a break." He started the audio playback.

*"Sayuz zdyehs, otvet.* Soyuz here, responding on 922.763..."

"Soyuz, responding on 922.763... Come in..."

*"Allahu akbar... Allahu akbar...* Come in..."

Marie felt a surge of satisfaction. "It's Sergei again. He's reaching out, responding to the message. And that last part, it makes perfect sense. He thinks the message might be Arabic, just like we did."

There was a click in the audio, a Russian profanity and some angry shouting, then another click. The next sound was a loud pop and a few seconds later a voice, weak and scratchy.

"What the hell?" Sergei said.

The audio playback ended. Marie let out a breath she didn't even realize she'd been holding in. Even lacking a visual image, or maybe because of it, the audio track was disturbing. Her heart beat rapidly and her imagination ran in multiple directions. Was the pop the same effect they'd heard at Fermilab? Somehow, it didn't sound quite the same.

197

"Wow, those guys saw something," she said. "Pixie, do we have a time stamp on the recording data?"

Pixie examined his screen. "Yeah, that last segment was 1051 UTC... 3:51 a.m. our time, so about two hours before Soyuz reentered."

"And there's nothing recorded beyond that point?" Pixie shook his head. "Two hours," she said carefully. "Lots of time for them to get out, but if they were still in the capsule, you'd think the microphone would have picked up something."

Daniel had been silent throughout the audio playback. He stood by himself, frozen, staring into space. His mouth opened but nothing came out. The demented soul, or Sherlock Holmes, was back again.

Marie stepped over to him and pushed his shoulder. "You've got to stop doing this, Daniel. What?"

He shook his head. "An idea. Colonel, can we get that yin thing down here?"

"Yeah, sure," the colonel replied. "I'll be right back."

While McGinn was gone, she asked Daniel, "Something to do with the final audio?"

He shook his head again. "No. Well, sort of. As I was listening, I was half-expecting to hear that vibrational sound again. You know... right after Sergei said, *what the hell.*"

It was a scary thought—an alien-sounding voice coming from inside the capsule. "But that didn't happen," she told him.

"No, it didn't," he agreed. "But it gave me an idea."

McGinn returned carrying the cardboard box. He unwrapped the contents and set the teardrop plate on the workbench. Just as before, it balanced on its tip with no effort. "What do you want to do with it?"

"Pixie," Daniel asked. "Pull up the other audio clip, the one with the vibrational sound."

Pixie had a puzzled expression. "You think? ..." He typed on the keyboard and the eerie sound began to play. They waited until the vibration *kak pashyevayesh* buzzed from the speaker.

As if responding, the yin-shaped object made a slight clicking sound, and suddenly a beam of light burst from the hole in its center. Hovering in the air, two feet in front of the teardrop, an image appeared.

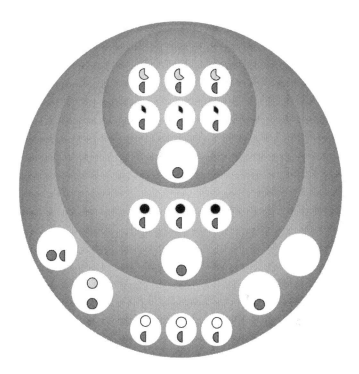

It was a multicolored circular shape, a drawing of intricate design, and it was projected into the air as clearly as if it had been drawn on paper.

"Oh, my God," Marie gasped.

The circular image didn't waver. The shapes within it were sharply defined, circles within circles, with a variety of colors—orange, blue, yellow and green. It was quite beautiful, though what it represented was anyone's guess.

"That's so cool," Pixie said. "The audio file triggered it."

Daniel reached out to the narrow base of the teardrop. Marie waved her hands rapidly. "Are you sure you want to do that?"

Daniel's fingers paused inches from the metal surface. He glanced at Marie, then back to the object, and grasped it. The image remained in place. As he lifted the teardrop from the workbench, the circular image rose along with it. Daniel slowly pivoted his hand and the image orbited around the teardrop as he moved. A smile broke across his face. "It's a projector."

Marie could faintly see light shining from the hole in the metal surface. It was undoubtedly projecting the image. But onto what? The air itself? "I've never seen any projection like this," she said. "It's so clear and sharp. How do you get that by just shining light into the air?"

Daniel turned the device, watching the image swing in the air. "It's like holding up a page from a laser printer, but without any paper."

The image was composed of multiple circles. Three large circles, gray, blue, and orange, nested within each other. They contained smaller circles of white, most with additional circles or semicircles inside them. Marie struggled with both the advanced technology and its clear link to the message. Replaying the buzzing voice had activated it, she had no doubt. Could the Chinese have created this? For what purpose?

"It's a diagram of some sort," she offered. "It almost looks like a schematic of a planetary system, with the little yellow moons across the top. But the pattern doesn't look random. It's very organized—grouped."

Daniel nodded. "Definitely informational. But projected into the air. Why?" He carefully set the yin object back onto the workbench. As it had done before, it straightened slightly and stood on its point. "Take a photo of it."

Marie pulled out her phone and took pictures from several angles. The camera captured the projection perfectly, relieving Marie of the bizarre notion that the image might be appearing only in their collective brains. She was about to take another picture when they heard a click and the floating image disappeared.

"Oh, no!" Pixie shouted. "Baby, come back."

Daniel peered into the hole. "The light is off. Maybe it's on a timer?"

Marie waved to Pixie's equipment. "Play the sound again, let's see if we can bring it back."

Pixie pulled up the list of audio recordings on his screen, but Daniel touched his shoulder. "Wait. Before you do that, could we try something else?" He bent down close to the device and spoke into it as though it were a microphone. "*Kak pashyevayesh.*"

The object clicked, the light came on and the projection appeared once again in midair.

"Yes!" Pixie said and pumped a fist in the air.

"Well, I'll be," McGinn said. "Voice-controlled."

Marie laughed. "Accuracy doesn't seem to matter. Your Russian accent is terrible. But a brilliant idea, Daniel." Daniel shrugged with an open hand.

McGinn spoke up from the back of the group. "So, we've got maybe two or three minutes until it shuts off again? I wonder if it's a battery thing."

"At least we know how to control it," Daniel suggested. "Even if we don't know what it's displaying."

Marie leaned in closely to study the details of the image. *How odd.* The investigation had certainly been a roller coaster of new experiences, but the technology in front of her was one of the most disturbing yet. The device was performing magic, standing on its point and projecting into air. They could touch it, hold it, take pictures of it, even speak to it. But understanding its purpose seemed out of reach.

Daniel leaned in next to her, their faces just inches from each other and from the object. They exchanged a very puzzled glance. "What do you think?" she asked.

"Photons don't glow." Daniel turned to the image. "They don't hover in the air. To reach our eyes, they have to reflect off of something. In this case, there's not much for the photons to hit—air molecules and maybe a little suspended dust."

"Lasers?"

"Well, it's true, a green laser can be seen at night. That's mostly reflection off dust and microdroplets of water. Red lasers don't even produce that much reflection. No, this is way beyond any laser we've ever produced."

"Maybe the Chinese have some new technology?" She didn't really believe it herself. The evidence was beginning to point in other directions.

Daniel reached out a finger and touched the side of the plate. "I wonder what happens when the projection hits something solid." He pushed the object to its side, as they had done before. The projected image also leaned and eventually intersected the workbench. It behaved as any projection would, displaying on the workbench surface instead of midair.

"Okay, that was thrilling," said Marie. Daniel smiled and released his touch. The object righted itself, the image returning to the air. Marie reached out to touch the hovering phantom, but as her finger passed in front, they heard another click and the image abruptly changed.

"Oh, shit, sorry," she said and quickly withdrew.

They both stood back. Floating in front of the object was an entirely new image, nothing at all like the previous one. It was a group of

202

orange balls mixed with smaller blue balls. But far more interesting, the image was no longer a flat page floating in space. It was three-dimensional. Each ball was a small sphere, suspended in the air in a specific three-dimensional position.

"Oh, wow," Daniel mouthed. He moved his head side to side.

Marie moved around the projection. It was like viewing a physical three-dimensional model of objects suspended by wires. She could lower her head and see the bottoms of the balls. It was similar to a 3-D visualization, but not on any computer screen.

She snapped several more pictures with her phone, each from a different view into the floating image. "Unbelievable. I love this technology. Can I have a computer display like this, please?"

"Oranges and blueberries," said Pixie.

"Oh, you're good," Daniel said. "Along with the Pixie Theory of Alien Communication, this image will forever be known as the Oranges and Blueberries Diagram. Are we going to have to pay you royalties every time you come up with this stuff?"

Marie recognized the importance of labeling the unknown. Planetary scientists named rocks on Mars or formations on Pluto. The often-silly names were simply a way to catalog the new discoveries in words they could all share. Oranges and blueberries would do just fine. She held a finger close to the projection. "You think there's more?" She looked around at their faces. "Shall I try?"

Daniel and McGinn both nodded and Marie stuck her finger purposefully into the projection path. Another click and the image changed to a flat diagram with circles.

"It looks just like the first image," she said.

"I think it *is* the first image," replied Daniel. "Try it again."

She waved her finger once more and the image switched back to oranges and blueberries. "Yup." Another wiggle and the circular diagram returned. "Looks like there are only two. But we can get to both of them as often as we like. And..." A clever idea entered her mind and she grinned. "*Kak pashyevayesh.*" The image changed to oranges and blueberries. "Aha! Flick your finger *or* voice command. Multimodal UX."

"Huh?" asked Pixie.

"UX, user experience. Software designers create multiple paths to reach the same functionality." She commanded once more by voice, and the circular image returned.

For such a simple purpose, the device did seem well designed. "Does it look smaller to you?" asked Daniel. "The image. It seemed bigger the first time we saw it."

"Yeah, I think you're right," she said. "Let me try something else." She placed her finger in the projection path and held it there. The image didn't switch, but a portion of it was missing where her finger crossed the projection path. She moved her finger towards the image and as she did so, it grew larger.

204

"Cool!" She smiled. "Zoom control, too." She brought her finger back toward the device and the image shrunk. When she withdrew, the image remained at the adjusted size. "Handy little projector they have here. I *so* want this technology on my computer."

Daniel spoke to McGinn. "We have a device that can project two images, an audio recording and a text message. But, we're only looking at half of what was left in Soyuz. The other half is still bolted, or glued, or somehow fixed onto the control panel."

McGinn nodded. "What do you propose?"

"We'll definitely want to try out voice commands on the other one too. Maybe we snap the two halves together again and see what difference that makes? There are several tests I can think of doing. None would take much time, and we might discover more functionality."

"I think my team is done by now," McGinn responded. "The capsule's just sitting there."

Daniel picked up the yin device and held it out to Marie. She reluctantly accepted it and felt a chill when her hands touched the cold, smooth metal.

Daniel seemed excited. She'd seen that look before—he had something else in mind. "Marie, you've got the best command of both languages, and you're a natural at advanced user interface. Can you take the lead? Find out what works."

"Okay. What are you going to do?"

He rubbed his chin. "I have one other idea, but first I need to make a phone call." He pointed to the yin in Marie's hand. "Then I might need to go back to Fermilab... and take this hunk of metal with me."

# 33 Yang

Marie lay prone in the commander's position of the Soyuz capsule, occupying the same space Sergei had just a few hours earlier. She felt his presence. It was a stupid idea, very unscientific with no basis in reality. But she felt him just the same.

At eye level to her left, a small window provided a view across the hangar. Pixie stood outside. Above her head, the unused emergency parachute still consumed most of the overhead space. The capsule felt just as claustrophobic as she had remembered from her cross-training at Roscosmos.

The control panel was more than an arm's length away and quite difficult to reach with the full force of gravity pinning her to the seat. It would have been easier in orbit. Soyuz was a craft designed for weightlessness, not for sitting on the ground.

Pixie's head appeared in the open hatch above her. "How ya doing?"

She acknowledged him with a half-smile. "Well, I got the two halves snapped together. Even that wasn't easy." Just as Colonel McGinn had described, she found the yang firmly stuck to the control panel with no obvious means for its attachment. It stood on its point, just touching the top of the control panel's metal frame. Unlike its partner, this version could not be pushed, tilted or perceptibly moved. She thought of Daniel's suggestion that the yin could be a four-dimensional object. Maybe the yang was too, with a mechanism of attachment that was not even located within her world.

The front of the yang was different from its partner. A vertical strip ran down its center with three black characters marked on it. They looked similar to the characters in the text message. Definitely not Chinese characters, but it was hard to know if they belonged to some other language. Now with the yin paired to its partner, the two formed a smooth oval shape like two commas, one inverted.

It had taken longer than she had thought to bring them together, and the effort of holding the heavy weight above her head for several minutes had tired her arms. She rested another moment. "Okay, here goes..."

She pressed the record button on her phone as a quick means of documentation. She wasn't sure how close she might need to be for the voice command, or for that matter, what to say. *"Kak pashyevayesh."* The basics were always a good place to start.

Nothing happened. She lifted as high off the seat and she could and spoke louder, and still nothing happened.

"Well, I was at least expecting to see the projection again, but the thing seems to work differently when it's attached."

"How are you?" she tried. The English version wasn't any better. Even if the device was voice-controlled, she had no idea which words to try. More Russian? Chinese, perhaps? If these devices had any relation to the Chinese, why did a Russian phrase control the yin's ability to project images? She wondered if Pixie's idea might be right. This device didn't look like anything made by humans.

*"Moskva, Sayuz, sdelanny."* Sergei would have said this many times trying to raise someone at Roscosmos. She waited, but the metal oval remained silent and motionless.

*"Peredachu na 922.763. Otvechat...* Houston, please respond..."

Nothing.

She tried several other radio phrases, both in English and Russian. Nothing seemed to have the slightest effect. "Damn," she mouthed. She had no expectations of what might happen, but she hoped for something. She felt stupid speaking to an inanimate device that provided no response.

She looked up through the hatch. Pixie was still in view, his eyes looking nowhere. "Sorry," she said. "I'm not sure what else to say."

"Maybe pull them apart again?" he suggested.

She nodded and reached up to the control panel. She pulled on the yin side and it snapped away from its other half like a refrigerator magnet. "Well, it's easier to take them apart."

She stood the yin on its point on the front edge of the center seat, hesitant to let go. "It sure feels like it's going to fall over." She released her grip, and the metal plate performed its vertical balancing act even though the seat itself was reclined at an angle. "Pretty amazing. It seems to balance anywhere."

"See if you can get the projection back," Pixie encouraged.

Marie nodded. "*Kak pashyevayesh.*" The yin device clicked and the circular image reappeared like a genie called from a lamp. "At least we got that part down."

"Your Russian is perfect," Pixie called down. "I know a little myself."

Marie shrugged. "*Yeshche odin dlinny den.*"

"Sorry, you lost me there."

She lifted up the yin device and turned it in her hand. "I said... it looks like it's going to be another long day."

The space was cramped, and she needed to get out and stretch. She stood up on the center seat and handed the yin up to Pixie. "Coming up."

She placed a foot on the top of the control panel, next to the yang. A flicker of light caught her eye. She wasn't sure what she'd seen and lowered herself back down. She squatted, directly in front of the yang, still marked with three black characters in a center strip. *That's strange. It looks different.* She pulled out her phone and took a picture.

~~~~~~~~~~~~~~~~~~~~~~~~~

Another military flight, another drive from the airport, and Daniel stood at the entrance to Wilson Hall, his overnight bag now ten pounds heavier.

It had rained since he and Marie had left Illinois only eight hours earlier. A mist hung above the grassy fields of Fermilab. *Ground fog by tonight*, the science in his head chimed. He entered the building and registered at the front desk. A few minutes later, Josh arrived, the same intern who had greeted Daniel and Marie less than thirty hours earlier. It seemed like a week ago.

"Where's Ms. Kendrick?" Josh asked as they rode the elevator.

"South Dakota, actually. Related business."

"Can you confirm the rumors?"

Daniel's eyes narrowed. "What rumors?"

"They're saying that the whole Soyuz flight was faked. That the astronauts died on board ISS, but NASA doesn't want to admit it."

Daniel shook his head. "Does that sound reasonable to you?"

Josh shrugged. "Well, no."

"Then it's probably just another conspiracy theory, isn't it?"

"Yeah, I guess so." Josh laughed. "I didn't really believe it." The elevator stopped at the fifteenth floor. "I can take you to Dr. Spiegel. Dr. Park isn't here."

Daniel stopped in his tracks. "Park isn't here? Where'd he go?"

"Washington. Some big meeting. Sorry, there wasn't any warning, he just left."

*Damn.* Daniel rubbed his forehead. Taking control of the nation's preeminent particle accelerator would have been easier through Park. But there were other paths. "Just let Dr. Spiegel know I'm at the facility."

He turned back to the elevator, leaving Josh with his mouth open and nothing to say.

As he stepped into the elevator, Daniel pulled out his phone and dialed. Voicemail picked up. "Nala here—well, my voice anyway. Leave me a message..."

# 34 Lockdown

Nala stood in front of the main entrance of the Stetler office building. She felt her phone vibrate. *Won't these people leave me alone? Let it pick up.*

She'd been on the phone for the past hour with two different authorities. The call from the congressional investigator was bad enough. Prosecution seemed a likely outcome. But the second call from the FBI had hit her in the gut. "Can you come in to the Stetler office?" a tough-sounding man had asked. "Or we can pick you up."

Whether he was offering a ride or threating arrest wasn't clear. Logic told her there was no other choice, so she got in the car. She told herself she had done nothing wrong, but that did little to dissipate her nervous feeling. Authority was authority, whether the FBI or the Illinois police, and possessing dark skin in America was always a risky proposition even if you were entirely innocent. Nala had experienced the consequences more than once.

She felt a chill as she started up the stairs. Only twelve hours before, she had climbed these stairs in the dark, with Yost's goon, McLellan, right behind her. *It's broad daylight. They can't hurt you now,* she thought.

The FBI vehicles in the parking lot didn't help. Yes, they represented protection from Yost and McLellan. But she desperately worried that handcuffs were in her near future. Her heart rate picked up as she walked slowly down the hall to the Stetler office. Her fingers stopped just short of the door handle, hesitant. Finally, she opened the door.

The previously immaculate reception area was now filled with cardboard boxes, each sealed with tape displaying the word *Evidence* in bright red letters. A young man stood near the reception desk. "Can I help you?" he asked.

"I'm Dr. Nala Pasquier. I was asked to come in."

"Agent Stevens, FBI." The young man shook Nala's hand. "We've been expecting you. I'll get Agent Townsend." He left the lobby and returned a minute later followed by a middle-aged man with wavy gray hair. The man wore a black suit and a thin black tie that screamed FBI.

"Dr. Pasquier, thank you for coming in." It was the same tough-sounding voice from the phone call. "I'm Agent Townsend, FBI. I'm managing this investigation. Am I pronouncing your name right, Pasquier?"

"You are, but you can call me Nala." Staying as friendly as possible was a learned trait.

"Thank you, but for now I'll just keep it formal if you don't mind. It's an investigation." He paused, his forced smile frozen on his face. "I must say, Dr. Pasquier, you've got some friends in high places."

The comment was nearly the opposite of what she was expecting; it didn't even make sense. "None that I know of."

"You'd be surprised." Agent Townsend looked at his phone. "Just this morning I was on a call directly to the White House and your name came up several times."

"What...?"

"Dr. Daniel Rice, White House OSTP. Someone you know?"

She hesitated, unsure how to answer. "He was in our office yesterday."

"And that was the first time you met?"

She nodded. *Okay, this is weird.*

"Hmmm." Townsend's voice was gruff, with no inflection to distinguish between question and accusation. "You were fired last night. After making an offer to Dr. Rice?"

The blood pressure in her head shot up. "I was fired for telling Daniel Rice what I know about this—"

"Oh, yes, I heard the reason," the agent said, nodding. "From Dr. Rice himself. But the story changes depending on who you talk to."

"Those ass... what did they say about me?"

The agent's stoicism remained unchanged. "Well, if you're referring to Mr. Stetler or Mr. Yost, they don't seem to think you're very trustworthy. They suggested that you had taken a thumb drive with classified software on it. I checked, and there is a drive registered in their security log that's missing. Any idea where it might be?"

"No, I don't. It's not with me." She knew the game. It was all too easy to create a security log and a story to go with it, but impossible to prove she didn't have something that had probably never existed.

Nala stepped closer. "Agent Townsend? Am I pronouncing that right? Let me give you another tip. Stetler and Yost? These are people who just make things up. They wouldn't blink an eye at falsifying whatever evidence you have in these boxes." She spread both arms wide. "You're looking for a nonexistent thumb drive? Search me."

Townsend paused. He looked like he might indeed kick her legs apart and pat her down. But his demeanor calmed, and so did his voice. "No need for that." He consulted his phone. "We do have a warrant to search your house and car, Dr. Pasquier. Acquired before Dr. Rice stepped into the picture. A search may not be necessary, we'll see."

His tone softened further. "Dr. Pasquier, you may be surprised to hear that I'm not an adversary. I'm an investigator, and I follow wherever the leads take me. You see all the boxes around you? So far, I'd say the evidence is in your favor."

Nala took a deep breath, calming her nervousness. There were no handcuffs yet, and maybe there wouldn't be.

The agent looked down the adjacent hallway, yelled for someone and returned his attention to Nala. "I'd like to have Agent Coffey ask you a few questions."

"Fine."

"And perhaps do a quick pass through your purse, if you don't mind?"

She held out her purse and Townsend held up his hand. "In a minute, no rush."

A thick middle-aged woman with short blond hair walked into the lobby. "You need me, chief?"

"Agent Coffey, this is our missing VIP, Dr. Pasquier."

"Ah, Dr. Pasquier, we've been expecting you," she said.

"I guess everyone has." The two shook hands.

Townsend spoke to Coffey. "Dr. Pasquier is kindly allowing us to look through her personal belongings for the misplaced equipment. And we'll need a full interview. Let me know when you're done."

"Right-o, chief." Coffey motioned to the hallway. "Follow me, Dr. Pasquier." As they walked away down the hallway, the conversation turned strangely casual. "You know, it's funny, we both have unusual last names. Pasquier. Coffey. Both kind of hard to spell, too. Coffey is with a Y, not like the drink."

They turned a corner toward the conference room. "You know, you look familiar. Have you been on TV? Or in a movie? You're not a movie star, are you?" Nala just smiled and followed the agent, who continued the one-way chat.

"I'm originally from Kentucky, but I kind of like Chicago. Except the winters. Have you lived here long?"

"Just a few years." Nala kept her answers simple.

Agent Coffey stopped at the conference table and looked at Nala like she was studying a photograph. "My brother once met that actress, what's her name? I can't remember, but you look like her."

Nala had heard the comparison before. Flattering perhaps, but it made no sense. It seemed there were always people in the world that needed to compare whomever they met to someone famous. This very odd agent seemed to exist in another world. "Don't you need to ask me some questions?"

Coffey seemed surprised. "Of course, that's why we're here."

"And you need to search my purse?"

"Yeah, I need to do that too. You don't mind, do you?"

Nala waved her hand in the air, put the purse on the table and pushed it over. Coffey dug around inside for a few minutes and pushed it back. She then pulled out a thin metallic wafer and placed it on the table. She touched a pad and it made a soft beep.

"Okay, so we're recording now. Go ahead, you can start. Let's see, just tell me about the events leading up to your being fired from Stetler. Oh, and anything you know about Mr. Stetler or Mr. Yost and their dealings with China."

Nala decided she'd better identify the key bits of information any prosecutor would need. It didn't look like Coffey was going to figure it out for herself. She started with her knowledge of Wah Xiang and her discovery that her computer had been hacked. She explained why a Chinese company might be brought into the project and talked about the new particle accelerator in China, The Higgs Factory. She detailed the events from the previous night, her meeting with Daniel in the bar and her confrontation with Yost and McLellan. Agent Coffey nodded and smiled and let the recorder capture the words.

"Anything else?" Agent Coffey asked after Nala had paused.

"Not that I can think of," Nala said.

215

"Great," said the agent. She switched off the recording device and put it in her coat pocket. "Just sit tight for a minute while I talk to my boss. I'll be right back and we'll get you on your way just as quick as we can."

It was more like ten minutes, but she finally returned. "I'm so sorry, Dr. Pasquier. That took a little longer than I expected."

Townsend was right behind her. Coffey took a chair but Townsend remained standing, scratching the side of his head. "Dr. Pasquier, I've just spoken again with Dr. Rice. It looks like you're going to receive immunity from prosecution, and I've agreed to proceed with this investigation on that basis."

Nala froze. *Damn, the guy came through, just like he said he would. Could this be real?*

Given the events of the past twenty-four hours and many months of working for this badly dysfunctional company, she was having difficulty in distinguishing friend from foe. But with this new information, Daniel Rice was now firmly in the friend column, maybe even in a new column reserved for saviors and superheroes.

Agent Townsend eyed her carefully. "However, in return for this immunity, we would like your continued cooperation on some specific items."

*That doesn't sound bad. A lot better than handcuffs.*

His voice was still just as gruff. "There are a number of documents we'd like you to review and provide notes where you may have personal information on conversations, meetings, and directives issued by leadership at Fermilab or Stetler. We will need you to sign a sworn affidavit after you have reviewed these documents. Will that be acceptable, Dr. Pasquier?"

She nodded. "Yes, of course." She breathed deeply and felt a warmth spreading across her. This was even better than "you're free to

216

go," better than walking out the door, better than being feet up on a barstool and a margarita in hand. This was an offer to help put away the scumbags who'd created this mess. She'd gladly do that even if they did put handcuffs on her.

Townsend turned to the door and then paused. "Dr. Pasquier, what we're doing is a little unusual, especially for an employee that was just fired from a company that seems to have broken a dozen security laws. Please don't do anything that will make me regret my decision."

Nala nodded. It wasn't easy to say to a cop, but she forced it out. "Thank you."

"You've got it from here, Agent Coffey." Townsend closed the door behind him.

Nala felt like she had just faced down a bull who had decided at the last minute not to charge. She had to consciously close her mouth. "Wow. That was a turn I wasn't expecting."

Coffey smiled. "I'm glad it worked out." She pushed a plastic badge across the table. "You'll need this back. Your access to Fermilab facilities has been restored—the same as you had before, but let us know if you see any mistakes, okay?" Coffey stood up. "Can you come with me? I'll get you set up on a computer."

Nala followed her down the hallway, her head in a daze. Things were rapidly changing for the better, yet chaos still reigned in the office. Cardboard boxes were everywhere and most desks had been cleared. Nala saw their IT manager working to disconnect some cables, but otherwise there were no employees in the office. "Where is everyone?"

"Most people were just sent home. Some were in tears, it was really sad. We've been calling them in one by one for interviews. We've only asked key people to remain in the building. Mr. Yost, Mr. Stetler and a few others."

She stopped walking. "Yost is still here?" She wasn't relishing meeting him in the hallway.

"Yeah, he's in his office, I think."

"Does he have access to anything?"

Agent Coffey shook her head. "No one does. We've shut all that down."

"So why are they still here if they can't access their computers?"

"I think Mr. Yost and Mr. Stetler are still meeting with each other," she said. "We pop in every now and then and ask them a question."

It didn't seem very thorough. Irresponsible, even. Why were Yost and Stetler still allowed to roam the building at all? She hoped this investigation didn't blow up through lack of competence. Agent Coffey stopped at a closed door, pulled out a key and opened it. It was a small office with no windows, one desk and one computer. There was another key lying on the desk.

"That'll be your key, Dr. Pasquier. This office is for your use only. You can take as long as you need to review the documents, but if you leave to go to the restroom or anywhere else, please close and lock the door, and don't allow anyone else inside."

She handed Nala a slip of paper. "It's your temporary login. There's folder on the computer desktop. Just follow the instructions and electronically sign the affidavit at the end. It's really pretty easy.

"Oh, and if you don't mind, just memorize your login and put the paper in the shredder in the hallway before you leave. My boss will get mad at me if you don't. Okay?"

"I can do that," Nala replied. "Thanks for your help. I hope you nail those guys."

"Mr. Stetler?" asked Agent Coffey.

"And Yost, especially Yost."

"I don't know about Mr. Yost, but Mr. Stetler seems like such a nice man." Coffey shook her head. "It's too bad, really."

"Don't let them fool you. If there was any money in it, Stetler would sell out his own mother." She sat down at the desk and turned on the computer. Agent Coffey waved goodbye and closed the door. Nala logged in. She was happy to see a familiar list of apps and file folders still available to her.

~~~~~~~~~~~~~~~~~~~~~~~~~~

Shawn Yost sat in the guest chair across from Terry Stetler. With no computer and no office phone, the desk seemed empty. But Stetler had adjusted and was making notes on paper and using his personal phone.

"I told you, I begged you to shut this thing with the Chinese down," Yost shouted. "Now we're both in it up to our eyeballs. They've got it all. The fucking FBI has everything they need, like we just gave it to them."

Stetler didn't flinch, his tone weary. "You're such a small-minded man, Shawn. I've tried to coach you. Lord knows, I've given you every opportunity to step up your game. But, it's clear to me now that you just don't have it in you. You're not executive material. Just a common personnel manager."

Yost was heated. "What the hell is wrong with you? You act like nothing is happening out there." He knew he was cornered, and he worried he was being set up for the fall. If he was going down, he'd take Stetler with him.

"Shawn, all of this"—Stetler waved his hands in the air—"it's just a temporary setback. The wheels are already in motion to bury this so-called investigation. The good senator from Oklahoma will come through. We'll be back in business in a few months. Well, I will. I'm sorry you

219

won't be involved in phase two, but I'm afraid I'll be needing a new chief technical officer. Shawn, it's been a good run."

"Fuck you!" Yost fired back. "You think Cummings is your savior. You think you can just do anything you want and no one can touch you. Arrogant prick."

"Shawn, get a backbone and shape up for God's sake. And don't even think about talking to the FBI. You'll be the guy who goes down, not me. I don't have to remind you that it's your signature on the Wah Xiang agreement. I'm also quite sure Jie Ping won't be testifying in your defense. But if you keep your mouth shut, this will blow over in a few weeks and then you can go find yourself another job. I might even write you a recommendation, if you're nice."

Yost stood up and paced the room. He knew he was in over his head, and the boxes piled up outside the office were a strong reminder. But if Stetler pulled this one out of the fire, it wouldn't be the first time. As it turned out, Yost didn't have to decide one way or the other. There was a knock on the door, and Agent Coffey poked her head around the door.

"Hi, guys," she said. "We're going to need to interrupt you now." She opened the door completely to show Agents Stevens and Townsend standing behind her. Stevens had a weapon drawn, pointing to the floor, and the look on his face made it clear he was ready to use it.

Townsend stepped into the room. "Do the honors, if you will, Agent Coffey."

Coffey approached Yost, pulled out a pair of handcuffs and took his wrist. With considerable expertise, she slapped the cuffs on one hand and reached around for the other. Yost was too stunned to move. She spoke to him as if she were awarding a blue ribbon for best brownies at a county fair. "You're being placed under arrest now, Mr. Yost. We'll read your rights in just a minute. If you wouldn't mind, just stand right there for now."

Stetler remained frozen in his chair, watching intently. Strangely, he still carried a look of confidence, as if he really believed his tall tale, and Senator Cummings would save the day at the last minute.

Coffey walked to his desk. "Would you mind standing up, Mr. Stetler? It won't take a second." Stetler hesitated, and Coffey repeated, "Yes, stand up, that's right." He looked at Stevens, at the gun in his hand, and back to Coffey. He finally stood up, a look of horror on his face as Coffey pulled another pair of handcuffs from her pocket. "You're under arrest too, Mr. Stetler." She slapped the cuffs on his wrists.

"Goddammit," Stetler yelled. "You damned incompetent bitch! What the hell do you think you're doing? He's the guy you need, not me! Yost made the deal. Check the paperwork, you've got it in one of those goddamned boxes out there."

~~~~~~~~~~~~~~~~~~~~~~

Nala heard yelling. She jumped up and peered out the door. It was coming from Stetler's office, and the FBI agents were standing in the doorway. "This, I have to see."

She padded down the hallway and came up behind Agent Townsend. He glanced at her and she lifted her eyebrows in a simple question. He nodded and she peered over his shoulder. Inside, Stetler stood at his desk, his arms behind his back. She could see the handcuffs on Yost. Her mouth dropped open. "Oh my God."

Agent Coffey carried on in her agreeable way. "Oh, of course you're right, Mr. Stetler. You know, I looked at that contract just this morning. And Mr. Yost had signed it, just like you say. But, you know, I got to thinking that maybe the whole thing was a little too simple. They taught me in FBI training to look at the big picture. You know what I mean?"

Nala couldn't believe her eyes. Agent Coffey was arresting Stetler and Yost. Cheery, sweet-natured Agent Coffey from Kentucky.

221

"So, this morning I got to thinking," Coffey continued, "about the big picture. I knew I'd need more information to get it right."

She walked to the credenza next to Stetler's desk, reached into a narrow space between the credenza and the wall and withdrew a thin metallic wafer that had been taped there. She held the recorder up in the air and smiled.

"I'm pretty sure this will help us with that big picture." She waved the device around like a proud mom. "It's really well designed, easy to attach to wherever you need it. Up to twelve hours of audio recording with a great mic that picks up conversations even in a room this big." She turned her head to Yost. "I put it there before you guys came in this morning."

Nala threw her hand to her mouth to suppress the laughter. "Amazing," she whispered. *She had me completely fooled too.*

Stetler hung his head down. "Shit," he muttered under his breath. Agents Townsend and Stevens each grabbed an arm and led the handcuffed men through the door, Nala pressing herself against the wall as they walked past.

She peered back in and caught Agent Coffey's eye. Coffey smiled back and Nala stepped into the room. "Damn nice work, girl. You've definitely got a style."

Coffey waved her off. "Oh, it's nothing. I'm just being myself. It seems to work well for my job. Kind of throws people off and gives me room to work."

"Masterful," Nala said in awe.

"Got to run now. Paperwork, you know. Oh, I almost forgot. When you get back to your computer, look for another file on the desktop. It's a copy of some documents that Dr. Rice received from the former security chief at Stetler?"

"The white envelope, I remember."

"Pay no attention to the content. Fakes, I'm afraid. Good ones, but not difficult to challenge in court. You're safe."

"Thanks, I appreciate your help."

"Well, you take care of yourself, Dr. Pasquier. And good luck."

"Call me Nala."

"Thanks, Nala. Call me Jean."

"Thanks, Jean. You're the best."

Jean Coffey, no doubt one of the FBI's best agents, just smiled.

# 35 Bliss

The office was little more than a hollow shell. No FBI, no Stetler, Yost, or any other employee for that matter. Even the stacks of cardboard boxes were gone. Nala was completely, marvelously, wonderfully alone.

She drifted slowly down the empty hallway, her shoeless feet barely touching the carpet. She looked up at the elegantly lit curved ceiling and down the hallway to the once-impressive reception area of the now-defunct Stetler Corporation.

A genuine smile broke across her face. Accompanied by beautiful music in her head, she danced.

She weighed nothing and floated effortlessly. One leg lifted and she performed a graceful pirouette on her toe, arms flowing in waves as her ballet teacher had taught more than twenty years before. She closed her eyes and reached both arms high overhead. She exhaled completely and then took a full breath of fresh, new, clean air.

She lifted onto one toe, tilted her head and touched her fingers in a circle. She turned around and leaped in a *tour jeté*, landing perfectly on her jump foot. The movements felt wonderful and the imagined music was magical.

She heard the clapping of hands behind her. She twirled, her eyes wide as they met Daniel's. He stood alone at the far end of the hallway. "Beautiful," was all he said.

Her face flushed at the intrusion into her private performance. But the joy inside would not allow embarrassment to spoil the fun. She placed her leg in front and bowed deeply to one knee, her arms forming feathery wings to each side. "Thank you, sir."

He waved a hand. "Please don't stop. Is there more?"

She flowed down the hallway on tiptoe, a *bourrée en couru*, stopping just short of Daniel and still on her toes. "*Un pas de deux, monsieur?*" She smiled, overtly sweet, took his hand and danced... as well as she could, dragging Daniel down the hall.

"Wait!" he cried out. Daniel dropped his overnight bag, and it hit the floor with a dull clunk. She stopped and turned to face him. "Ah, ballet's not your thing. A ballroom dancer, I think." She placed his hand on her waist, her hand on his shoulder and their free hands together. The music in her head changed to a waltz and she hummed for his benefit. She led, he followed, in a clumsy sort of way. But the effort was there, and that was all that mattered.

They danced together. She looked up into his face and beamed. "Pure joy is fleeting, to be treasured when it comes." Daniel nodded, his face still more surprised than overjoyed.

They spun, lifted and twirled, not elegantly but with enthusiasm. When he almost stepped on her foot, he lost his balance, and together they crashed into the wall. She buried her face in his chest, laughing as hard as she'd laughed in months. She looked up at him. "Oh my God, Daniel. You're great!"

"Since when is terrible the same as great?" He still held her hand. "You, on the other hand, have a wealth of hidden talent."

She leaned her head against him and took a deep breath. He smelled nice, a scent she couldn't place. She remembered a similar dance years ago, on a tropical beach at night. The dance had ended much the same way, with a crash. But, helped along by tequila, it had also led to a night of pleasure.

His face was near as he spoke. "I saw the parade of felons in the parking lot. You must be relieved."

He wasn't a surfer, and this wasn't a beach. She released his hand and stepped away. Her ballet slippers returned to being ordinary socks, and she walked through the doorway of her temporary office. "It's a new day, Mr. Government Investigator. And the rain clouds are parting."

She rounded the desk and sat down in the chair. Daniel stepped into the doorway, and she held up a hand. "You're not allowed in here. So says the FBI. Only me."

"I see." He stepped a foot backwards. "I hope things worked out with... Agent Townsend, I believe?"

"You've spoken with them, and apparently very persuasively." She grabbed her Fermilab badge from the desk and held it up. "I've been redeemed. Thank you again, sir."

Daniel leaned against the doorway. "I wouldn't have made it very far without your help. You were brave to come forward, and I'm very grateful."

The past twenty-four hours had certainly been dicey. An emotional roller coaster, as they say, with an outcome that could have gone either way. Without his intervention, she wouldn't be sitting in this office.

"Buy me dinner sometime." She smiled. "How's tonight?"

Daniel laughed. She knew he would.

"You know, that sounds wonderful, and I wish I could. But..."

And she'd also expected his answer. "Yeah, I get it. Duty calls. Astronauts still missing and all that." She stood up and grabbed her car keys from the desk. "Well, it's nearly six. I'm done here, so I think I'll head home. Thanks for the dance." She poked a finger in his chest and lifted her eyebrows. "You were fantastic."

Daniel straddled the doorway, blocking her exit. His mouth tightened. "Nala, I need your help. Again."

# 36 Circles

"Nala, I need access to the lab... and your talents."

He couldn't stop her from leaving, and he would let her pass if she insisted, but Daniel needed her cooperation. He had used his leverage to ensure no charges were filed against her, and his effort had not been solely for her benefit.

Their hallway dance had been a delightful diversion. She was an impulsive, intriguing woman, and he would have gladly spent the rest of the evening locked on to those beautiful eyes. He could see the change in her. The nervousness and frustration were gone, replaced by an aura of self-confidence that made her even more alluring.

But right now, he didn't need an attractive woman on his arm or an exotic dance partner; he needed the particle physicist who stood before him.

"Park was called away to Washington," he said. "It's past six, and somehow, I need to tap into the power of this facility. Tonight. Can you help?"

He was significantly taller than Nala, and she looked up to answer. A twisted smile formed on her lips. "Sounds like a man who needs neutrinos. I'm at your service."

"Thank you, I do appreciate your help." Daniel held up a hand. "But first I need to show you something."

She shook her head. "Not here. The FBI owns it now. I gave them what they wanted, I'm done with this dump." She wiggled her index finger in his face. "Come on, I know the perfect place."

She closed and locked the door. Daniel followed her down the hallway and out of the building. They took her car the short distance to Wilson Hall, and then the elevator to the lowest levels of the labyrinth beneath the ground. She cheered at each security door as her badge flawlessly provided access.

They dropped down another level by stairs before reaching a door marked *MINERvA*. Inside was a large room that looked half-finished, with scaffolding reaching up to an exposed rock ceiling. In the center, a massive steel hexagon as big as a car and probably ten times as heavy was suspended in the air by a structure of steel I-beams.

"We're at the deepest point underground now," she said. "More than a hundred meters of rock are above us." She pointed to the steel hexagon. "They slam neutrinos into iron atoms here. The beam passes through that steel block on its way to Minnesota."

She walked to the corner of the room and opened another door. "But I didn't bring you here for any of that. The MINERvA team has the best analysis room at Fermilab. Cozy and quiet, with comfy chairs and a fridge."

Daniel set his bag on the table with a noticeable clunk. "Perfect."

"What? Did you bring your free weights with you?"

He laughed. "Just as heavy. Something very unusual we found in South Dakota." He pulled out his laptop and turned it on. "Soyuz landed there."

Her head spun. "Landed? Are you kidding me? That's huge."

It *was* huge, and he hated to let her down. "They weren't in it. The capsule was empty."

She shook her head. "Wait a second... the capsule landed, but without its passengers?"

Daniel nodded. "We don't know what happened. We're working on it."

"Then what the hell are you doing here? Shouldn't you be in South Dakota, figuring this out?"

"My partner is still out there. I came back because I think some of the answers we need are right here." He reached into his bag, pulled out the silver teardrop-shaped plate and handed to her.

She took it in one hand and added a second hand. "Heavy, what is it?"

"We're not sure. We're calling in the *yin*. There's a similar one back in South Dakota, the *yang*. These things were inside Soyuz."

Nala squinted and shifted the thick plate in her hands. "Mysterious. No people, but heavy metal returning from quantum space." She looked up with a worried expression. "You sure Soyuz was empty? I mean, really empty?"

Daniel nodded. "Yeah, I thought the same thing. They searched for human remains. Somehow those guys got out. Personally, I'm suspecting a fourth-dimension-style exit. You know, where they jump right past the metal walls of the capsule like they weren't even there? The usual stuff that you deal with every day."

She tilted her head. "I'm not sure how that would work. They were already in 4-D space. Expand a fifth dimension? It's either that, or solve the problem of anything alive returning to 3-D space. I don't know, this is quickly getting beyond my experience."

"It's possible the Chinese have advanced well beyond Fermilab."

She shook her head. "You shouldn't put so much faith in Wah Xiang's abilities. This stuff is not easy. It took us years to get to where we are. They've only had our software for a couple of months, and right away they fucked up. They may be good hackers, but in my opinion they're crappy scientists. Don't expect them to unfuck this mess... if that's a word."

"But their Higgs Factory came online faster than anyone anticipated, and we agree they're targeting at much greater distances."

She shrugged. "Yeah, but those are really just the same thing. Bigger accelerator means greater energy, which helps the neutrino beam stay coherent to greater distances. I grant you they've built a larger accelerator. But I'd still say they don't know what they're doing with it."

It was good to get her view, even if neither one of them knew exactly what the Chinese could or couldn't do. "I'm just looking at the possibilities," he said. "Unfortunately, the competing explanation takes us out on a limb. Technology not of this world. Alien. Some of the people out in South Dakota are taking that option seriously."

Nala straightened. "Really?"

Daniel took the device from her and set it on its tip in the center of the table. "Watch this."

Her eyes grew wide as the yin stabilized in a vertical position. "Holy... it does a hell of a good *en pointe*."

"That's just a warm-up." He spoke the Russian phrase, the device clicked once, and the circular image snapped into view.

Nala leaned in close. "Wow!" She positioned her head to the left and then the right of the object. The flat image floated in the air like a piece of paper glued in place. "This is real?" He nodded. She reached out to touch it, and suddenly the image grew larger. She held her hand in the path of the projection, moving it slowly and watching the image resize.

"I love it. I want one, to put on my coffee table." She looked back at Daniel. "Personally, I'd go with your alien hypothesis. This thing ain't Chinese."

"It's not my hypothesis."

"But you're leaning that way."

"No, I don't think so." He tried to sound convincing. "Look, this is my professional background. I started my career thinking I would be involved in a SETI group or follow the trailblazers of the Kepler program and search for habitable planets beyond Earth. But I learned quickly what

230

it takes to declare you've found life elsewhere, and it's a lot more than we have right now."

"But you're holding physical evidence." She pointed to the yin. "Diastasi never had that—we only speculated what we might find."

"What do you mean, you speculated?"

She lowered her head. "Daniel, Daniel. You're living the dream. Around here, we've talked about this for the past year and a half."

"What, aliens?"

Her expression was serious. "Yeah, first contact, all of that."

She was heading down a path that had been lingering in the back of his mind ever since their meeting in the bar. He'd pushed it to the corners of his thoughts, probably to avoid dealing with it. But he really wasn't surprised at her disclosure. "It's the compression, isn't it? We've opened a door."

Nala grinned. "It's finally sunk in, eh? I did try to tell you. Compression is the crown jewel. It's what this discovery is all about. Spatial compression, reducing real distances to almost nothing. You bet it opens a door."

"And you... or the Diastasi team, have been talking about what you might do with it?"

"Jan Spiegel laid out this exact scenario more than a year ago. He knew, we all knew, there were dangers with compression—getting too close to a star or a black hole. But there were also opportunities. If you can compress space in any chosen direction, you've got a pretty good tool for scouting the galaxy by remote control. Send a camera out there. Who knows what you might see?"

Daniel took a deep breath. It was good to know he wasn't the only one with these thoughts. "And now it's happened. But instead of a camera, living, breathing astronauts became unwilling guinea pigs."

Nala swiveled her chair and they sat face-to-face. "Daniel, I have no idea how far those guys were pushed in the *kata* direction. We'll have to ask the Chinese about that. But if it was more than a thousand kilometers, then some other direction of real 3-D space compressed by a factor of a billion, maybe more. This is the bottom of the Spiegel curve— a small tweak in *kata* and you can bring stars into your backyard. These guys may have been sent to a place where Earth was on one side and who knows what... the Orion Nebula... was on the other."

Daniel released the tension in his clenched fists. The idea was disturbing. *She* was disturbing, probably because she might be right. All his training as a scientist told him to be very careful, but his instinct was leaning the other way.

Nala slid a finger along the curved edge of the yin. "And you say there's another one like this inside Soyuz?"

"Similar. It has two colored sockets on the front and a panel with characters printed on it—at least we thought they were printed. My partner, Marie, is studying it as we speak. She says the characters have been changing."

"Changing, how?"

"I'm not sure. She sent a text just before I arrived. What looked like black paint might be more like a computer display. She's still trying to figure it out."

Nala returned her attention to the floating image. Three circles of different colors, nested one within another, with many smaller circles inside. Amazingly sharp and clear. "What do you think it is?"

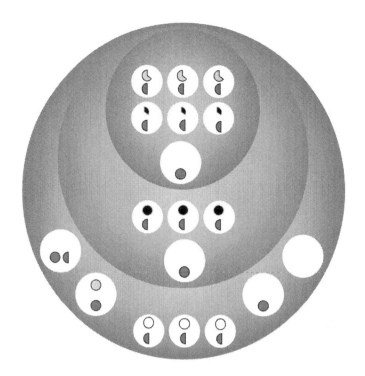

Daniel put both elbows on the table and brought his face close to the image. "I don't know. Marie thought it might represent a planetary system. The shading makes the circles look spherical. Plus, the little yellow moons across the top."

Nala nodded. "They do look like moons... well, sort of. They're not so much crescent-shaped as they are..." Nala stopped and covered her mouth. "Holy shit."

Daniel turned. "What?"

She touched her forehead and stared intently at the image, her mouth open.

"Holy. Fucking. Shit." Her index finger tapped in the air, counting. "Four sets of three, grouped, it's all there."

Daniel looked at the image and back to her. "What!"

233

She turned to face him, her expression a mix of surprise and joy. "Daniel… it's the Standard Model."

He was slow on the uptake, or maybe he hadn't heard her right. "Our Standard Model? The components of the universe? That Standard Model?"

"Yes, our Standard Model. That's exactly what it is." The excitement of discovery poured out of her, and she spoke quickly. "Daniel, I've seen dozens of versions. Every particle physicist has their own way of drawing it. I've never seen one quite as circular as this, but still, it's got all the particles. Look at it."

She pointed. "Six white circles at the top. Six quarks. Grouped two by three, just as we do. These yellow moons, they're not crescents at all. Daniel, they're pies. They're showing two-thirds of a whole. Two-thirds! That's the electrical charge for the top row of quarks."

She pointed again. "And the green half circle below? That's got to be the spin. Each quark has one-half spin. Do you see it?"

Daniel stared intensely. The shapes were as she described, but how had she determined their meaning? And so quickly?

Her words came rapidly. "Look, the second-row pies are all black. And the second row of quarks has what charge?"

"Um… negative one-third? I think."

"Correct, minus one-third. Doesn't that look like one third of a pie? And look at it. It's a black interior with a yellow border. Opposite colors from the top row pies. A pretty good way to indicate a negative number."

She leaned back. "Daniel, those first six circles are quarks. There's no doubt about it."

He was stunned, mostly because he could tell that she was right. "How could you possibly see this so quickly?"

She laughed. "Daniel, I live this stuff. I could recite the details of the Standard Model in my sleep. I've seen this diagram a million times. Well, not with circles." She looked back at the image. "But you know, now that I've seen it, I kind of like this version. There are no numbers at all, but it gets the point across perfectly."

"What about the rest of it?"

She studied the image again. "The white circle at the top with the full green inside? That's got to be the gluon. It binds quarks together and has a spin of positive one. And see? The green circle is a full pie, representing one."

She rapidly dissected the rest, like a kid unwrapping Christmas presents. "Look at the next group inside the blue circle. Three leptons, with negative one charge and one-half spin. And three neutrinos at the bottom of the gray circle. No charge at all and half spin. Daniel, it's all there. Compare it to any diagram we've ever drawn."

She laughed. "Oh my God, this is great! Z and W bosons at the bottom. They've even got the Higgs. That plain white circle on the right. Zero charge and zero spin, and that's exactly where most physicists draw it. But..." Her eyes scanned across image. "What's this other thing?" She pointed to the white circle on the left side. It contained a full green circle and another half-circle. "A graviton? That can't be right."

"Maybe they discovered gravitons, even if we haven't."

Nala shook her head vigorously. "Theoretically, gravitons have a spin of two—if they exist at all. This shows one and a half, so it can't be a graviton. But what else is there? There aren't any other forces."

"Well... none, that we know of."

Nala bounced in her chair like a little kid. "Holy shit, I'd love to talk to these people. Two questions right away: where's your graviton, and what's this extra boson?"

*These people*. It was a leap into the fantastic, but she was going there willingly. Daniel didn't blame her. She had uncovered meaning and there was no question she was right. While she was pointing, he had noticed something else about the diagram. "Look at the symmetry," he said softly. "Six quarks, six leptons, and now six bosons. We only had five."

"Feels complete, doesn't it?" Nala broke into a huge smile. "Daniel, this is monumental. Somewhere out there is my counterpart. Some other man-woman-thing living on some other planet. Someone who knows all about quantum physics just like I do. You have no idea how thrilling that feels."

Daniel took a deep breath. The battle of fact versus fantasy had played itself out. This was a first communication. "They sent something they knew we'd understand. They sent science. It's not the Chinese."

Nala looked at him and their eyes connected. "No Sir, it's *definitely* not the Chinese."

She jumped up out of her chair as if she could no longer be constrained by furniture ever again. She almost bounced around the room. "Wow, am I glad you came back to Fermilab. That thing is amazing. I feel... honored to see it. To be a part of your investigation."

"It may not be my investigation much longer," he said. "It's bigger now. But that's the way science works, isn't it? You look for one thing, and you find something else entirely."

"Do you think this is a test? You know, to see if we're literate?"

Daniel shrugged. "If it is, we're only halfway there. I haven't even shown you why I came here. Flick your finger through the projection."

She reached out, waving a finger in and out. The yin clicked and the image changed. She broke into a huge smile. "Oooh."

"We've been calling this one oranges and blueberries."

236

"Very interesting. Three-D!" She leaned to the left to view the side of the projected image.

Daniel let her absorb the view. It *was* impressive technology. "I have some ideas about this one."

"Do tell."

"It may be a star chart. But I'm not sure which stars. That's the next step."

"They don't really look like stars. Why two different colors, and sizes?"

"It could be representational. Their size is exaggerated. And all stars aren't the same size or color anyway. The orange ones might represent red giants."

"Like Betelgeuse?" Nala asked.

"Exactly," answered Daniel. "And the blue ones might be white dwarfs, which are really the same star type, just at a different point in its evolution. Red giants eventually become white dwarfs."

"So why are they orange and blue?"

"Yeah, good question. Astronomers often make up names that don't quite match the object. Red giants are actually closer to orange in color, and white dwarfs tend to be bluish-white."

Nala shrugged. "Wow, this really is a test. You've been handed a map to the stars. What do you think happens if you follow it?"

A sly smile crept across Daniel's face. "There's more. A text message, and writing too."

"Daniel, you're just full of surprises, aren't you? Any minute now, you're going to pull a Wookiee out of that bag, I just know it."

"Too ordinary. You already know what a Wookiee looks like. The unknown is always more interesting, and scarier too. But that's where this is leading, and I need your help to get there."

"Well, that's clear as mud. Last night you accused *me* of being vague."

He pointed to the yin. "Nala, I think there's more to this device. Something we can't see."

She looked at the yin and the 3-D star map hanging in the air. A faint flicker in her lips gradually turned to a smile and her eyes lifted to Daniel. "Oh... Mr. Scientist, you are so clever."

~~~~~~~~~~~~~~~~~~~~~~~

Nala led Daniel down a long hallway and turned into a large, brightly lit room. A long curving desk was covered with computer displays and electronics equipment. At one end sat a man with long hair pulled into a ponytail. He studied a complex set of graphs on the displays in front of him.

The man turned around as they approached. "Nala, how are you? Long time, no see."

"Hey, Tony. Yeah, I've been pretty busy over in Diastasi. I should drop by more often. You guys have all the best late-night snacks." She motioned to Daniel. "Tony, this is Daniel Rice. We're working together."

Tony stood up and they shook hands. He quickly returned his attention to Nala. "Somebody said there was trouble over at Stetler. I hope it didn't affect you."

Nala laughed. "Touch and go for a while, but I think I ended up better off." She glanced at Daniel and caught his eye. "I got some help from high places." Daniel smiled and lowered his head in a small bow.

"Hey, Tony," she continued, "we need some protons tonight. Can you make it happen?"

He studied his computer display. "Yeah... should be okay. Maintenance put up some shielding around the NuMI horn a while ago, but they're done now. You need anything special?"

"Nope, just the usual. A few trillion protons at light speed. Give me that and I'll take it from there."

"No problem," Tony said with a grin. "Magic coming up. Give me about thirty minutes."

She patted him on the shoulder. "Thanks. Have a good shift. I'll bring the donuts next time."

They left the control room and went back into one of the many long corridors of concrete. "You have surprisingly easy access to some impressive power," Daniel remarked.

She nodded. "It takes a big crew to keep this place running, but the acceleration and test benches are all computer-controlled. Tony gives me protons, I smash them into graphite atoms. Voilà, we have a focused beam of neutrinos."

"It can't be that easy."

"It's not. Tony will be busy. Security and safety protocols, electrical pretests, power up. It's not quite like starting your car."

"But still, all you had to do was ask. You have full command of one of the most advanced scientific instruments ever created."

Nala beamed. "Yeah. That's pretty cool, isn't it?" They turned a corner and climbed some stairs. "How about you? You like what you do?"

"Most of the time," he said, walking beside her.

She looked up at him. "Except when you have to call in the FBI?"

He shrugged. "Or when I grill someone who turns out to be innocent." They walked a few paces with eyes locked on each other. "Sorry," he said.

She smiled. *"Je vous pardonne, monsieur."*

# 37 Qinhuangdao

Lao Yan looked displeased even as his words declared the opposite. "It is good news, Jie Ping."

Zhu Jie Ping had expected the worst. Their associate in America had reported FBI activity at the Stetler Corporation. He had even provided telephoto pictures of Terry Stetler being led away in handcuffs. The situation did not look good, and now he worried about his own future.

Lao set the page down on the table and turned it toward Zhu. "The crisis is over. Soyuz has landed. This briefing paper is from General Ji. It includes satellite reconnaissance of the ship coming down in a northern state of America and collected by their military."

Zhu was elated, but confused. He knew his team had nothing to do with the landing. They had attempted to locate the spacecraft in every way they knew how, but it was like hunting for a gnat across the emptiness of Tibet.

"We made every effort. I am happy for the success, even if I cannot claim credit." Zhu knew that Lao had been provided regular reports—probably from one of his own team members. There was no point in denying their failure, but he was curious how anyone else could have accomplished the impossible task. "Do we know how they returned?"

Lao's grim face still hid information that Zhu could not discern. "General Ji provides no additional information. Perhaps the expanded space collapsed on its own?"

Zhu couldn't think of any mechanism for such an event, but then he really had only a vague understanding of how any of this technology worked. "My team will investigate and find out."

Lao shook his head. "Your team no longer exists, Jie Ping. You will need to assign each person to a new position at The Higgs Factory."

"You're disbanding my team?" This was a greater crisis than an accidental displacement of a Russian spacecraft. It was personal ruin.

"I am sorry, Jie Ping. Perhaps it is a temporary setback. Perhaps we shall start again in the future. For now, the political damage is high and must be contained." He swiveled his chair and looked away. "All personnel must be reprocessed. All data and all software must be sent to Records Archive. Once this is complete, your team—officially—never existed."

# 38 Layers

The Diastasi lab was pitch dark. Daniel could dimly make out some overhead pipes, but nothing else. Nala ran her hand along the wall. "Lights, lights. Where's that switch?"

Daniel laughed. "So… you're about to single-handedly operate a machine that can compress space itself, but you don't know where the light switch is. I'm not getting a good vibe."

"You know, Daniel, I've told people to fuck off for less than that."

He had no doubt about the veracity of that statement. "I can see that I'll need to be more careful around you."

"You do. I'm very dangerous." She located the switch and the room was illuminated. "Make yourself comfortable. I'll be a few minutes on the computer."

She pulled a chair up to the workstation that had been occupied by Thomas the day before. Daniel took a seat next to her and set his bag on the desk. "You won't need any help to make all this work?" he asked.

"I'll manage. Why don't you get your magic plate set up?" She motioned to the plexiglass box. "You have any specific destination in mind?"

Daniel lifted the top of the plexiglass box and carefully placed the yin projector on its point. It balanced in the center, still within range of a voice command. "I think anywhere in 4-D space will do. But we'll also need that webcam that Dr. Park was using."

She pointed to the shelf where it was stored, and Daniel turned it on. A window automatically popped up on the computer, transmitting the webcam's view. He set the webcam next to the yin. "When you send this thing into a fourth dimension, I guess it won't be able to hear me, right?"

"Definitely not. It'll only be a meter away, but of course your voice is nothing but a vibration within three-dimensional air." It made sense. Thinking in four dimensions was becoming intuitive... almost.

"That's all right, we'll do them one at a time. The first projection was a flat 2-D image. The star map was 3-D."

"And you think you're going to get something different in four dimensions, right?"

Daniel's brow arched. "We'll see."

A background hum filled the room. "Ah, we've got protons." She picked up a handheld radio from its cradle and keyed the mic. "Control, Diastasi. Confirm power up."

The radio hissed, followed by Tony's voice. "Hi, Nala. Yeah, we're all set. You can go anytime."

"That was quick," Daniel said.

"Yeah, Tony's good. Why don't you tell that projector to do its thing?"

Daniel nodded and provided the voice command and the yin performed its job. He adjusted the webcam until the projection was in view. "Really, this is just a guess. It might look exactly the same in 4-D."

"But that's how science works," she offered. "You make an educated guess, you try a few things, you measure your results, and repeat."

*Mostly,* Daniel thought. *Along with a willingness to revise your viewpoint in the face of contrary evidence.* Most people forgot about that last part.

She flipped a few toggle switches on a panel and typed once more on the keyboard. "Ready?"

"Into the unknown."

She pressed a key, and a loud buzz filled the room, followed by a bright flash and a loud pop. The yin and the webcam disappeared. Daniel shook his head. "I don't think I could ever get used to that."

"You're not the only one," she laughed. "I've done it hundreds of times, and it's still amazing."

"Why does it pop?"

"We think it's an interaction with oxygen molecules. Like a mini flash fire, but without flames."

They both pressed close to the computer display. The yin was partially in view, its metal surface only dimly lit. Daniel could make out the gentle curve of the metal down to its point, but it no longer stopped there. The metal extended lower, its curve flipping upward at the end, like the bottom of a lowercase *j*. *It's a four-dimensional object.*

Nala saw it too. "Damn it, Daniel, are you always right?"

"More structure, below its point." His finger drew a line along its j-shaped edge. "That's how it balances."

Nala nodded. "Probably also why it feels heavier than you'd expect. More mass, hidden from our view. But the projection looks the same."

As dim as the yin's surface appeared, its projection stood out bold and bright. The circular depiction of the Standard Model was the same as before.

"Take a screenshot and let's try the other projection."

Nala typed, and the webcam and the yin popped back into the plexiglass box. Daniel flicked his finger and the projection switched to the 3-D star map. A few more keystrokes, and the device and its projection disappeared once more into quantum space.

Daniel leaned over her shoulder and stared at the yin's projection, displayed clearly on the computer. The oranges and

245

blueberries were still there, but now there was much more. Lines connected the orange spheres, and surrounding them were boxes with script inside.

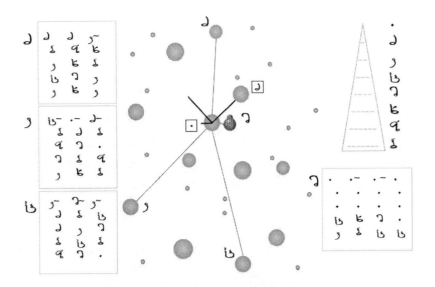

"Wow," he shouted. "This is fantastic! It was projecting four dimensions all along, but we could only see three." There was a lot to examine, but he pointed to one of the boxes. "The characters look similar to the text message script that I told you about."

"Reminds me of boxes under a Christmas tree." Nala pointed to the triangular shape on the screen. "And what's the thing in the center? It looks like a hand grenade."

Daniel laughed. "Yeah, it does. Oranges, blueberries and a hand grenade."

"Kind of an odd species," she said without a hint of sarcasm. "They enjoy a diet rich in fruit and explosive metal. But I'm starting to like them as I get to know them better."

Daniel pointed to the lines. "Some of the oranges are connected by lines. Important places on a map?"

"Transportation links?"

"And the hand grenade is at the center?"

"Your guess is as good as any." She paused to take a screenshot of the image. "We can study this thing all night, but there's no need to keep the neutrino beam running. Anything else you want to try while we're in 4-D?"

"There's a lot here, we just need to figure out what it's telling us."

"Okay, I'll power down for now. We can always restart if needed." She saved the screenshot and attached it in an encrypted message to herself with a copy to Daniel. "Okay, captured and safe." She hit a key and the buzzing sound lowered. The yin and webcam reappeared with a light pop, exactly where they'd started. Daniel retrieved both objects from the box, and Nala called Tony on the radio to power down.

She grabbed a laptop, pulled up the message she had just sent and opened the attachment. "Okay, same image, but now consuming one millionth the amount of power to view it."

"The taxpayers thank you."

Daniel studied the image now on the laptop screen. He noticed that the lines varied in thickness and that one ended without pointing to anything else. There were several rectangular tables of characters, a triangle shape and another column of characters.

Nala waved her hand with excitement. "Ooh, look. The labels match with the tables. The tables on the left match up to some of the oranges. And the table on the right matches the hand grenade. Four tables, four labels. Except that column next to the Christmas tree doesn't have a label."

Searching through the details generated questions, and Daniel had plenty. He pointed to the center of the diagram. "Why are two of the

247

labels inside boxes? And what's that little stubby line going to one of the boxes?"

Nala shrugged.

He could keep asking, but neither of them had answers. "Okay, hang on, let's think from the top. What do we have so far?" He paused and she waited. "Well, we've got another diagram that looks like a star map. And it's in two parts. To view the second part, we had to place the map into four-dimensional quantum space. So, what does all of that tell us?"

Nala paused. "It's a test."

Daniel squinted one eye. "Well..."

"Hey, I'm brainstorming. Isn't that what we're doing? There's no bad answer when you're brainstorming."

Daniel held up his hands. "Okay, you're right. For the sake of expediency, let's brainstorm. If we get nowhere and need a more structured approach, we'll bring in a project manager and a team of analysts. For now, it's just you and me."

"Then, I'm not withdrawing my brilliant hypothesis," she said with a smile. "It's a test. They're wondering if we have control over quantum space. You don't get to see the details until you pass the test."

"And we passed."

"We did."

Regardless of the brainstorming format, Daniel still felt the need for some structure. Start from the top, use the evidence, set aside claims that don't conform, and arrive at the most likely answer. He advanced using a smaller step. "The Chinese have placed a satellite in orbit around another star."

"Overruled. Daniel, you've really got to let go of that notion. This thing is not Chinese."

"Just examining the alternatives. I thought we were brainstorming."

"Got me there. Okay, I'll allow it." She held up a hand. "My turn. They've placed a device inside a human spacecraft that can only be activated by a password they delivered via radio to that same spacecraft. Using the password—your Russian phrase, *kak*-something—the device displays a scientific calling card, their version of the Standard Model, along with a hidden treasure map that points to their secret cache where they have stockpiled gold and diamonds, or possibly hand grenades. How's that?"

Daniel tapped mindlessly on the table. "Pretty accurate, I'd say. Except for the gold and diamonds." He stopped drumming his fingers and looked carefully at the image on the screen. "My turn now. There's nothing secret about this location, the hand grenade. Even if we don't know what all these characters mean, they're showing us how to get there."

Nala's playfulness in brainstorming switched instantly to serious. "Daniel, that's exactly what they're doing. They're showing us how to get to the hand grenade. It's a place. It has coordinates. And with the right spatial compression, we could be there in five minutes."

Daniel smiled. He looked away, absorbing, and there was a lot to process. If any of this was true, the map represented intent—a plausible reason for the message sent to Soyuz. A request of some sort, but designed only for the scientifically literate. The terrestrial explanations for this device were disappearing fast, and it was making him nervous.

He thought about the missing astronauts. Soyuz had returned, empty, except for a device that had provided a scientific greeting, followed by a map and instructions. *Uncover the meaning and you'll find the astronauts.* Maybe, or maybe not, but the possibility was hard to ignore.

"Nala, I have to coordinate with the White House on this."

Nala glanced at the clock. "While you're doing that, can we get something to eat? Figuring this out could take all night. It's already past eight and I'm starved."

"Yeah, sure. Sorry, I was so focused…"

She shook her head. "That's an understatement. You haven't let up since you arrived."

"All day, really." He had taken enough of her time. If this map led the way to missing astronauts, following it was going to involve high-level people. "I don't want to impose on you any further. I have what I need for now. Why don't you go home? I'll make my calls from the hotel."

She scowled. "Daniel. You came to me for help, right? I helped. Don't disappear on me just when things get interesting. We're going to solve this—tonight. And once we do, I'm the person who can take you wherever this map is leading. No way am I missing out on the biggest story of the century."

"Fine, you're right, and I do appreciate your help. But this is no longer just me and you."

Nala's scowl deepened. "Once you make those calls, are they going to come and take this thing away? Lock it up in a vast government warehouse? You know the one. Don't you think the public has a right to know what you've discovered? With significant help from myself and Fermilab, I might add."

Her paranoia about authority was strong. Daniel was the first to admit that governments didn't always do the right thing. But he also felt sure that the right argument could persuade the bureaucrats and allow the scientists to lead the way.

"Don't worry, I see the whole picture," Daniel started. Their eyes connected, and he could tell she was resolute in her participation. There was also no doubt she could be very valuable. "Let's do this… I'll make my calls. But then, we'll see what we can figure out—just you and me. If this really is a map to a hidden location among the stars, the Diastasi technology could be the path to get us there. The bosses are going to want that option."

The scowl disappeared. "I can work with that." She picked up her car keys, put a hand on his shoulder and leaned in close. "Get your calls done. I'll be back in twenty minutes with hot food."

The scent of her perfume was a strong reminder of their very personal dance in the hallway. She had become a key part of the investigation, and her mastery of the science was invaluable. But he couldn't deny a physical attraction. His eyes followed the intriguing and complex woman as she walked out the door.

*Focus, Daniel, focus.* He took a deep breath and picked up his phone.

# 39  Puzzle

Daniel's first call was to Spencer Bradley. He wasn't sure where to start. How do you explain to your boss, who happens to be the president's science advisor, that you've discovered a star map with extra information hidden in a fourth dimension? Or that whoever had sent this message had led with their own, fully-symmetric version of the Standard Model?

Bradley was strangely accepting, and most of their conversation was nearly normal. It was only when Bradley began to summarize that Daniel could tell the implications had hit home. "An extra dimension of space was a leap forward, but now… a message from…" He didn't finish the sentence. "You know, Daniel, when I was out at Fermilab last spring, I knew they were onto something very big, even bigger than the technology they were demonstrating. I guess I shouldn't be surprised now that it's happened. But Jesus… this could be historic."

By the end of the call Bradley made it clear he would be on a plane to Fermilab as soon as he could. He suggested that Daniel continue to explore the meaning of the message, but cautioned that more people from a variety of disciplines would soon be involved.

His second call was to the NSA, Christine Shea, and it was far more routine. He left a message with a White House staff member and highlighted that 'new discoveries had been made.' He outlined his proposed next steps, even though she might ignore them. Shea would probably call Bradley and the two of them would decide exactly what happened next. It was possible that all hell was about to break loose, but at least for the next few hours, Daniel was still on his own. He liked it that way.

The third call was to Marie. "How's it going out there?" he asked when she answered.

"Tiring. The yang is still immobile, still stuck on the console. I've been speaking to it, making loud noises, tapping it. I even sang a song. No effect. The only thing changing is the writing on the front. I sent you some photos. We decided to work on it some more in the morning, before Roscosmos arrives to claim their vessel. How are things on your side? Any progress?"

"Directly? No, we still have three missing astronauts. But indirectly? Coming back to Fermilab was the right thing to do. Marie, we know what they mean... the yin images. The first image—the one with all the circles—is a version of the Standard Model, just like we were reviewing on our flight to Chicago. Nala recognized it immediately."

"Really? Wow, that kind of tips the scales, doesn't it?"

"No kidding. Tell Ibarra, I've already told Shea and Bradley. Whoever we're talking to, they're scientists."

~~~~~~~~~~~~~~~~~~~~~~~~

Nala set the brown paper bag on the table in the MINERvA analysis room. She withdrew several white boxes.

"Chinese food," Daniel said. He was hungrier than he'd realized and opened a box of fried rice.

"Given the circumstances, I thought it was an appropriate choice." She grinned. "Did you get your calls done?"

"Two of three, with one message. The White House staff is pretty good about keeping the right people informed. My boss said he'll be on the next flight out, so expect some company here in a few hours."

There were other thoughts running around his head, but he didn't verbalize them. He could gauge Bradley pretty well, but Shea's reaction could be tricky. She was a political player, and security was her overriding focus. Her first priority would continue to be a safe return of the astronauts. But the message, particularly the 3-D star map, might bring another issue into play—the potential that this communication represented a threat. He had no reason to believe it did, but not everyone thought the same way.

253

Nala plucked a ball of sticky rice with her chopsticks. "I'm surprised your partner didn't come with you."

"Marie? Yeah, I just talked to her. She's working with the counterpart to the yin. It's the same shape, but it has lights on the front and a panel with some of these same characters drawn on it. The whole thing is literally stuck to the Soyuz control panel, back in South Dakota."

"She sounds like a good partner. I like her."

"You haven't even met her."

"No matter. I know enough." She pinched a chunk of pork.

"Marie trusted you right away," Daniel confided. "Did the FBI show you the documents I sent? That white envelope that McLellan gave me at the bar. It was a full dossier on you, complete with phone records of calls supposedly placed to China."

Nala shook her head. "Shitheads. The calls were probably real— except Stetler was the one who made them, not me."

"Marie took your side. She didn't hesitate."

"There you go." She lifted an eyebrow. "That's why I like her."

Daniel nodded. "Yeah, I do too." He opened his laptop and pulled up a copy of the text message received by Soyuz, along with the 4-D image star map. "Looking at them side by side, it's easier to see what matches." He waved her over. "Take a look."

She rolled her chair around the table, next to Daniel's. "That's the message? Interesting script. You sure it's not Arabic or something like that?"

"It's not. The guys at Ellsworth compared it to several languages. I did too on the flight out here. We'll need a linguist to double-check, but so far it doesn't match any known language." He explained the three lines of script and their relation to the Russian phrase, *kak pashyevayesh*.

"Ah, so that's how you discovered the link between the text message and the yin thing. It was like a password. Pretty smart, Daniel. I don't think you need the linguist."

"Well, the characters in the message were fairly easy. They're just phonetic matches to a phrase we already knew. But there's no meaning involved, it's probably just an echo, like a parrot saying 'cracker.' But the map is different. If we're going to make sense out of these characters, we'll need to understand what they mean, and that's much harder."

"Seems like you'd need something to translate," she offered. "A book of photographs, with the corresponding script next to each picture. Like a children's book."

"That would certainly help, wouldn't it?" He recalled several exobiology seminars he had attended, including a panel discussion on communicating with another intelligence. "A primer is useful for concepts that two civilizations share, like 'water' or 'star.' But it breaks down quickly. Reverse the scenario. What if we showed them a picture of say, a pencil or a spoon—would they know how these objects are used? Very doubtful, at least not until they understand more about us. Many of our manufactured objects are designed for our bodies. Even chopsticks." He fumbled trying to pick up a piece of pork. "As simple as they seem, chopsticks are extensions to our fingers. The same would be true for them."

It was an age-old debate. Would evolution work the same on other planets, producing similar body parts? Or would alien life be entirely foreign, even unrecognizable? An octopus doesn't have fingers but can grasp a variety of things. If their bodies were entirely different, wouldn't their thought process be different too?

Daniel looked back at his computer, carefully studying both images side by side. "Huh."

"What do you see?" she asked.

255

"Nothing, but that's just it. Not a single character in the text message matches any character on the map. What does that tell you?"

"I don't know. What does it tell you?"

Daniel paused. "Numbers."

"Sorry, I'm not following your logic there."

He set down his chopsticks while he pondered his own statement. "Are numbers a universal math concept? Who knows? But numbers were invented independently multiple times in human history, and it's pretty hard to imagine mathematics without numbers. And without math, you don't have science."

He pointed to the text message. "Phonetic characters, representing speech. We've already figured that out." He pointed to the star map. "And we have a map with characters, none of which are shared with the message. These characters around the edges could be numeric representations of positions on the map."

"Maybe, but they've already shown us their numbers. Their fractions were little moons."

Daniel thought for a minute. "The pies are visual fractions, but I can't see how you could extend that into a full-fledged math system. To have any meaningful math, you've got to have numbers. Of course, I'm human, so my bias is guaranteed."

She set her chopsticks down. "Okay, still brainstorming, so I have another idea. It's probably nothing, but I was just thinking about the old connect-the-dots game we played as children. The book gives you some part of the picture already drawn, and you fill in the rest yourself. Let me see that diagram again."

Daniel had to admit he would have never thought of it. They looked at the diagram together. Some oranges were connected by lines, but it was a radial pattern from a central point. He mentally connected some of the other oranges, but nothing popped out. He shook his head.

"Yeah, maybe not," she said. "It was just a thought."

Daniel turned to her. "You know, you're really good at this."

"Good at what?"

"Brainstorming, coming up with ideas, thinking through a problem. You're good at it."

She smiled. "Thanks. It's a fun problem, like a difficult puzzle with no hints. I keep wondering if these people are challenging us."

"Maybe they think it's simple. Not a puzzle at all, but just a communication. I have to say, though, displaying portions of the map in 3-D and the rest in 4-D sure seems intentional."

"So, do you really think it's a test?"

Everything about the intelligence on the other side of the message was unknown. With such limited communication, even the reason for the message not clear. It could be a test, but it could just as easily be something trivial.

Daniel had been down this road before. "I've often thought that the reason we had never heard from other civilizations was not because they weren't out there. It was because they didn't really care. Just because some yokel from the backwaters of the galaxy comes calling doesn't mean you invite him into your house. So, even if they knew we existed, maybe they just didn't care. Or at least, that's what I used to think."

"And now?" she asked.

"They care, at least enough to communicate. They're not treating us as insignificant."

Nala took a sip of water. "Maybe I'm good at ideas, but you're really good at that."

"What, bloviating?"

"No. Summarizing, making sense of things, asking the right questions to find the meaning. You're a natural." Her look was sincere.

"You're very kind. I get my inspiration on occasion."

She laughed. "I do too, in weird ways."

He bared a bit of private information. "My inspiration comes when I'm in the shower."

"No, really? That's funny, we both use warm water. I have a float pod."

"And that is…?"

"An immersion tank. You've never heard of floating?"

"Never tried it, sorry."

Her eyes were downcast as she revealed what was certainly a private moment of her own. "It's meditation without distraction. When you're floating, you feel your breath, your heartbeat and nothing else. You get into a state of total relaxation and your mind wanders. You hallucinate."

"Really?"

She laughed. "Yes, really. Deprive your brain of external stimulus and it creates its own. Weird shit, sometimes. Like in a dream, except you're fully awake."

"So how does that inspire you?"

There was a sincerity in her eyes. "Promise you won't laugh?" He agreed. "I've developed my own technique. You fill your conscious mind beforehand with whatever you want your subconscious to process. After you've been in the no-stimulus environment for a while, your subconscious takes over. It's like being on autopilot. You don't even think about it, insight just comes to you. Remember what I told you about Wah Xiang? I figured that out while I was in the pod."

"I'll have to try it sometime." He meant it.

The conversation stopped and they both sat silently. She finally broke the silence. "I have an idea."

Daniel raised his eyebrows high. "Involving warm water?"

She admonished him with a finger. "Perfectly wholesome. But it will give you a good idea how to find inspiration through your subconscious."

Daniel twisted his head. "I wish we had time, but really—"

"Look. You have a problem right in front of you that you haven't solved, right?"

"Well, yeah, but—"

"This could help you solve it. Give me five minutes. You can spare that. The technique works, really."

Before Daniel could put up any other objections, she stood up, flipped the room light off and moved behind his chair. The room was darker, but his laptop screen provided enough light to see. She put her hands on his shoulders and bent down, her mouth close to his ear, and whispered, "For science."

He laughed and turned his head towards her. "I've heard that line before... well, actually I haven't."

She put her hands on his temples and turned his head to look forward at his computer. "No jokes, this is serious. Now, examine the image on your computer. Mentally absorb everything you see."

*Five minutes. I can spare that.* He did as she asked and took one more look at the image of oranges and blueberries surrounded by characters.

"List what you see. Describe the components and their relationships with each other."

"A central sphere, with spokes to other spheres, four tables of rows and columns…"

"Good. List everything." Daniel continued and described the items on the screen until there was nothing left to itemize. "Now… close your eyes." She removed her hands and whispered into his ear, "Relax your body." He tried, but he could still feel her standing behind him and the unusual situation was hardly relaxing. She began to rub his shoulders gently and his muscles relaxed, a little.

"Good, relax. Now, I'm going to stay behind you, and as you hear me breathe in, you count in your head—one… two… When I breathe out, you count again—one… two… We'll keep a tempo, together. It's easy, and very repetitive. I'll tell you when to stop. Just count silently and listen to my breath, nothing else. Okay?"

"Okay," he said softly. It seemed odd, but he was game.

She leaned in very close, her lips grazing his left ear. She breathed in, and then out, at a normal rate but with a stronger breath. She let the air blow across his ear. In his head, Daniel counted in time with her breathing—one… two… He kept very still and felt her lips occasionally touch the side of his ear. It was sensual, even if she didn't mean it to be. Or maybe she did, he wasn't really sure.

At more than a hundred meters below ground, the room was intensely quiet, and relatively dark. It *was* relaxing. He listened carefully and could hear a slight vibration in her breath. Her heartbeat. After a minute, she whispered again. "Hear nothing but my breath. Think of nothing and count." She continued her slow but purposeful breathing, and Daniel continued to count. He thought of nothing. Well, almost nothing.

Time passed, and even the thoughts of the sensual woman behind him began to dissipate. The slow, rhythmic tempo of her breathing was relaxing to both his body and his mind. For a brief time, he felt like he was dreaming, yet still awake. It was entrancing and timeless, and he enjoyed it.

The spell was interrupted as her hair fell across the back of his neck. His heartbeat picked up. "I hear that, Daniel," she whispered. "Your heart gives you away. Good job focusing, but you'll need practice."

"I did start to..."

Nala put her finger to his mouth. "Shhh."

# 40  Inspiration

Daniel sat motionless, his eyes closed. The stillness of the darkened room eliminated all but the weakest of sounds—the gentle rhythm of his own heart, the occasional creak of the chair. He felt tranquil, but fully conscious. Like *sav asana*, the yoga technique for rest and contemplation.

Nala whispered in his ear. "Ready to think again?"

He turned around as she flipped the lights on. "An interesting exercise, but I'm not sure it did anything."

She sat in the chair next to him. "You mean your brain's not suddenly sparking fabulous new ideas? But why should you expect that? The exercise wasn't for your conscious mind. And, unless you're dreaming right now, your subconscious is in the backseat."

"True enough. Thanks for the lesson, your technique is very... physical." *And sensual*, but he left that part out. It didn't matter; she had affected him and there was little doubt she knew what she was doing.

She rested her elbows on the table and turned toward Daniel's laptop. The image of oranges and blueberries, along with connecting lines and characters, still filled the screen. "It's all very tabular. Columns and rows." The smart physicist had returned to the decorous side of the social boundary line. "Except for the single column next to the Christmas tree."

Daniel eventually turned his focus to the computer. He gravitated to the triangular shape, the Christmas tree, as she called it. A triangle filled with small lines, like dashes. One at the top, then two. "Look at that," he said, his mind racing. "There's our list of numbers."

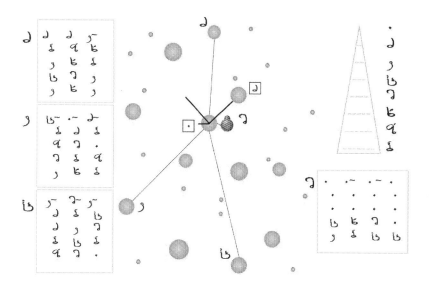

"Where?"

"Inside the Christmas tree. The dashes. One at the top, then two, and right on down. At the bottom, there are seven dashes inside the triangle."

Nala smiled. "They line up with the characters in that single column. Except for the topmost character."

"Zero. It's zero at the top, the point of the Christmas tree."

She used a finger to count the characters in the vertical column. "Eight characters. Representing zero through seven? A base eight counting system. You think it's that simple? We use different bases all the time in computer programming."

"Yeah, it could be. All the other tables have columns of characters too. Maybe they write all their numbers vertically."

The realization hit him like a brick in the face.

"It's a countdown," he whispered.

Nala squinted at him. "What's a countdown? This image?"

263

Daniel slowly shook his head. "No... the yang... in South Dakota." His mind was gripped with the concept of a countdown and his imagination filled in the blank of what might happen when the count reached zero.

He grabbed his phone, fumbled it, but managed to dial. He heard a ring. *Oh, hell, this can't be true.* Another ring and a familiar voice answered.

"Marie, where are you? Anywhere near Soyuz?"

"Hi, Daniel. Yeah, sitting inside right now. Still trying to get this thing to respond. Nothing so far, except the characters on the front keep changing."

"Get out. That thing is counting down."

"The yang? Counting down, you mean, like a timer?"

"Exactly. Those characters are numbers."

"Yeah, I'm coming to the same conclusion."

"We don't know what it's going to do. You shouldn't be in there. Get out, now. Please!"

"What... you think it's going to blow up? Or launch, maybe?"

"I have no idea, but it has me worried. Humor me, okay? Get out of there."

"Okay, I will. I'll need two hands to get through the hatch. I'll call you back." She disconnected.

Daniel's heart raced, and images of thermonuclear explosions filled his mind. It was a gut reaction, he knew that. A minute passed and his thoughts coalesced into a more logical form. There was no reason to panic. Even if the yang was counting, he didn't know whether it was up or down. Maybe it didn't matter. It was a clock, it was timing something, and the outcome was unknown. He felt the adrenaline pumping through his body. *Don't beat yourself up*, he thought, *it was a normal human reaction.*

Nala looked at him with wide eyes. "Wow, that doesn't sound good."

Daniel shook his head. "I don't know, maybe I overreacted. But we should be more cautious with these things. They could easily have hidden functions that we haven't guessed yet."

He pointed to the screen and spoke with certainty. "These are clearly numbers, and they're putting them in order. The Christmas tree is spelling it out. These same characters are scattered around in the other tables."

Daniel's phone rang and he quickly picked up. "You okay?"

"Just fine," Marie replied. "I understand why you're worried, but really, it's okay."

He could feel his heart rate calming just from hearing her voice. "Marie, we sent the yin into 4-D, and just like I thought, there was more. That oranges and blueberries diagram? It now has tables of characters. They're numbers, I'm sure of it, and they match the photo you sent of the yang."

Her voice was steady. "Yeah, I came to the same conclusion, just from a different perspective. I've watched the pattern long enough now to see how it's repeating. The bottom character changes every two and a half minutes. The middle character changes about every twenty minutes. The top character hasn't done anything at all yet, but based on the pattern, I can predict it will change in less than an hour, and I even know what the next character will be. There are eight characters and they're flipping in a specific order."

"Marie, it's a clock."

"I agree. And you think it's counting down?"

265

Daniel pressed a few keys. "I've just sent you the screen shot of the tables. There's a column on the right side, and I'm sure it represents zero through seven. Compare those to what you're seeing on the yang. It shouldn't be hard to figure out where it stands."

"Got it." There was a pause. "Yeah… definitely. Those are the same characters I'm seeing. If that one on top is zero, then yes, it's counting down. But let's not get ahead of ourselves. Counting down is not necessarily a bad thing."

She was right, but we're all preconditioned by the cultural references in our world—the climactic movie scene with a clock counting backwards to an impending catastrophe. Even with a rocket launch, the countdown was a warning to be ready and keep your distance. *Human bias? Sure.* But there were still a lot of unknowns.

He recognized the right course of action. "You might want to report this to Colonel McGinn. The safety of the area is his responsibility."

Another pause. "Yeah, you're right. For now, we'll keep our distance. Let me calculate when this thing hits zero. I'll call you back… and thanks for the heads-up."

Daniel hung up. Whether his concern was sensible or irrational, he couldn't help the feeling of relief that Marie was out of the capsule.

"You did the right thing," Nala said. She leaned close to the computer screen. "While you were talking, I've been studying these tables. If these are digits, zero through seven, then the tables are coordinates, and we should be able to translate them to our numbering."

Daniel looked at the screen again. "Possibly, but there's more to a numbering system than just digits. Order, fractional amounts, negatives, even the concept of a digit representing a power of the base. Our current Arabic numbering system has all those concepts, but people have used other systems that didn't—Roman numerals, for example."

He studied the tables next to the oranges and blueberries. "But what if they do have those concepts? Every table uses vertical columns. Except..." He paused and traced a finger down one of the columns. "There's a distinct offset from the character at the top. The ones below it are shifted slightly to the right."

"I see that," she said. "And what's the squiggle?"

He studied the detail. Each column used a combination of the eight characters, except for a curvy line that sometimes appeared on the top row, but not always. The curve was unique among the characters. "What if the offset represents a decimal point? And the squiggle represents a negative? If so, then our numbering systems are similar in concept, if not format."

She shrugged. "Why not? Okay, so, translating... the first column in the first table is one... point seven... two... three... two."

"Yeah, exactly. Then the second column would be one... point six... five... four... five."

"And the third is negative two... point five... seven... two... two." She lifted her hands in the air. "Hey, we can read Vulcan!" She punched him in the shoulder. "And you didn't think the breathing exercise did you any good."

Daniel laughed. "*Maybe* we can read Vulcan. It's only a guess. It would help if we had some way to validate. Otherwise, this interpretation could be way off." He looked back at the screen. "But wait... they did give us a way."

She shook her head and smiled. "The genius is pouring out now. Lay it on me."

He enlarged the image on his screen. "So, what are we looking at? A 3-D map and a bunch of numbers we think are coordinates. But to validate, we need a coordinate *system*. An origin, a unit of measure, and three axes." He pointed to the center orange where all lines connected.

"Voilà, I give you an origin. And three axes radiating from it, the thicker lines. See? Even in this flat-screen shot, they certainly look perpendicular."

"Nice."

"They may also be giving us the unit of measure. The thick line between the two oranges. It has boxes on either end, which are labeled with their zero and one. One unit of distance? Like the parsec that astronomers use."

"One unit," she echoed. "That could mean anything. How are we going to translate it to our measurements?"

"We'll have to overlay this map onto a chart of known stars— digitally, of course. It takes the right software and a good star database, but backyard telescopes do something similar every time they initialize. If we can match the oranges to real stars, we'll know exactly what one unit means."

She grabbed a piece of paper and wrote 1.7232. She looked at the other columns and wrote 1.6545 and −2.5722. "Let's see if your guess about the decimal point is right. Does this look like a valid coordinate for the top orange?"

Daniel compared the numbers to the presumed axes. With only a flat-screen shot, the $z$ dimension was impossible to determine, but the $x$ and $y$ coordinates matched well. He looked up at Nala and broke into a smile. "Madame, I'm somewhat astonished, but I think we may have broken the code." She held up a hand and he slapped it.

Daniel leaned back in the chair and looked around the room. His mind surfaced from the math problem and he took a moment to absorb the accomplishment. In this small room, with nothing more than a pen and paper, two people were decoding a message from the stars. Communicating with another species? No flying saucer had landed in Washington, D.C., to mark this momentous event. There was no invasion of sleek metal ships, blasting our buildings with unknown energy. Communication had begun with a simple message of science and math.

"My subconscious is on overdrive," he stated grandly.

She hit him in the shoulder again. "Nobody likes a snarky scientist."

He winced at her punch, though it was mostly fake. "Hey, we've done well, don't you think?"

She nodded, her smile sincere. "Yeah, amazing stuff. Who would have dreamed we'd be here?"

Daniel shrugged. "Well, I did. Ever since my first astronomy class in college. It was built into my plan. Biology and astrophysics, the two degrees I figured would put me here. It's crazy but it feels like this day was meant to be—a hand that was dealt years ago. And now I'm living it."

"That's nice. Really nice." She patted his semi-sore shoulder. "Sorry."

He looked at the clock on the computer, 10:40 p.m. "Let's get the other coordinates into our math format. I'll decode, you write." Daniel looked again at the three tables of alien numbers on the left. But he stopped at the fourth table, the one on right side. "Wait a second..." He compared the tables left and right. "This one is different. It has four columns."

Nala moved closer to the screen and squinted. "It does."

Daniel spoke softly, almost to himself. "It's the coordinate for the hand grenade. Four columns, not three." He turned to Nala and they both smiled together. "This focal point, this thing we call the hand grenade. It's a place they want us to know about." He brushed the hair back from his forehead.

"And it's located in four-dimensional quantum space."

~~~~~~~~~~~~~~~~~~~~~~~~~~~

The message on his phone was from Marie.

*Yang now reads 215, base eight. Decrementing every 146 sec. Will hit zero in 5.7 hours, at 3:20 AM MDT. McGinn went ballistic and is clearing the base of nonessential personnel. So far he's letting me stay, but no guarantees. Apparently, the base has an old fallout shelter we can use! Would be helpful to know what's going to happen <understatement!> Your move.*

Less than six hours to figure this out. The military reaction was predictable: assume the worst in the face of the unknown. Daniel couldn't fault them. He'd done the same thing.

# 41 Giants

Daniel did his best to wrap his mind around the disturbing sight. A coaxial cable, one end connected to a radio transceiver on the shelf, the other end disappearing into nothing.

He pieced together a mental image of the electronic components, most of which were now somewhere off in that mysterious *kata* direction. The radio he held in his hand transmitted to the receiver on the shelf, which connected via the cable to a signal repeater. The repeater, which Nala said was only a few feet away at the other end of the coax cable, then transmitted his voice to a second receiver that was floating somewhere in a void of darkness, along with two cameras and the yin.

It was a lot of equipment just to test voice commands to 4-D space. Normally, he'd set the yin down and speak. But as soon as a fourth dimension was added to the mix, this was the only way to "uplink," as Nala had described it. A way to control any device sent into quantum space, no matter how far. He dearly wished this radio setup had been available to NASA ground controllers when Soyuz was still lost.

Identifying how the electronics worked didn't normalize the bizarre visual. The coaxial cable hung in midair, cleanly sliced at the point it entered the top of the plexiglass box. Everything else in the box had vanished in a pop.

Nala didn't seem disturbed in the slightest. "Our design engineer thought we'd need this capability for phase two. He was right, just wrong about the timing. Turn the yin on again."

Daniel picked up the handheld radio and spoke the Russian phrase, *kak pashyevayesh*. The chain of radio components worked as planned, and the view on Nala's computer screen instantly changed. With two webcams in the box this time, the yin's projection could be seen both from behind and from the side. She reached to a small joystick and pushed it to the right. The webcam view swung along with her

271

motion. "It's not just voice, this setup is great for controlling the camera view, too." She panned up and down. The camera view tracked as smoothly as if it were attached by USB.

She beamed. "Right now, compression is negligible. The camera's only a meter away in the *kata* direction. But, once we go big-time, I'll still have the same camera control even if we're looking at something a million miles away."

Daniel looked at the clock. "Past midnight now. Are we okay on the accelerator?"

"We can have it all night if we need it. I convinced Tony to extend his shift. He understands how important this is."

"I have no idea when Bradley arrives," Daniel said. "But we've got about four hours before the yang countdown finishes and it does whatever it's going to do." He pushed a hand through his hair. "I'd sure like to have some options when he gets here, but we're still missing one key to this puzzle."

"The origin?"

"Right. We've got a map. We understand the coordinate system. We can see they're pointing us to a special place... the hand grenade, the focus point, the hub, whatever you want to call it. But to get there, we need a starting point."

"And software changes. Don't forget about that."

"Sorry, I know you're working on it, I just have no idea what you're actually doing."

"Neutrino oscillation amplitude. It's not hard to control, but it will require testing. A few baby steps would be helpful before we jump off to a star."

Baby steps. She was being glib, of course. At the moment, this was a two-person operation, and one of them was doing little more than pouring coffee. Using cobbled-together equipment and a particle physics

272

test bench, they might soon have controllable cameras positioned a long way from Earth. He imagined what an equivalent deep space mission at NASA would look like—and how many people would be involved. He wasn't sure which emotion was winning, his nervousness or his curiosity.

Bradley would be there soon, and Daniel wanted viable options to give him. "Let's line up all the dominoes. You work on the software, I'll check with Marie again on those star charts."

Daniel assembled the pieces in his mind. The yin, a device that informs. The yang, a device that counts toward some unknown event. The easily solved number system was not just good fortune. *They wanted us to know. Their clock is ticking for all to see.*

He fired off another in a series of messages to Marie. Ten minutes later, his phone rang. "Marie, good evening, or morning, or whatever it is."

She laughed. "You sound tired too. How are things going?"

"You know… we have a surprisingly useful electronics setup. You'd love it. Now all we need is some idea where we're going."

"I think I can help," Marie said. There was some background noise on the phone. "Sorry for the noise, I'm in the communications building now and they're moving a lot of people in here."

"Keeping your distance from Soyuz?"

"Right. I think they're just being cautious. The hangar is already isolated from the rest of the base. But there are a few strange ideas floating around here. Their base security guy asked me if I thought a portal was going to open. He was deciding what kind of weapons he might need to kill the Klingons that would be pouring out."

Daniel knew what he'd tell the guy, but Marie had probably been more diplomatic. "What'd you say?"

"I asked him to give me two minutes to try a friendlier approach before he pulled any triggers. In truth, it is a bit nerve-wracking, but we still have hours to go in the countdown. While it's still ticking, I'm going to try to get back into Soyuz for another check."

"Be careful, will you?"

"Yeah, I get it, and I'm okay with the risks. Hey, I found the stars you needed. Ever heard of VY Canis Majoris?"

"Not really, but I'm guessing it's in the constellation Canis Major."

"Yup. A red hypergiant, one of the biggest stars in the galaxy. That's your origin. Hang on, I'll send you the full list."

His phone vibrated and a message popped in. He opened it and looked at a list of names. A few he recognized: Antares, KY Cygni, Betelgeuse. Big stars, giants compared to our own sun. Several others he knew only by their constellation names: AH Scorpii, UY Scuti, V354 Cephei. "How did you come up with the list?"

"An astronomer at UC Berkeley," Marie answered. "I've worked with him in the past. He's remotely operating one of the telescopes at Mauna Kea right now. Pretty handy for us that astronomers work at night, huh? I gave him the image and he had it figured out within an hour. Turns out you were half right. The oranges aren't just red giants— they're supergiants and hypergiants, the very largest stars in the Milky Way."

"That's fantastic, Marie. Sounds like you got to the right person. How sure is he about the origin?"

"Very sure. He said that having multiple stars made the difference, especially the blue-white stars. Comparing four or five might give a match, but with low confidence. Matching all twenty-eight stars could produce only one possible solution. The origin is certainly VY Canis Majoris."

The last puzzle piece fell into place—a map of stars. He called out to Nala, "We've got it. A star named VY Canis Majoris."

Nala looked up from her computer. "How far away?"

Daniel put the phone on speaker. "Marie, Nala's right here, too. We're both pretty excited about this."

"Nala, good to meet you," Marie said. "Sorry I couldn't be there in person."

Nala rolled her chair closer to the phone. "I hear you're taking good care of the yang, who seems to be deaf, but ticking."

"Yeah, a tough nut to crack. Hey, by the way, we're located on that map. Us... I mean, Earth. The two oranges at the bottom? The one on the left is Antares, and the one just to its right is Betelgeuse. Neighbors, relatively speaking. Earth is in between them."

Daniel quickly pulled up the star map and placed the computer cursor where he thought Earth might lie. "Well, I know it's about five hundred light years to Antares, and maybe six hundred to Betelgeuse. That would put VY Canis Majoris... several thousand light years away."

"Three thousand eight hundred and forty," Marie said. "Give or take. I looked it up."

Daniel turned to Nala. "Can we go that far?"

She wrinkled her nose. "Maybe. Depends on what's along the line of sight. If there's another star in the same path, then no."

It was a question that had come up in Daniel's own observations of the night sky. How often does one star block another? The answer, it turned out, was only rarely. Within four thousand light years of Earth, there were millions of stars, but there was also a *lot* of empty space. Two stars rarely aligned exactly.

Marie answered the question. "Nala, I was wondering the same thing, so I asked him, if I needed to fly to this star, would I hit anything?"

Nala laughed. "You didn't give away much."

275

"Well, I couldn't think of any better way to put it. His answer was... it depends. He said we currently have a direct line of sight to VY Canis Majoris, but we're seeing this star as it was four thousand years ago, and stars move. Where it is *now* is harder to determine with any precision. So, the bottom line, there's some uncertainty."

"Sounds like we're clear to go," Nala answered. "As of four thousand years ago. Not the most up-to-date information, but I can work with it."

The background noise became muffled, like Marie had put a hand over the phone. "So, you're really thinking about going there? I mean, with a camera?"

"We'll let Bradley make that call," Daniel said. "But we'll be ready to go."

There was a pause. "Daniel?"

"Yeah, what?"

"Can you patch me in somehow? I really have to see this."

Daniel looked at Nala and she nodded. "We'll figure it out on our end," he said. "You're in a communications center—do they have video conferencing somewhere?"

"Duh. That's why I moved over here."

"Marie, you have my word. If we launch anything, we'll make sure you're on board."

~~~~~~~~~~~~~~~~~~~~~~~~~

Nala kept her head down, eyes focused on the computer screen as Daniel refilled her cup with fresh coffee. He saw the lines of software code scrolling by, but his understanding was limited to what she had told him. Adjustments in the neutrino oscillation amplitude. A larger amplitude would increase quantum expansion, and greatly increase the corresponding compression of normal space.

A version of the graph she had sketched in the bar was taped on the wall, more carefully drawn. Expansion versus compression. Expanding quantum space to a thousand kilometers would give a ratio of compression equal to 0.0002. The tau ratio, they called it. Ordinary space would compress by 99.98 percent. In practical terms, it meant that orienting the beam in the right direction could compress real space enough to put a camera next to Mars. Point in a different direction, slightly tweak the expansion, and the camera would suddenly be at Jupiter. The capability was startling.

Daniel set his laptop on the desk. "We'll need a target for a test run, right?" He pulled up an app that displayed a view of the night sky from Earth. It tracked stars, planets, even satellites, all in real time.

She looked up from her work. "It doesn't matter that much. Anything a few million kilometers away will do. But pick a place that's roughly overhead, with nothing else in between. A planet would be nice."

He looked at the constellations marked on the screen. "Canis Major is just rising now." He zoomed in to see the dimmer stars. As expected, a reddish star appeared with a label *VY CMa*. "Cool, I found the origin star."

Nala swiveled her head and did a good impersonation of a scowling mother. "Something nearby, Daniel. Baby steps."

"Okay, just checking." He clicked on an icon to label the current planetary positions and rotated the view to point straight up into the night sky. One planet stood out.

"Perfect, the rings should be beautiful this time of year," he said.

"We're going to Saturn?"

"It's nearly overhead right now. Mars and Jupiter are below the horizon, and the moon is nowhere near. Unless an asteroid happens to be in the way, it's a clear shot from Earth to Saturn."

Nala rolled her chair over and looked at Daniel's computer screen. "Saturn, it is. What kind of position data can you give me?"

"Right ascension and declination, plus current distance. Will that work?"

Nala nodded her head. "That works. I'll need one more software change. And a few hardware adjustments to survive deep space. Give me twenty minutes."

Daniel clicked on the label and zoomed in. His night sky app displayed a photograph of Saturn, likely taken by NASA's Cassini mission.

*Robotic reconnaissance missions are now ancient history*, he thought. To deliver a package of scientific instruments to Saturn in 2004 had taken thousands of people, many years and hundreds of millions of dollars. Using Diastasi technology, NASA could do the same thing within minutes at a tiny fraction of the cost.

Rockets were now obsolete. Space flight itself was obsolete. All future planetary science would be conducted simply by *positioning* instruments in a *kata* location, taking measurements, photographs, maybe even rock or air samples, and then returning the package to Kata Zero.

*No*, he thought, *we definitely won't be shutting this program down. Even if three astronauts had to give their lives to make it possible.*

But, of course, there was much more to think about. Our solar system seemed small in comparison to the vast collection of stars, many with their own planetary systems, each waiting to be explored from the comfort of a laboratory on Earth. The likelihood of at least one other civilization beyond Earth made the quest even more important.

Regardless of the knowledge that might be gained from this marvelous technology, Daniel's original objective remained front and center. He had been tasked with finding three men and supporting their rescue, if feasible. That rescue, or perhaps the recovery of bodies, was somehow interwoven with the alien message, the yin-yang devices and a map to a location far from Earth. Was it also tied to the countdown? They had less than four hours before the device in South Dakota hit zero.

Daniel looked over at Nala, her head immersed in her work. She was single-handedly harnessing the most significant technology ever created, and like any advanced technology, it could also be dangerous. She had pointed out its dangers several times. She said it herself. *You have to know what you're doing.* Did she?

Nala motioned in the air as if talking to someone not there and then typed furiously on the keyboard. Smart, diligent, with attention to detail. She had each of those qualities. But she was also impulsive. *Pick a planet*, she had said. Not exactly a rigorous scientific analysis. But then, what was the downside? They might lose a camera by slamming it into an asteroid?

*The yin stays here*, he decided. If it had some additional purpose out in the depths of quantum space, there would be time to learn its secrets. But there was no reason to risk sending it off to Saturn... or VY Canis Majoris. Only expendable electronics would make the trip.

Nala finished her computer work and turned her attention to the equipment. She wrapped the radio and its battery pack in a large thermal blanket. "Our engineer thought of this," she said. "It adds some radiation shielding and should help to keep the battery from freezing." She taped the ends of the blanket and then taped two webcams to the top. She plugged their USB cords into the back of the radio.

It made a compact package. Certainly nothing NASA would send into space, but it had a chance of being functional. Daniel recalled an article he'd read about an ordinary Nokia phone that had been strapped to the outside of a satellite, and was still able to take photos, even in the vacuum of space.

But there were more questions in the back of his mind. "We're not really sending any of this into space—I mean real space—right?"

"Correct. We're going into *kata* space, 4-D space, quantum space. We're essentially creating a bubble of new space that never existed. There won't be anything in it, not even at the molecular level. But from the bubble, we'll be looking into real space that has been highly compressed. Some of that light and radiation that exists in real space will leak into quantum space. Photons are quantum particles, too, just like neutrinos. So, yes, if we got close enough to a star, this equipment could get fried."

The geometry of this new form of space was hard to grasp. He knew that a fourth dimension was easier to comprehend by using the imaginary Flatland world. He pictured a 3-D bubble, like a soap bubble, attached to a flat piece of paper, and then imagined folding the paper like an accordion to compress it in one direction. Nothing about the soap bubble would change, but a camera inside would suddenly be very near what used to be the far edge of the paper. He made a mental note to remember the metaphor for future use. Something told him he might be explaining all of this to higher-ups.

Nala finished her work and turned a beaming face toward Daniel. "Software is adjusted and unit tested. Hardware is as protected as we can make it. I think we're ready to fly, cowboy."

# 42  Intuition

Pixie drove past a long row of helicopters, each tied down by thick orange straps. The car shuddered with each gust of wind as they drove across the darkened tarmac. Marie wondered how anything stayed in place, tied down or not. The car's headlights illuminated the hangar and they stopped near its entrance. She grabbed a canvas bag from the seat and pushed the car door open.

The cold wind whipped open her light jacket. "Jesus." She pulled it tight. *Does it ever stop blowing?* Pixie ran ahead and pulled a key ring from his pocket. She hurried through the open doorway, glad to be out of the storm. "Thanks, Pixie, I really appreciate your help."

"No problem, ma'am." He pointed into the dimly lit hangar. "You sure you want to go back in there?"

No doubt, he was nervous about Soyuz. Everyone at the base was. "We've still got time before it hits zero, and I won't be long. Just have to get this camera in place." She held up the canvas bag.

Pixie looked pale. "I can stay if you want me to."

"That's not what the colonel said. Limited exposure—that's what I heard."

He didn't argue. "Yeah. You have my number. Call me when you're ready and I'll pick you up. If I don't hear from you in twenty minutes, I'm coming anyway."

She nodded and he wished her well. The door clanged shut with an echo across the empty hangar floor. She stood alone in the near darkness. A sole spot light illuminated Soyuz.

She walked purposefully to the capsule and climbed the metal stairs to the top of the scaffolding. Someone had left an extension cord with a lamp attached to the end, and luckily it worked. She dropped it through the hatch and lowered herself down.

The lamp provided enough light to see, but the long shadows it created on every surface made the capsule feel… haunted. It was not a word she would have used in front of anyone else, but it matched her internal emotions perfectly. She sat in the left seat once more, Sergei's seat, feeling the curves in its cushion imprinted by his body. She didn't move for several minutes and absorbed the surreal experience; the empty seats, a spent oxygen bottle wedged into a corner, the blank control panel with the yang still attached firmly on top.

As she watched, the bottommost character on the yang changed. It was a quick flick of black and gray, a change hardly noticeable unless you were looking directly at it. *Two and a half minutes closer to zero.*

She pulled out her phone and compared the characters that Daniel had sent to the yang. *104, base eight.* About two and a half hours to go and still on track to hit zero at 3:20 a.m. local time.

She took a picture of the yang and then started a video for good measure. She panned around the cramped cabin and narrated. "It's nearly one in the morning. The yang is still doing its thing, I don't see any changes. I don't know why I should expect anything different. People are scared of it now, like it's packed with explosives or something. Blowing up the capsule seems farfetched to me, but this thing must have a purpose. I'm going to hook up a camera so we can watch remotely when it gets to zero."

The yang ticked again. 103.

She pulled a camera from the canvas bag and wedged it firmly between the seat backs, pointing at the yang. McGinn had also provided a "field pack," as he had called it, a portable network router that could send a secure signal to a base unit. She plugged in a cable from the camera and powered up. A green light lit on the camera and she leaned into its view, smiled and waved. "Camera secured and tested."

The yang ticked. 102.

Her primary task complete, she dropped back into the seat. She closed her eyes and thought of Sergei and Jeremy. Mostly Sergei. The chances of seeing him alive again seemed remote. All conventional means of returning safely to Earth had come and gone. She imagined him stored away in some alien test tube filled with clear gel, a line of cables plugged into his vertebrae. But, of course, that was a fear implanted into her brain by writers of fiction. *Push it out of your head.*

*Remember the man. Kind, funny and playful. Forever dedicated to his mission.* She would sorely miss Sergei. Yet somehow, she felt him. It was more than sitting in the contours of his seat. More than a lingering scent of a missing man. She felt him directly.

The yang ticked to 101. There was no sound, but she opened her eyes on cue, her brain in complete synchronization with the two-and-a-half-minute count. The yang seemed to stare at her. Taunting her. Her anger built.

"Stupid thing," she growled. "What the hell are you doing?" She lifted a leg and kicked it, which did nothing except to hurt her ankle. She screamed at it. "This is torture. You take away my friends and act like nothing happened. You sit there and just count down. To what? What the fuck is your problem?"

She took several deep breaths and tried to calm down. She remembered the camera was rolling and felt embarrassed by her outburst. Lashing out wouldn't help. The challenge she faced was something that could not be solved with fists or yelling or weapons of any kind.

The yang ticked. 100.

It made a clicking sound, and from the left hole, a green laser projected straight ahead, hitting the middle seat just a few inches from her right shoulder.

She jumped, banging her knee on the control panel. "Oh, shit!"

The laser light flicked to the empty right seat.

"Oh no, get me out of here!" She managed to get one leg on the seat, squirming to shift her weight in the confined space. "Oh, please…"

The laser flicked to the left seat and its beam hit her squarely in the chest. The yang's silver panel slid open and a slender tube extended into the air. She got a second leg onto the seat and frantically pushed up. The tube extended further, its tip sharpening to a point. Her hands slapped the edges of the hatch tunnel, searching for a grip. "Nooo!" Her hand finally grabbed onto a bar and she pulled as hard as she could. She launched upward and out the hatch.

Her heart pounded, her breath stuttered with a voice that would not come out, and she collapsed onto the metal scaffold.

# 43 Saturn

The photon was like any other of the googolplex photons in the universe—a simple string vibrating in ten dimensions in just such a way that it existed as a boson capable of transmitting electromagnetic force. Light, as it was called.

If a photon could be happy, this one would be. It sailed unrestricted through routine three-dimensional space on its way from the star called Sol toward the planet called Saturn. But like all photons, it didn't spend all of its time in the wide-open space of three-dimensions. Occasionally, its vibration carried it into one of the very narrow quantum dimensions—the back alleys of space, just wide enough for particles of its size to pass.

Moving at very high speed, the photon approached the giant planet. Its surface was covered in swirls of yellow and blue in long horizontal bands. At its somewhat flattened pole, a hexagon shape stood in contrast to the vigorous churn elsewhere in the atmosphere. Enormous rings of shimmering white stretched around it, raked into perfectly parallel lines like a Japanese rock garden.

The photon approached one of the many moons orbiting the planet. At its current speed, it would blow past in a fraction of a second. But it didn't.

At the precise instant that the photon happened to be vibrating in a fourth dimension, space radically deformed. The quantum thickness suddenly burst into a colossal bubble, and the photon's direction of travel collapsed to a tiny fraction of its former size. New space had come into existence—a deformity that was attached, yet separate from the routine set of dimensions where the photon existed only a moment before.

At the center of this new void, wisps of frozen fog drifted into surrounding emptiness. The fog cleared, revealing an array of electronic equipment floating in place—a radio receiver and two webcams.

From inside the bubble, the view of the planet was very different. The enormous breadth of its rings was compressed into an elliptical shape pressed onto a flat wall that stretched to infinity up, down, left and right. The massive planet within the center of the rings had also collapsed to an ellipse and was embedded in the same infinite wall. The planet's colors had not changed, its atmosphere swirls were still there, but its bulk was gone like a deflated balloon.

~~~~~~~~~~~~~~~~~~~~~~~~~

"Holy crap." Nala stared at her computer screen. Two windows, one for each webcam, and both were filled with a gloriously complex but bewildering view. The gentle curve of the planet's edge filled the view from top to bottom. Striated rings of white stretched out of view to the left. She touched a joystick and panned one of the cameras further left. The rings seemed to end prematurely, misshapen as though their circular shape had been compressed. She panned back to the planet. The camera revealed an enormous oval with bands of yellow and white waves across its surface. It was beautiful, and odd at the same time.

Daniel sat next to her, his face close to the screen. "It looks like Saturn, but squished."

"Spheres compressed to discs. Predicted by theory, but still amazing to witness." She had known their program would get to this stage, but she'd never thought it would be this soon. *Lost astronauts turned out to be pretty useful.* It was a selfish thought and she banished it from her mind lest she say it out loud.

The background was entirely black, but otherwise the view was brightly lit. She switched to the second camera. In the foreground, she could see the first webcam attached to the thermal blanket, a visual confirmation that the scene was very real. She turned the camera until its view settled onto a second ellipse, this one smaller and colored yellow. Its edges were somewhat fuzzy and it had a distinct reddish glow in its center.

Daniel pointed. "There, that's got to be Titan. The yellow color is right, and it has an atmosphere."

"With a red center."

Daniel peered closely. "Yeah, that answers a hotly debated question. Planetary geologists thought Titan's center might be slushy water, but it looks like it's molten."

Nala laughed. "Pretty handy to see inside things, huh? How much did NASA spend on that Saturn mission? And look what we found out in just a few minutes."

Daniel shook his head. "Planetary research will never be the same."

Behind them, the lab door swung open and Jae-ho Park walked through. He was followed by two others. The bald man looked friendly enough, even familiar, but the woman exuded authority—never a good sign as far as Nala was concerned.

Nala reached out to Park. "I wasn't expecting to see you tonight."

Park held both of her hands in his. "I am so sorry, my dear—this Stetler business. You stood up and did what was right. Had I recognized the problem sooner... nevertheless, I will make it right."

He'd always been good to her, in many ways a father figure. Flaky at times, but kind. "Thank you, Jae-ho, you know how much I love what we're doing."

Daniel shook hands with the unannounced visitors and introduced Nala to Spencer Bradley and Christine Shea. "I'm glad you're here," he told them. "We've learned a lot in the past few hours. I think we have a realistic opportunity to resolve this mystery."

Shea nodded but made no comment as she looked around the room. Nala recognized the authority type immediately. *Give away nothing and observe everything.* It was a style designed to be intimidating.

Park looked subdued, like he'd just returned from a whipping at the woodshed. She imagined the sparks in *that* meeting. *Poor Jae-ho. Well, maybe he deserved it.*

Shea walked quietly around the small lab, examining the shelves of equipment and picking up the blue plastic tesseract. She had clearly not been here before. Bradley pointed to the pipes overhead. "I hear the protons. You're in 4-D space now?"

"We're testing a software change," Nala replied. "And some additional hardware. So far, it's working well." She recognized him; Bradley had been at the lab, many months before.

"We've decoded the star map," Daniel added. "We have a known destination."

Shea leaned against the work table and stared up into the plexiglass box above her. The radio's coaxial cable entered near the top and disappeared into nothing. She didn't seem to be concerned. "Soyuz first, Dr. Rice. We've had several calls with Colonel McGinn at Ellsworth, including a disconcerting call just now. The device they have quarantined there is counting down, and it will reach zero in just a few hours, I believe. What do you make of it?"

Daniel sighed. "Honestly, we don't know what it's doing. The precautions are wise, but it would be a mistake to jump to any conclusions."

Shea's voice was clear and cold. "The device revealed its intent just a few minutes ago. Your partner in this investigation, Ms. Kendrick, was nearly killed by it."

A surge of anxiety hit Daniel hard. "What the...?"

"She escaped the attack unharmed. But it *was* an attack. The device apparently contains a laser."

Daniel already had his phone out and was typing furiously. "You're sure she's safe?" His face reddened and his fingers fumbled on

288

the keypad. A few seconds later, he looked up from his phone and sighed deeply. "She's says she's fine."

*Well, that was tactless*, Nala thought. She tried not to convey any negative body language toward Shea, but it was impossible not to feel antagonistic.

Shea leaned against the lab table and folded her arms. "I wish Ms. Kendrick hadn't put herself at risk by going into that capsule. We're taking action to secure the area and will destroy the device if needed."

Daniel looked up from his phone. "Destroy it?"

"Yes," she said. "They're preparing as we speak for a Modified EOD—explosives ordnance disposal. They're moving the capsule to an old missile silo near the base. Once it's at the bottom, they'll place a high explosives pack on top."

"And you intend to blow it up before the count reaches zero?"

"Possibly."

Daniel became animated, waving both arms. "But you have no idea what it's going to do when it reaches zero."

"No, I don't. Do you?" Shea's eyes were piercing, her expression deadly serious.

"Of course not. But if we're being attacked, why would it count down? Why give us a warning?"

"Why does any enemy give warning? We surrender, lay down our arms, and they don't have to fire a shot."

Shea had intentionally put Daniel on his heels by suggesting Marie was in danger. This woman was a menace. Maybe paranoid, too.

Daniel seemed to be in agreement. "Do you really believe that ludicrous scenario?"

Shea turned a cold face to him. "The president expects me to consider all possibilities, and to protect the country and its citizens."

Daniel raised his voice. "Then consider this possibility. We've been contacted for the first time by another intelligence who has so far been nothing but helpful. We've been greeted by a declaration of scientific knowledge and we've been invited to a place of some significance. Exactly what we'll find there, I don't know. *That's* our risk, the risk of the unknown. But if we're wise enough to set aside the irrational worst-case scenarios, we might recognize that this is also our opportunity."

Shea listened with no reaction.

"Ms. Shea," he continued, "just in the past hour we have determined the precise location of the destination, and thanks to Dr. Pasquier, we have the technology to go there."

He glanced at the clock on the wall. "We have about two hours left in the countdown. Yes, you could proactively destroy Soyuz, and along with it, one of the devices they sent to us. Or… we could take a different course of action. We could seek out answers to our questions, including where those astronauts went."

Shea remained impassive, but she wasn't stopping him.

Daniel picked up his laptop and turned it toward her. "This is what we found when we projected the map image from quantum space. Labels, axes, and a coordinate system. Over the past several hours, we've decoded it. It's a star map, and we now know which stars are represented here."

Bradley and Park drew in closely behind Shea. Daniel pointed to the hand grenade. "I believe this is where we'll find those answers, the hand… the… the hub. The origin. Grand Central Station, whatever you want to call it. All lines lead to it, and it's located in quantum space. A fourth dimension where only the scientifically literate and technologically advanced can go."

Nala laughed to herself. *Nice pivot on the name, Daniel. No explosive devices around here!* She caught his eye and smiled. Daniel shrugged.

"Look... here's the bottom line," Daniel said. "I believe there's a relationship between this invitation, this place, and our missing colleagues."

Shea lowered her head and tapped all ten fingers together. After a minute, she lifted her eyes. "Find this place and we find the astronauts?"

Daniel nodded. "Something like that."

Park had remained in the background through the debate, but he finally spoke. "Compression of space is understood, theoretically. But we have not attempted such distances." He looked toward Nala and his brow lifted.

Nala rolled her chair to one side, revealing the computer display behind her. "Jae-ho, I made the software changes we'd talked about. All of them. The oscillation amplitude changes, the beam directional control. It all works."

Park moved closer to the screen, with Bradley and Shea not far behind. Nala reached for one of the joysticks and panned the camera across the rings stopping on the curvature of the enormous planet. "Saturn," she said.

"You have a camera at Saturn? Right now?" asked Bradley.

"Controllable, too." She beamed. "I rigged up new equipment that Rohrs designed—he's our team engineer. Works like a charm." She pushed the joystick further, and the view moved to the planet's polar region. The recently discovered polar vortex with its hexagon shape stood out bold and bright. Daniel gave her a thumbs-up.

Shea sat in the chair Daniel had been using and looked closely at the computer screen. She turned back to Daniel. "Okay. So, tell me how you would do this. And more importantly, give me the risks."

Daniel motioned to the plexiglass box. "Nala, can you bring the equipment back?"

She nodded. "Everyone might want to cover their ears. At these distances, the pop is loud." She typed a few keys and everyone did as she instructed. It sounded like a small gun had fired and the radio in its thermal blanket with webcams on top materialized inside the box. The coaxial cable magically reconnected to the radio repeater on its other end, as if denying that it had ever been involved in anything unnatural.

"A lot louder than I remember," Bradley commented.

"Daniel and I learned the hard way when we sent this equipment to Saturn," Nala replied. "Pushing to greater distances does involve more energy."

Daniel pointed to the cable. "Normally, communicating outbound to a device in 4-D space is impossible, but this little setup was ingenious. We can send and receive both voice and data, and control the cameras. This setup is protected by a firewall at the receiver on the shelf, so our only risk is to the equipment we're sending. We get it too close to a star and it's fried. Relatively cheap stuff, though. Expendable. Did I get all that right, Nala?"

She nodded.

"Devil's advocate," Bradley interjected. "What do we know, theoretically, about expanding further than we've gone into quantum space? I understand the compression part, that's how we're jumping off to a star. But are we at risk of doing some irreparable damage? Tearing a hole in the universe? Anything like that?"

All eyes turned to Nala. "Dr. Bradley, I'm sorry, I'm not the theorist. For that, we need Jan Spiegel in here. But I can tell you that Dr.

292

Park and I were both in several sessions where Jan presented, and we all did our best to blow holes in his theory. Somebody even asked a question similar to yours—we called it the Donnie Darko scenario. I think Jan did a good job of taking it down."

Park nodded in agreement. "I agree. The mathematics of expanding quantum space work precisely the same way whether you're growing space by one micron or one kilometer."

"Except the pop is louder," Shea said. "Larger scale is obviously different."

It was a valid critique, and Park responded. "We believe the pop is a local phenomenon only, related to the oxygen molecules in the test chamber. A flash fire, so to speak, but at the atomic level. We conducted a test a few months ago, replacing the air in the box with pure nitrogen. There was no pop."

Shea had no reaction, but she wasn't saying no. "Can we do this incrementally and abort as needed?"

Nala had the answer and was surprised to find common ground with Shea. "Got it covered. The destination on this star map is nearly four thousand light years away. I thought the same thing—a single large jump could be dangerous to the equipment, not to mention what the pop might do to our ears. So, I set it up to move in increments, a software loop. The system will push the equipment in steps, while we watch. From the camera view, I think it will look like we're zooming in."

Bradley's face was distorted. "Four thousand light years? You're proposing we send a camera that far into space? Can you even do that?"

Daniel nodded. "The hub, our destination, is near a star called VY Canis Majoris. It's one of the largest stars in the Milky Way galaxy, and there's something in orbit around it, or near it, in 4-D space."

"And remember," said Nala, "we're not really going that far. We're only sending the equipment a few thousand kilometers in the *kata* direction. But from the camera's perspective, the space between Earth and the destination will compress by a factor of…" She looked down at her notes. "More than a trillion. From the camera's perspective, the Earth will be about a thousand kilometers away—satellite distance. And so will this… hub."

The room became quiet. Shea looked at the floor, her hands clasped together. She looked up at the clock on the wall. "You're sure you can abort?" Nala nodded. "Quickly?" Nala nodded again.

"Jae-ho? Spence?"

Both men appeared in agreement.

Shea took a deep breath. "Okay, let's do this."

## 44  Hub

The Soyuz capsule hung precariously at the end of a steel cable and wobbled in a small circular motion as the hoist operator positioned it over the center of the flatbed truck. Marie watched from a safe distance on the hangar floor and wondered how all of this would turn out. A spaceflight disaster, an international incident between superpowers, and the intentional destruction of Russian property. The terrestrial issues alone were stupefying. When she added alien messages and a device counting down to who-knows-what, her head was swimming.

She took out her phone and connected to a secured Wi-Fi network for the Air Force base. She located a link to the camera she had positioned inside the capsule. The live video feed displayed a somewhat different scene than she had escaped less than an hour earlier. The yang was now inert. No laser, no protruding silver spike, and its panel once again closed. Three characters were still displayed on its surface, and she quickly translated them to 057, base eight. Just under two hours.

She closed the video window, opened Daniel's last text message and responded.

~~~~~~~~~~~~~~~~~~~~~~~

Daniel heard a beep and reached for his phone.

*Really, I'm fine. We've got bigger things to worry about. They're taking Soyuz out now, camera is working. We have to see what happens at zero. Tell her—convince her to wait. McGinn will do what she says. No explosions, please!*

He typed back and her response was immediate.

*Hogwash, it wasn't trying to kill me. Think about it, the countdown was at 100. Not sure what was going on, but seems more like a preflight checklist than a murder. Convince her.*

Convincing Shea wouldn't be hard. She was being cautious, but she wasn't stupid. If a portal was about to open with Klingons pouring out, they probably wouldn't be stopped by C-4 explosives. It was a ridiculous scenario, and he refused to believe she would carry it out. He could convince her, he was sure.

More useful, and more believable, would be a holographic ambassador that popped out of the yang at zero hour and provided a much-needed lesson on first contact etiquette. He was beginning to think he'd rather be in South Dakota. It might get interesting there very soon. He typed to Marie. *Got the camera working? Send a link.*

He switched thoughts to their destination—the hub, formerly the hand grenade. What would they find there? He had no clue.

Nala was busy cleaning the lens on the webcam. The "flight" to Saturn hadn't caused any obvious damage. Daniel laughed to himself. Things had moved quickly in the past forty-eight hours. He was intensely curious to see where they would go from here.

Nala placed the equipment pack back inside the plexiglass box, the coaxial cable trailing out and to the radio unit on the shelf. "Ready to go when everyone else is," she announced.

"Marie's on a secure connection out at Ellsworth," Daniel told her. "Can we get a video link set up?"

Nala nodded and sat down in front of the operator's console. It wasn't long before another window appeared on a second monitor with a text box: *Waiting for connection.* A few seconds later, Marie's face appeared in one half of a split screen. In the other half was the camera view from inside Soyuz. Nala spoke into a computer microphone on the desk. "Marie, good to see you. We're receiving the Soyuz cam on this end."

The video link was reasonably good, with only a few motion interruptions. "I've got you too, Nala. Thanks for connecting me in."

Nala typed, and two more windows popped up on her main screen. The video feed presented a live view of the lab. "Can you see the lab cams now, Marie?"

"Got the feed, thanks, and I can see everyone in the room." Daniel had kept his promise to Marie and they had gained a view of Soyuz at the same time. "Ms. Shea," Marie called, "I just want to reiterate what I know Daniel has already said. In my view, the security of Soyuz is critical, now more than ever. We'd all benefit, I believe, if you'd ask the military to stand down."

Shea answered quickly. "Not just yet, but thank you, Ms. Kendrick. I am in contact with the president, and he has authorized me to make the decision." She added, "Yes, he's awake and aware of what we're doing."

Daniel watched the exchange and felt proud to call Marie his partner. *Shea will hold off. She's not crazy.*

Park walked around the lab and handed each person a set of earplugs. "I picked these up from the maintenance shop. I suggest we use them."

Nala looked around after each person had inserted the plugs. "Everyone ready?"

At two o'clock in the morning, from a laboratory outside of Chicago, with five people in the room and another watching remotely, Earth's first interstellar flight launched. There was no rocket, no ion engine, no warp drive and no hyperspace jump. But there was a sharp sonic boom that rattled everything in the lab that wasn't screwed down.

The plexiglass shook but didn't break, the plastic tesseract cube fell off the shelf, and Nala's cup of coffee sloshed out onto the desk. "Wow!" she yelled. "Love that effect!"

"It makes it pretty clear we've jumped a long way," Bradley said, smiling.

The target box was now empty and the cable disappeared at its midpoint. The jump was clearly their largest yet. Daniel looked at the webcam window and saw nothing but darkness. "Where are we? You didn't jump all the way to VY Canis Majoris, did you?"

Nala shook her head. She studied a panel that displayed rapidly changing numbers. "Nope, moving incrementally, just as planned. Tau is now $2.9 \times 10^{-4}$, just approaching the bottom of the Spiegel curve." She pointed to the graph on the wall. "We've still got a long way to go."

"Are we out of the solar system?" asked Bradley.

"You can't really think of it that way," said Nala. "We're not flying through space. It's better to think of space collapsing in front of us. Our solar system is collapsing, the stars beyond are collapsing, but it's all still in front of us."

"More like a telephoto lens?" Daniel offered.

"Exactly. Good analogy." She turned around and smiled. "You're so good at that," she whispered.

The numbers in the panel continued to change like a car's odometer and the on-screen view did too. There were a few stars in view, dim, but visible. After a few seconds one of the stars to the left side became noticeably brighter and its position shifted further left. Eventually it disappeared completely out of view on the left side, while other stars closer to the center replaced it.

"Tau passing $10^{-6}$."

"Meaning?" asked Shea.

"Distances have shrunk by a million times. A light year is now less than the distance to Mars." Nala pointed to the screen. "This is so cool—the stars on either side of the target line move toward the edges, just like we're flying."

Daniel stood directly behind Nala and put a hand on her shoulder. She looked up, her face filled with pride. He glanced at the

298

faces gathered around, Shea, Bradley and Park. They were each mesmerized by the changing image on the monitor.

A star near the center of the view grew brighter. As the seconds passed, it separated into two stars, one white and one orange. The white star grew brilliant.

"Tau passing $10^{-8}$. We've got a star coming up almost right on line. This one's going to be close."

"Risk?" Shea demanded.

"I can't tell," Nala called out. "It's so close to the center. It needs to start moving left or right, or we'll hit it."

"Or be sucked in by its gravity," Park pointed out. "Fundamental forces still apply, even in quantum space."

Shea was about to speak when Nala held up a hand. "Wait... I think it's shifting." The star appeared incredibly bright now, but its position drifted slowly to the right. The light filled the screen, briefly washing out everything else, but then shifted rapidly out of view. Beyond it, the orange star remained steady, dead center.

"Sorry, a little too close, but we're still on track." Nala shook her head as she studied the numbers. "Tau passing $10^{-9}$. Compression of one billion." Daniel was having a hard time believing it too. *This is the best telescope ever invented.*

Daniel pointed. "The star in the center. VY Canis Majoris?"

"It must be. We're still light years away, but it's getting big fast."

The star was no longer just a bright point of light. Its spherical shape was noticeable, a brilliant blast of orange. As the seconds passed, the ball grew rapidly and began shifting to the left.

Nala typed on the keyboard. "I'm slowing down now, for better control. We'll ease into this."

The star had shifted to the left side of the screen but was now so brilliant that it was impossible to tell what might lie directly ahead. It was like looking for an object next to the sun. Would the webcams hold up to this intense light? It was strange to think of the equipment package so far away. Or was it? More accurately, the equipment hadn't moved much, but these stars had become much closer. *Stupefying, astonishing, mindboggling, staggering.* Daniel ran through all the appropriate words in his head. It had taken just a few minutes, but they were almost there. Three thousand eight hundred and forty light years from Earth.

~~~~~~~~~~~~~~~~~~~~~~

Intensely bright light flooded the darkness of space from a binary system, one star enormous and of deep orange color, the other tiny and white. The white star was larger than most, but it was virtually lost next to its big brother, which dominated both in size and in brilliance. The behemoth's gravity ripped a fountain of flaming gas away from its smaller companion. The flame arced between the two stars like a torch in the wind.

Near to the stellar drama, and separate from it, was a special corner of space—a bubble of quantum space. A place that had been created ages ago by a civilization hardly remembered. Its distinct boundary with the ordinary space of stars permitted only bosons to cross, the energy of light and gravity. Quarks and leptons, the bits of matter, were required by the dimensional laws of the universe to remain behind.

But this bubble of quantum space was anything but empty.

An enormous sphere, surrounded by a hundred smaller objects of varying sizes, filled the space. The sphere was brightly lit by the nearby star and glowed in an orange tint. The smaller objects floated around it, some orbiting, some hovering over a single position.

The sphere's surface was covered with a mix of light and dark panels in regular rows and columns, as if it had been wrapped in a checkerboard. At the top, a second and smaller half-sphere was grafted to its larger base. The smaller hemisphere also displayed the same checkerboard pattern on a smaller scale. There was nothing natural about the configuration. This was a construction.

For a brief instant, a flash of blue light crashed through the boundary of the bubble of space, and a rectangular package popped into existence. The bright light from the nearby star flooded two cameras mounted on its upper surface, making photography in that direction impossible. But the cameras began a gentle counterclockwise rotation, turning away from the intense glare. They panned across a beautiful splash of stars, darker dust and the deep red of hydrogen gas that, along with the brilliant orange star, were embedded in a wall stretching infinitely in every direction.

The cameras continued their slow pivot and then stopped, pointing directly at the enormous sphere.

~~~~~~~~~~~~~~~~~~~~~~~~~

"We made it. The hub," declared Daniel, his mouth wide open. "It even looks like..." *An enormous hand grenade.* He shook his head. "The regular rows, the parallel lines. This thing is definitely a design. There's no doubt it's technology."

"Big, too," Nala added. "Right when we stopped, the Tau value tripled, and it wasn't from anything I did. I think our bubble of quantum space intersected a larger bubble that was already here. I'd estimate this thing might be a couple thousand kilometers in diameter."

*More like a small moon.*

The surface glowed orange. The darker panels looked smooth and featureless. The lighter panels were covered in a maze of tangled lines, curves, and dots, brighter and slightly whiter.

The foreground was alive with activity. A small bean-shaped object near the top of the screen drifted across the view, a bright yellow

301

light blinking on and off. A larger cylinder composed of several rings, some that were slowly turning in place, rose from the bottom. A black wedge with a red light floated to one side. More objects floated, twisted and blinked within the scene. Some had long poles extending from them. Others were covered with smooth metal surfaces that glinted in the starlight as they rotated.

Without familiar reference points, it was impossible to tell the absolute size of any of the objects, only that they were all much smaller than the sphere.

"If this thing has enough mass, they may be in orbit, like satellites," Daniel offered.

Christine Shea stood directly behind Nala. "Amazing." She seemed as absorbed in the view as anyone.

Nala's head snapped upward. Daniel noticed it too. A flickering red light came from the radio receiver on the shelf. "We're getting something," she said. "Daniel, turn up the volume."

He reached over and dialed a knob on the radio's panel, bringing a speaker to life. It was a scratchy sound, a buzzing sound, like a stringed instrument.

"*Kak pashyevayesh,*" buzzed from the speaker.

"Contact," Daniel called out. Every nerve ending in his body was triggered. He looked over at the monitor. "Marie, did you hear that?"

From her video feed, she nodded. "Yeah, I did. What frequency is your radio on?"

"It's on 922.763, just like you suggested," Nala answered.

Marie's smile broadened. "Contact indeed. Can you respond?"

Nala motioned to Daniel. He picked up the handheld transceiver from the shelf, looked at Nala, then Bradley, and shrugged.

"Just respond," Bradley encouraged. "It probably doesn't matter what you say."

Daniel swallowed hard. "We're doing well. How are you?"

There was only a moment of silence, and then the speaker buzzed again. It made little sense, except for the faintest recognition of a few syllables.

"*Bezhaarz auzh nazh ghesh ruzhpon onge nigzh zhuzhu zovzhez deezh.*" The tone varied with high and low frequencies, sometimes mixing both, as if two instruments were being played simultaneously. It was not spoken; it sounded far more like something synthesized.

"Did I hear *respond* in there?" asked Marie. "It sounded like *respond*. That's all I could make out."

"I have no idea," Daniel replied. "Lots of buzzing, but I didn't hear anything recognizable. Did you hear anything Russian in that?"

"No, not a word. Say something again."

Daniel nervously keyed the mic. "Respond."

The buzzing tone came back immediately and was higher-pitched this time. "*Ruzhpon.*"

Daniel dropped his head. "Oh, wow. That's incredible." Nala wore the widest smile Daniel had ever seen.

Their elation was interrupted by a tone from the console. "A message, inbound," Nala snapped. She swiveled her chair and studied the screen. "It's being transferred to the console as formatted data." She typed some keys and displayed the message on-screen. It was short, but required no translation.

*Data on 922.763*

# 45  Paradox

Daniel leaned against the edge of the lab desk, lost in his thoughts as he pondered the meaning of words.

*Data*. A set of numbers, but it could just as easily represent speech, or text, or communication in general. But what if they had assigned some other meaning? From the human perspective, an error, but no less likely.

*On*. A path, a conduit, a choice. Or again, something else entirely.

*922.763*. A radio frequency in megahertz, millions of cycles per second. Radio waves are a natural part of the electromagnetic spectrum. But one second of time is a purely human measure, meaningless to anyone else. To them, the number might be no more than a tag for a given frequency.

*Data on 922.763.*

It was very similar to the original message. It could be another echo with no meaning at all. Something they'd pulled from a text message sent by Soyuz. But then again...

Daniel emerged from his trance. All eyes in the room were on him, even before he spoke. "They're asking for input. Fodder. Fuel for our conversation."

"For what purpose?" Shea asked.

"Probably to learn about us. They may not know much. We're communicating, but not very well so far."

Marie was still connected via video link. "We've got one word. *Respond*. It's a start."

"Communication is a first step when two civilizations meet. At least, it has been throughout our history. My guess is they will learn our language faster than we'd learn theirs... if we give them something to work with."

"What do you propose?" Bradley asked. "Send a dictionary?"

"Simpler," Daniel responded. "We'd need a primer. Like a children's book."

"You're going to read a children's book over the radio?"

"Not exactly." Daniel looked at Nala. "Could we send a web page?"

She nodded. "Sure. But would they decipher the format?"

"They've already figured out our message format."

"Wait a second," Shea interrupted. "You want to send them web pages off the Internet so they can learn about us? I think we're going to need a more structured approach, and probably a team of linguists."

Daniel looked at the clock. 3:20 a.m. *No sleep tonight.* "We've got exactly one hour until the yang countdown hits zero out in South Dakota. I think we have a realistic chance of learning how Soyuz is tied to this hub… this alien structure. If you can get a team of linguists in here in the next thirty minutes, I welcome their help. But otherwise, we're probably on our own."

Shea held her hands to her forehead.

Daniel took the opportunity. "The missing astronauts, *and* that thing counting down inside Soyuz, *and* the map that sent us out here, *and* this initial communication. They're all tied together, and honestly, I think we have a shot at finding out how. But before we can solve that mystery, we have to communicate. I think whoever is on the other end of this radio is saying the same thing."

Shea kneaded her forehead with her fingers and finally spoke. "Find something simple to send. One page. Let's see what they do with it."

Daniel leaned over to Nala. "Try a Wikipedia page. Maybe something about humans or our language."

She typed at the console and located a page on languages that looked appropriate. She responded to the message, including the page. For good measure, Daniel picked up the handheld and keyed the mic. "Maybe you're asking for audio communication, too. We've sent data. We hope it will help. We'll stand by."

There was silence in the room and on the radio. "What now?" Shea asked.

"I guess we wait," Daniel said. "Making any sense of this seems like a long shot, but if we give them enough time to process it, we might—"

Nala yelled out. "Got another message." She put it on the screen.

*Good. Language. More. Data on 922.763.*

Before anyone could react, the radio speaker burst into a strong vibration. The synthetic voice said, "*Gudzh.*"

"Ten seconds," Nala said. "Damn, these people are fast! Either that, or they've got some really fine technology."

Bradley held up a hand and waved until he got everyone's attention. "Wait a second. Something's amiss here. We seem to be at square one. If these *people* had something to do with Soyuz, if they are the owners of these two devices, the yin and the yang, then why don't they already know about us? Why not send a ship to Earth? They know where we live. Why bring us all the way to this hub and then ask for data?"

They were good questions with no certain answers. But Daniel had already thought about the bigger picture. "I'm not sure, Spence. Questions about intent are going to be hard, but I can throw out a few possibilities. The most obvious is that this sphere—this hub—is somehow very important. They needed us to find it. Maybe it's a communications platform, the easiest way for us to begin a conversation. Maybe it's an artificial intelligence, a machine that makes communication possible, or easier."

"An official interpreter," Bradley offered.

"Could be," Daniel agreed. "And what if we're not the only ones? I've often thought about how hard it would be to have a galactic conversation among many species. You'd not only need the interpreter, you'd need an advisor familiar with the customs of each civilization and a diplomat who is careful not to say or do something that might be threatening. First contact would be daunting. What if this thing is more like an ambassador, or even a meeting place like the UN?"

Bradley nodded thoughtfully. "A galactic conversation among many civilizations. That'd be a hell of a thing to tap into."

"A conversation that might have been going on for many years, maybe centuries. And to our good fortune, we have an invitation to join." Daniel stopped talking to let that point sink in.

Shea looked around the room. "All good, assuming they are friendly. But what if they're probing for weakness? You scientists might say that's nonsense, but what do we know about them or their intentions? Personally, I'd rather see them, face-to-face, on our territory. Come out of the shadows. Show yourselves."

"I'm not going to say you're wrong," said Daniel. "It's wise for us to take precautions, and yeah, I'd like to see them too. But I would add that if they meant us harm, they'd probably just do it. They wouldn't be politely asking us to provide information."

Bradley rubbed his chin and spoke to Shea. "Except for that incident with Ms. Kendrick, they're showing no signs of hostility." Daniel tried to interject, but Bradley held up a hand. "Yes, I agree there are other explanations for her experience inside Soyuz. Their technology is clearly more advanced, and we don't know what it's doing." He pointed to the screen, where the image of the checkerboard sphere remained in place. "Look at this thing! They not only know about quantum space,

307

they're building huge structures in it. If you look at our history, we've had our stops and starts, but it's always been true that the most advanced societies on our planet are also the most peaceful, the least likely to intentionally harm others. Why should we expect any less from them?"

Shea's response was clinical. "More people died from war in the twentieth century than any other century in history. The twenty-first century is not looking any better."

Bradley countered. "Body counts are not a good measure of war or peace. We have seven billion people on our planet now. In the twelfth century, when Genghis Khan was ravaging Asia, we had less than five hundred million. Even less in the eighth century, when wars in China massacred a large portion of their population. Percentage-wise, the twentieth century was pretty good. We *are* advancing."

Shea didn't react. It wasn't clear if she was agreeing or not.

Bradley wasn't finished anyway. "What I can't understand is why we haven't found each other before. We have astronomers all over the world who listen for signals from deep space every day. In fifty years, no one has heard a peep. And our civilization is not exactly quiet. We broadcast daily on every frequency in the electromagnetic spectrum. No one's ever heard us?"

"It's Fermi's paradox," Daniel answered. "Billions of planets in our galaxy alone. Millions within habitable zones. If they were out there all this time, why haven't we heard from them?"

Bradley nodded. "Exactly."

The famous physicist, Enrico Fermi, had first asked this question in 1950. With a galaxy as big as the Milky Way, the probability of intelligent life was high—yet there was no reliable evidence of contact in the history of human civilization. The solution to the paradox had remained elusive ever since Fermi had proposed it.

But Daniel had the answer, he was sure of it. The discoveries made at the laboratory that bore Fermi's name had provided it.

"Light speed is too slow."

All eyes in the room turned to Daniel. He stared at the floor. It was time to release an idea that had been circulating in his head for years. He had even rehearsed it, privately. It was an answer to the paradox that Fermi himself would have enjoyed hearing.

Daniel lifted his head. "The speed of light... it's too limiting. Radio communications, space travel, everything... it's all too slow. The cosmic speed limit doesn't meet the requirements of interstellar space, much less intergalactic space. The distances are just too big. A single message sent from one inhabited planet to another could take hundreds, even thousands of years. And thousands more for the response. A useful conversation is impossible when wait times are longer than lifespans. 'How are you?' Wait a thousand years... 'We're fine.' Wait another thousand years. It's absurd."

Daniel paused. "Radios are utterly worthless for communicating between stars."

He shrugged. "A technology that's not useful doesn't get used. Every civilization must figure this out, probably not long after they become spacefaring. There's simply no point in listening for electromagnetic signals from the stars. It's like searching for a phone booth on a city street. You're not going to find one—that technology is no longer useful."

He held up a finger. "But... if, by chance, they uncover the true nature of the universe, as we recently have, and they learn to control the dimensions of space, as we can now... then the problem is solved. Expand quantum space, compress normal space, and those enormous distances disappear. Even a star that's four thousand light years away is no problem at all. We just did it. We're doing it right now."

Bradley shook his head. "Fermi's paradox, resolved." He put a hand on Daniel's shoulder. "Good insight. It makes sense."

"But they haven't abandoned radios," asked Nala. "We're communicating right now by radio."

"Perhaps radio is still useful at orbital distances," Daniel answered. "And, yeah, given that they have radios, it's possible they could have even picked up our transmissions. Maybe they compressed space somewhere in the direction of Earth at some point over the years. Who knows? But we would be like a rowboat in the ocean, shining a dinky little flashlight at planes flying thirty thousand feet overhead. We shouldn't wonder why they never saw us, or heard us."

"And so, you think they know nothing about us," said Bradley.

Daniel nodded. "They probably didn't know we existed. We're newcomers. We only recently figured out how to compress space." He turned to Shea. "Which brings me back to my original point. They're asking for more information about us. I think we should provide it."

Shea's eyes were cold and her face expressionless. "You've made a good point, Dr. Rice. Very well done. But I'm going to require a short delay." She held up a hand. "Yes, I realize the countdown out in South Dakota is quickly approaching a point of no return, and I just received an update. Soyuz is now secured in a missile silo and there's a half a ton of high explosives sitting on top of it. I'm inclined to keep a finger on the trigger... but not fire just yet. Before we go further with this communication, I want to bring in the president."

There was motion just behind Shea. Nala's attention was now consumed by a window that had popped up on the operator's console. Bold red lettering in a large font made it clear why.

*Malware detected. Quarantine?*

"What the...?" She hit the enter key several times. "Why won't this work?"

Daniel moved closer. "What's going on?"

"Something is running on the system. It's not supposed to be there."

Shea noticed it too. "Shut it down!"

Nala's eyes were moving as fast as her hands. "I'm trying. The system won't isolate it. Whatever it is, I think it's accessing the Internet."

"Shut the computer down."

A tone sounded and an alert appeared at the bottom of the screen. *New message.* Nala hit the system power key on the keyboard, but the screen remained lit. "It won't even shut down."

Daniel reached to the radio on the shelf and pulled the coaxial cable out of its socket. He looked at Nala anxiously as she peered at the screen. "It's stopped," she said. The virus warning message changed. *Malware successfully quarantined.* Daniel took a deep breath.

"What the hell just happened?" Shea demanded.

"Something got through the firewall. I don't know how." Nala pulled up a log file. "Looks like it was hitting URLs out on the Internet and downloading."

"Damn!" Shea spat. "It could have gotten to anything. Does this machine have access to government servers?"

Nala nodded. "Fermilab, at least. Argonne too, maybe more."

"Oh, great." Shea shook her head. "Find out what it took, can you do that?"

"I'll try." She clicked a link in the security log file. It was a list of URLs accessed, with date and time stamps for each. "Looks like it hit about twenty different pages."

"What? Data files? Secure sites?"

Nala scanned down the list. "No, actually. Pretty ordinary stuff. A couple more Wikipedia pages… the *Wall Street Journal*… MSNBC… Disney.com… even YouTube." She looked up, very perplexed. "It was web surfing."

Shea looked pale. Bradley started laughing, and then tried to control it. Park hid his face in his hands.

*Plug it back in*, Daniel thought. *Maybe they'll open a Twitter account.* But he didn't say it. Instead he silently pointed to the message indicator at the bottom of the screen. "A message came in just before I pulled the plug."

Nala first ran a quick scan. No malware detected. She opened it.

*Please sorry. More data. Good language.*

Daniel pulled his hair back with his hand. "Oh my God, they're apologizing for aggressive behavior. This is really remarkable." He couldn't help but laugh, regardless of who else was in the room.

Shea took a deep breath. Her face was a combination of pissed and wounded, but there was hint of a smile coming on, deep down in there somewhere.

Bradley kept his composure. "We've just been attacked by an alien virus—and maybe that's exactly what we needed."

# 46 Galactic

The clock nearly screamed its message: 3:50 a.m. Thirty minutes left in the yang countdown. Daniel was using those final minutes one-on-one with Christine Shea. His first point was the effectiveness of a simple coaxial cable. Pulling the plug had shut down the intrusion, and the option remained available. Just when he thought the impact of his argument was waning, she stopped him and simply said, "Plug it back in."

His second point led from the first. Further communication provided more information, and unless there were signs of hostility, there was no logical reason to detonate explosives. The device inside Soyuz might even be a key component to their communication. The argument seemed to have some success, but the clincher came from an entirely different direction. How would she explain to the Russians that she had destroyed their spacecraft and all evidence it might have held? She agreed to play it minute by minute, but Daniel noticed she tightly clenched her phone, and he had no doubt McGinn was standing by on the other end.

It seemed odd, reconnecting only half of a cable that disappeared into nowhere.

"But be ready to pull it, if we need to," she added.

He pushed the cable back into its receptacle and queried Nala, "Anything else we need to do?"

"Don't think so," she responded. "We should be back on the air. You might offer them a clue, though." She motioned to the handheld radio.

Daniel picked it up and marveled at the simple electronic device in his hand. In ways never envisioned by its designer, it represented the first link in a communication crossing an immense distance. Maxwell, Einstein, Hertz, Marconi and others had contributed to this moment. One discovery leading to the next. There would be new names to add to the list, several from Fermilab. Scientific progress spanning several centuries had put into Daniel's hand the power to reach the stars.

"My voice comes to you as a modulated radio wave sent across four thousand light years of space compressed to a small fraction of that distance by coherent neutrinos. I hope the reception on your end is good."

Nala looked at her screen and back up to Daniel. She gave him a thumbs-up. They waited in silence, but not for long. The radio's speaker crackled with the vibrational voice, and this time it was far clearer.

"*Honor to meet you.*"

Daniel felt a surge of scientific pride, and a validation that his instincts had been right. There was nothing to fear from this voice. It was first contact with an intelligence who likely shared our curiosity. At the very least, it was an intelligence benevolent enough to provide an invitation to meet.

He looked at Shea, and this time she encouraged him to continue. Bradley held his phone up to the radio speaker, and Nala whispered to him, "Don't worry, I've got a recording started. We're capturing the webcam video too."

The webcam window still provided the same view. The spherical hub more than filled the screen. Several smaller spacecraft—satellites, whatever they were—moved across the foreground. The black wedge with the red light had moved closer to the center. There was really no way to know what any of these machines were doing, but it was fascinating to watch.

Who was on the other end of this radio connection? And speaking from which object? This, too, was unknown. The spherical hub had no windows and nothing that resembled a control room, or a "bridge."

He keyed the mic again. "You have created a very great technology. We are inspired by what we see."

*"Thank you. Welcome. I am Core. I come from many."*

Daniel smiled. Real communication; this was no echo. Absorbing a few dozen web pages and YouTube videos was apparently sufficient to get you this far—if your cognitive abilities were high enough and your computers were fast enough.

He spoke to the room. "I'm not sure what that last part means, *I come from many.*" No one else had an answer. Daniel held the radio up. "We have many questions for you. In our language, do you understand the difference between a statement and a question?"

*"Yes."* The vibrational voice made it sound more like *yezh*, but it wasn't hard to figure out. *"I help your questions."*

"Thank you. Are you technology? Or biology?"

*"Many are biology. Many are technology. I am both."*

Daniel grinned as the meaning hit home—he was conversing with a hybrid intelligence, a cybernetic organism. For decades, science fiction in books and movies had provided a single view of cyborgs—and it wasn't pretty. This particular disclosure might be a hard sell to the average joe. *Don't worry, they're nice cyborgs.*

Shea might have picked up on the disclosure too. "Ask him why they haven't shown themselves to us," she suggested.

Daniel decided to rephrase it in a simpler and friendlier way. "Thank you. We would like to meet you, in person. Will you come to Earth?"

*"No. I am Core. I am what you see."*

Daniel had assumed the sphere was a ship, but it was possible the whole thing was one living entity. "Will anyone visit us on Earth?"

*"No. Too soon. You will learn."*

Daniel shrugged. "He seems pretty certain about protocols. Maybe we leave it at that for now."

Shea glanced up to the clock on the wall. There were now less than twenty minutes. "Okay. Then I want to know about our astronauts."

Daniel agreed. There had to be a connection, and this was a golden opportunity to find out. He keyed the mic. "Our astronauts... our humans in space. They're missing and we're worried. Can you help us find them?"

*"Not missing. They are home."*

It was an interesting response, perhaps even promising. "Did *you* send them home? Where?"

*"Not in your space or your time. They are alive. They are home."* Simple words, but potentially packing a lot of meaning. Alive was good, but the rest could go either way. Not in our space *or* time?

"I don't understand. How can we bring them into our space? We think they will die if they return. Anything alive will die."

*"Yes. Alive will die. Time answers. You will learn."*

Nala turned around. "I think he has an answer to the cell degeneration problem. At least I hope he does."

*"Time answers,"* Bradley repeated. "Something to do with the countdown?"

Daniel shook his head. "Maybe, but it could be more than that." He keyed the mic. "Your device is counting down. What happens when it finishes?"

*"Be ready. Humans are alive. Time answers. They will not die."*

Daniel pivoted to Shea, and she was already dialing. "I'm on it," she said.

316

*Be ready*. The connection between the astronauts and the yang countdown was plain, even if the details were still obscure. Soyuz was ground zero, but not for any alien invasion, and McGinn would surely be getting new instructions.

Daniel glanced to the second monitor, where Marie's video link was displayed. *Attendee has disconnected*, it read. His heart raced and he wished the best for Marie. Somewhere at Ellsworth Air Base, he imagined she was probably running as fast as she could go.

He keyed the mic. "Thank you, we appreciate your help. We'll be ready."

"*I help many. Add your voice.*"

"When you say *many*, what do you mean?"

"*Many voices. Many people. Many planets. Do you add your voice?*"

"Yes, of course," said Daniel without hesitation.

"*Welcome. You will learn. Data voice more. Many ideas. Many people.*"

A tone chimed on Nala's console, and the new message notification lit. She opened it and her face lit up. "Two attachments. Wow, formatted JPEG and MPEG. They're making this pretty easy."

The vibrational voice continued, no longer waiting for questions. "*Observe. One of many. They are people like you. Their planet is near. You will be friends.*"

Nala already had one of the files open, and Daniel looked over her shoulder at an alien landscape with intriguing but indecipherable shapes in the foreground. "Is that why you sent these images to us?"

"*Yes.*"

"Thank you. I hope we will be friends."

*"It is time. Return later. I will help."*

"It's time to end our conversation?" asked Daniel.

*"Yes."*

"Why?"

*"It is time. A new count will start. Return then. Goodbye."*

A new count—the yang. Daniel looked up at the clock. Ten minutes until the yang did whatever it was designed to do. The lives of three astronauts were intertwined with this specific time, and according to Core, they were alive. Marie would be there.

A message icon on Nala's display lit up again. She quickly opened it, and Daniel stood close behind.

*1 complete. 7 remain.*

She laughed. "Well, well, it looks like we're on a lesson plan. Eight in all and we've just finished the introductions." There was another attachment, and she opened it to find a multiple-page document. On the first page were many intersecting circles with hash marks around their perimeters, each connected to other circles by lines at various angles. There were numerous notations of unknown purpose. A second page was mostly script text with an embedded graphic that looked like a vehicle.

She turned around to Daniel. "I think our lesson plan comes with homework."

There would be time to study the document, hopefully with some help to understand its meaning. "What's in the video file?" Daniel asked.

Nala clicked on the MPEG attachment, an act strangely foreign and familiar at the same time. She enlarged the video window to full screen while all five in the room gathered around. Together they witnessed moving images no human had seen.

318

Nala gently shook her head. "They're beautiful."

# 47  Reunion

The Air Force staff car accelerated down the narrow country road, creating a plume of dust and gravel that blasted into the grasslands on either side. Sergeant Peabody held the wheel, with Colonel McGinn in the front passenger seat. Marie and Pixie sat in back. Marie tightly gripped her phone, which continued to display the video feed from inside Soyuz. The markings on the yang showed the equivalent of 003. Seven minutes.

McGinn twisted around and yelled over the noise of the speeding car and the potholes in the road. "Not much farther. They've removed the explosive pack and are getting a cable on Soyuz now. They should have it up in a few minutes—about the time we arrive."

"Can we get an ambulance out here?" Marie yelled back.

"Already called. Base EMTs should be right behind us."

The early-morning darkness hid the grassy hills of South Dakota. Marie could see a few telephone poles flying past, but little else. *We're so close. Please let this work.* The knot in her stomach was getting worse, as was the tension in her temples. Her hand shook as she touched the face of her phone to prevent it from shutting off. The yang showed 002.

Not far ahead were lights. A flatbed truck loomed out of the darkness, with crew members working under a floodlight attached to the back. Peabody slowed the car and they stopped a safe distance from the activity.

Marie jumped out and ran to the light, with McGinn and Pixie not far behind. A man stood next to the truck, operating a large hoist. Its cable disappeared into the depths of a large circular hole in a concrete pad. He turned as she approached. "Stand back, ma'am, it might swing a little when it comes out." She moved back a step, but the intensity inside her would not allow much more.

The floodlight illuminated the upper portion of the hole and she could see the cable was moving. A second later the top of the capsule was visible, and then it was out, swinging to one side. One of the other men got a hand on it and steadied its swing. "Make room!" the operator yelled out over the noise of the hoist. He swung the capsule away from the hole and set it down on the concrete pad. Another man tilted the floodlight to shine on Soyuz's resting place. The operator turned off the hoist.

It was suddenly quiet. The only sound was the wind blowing through the surrounding grasslands. They gathered around the capsule as one of the men climbed to its top and began to open the hatch. Marie peered through the circular window on the side. As the hatch opened, enough light shone in that she could just make out the yang on the control panel. The last character on its face flickered. 000.

A piercing high pitch, like a whistle, interrupted the stillness. An intensely bright yellow light flashed inside the cabin and blasted out through the window and the open hatch. For a brief moment, night turned into the brilliance of day. Marie pulled her head away, shielded her eyes and dropped backwards. The man squatting on the top of the capsule fell back, grabbing the hatch at the last instant to keep from falling off. The screaming sound stopped and the flash quickly faded, while blinded eyes took a few seconds longer to recover. The man on top of the capsule readjusted his position and carefully leaned over the edge of the hatchway.

"They're here!" he yelled.

Marie raced back to the Soyuz window, her heart pounding. She held one hand to block the glare of the floodlight and peered inside. Three men in flight suits sat side by side in their seats. Sergei turned toward the window, his eyes bloodshot, his chin covered in a two-day growth and his head sweaty—and he smiled. "Marie," he mouthed through the thick window.

"Sergei!" she screamed back. "Oh my God, you're back! It worked—you're back!"

She pressed a hand to the window, and Sergei slowly raised his own to match it. They smiled to each other. Only the thickness of the glass separated their palms—a few millimeters. She felt it again, his presence. The same feeling she'd had a few hours earlier while sitting alone in the capsule in the middle of an empty hangar. She now realized that even then, he had been close to her. A few millimeters, perhaps, but pushed ever so slightly in a *kata* direction. He had been inside Soyuz all along.

She looked up. The man on top was pulling Jeremy out through the hatch. He looked weary, but still able to move. Jeremy sat on the edge of the capsule and reached down. "Marie, you're a sight for sore eyes." She reached up and touched his fingers. A second later he was gently lowered down, and she held him up from the gravity of Earth, wrapping her arms around him.

The tears flowed. "Jeremy, I thought we'd…" Her voice broke.

He put a hand on her cheek. "Me, too. I don't know how we got here, but I'm sure thankful."

An ambulance pulled up, its emergency lights turning the scene into a chaos of red and blue. Two EMTs rushed out and took Jeremy out of her arms. Another brought a stretcher.

"My dear Marie!" the familiar Russian voice called from above. Sergei sat on the edge of the capsule, his legs dangling down. "My darling, where have you been? I've missed you!"

She burst into tears all over again, laughing even as the tears streamed down her face. Sergei was lowered and soon in her arms. They embraced, her face beside his, not wanting to let go. "Oh, Sergei," she sobbed. "I was so worried. I…"

"It's okay. It's over now." She felt the drips from his face too.

322

She gently pushed back, laughing while she brushed her swollen eyes and wet cheeks. "I must look terrible."

Sergei held her shoulders in his hands as he studied her face. "On the contrary, my dear Marie, you are the loveliest thing I have ever seen."

As promised months before, a promise made even before he had departed for launch, a promise made between colleagues who had become cherished friends—she kissed him full on the lips. She kissed him for all the time that had passed and all the emotions that had exploded over these grim and inconsolable days. She kissed him hard, and he kissed her back.

"I told you I would," she said as they pulled apart.

"I remember. I'm glad you did, too." He laughed. "Can any of this be real? Kiss me again."

"In America, we say 'pinch me.'"

"What a terrible custom," Sergei declared. "Why would I want to be pinched when I could be kissed?"

"Couldn't agree more." She kissed him again.

She felt the EMT tap her shoulder with a gloved hand. "Sorry, ma'am, we need to get him under care."

"I've never felt better," Sergei shouted.

"And, ma'am," the EMT said, "given that you had… uh, contact with him, you might need to spend time in quarantine too." *Gladly*, she thought as the EMT helped Sergei to the ambulance.

Anton was out of the capsule now too, lying on a rolling stretcher and sipping from a bottle of water. Another ambulance pulled up, adding to the chaos of lights flooding the surrounding sage. Marie approached the stretcher. "Do I get the same greeting?" Anton asked sheepishly.

"Close," she replied with a smile. "But I don't know you as well, so you'll understand why I'm shy." She kissed him on the cheek and wrapped her arms around his neck. "Welcome home, Anton."

As she pulled away, she noticed a spot of blood on his forehead. "What happened here? Sergei had that too."

Anton reached up and touched his forehead. "I don't know. There was a floating thing, like that Chinese yin-yang shape, then a flash of light, and we were here. That's all I remember."

Marie laughed. "There's a lot you don't know. We'll debrief when you guys feel better."

He nodded. "Marie, thanks for getting us home."

She shook her head. "Don't thank me. Somebody else brought you home—they're not from around here." She patted him on the shoulder. "We'll talk."

Pixie ran up beside her, his excitement obvious. "I need to show you something." He motioned toward Soyuz. Marie followed him to the side of the capsule. "Inside," he said. "Can I give you a boost?" She nodded and he boosted her up. Grabbing some handholds, she pulled herself to the top.

She peered inside the capsule, now empty once more. She looked back at Pixie below her. "What?"

"Climb in and take a look at that thing. Don't worry, I'll help you get out."

She hesitated. Her last time alone in Soyuz had been a terrifying experience. Still, if there was one last job to do...

She summoned her courage and dropped down through the hatch. Inside it was cold and only dimly lit from the floodlight. Sergei's handprint was still on the window, but otherwise the cabin hadn't changed since she had sat there a few hours before.

She looked up at the yang device. It was still in the same position on the control panel, but the characters on its front had changed. Instead of three, there were now four. She'd seen the characters enough to have them memorized. The yang read 7773. A quick calculation told her the time represented a little more than six days. The yang was counting down once again.

On a hunch, she reached up and touched it. The yang moved easily to one side and righted itself on its point. "You weren't doing *that* before," she said aloud. Without any effort, she lifted it from its place on the control panel. "Full of surprises, aren't you? Just like your mate."

She looked up into the hatchway and saw Pixie staring down. She wrapped one hand around the stem of the yang, like a movie star grabs an Oscar, and shook it in front of her face. "This time, you're coming with me."

Overflowing with pride and confidence, Marie hoisted herself up through the hatchway and toward a night sky filled with stars.

# 48 Humans

The sound of Daniel's measured steps on the marble floor produced small echoes as he walked the empty corridor of the West Wing. He visualized sound waves bouncing off the far wall and expected the slight delay to decrease as he approached. It did.

A day of rest, another flight, and he was back where he had started. Near the end of the corridor, bright light streamed into the hallway through an open door. Daniel turned and entered the Roosevelt Room. Teddy hung on one wall, Franklin on another. In between was a long conference table where one woman sat alone. She turned as he entered and burst into a broad smile.

"Daniel."

He wasn't going to let the formality of the White House ruin this reunion. Daniel embraced Marie and hugged her tight. "You had me worried for a while," he said. They held hands and smiled at each other.

"Daniel, that was no attack. The yang was watching over that space, making sure it would be clear when the countdown hit zero." She hugged him again. "But thanks for being worried. I'm fine, really."

"Not a bad interpretation," he said. They took chairs at the table. "That thing turned out to have quite a few functions, beyond just counting."

"I carried it out with me. It somehow unlocked itself from Soyuz—I could just lift it up." She pointed to a direction that could have been anywhere in the city. "It's over at NASA HQ right now—some of the engineers are studying it. You know, it's counting again."

"I heard. It restarted at 7777, right? About six days, our time?"

"You'd think they'd just send us a calendar invite." She laughed. "Maybe we have something we can teach them?"

Daniel smiled. "You'd think they already know. They learned our computer formats pretty quickly. They were inside our Internet for less than two minutes, downloaded twenty pages and a few YouTube videos. And that was enough. The quality of the conversation really picked up." Daniel ran a hand through his hair. "His ability to absorb the nuance of our language was incredible. I'm not sure how much of that you heard."

"Some of it," she replied. "But as soon as he said the guys were alive and they were home... well, I knew exactly what that meant. We went straight to Soyuz." She looked down pensively. "Daniel, it was so strange, but I absolutely *knew* they were there. I'd felt it when I'd sat in there alone. It was like Sergei was sitting next to me."

"And in a sense, he was."

She nodded. "But they weren't just in 4-D space. They were frozen, suspended somehow. None of them had any recollection beyond their first twenty-four hours. All that time Soyuz sat in that hangar—those guys were right there. Maybe offset just a little from our space, but suspended. They don't remember any of it."

"And the doctors at Ellsworth checked them for medications?"

"Yeah. They'd each been stabbed in the forehead—probably by the same needle that was pointed at me. But there were no drugs in their systems, nothing that would have put them to sleep. Their body temperatures were normal, so it wasn't cryogenics either. They were suspended in a physical sense, not medically. Pushed into quantum space, but also frozen in time."

Daniel didn't disagree. "*Time answers*, he told us. The solution to returning anything alive from 4-D space. If they've got control over both space and time... well, as he said, *you will learn*."

Marie beamed. "We have so much opportunity. I really want to be there."

"Is Ibarra going to keep you involved? Really, except for the debrief today, our job is done. Shea told me the government has initiated a discussion with the Chinese, and apparently, they're already hinting they might make an official apology. I'm heading back to Fermilab tomorrow to make sure we have a solid plan for the next event with Core. But even there, other people will step in to handle the conversation itself."

She put her glasses on, and she did look five years older, just as she'd told him—was it months before? "Ibarra should be here in a few minutes, and a bunch of other NASA people. Once we're done briefing the president, Ibarra's going to ask him to appoint a team for all future contact. I *so* want to be part of that. It's the chance of a lifetime and I'm not going to miss out. Help me, will you?"

Her face was bright with the wide-open potential of her future. "Of course," he said. "You earned a slot. You think you're ready to do some *kata* traveling?"

Her eyes widened in mock shock. "Maybe we'll stick with radios and cameras for a while. We're lucky we have those guys back in one piece."

"By the way, where are they now?"

"Sergei and Anton are on a plane to Moscow. They've got their own debrief to do. And Jeremy should be back in Houston by now. He's got two of the cutest kids you've ever seen, and his wife Elise..." She stopped and her eyes filled with tears. "I can't imagine what she must have gone through."

Daniel reached for a box of tissues on the credenza and handed her one.

"Thanks." She dabbed her eyes. "Sorry, some of these things get to me."

"Sergei, too," Daniel said. "He's special, I think."

She nodded and scrunched the tissue in her hand. A large smile broke out across her face. "He's coming back, once he's done in Moscow. I'm going to meet him in New York, show him the city. R and R, as they call it."

"That's great, you'll have fun. Marie, I'm really glad you were there when they... *materialized*."

She laughed and looked up at Daniel. "What a strange world we live in now. I know it sounds clichéd, but everything is completely different than just four days ago, isn't it?"

Daniel had the feeling that there was a great adventure to come for the young woman in front of him. He was proud to have partnered with her. She was going places.

They both looked up as Augustin Ibarra walked into the room, the very man who could help make her wish come true. Daniel stood up and shook his hand. "Director Ibarra, good to see you again."

"Ready to talk to the president?" Ibarra seemed as relaxed as anyone could be when just minutes away from explaining one of the most bizarre tales ever told to the most powerful man on Earth.

"I am. Do you think he's ready to listen?"

Ibarra squinted. "He'll listen to you... and to Shea. But show him what you learned, and don't be afraid to speak your mind. In the end, I think he'll see things the same way we do."

Marie interjected, "There'd better not be any nukes sent out to VY Canis Majoris."

Daniel wasn't overly concerned about a war scenario. It didn't seem likely that an advanced species would reveal the location of their communications hub to an unknown civilization without defenses of some kind. But then, who knew? Earth might be the only aggressor among a sea of pacifists. Maybe the *many people* Core had referred to were the Federation, and humans were the Klingons. There was so much

329

yet to learn. But if any fear-mongering developed, he was ready to counter it.

Ibarra put an arm on Daniel's shoulder. "Before the briefing, I wanted to get your input directly. The hub. What do you think it is? Why is it out there?"

With only a day to ponder their discovery, Daniel didn't have the answers. They might come with time—and lessons from Core. "We at least know it's a communications center. The swarm of objects around it—they could be equivalents to our geosynchronous satellites. Communication relays that use 4-D space to send messages back to a hundred home planets. Plus, Core made it clear we're expected to return to the hub. They're not coming to Earth—we go there."

"Why there?" Ibarra asked. "What's important about that star?"

Daniel shook his head. "VY Canis Majoris? Well, it's big—that's an understatement, it's enormous. It makes our sun look like mote of dust. Who knows why they picked that spot. Maybe it really is a central location to lots of civilizations—the *many people* he told us about. But maybe we've only seen a small part of what's out there. There could be more hubs like Core. Maybe more quantum space, too. For all we know, there might be a maze of constructed space, filled with more technology like the hub. We may have just found the entrance to a cavern we never knew existed."

"We *are* brand-new to all of this," Marie added. "All we've seen is one pathway between Earth and the hub."

Daniel nodded. "One small slice of a galaxy filled with billions of stars... and maybe much more."

~~~~~~~~~~~~~~~~~~~~~~~

At eight o'clock that evening, the downtown Chicago bar was alive with laughing friends, after-work colleagues, and happy people simply enjoying the evening in the company of others. Daniel and Nala sat on high barstools at a small round table covered with plates of food and tall glasses of beer. Every other table in the bar was similarly covered, with one exception. Only their table displayed a blue plastic cube in its center, unique not only within the bar, but probably within the entire world.

Daniel picked up the tesseract. "I'll have to find a place of honor in my office for this."

"Jae-ho is giving it to you?" Nala asked.

He shrugged. "He said he could make more."

Daniel studied the tesseract in his hand. It was nothing more than two sets of eight vertices attaching one cube inside another. He flicked his wrist and felt the odd delay in its momentum shift—a clear indication of additional mass, unseen. The feeling and the thought were fascinating.

His eyes focused beyond the plastic cube and absorbed the fine features of his dining partner. A day of rest, a chance to groom and change clothes, and the talented physicist had transformed into an exquisitely beautiful woman. Her hair was pulled back, her eyes sparkled and her smile dazzled. In a word, she was stunning.

"You'd make a good representative from our planet," he said, grinning.

Nala burst into laughter. "Where'd that come from?"

"You're smart, you know your science, you're beautiful. Perfect. Except..."

"Except?"

"You'd probably have to clean up your language."

She rolled with laughter again. "Fuck that!"

"Or maybe not." Daniel laughed.

"Sorry, no interest in being a *representative*. I'll stick with my current job, thank you very much. Hey, I'm employed again."

"Park made it official?"

She took a sip of her beer. "Close enough. He said he'd create a permanent spot on the Fermilab staff as soon as he can get the paperwork through the system. In the meantime, I'm on temp status, and there's lots to do. Only four days until the second conversation with... Core. This is going to be weird... but really interesting."

"You know there's going to be a parade of self-important stuffed shirts passing through your lab now, don't you? Likely a few arrogant pricks in the bunch, too. Can you handle that?"

She lifted one eyebrow. "Will you be one of them? Either a stuffed shirt or a prick?"

Daniel laughed out loud. He could easily hang around this woman—tonight, tomorrow, the next day and the day after that. "Something tells me that Fermilab is going to be high on my priority list for quite a while."

"Good then. We'll be happy to have them," she said. "It'll be fun." Her face turned down but her eyes lifted up, meeting Daniel's. "You're going to be famous pretty soon. Can you handle that?"

Daniel couldn't deny it. The president's press conference just a few hours earlier had provided only the most basic of information—the missing astronauts had been safely recovered with help from a nonhuman intelligent *device*, as he had phrased it. But the floodgate was open and the crush of international press would be coming Daniel's way—as soon as they learned about his role in the discovery.

"I'll figure that out, too."

"There are going to be a lot of questions, Daniel. I'm really not sure how we're going to explain it. Most people won't understand any of it—the technology, the hub, multiple dimensions of space. It's just too

332

much ground to cover and still be believed. My mom, for example. She's not dumb, but everything I do is way over her head."

He picked up the tesseract and tossed it in the air a few times. "For everyone in this bar, it's just a piece of plastic with an interesting shape. Only you and I know what it really is."

Nala nodded. They were on the same wavelength. "Yeah, I get it. Most scientific discoveries have that problem. Only a select few people have the privilege of experiencing it directly. Everyone else hears about it secondhand. They believe it or they don't."

"Exactly. Which means that every scientist has an obligation to lay out the evidence, clearly and truthfully, and in a way that the average person might grasp. Your mom, my sister, everyone. The same goes for educators. Children are pretty accepting of whatever they're taught, which puts the burden on teachers to present a reality supported by evidence and not just throw out a bunch of alternatives and hope the kids figure it out. Evolution, not creationism. Climate change described by science, not pulled from some energy lobbyist's pitch."

He patted the tesseract. "This discovery will be the same. How did we get there? Who are they? Can we accept them, or will we fear them? Those of us who had direct experience in the discovery have an obligation. We all have some work to do."

"Are you going to help?" she asked.

"I'll do my part. You?"

She nodded. "I'll try. In a way, I feel like one of those kids. I'm really excited to find out what's next in our lesson plan. I only got a glimpse of that document they sent, but it looked pretty amazing."

"Yeah, they seemed to be prepared for us. I wonder how many times they've done this. Eight lessons, then they turn us loose?"

"Into the galactic conversation."

Daniel nodded. "*Many people*, he said. *Many planets*. Each bringing their own unique knowledge and perspective. The galactic conversation. It's hard to imagine what we might learn."

"Even better than the Internet. I say cheers to that." They held up their glasses and clinked.

A young couple approached their table. The man wore a fashionable hat skewed to one side and the woman hung on his arm like a similar accessory. "Hey, man, I was watching you play with the plastic block. What's it for?"

Daniel handed the tesseract to him. The young man turned it over in his hands while Daniel explained. "It's called a tesseract. It's a four-dimensional object. Most of it you can't even see because it exists beyond our three-dimensional world. If you turn it enough, you might feel the extra mass that your eyes can't see. It feels like it's not quite in balance."

"This is for real?" The man turned it a few times and bounced it up and down in his hand, and his eyes widened as it shifted. "That's so cool, man. I gotta get one of these."

"Not in production yet, sorry. But stay tuned. I think you'll be hearing a lot more very soon."

The man handed the tesseract back. "Make sure you get it into stores before Christmas, man. You'll probably get rich." He waved, and the couple wandered off to find their friends.

Daniel set the tesseract back on the table. "There you go, a side business for Fermilab. You can sell these things in the gift shop."

Nala's elbows rested on the table, her chin in her hands. "I'll suggest it to Jae-ho, but don't hold your breath. We're not exactly a marketing machine." She pointed to her phone. "Those two should see the video—now *that'll* blow their mind."

"You have the video on your phone? *That* one?"

"Yeah. No big deal. It's going to be on every website in the world by tomorrow."

Daniel looked both ways to see if anyone was watching. It probably wouldn't matter anyway. "Play it, I'd like to see it again."

She opened a file, and they huddled closely together to watch.

Blue and green plants waved gently in a watery environment. The plants moved in slow motion with ripples spreading slowly across their flat structure like a flag in the wind. Beneath the plants, a solid surface was covered with what looked like miniature structures of some kind. But the view changed, zooming in closer. The scale of the structures became more apparent—they were buildings beneath enormous kelp-like trees.

The view continued to magnify, showing detail on the buildings, windows perhaps, and some vertical banners of various colors. There were small white objects floating around and above each building. As the view clarified, it was clear the white objects weren't just floating. They were living creatures, who were moving—swimming—in every direction. Their soft white bodies expanded and contracted as they moved, like jellyfish. They even had tentacles drifting gracefully away from their propulsion end.

The view magnified further, focusing on a single building and dozens of creatures around it. The zoom stabilized and something remarkable happened. The white creatures interrupted their random movements and formed into several groups, with exactly five members in each group. And they started to dance.

It couldn't be described as anything else. They danced. In complete unison, each member of each group dipped left, dipped right, spun in a circle, expanded and then contracted their bodies. A soft rhythmic beat could be heard that coincided perfectly with their movements. The effect was beautiful and artistic. It had the feel of a delicate performance, a water ballet of sorts, performed by creatures with the softest and smoothest of bodies.

"They're really beautiful," Nala said. "Like ballerinas, except that it's the tutu dancing by itself."

"I love the grouping thing they're doing," Daniel replied. "It seems very social. Obvious intelligence."

"And they're our neighbors—at least that's what he said. I noticed he didn't reveal where they actually live."

"Doesn't trust us yet?"

"Would you?"

It was a fair point. Tribes of humans weren't exactly accepting of individuals not of the tribe. Looking different or behaving differently often meant a newcomer was ostracized. How much worse would it be adding nonhumans to the mix? Creatures whose looks and behavior were utterly foreign to us? Would we extend compassion and respect as equals? Or would we revert to our long and sordid history of conquering those who could be conquered? The video provided some hope. Beauty and elegance went a long way to overcoming primal fears.

She closed the video file but left her phone on the table. A mischievous look crossed her face. "I was thinking about posting it to Facebook." She smiled.

"You might want to wait on that," Daniel offered. "Something tells me that high-level people are putting together a communications plan right now. You don't want to be the rogue factor."

"True," she said. "Probably wouldn't be a good idea to get fired twice in one week. But..." She shook a finger. "But they'd better not bury this. Otherwise, I'm going public."

"They won't. They can't. Government bureaucrats don't have that much control."

"You have a lot more faith in authority than I do."

Daniel leaned in closer. "Yeah, I noticed that with you. What's that about?"

She shook her head. "My history with authority? It's a long story. Not much fun."

"I've got time."

She reached out and put a hand over his. "Daniel, we're out for the evening. Together, you and me. Semi-alone, if you don't count the five hundred people in this bar. Relax and let it unfold. There's a lot of fun things we can do tonight." She smiled.

Daniel turned his hand over and held hers. He looked into her sparkling eyes. "What'd you have in mind?"

She locked eyes with him. "Well, I could take you home and make those fabulous enchiladas that I have in my refrigerator. Or you could try out my float pod. But, really, I think we should climb onto my workout bench and make passionate love. Or my bed, if you're feeling traditional."

There was never anything coy about this woman. Daniel's response was easy. "Good options. Can I choose all of the above?"

She nodded, and her mischievous smile returned. "You can. But I do have to warn you, sir…"

Daniel's brow raised. "Yes?"

"That little mental exercise where I blew in your ear?"

"Yes, I do recall. Very… ah… stimulating."

"You haven't seen anything yet."

Her smile alone was enough to cause a meltdown. Daniel held it together, just barely. She held out another hand and he took it. They both stood up and he pulled her close, her perfume filling his senses. "Shall we get out of here, Dr. Pasquier?"

She looked up into his eyes. "I'm all for that, Dr. Rice."

They left the noise of the bar behind. Outside, the night was cool and clear and a few stars shone overhead. The lights of Chicago didn't help, but the view to the east, across the darkness of Lake Michigan, was much better. The bright star Sirius was rising. Somewhere beyond it would be VY Canis Majoris, and Core. Daniel absorbed the view and their newfound knowledge. This part of the night sky would never be the same.

Several of the brighter stars were also visible, and he knew them all by name. Capella, Procyon, Pollux and Aldebaran. All neighbors, only a short hop away—when you had technology that could compress space. One of these neighbors might have an orbiting planet, an ocean planet that was home to an intelligent water species. Dancers. It would make a good name for them, at least until we knew them better. Perhaps the Dancers could swim to the surface of their ocean and even look up into their night sky. They might see the star we call Sol, our sun. What name had they given it? Daniel was curious.

His trance was broken when Nala lightly kissed his lips. "Hey, scientist. The door's open. You ready to step through?" She grabbed his hand and pulled him toward the waiting taxi.

# Afterword

I hope you liked the story. There will, of course, be another book in the Quantum series—more on that below. For now, allow me to step outside the narrative and look back.

For me, science fiction is best when it starts from a solid base in reality and extends from there into fiction. How far the book extends is up to the author, but it's the base that makes it science fiction. Without real science, the story is better cataloged as fantasy.

If you're not a particle physicist but you're curious, (you are curious, aren't you?) I thought I would use this section to distinguish the reality in this book from the fiction. It also gives me an opportunity to provide supporting information in case you're interested.

Writing the fictional portions of this book was tremendous fun, but the reality of the quantum world is just as fun. Our real universe is sometimes so bizarre that it's hard to know what's demonstrably real, supported by solid evidence, and what is speculation. But the refusal of the universe to behave the way we think it should is also what makes science fun. We have this fantastic opportunity to discover how the universe really works, not how we think or hope it works.

The science of quantum physics gets going in Chapter 5, "Quantum." Spencer Bradley describes the Standard Model, quarks, leptons and bosons and the discovery of the Higgs boson at the CERN laboratories in Geneva in 2012. Of course, all of this is real, and most people have heard about the Higgs boson because it was plastered all over the news at the time. But ask the average educated person what the Standard Model is and you'll get a blank stare. This is a shame, because it's one of the fundamental achievements in the realm of physics in the past hundred years.

The Standard Model is a terrible name, as several characters mention. It really should be called the Architectural Diagram of the Universe or something grand like that, because that's exactly what it is.

We, and by "we" I mean humans, have discovered the fundamental building blocks of our universe, the Legos, as Bradley called them. Yet most people don't even know this fact, much less have any notion of what the model looks like. It's not anyone's fault, but I do wish we had a better method of science education for adults. Most people stop learning anything about science once they graduate from high school or college, but discoveries continue throughout their lifetimes.

The Standard Model is one such discovery. When I was in high school in the 1970s, the Standard Model diagram that I show in this book didn't exist. In just the past several decades, scientists at Fermilab (yes, of course it's a real place!), Argonne and elsewhere have pieced together the basic structure of all matter in the universe. And not only did they discover the elemental particles (quarks, leptons and bosons), but they figured out the relationships to particles that we already knew about (protons, neutrons and electrons) and the relationship to the forces (electromagnetism and the strong and weak nuclear force). During this process of discovery, the theorists described what particles *might exist*, and the experimentalists started searching for them.

Not only did they find these particles, one by one, but they were clever enough to put all of this knowledge into a single-page diagram that exquisitely shows the building blocks and their relationships, the Standard Model diagram. It's an amazing scientific achievement, and it all happened in the past forty years or so, and mostly in the suburbs of Chicago at Fermi National Accelerator Laboratory. Americans should be immensely proud, yet most don't even know this history.

Daniel shows the Standard Model diagram to Marie in Chapter 8, "Chicago." He says, "In this single diagram, you're looking at the underlying structure of our universe. It's a parts list, but it's also an architectural drawing. Everything you've ever touched or felt is here. The air you breathe, the ground you stand on, the sunlight that pours down, the stars in the night sky. All in those seventeen boxes."

340

Of course, I asked him to say that. Characters are pretty compliant in that way. I also believe that in the future, a real person will present an even better diagram, the so-called Theory of Everything. (Definitely a better name!) The Theory of Everything diagram will look pretty much the same as the Standard Model, but it will have a graviton on it, another theoretical boson that has yet to be experimentally discovered. This future diagram might also explain things like dark matter and dark energy, which we don't fully understand yet today.

When this happens (2030? 2040?), we might be finished. We will be able to list all of the fundamental components of the universe and describe its architecture in detail. I know that this goal is perfectly achievable. Why? Because we've already done it with atoms. The Periodic Table of the Elements has stood rock solid for more than a century, with the only additions coming in the form of elements that decay so rapidly they don't exist outside of the laboratory. The ultimate version of the Standard Model diagram will take its place next to the Periodic Table as a major achievement of science.

We're actually pretty close right now, and from my perspective, missing a graviton or a dark matter particle is like having a jigsaw puzzle that is 95 percent complete. There may be a couple of holes, but you can still see the picture. If you want to know more about the Standard Model, Wikipedia has a pretty good page: https://en.wikipedia.org/wiki/Standard_Model, and Fermilab has a great public outreach program: http://www.fnal.gov/pub/science/particle-physics-101/index.html.

How about neutrinos? Are they real? Yes, of course. There are three flavors of them in the Standard Model. And, yes, Fermilab today is using a concentrated beam of neutrinos in their experiments, including shooting this beam straight through the Earth to detectors in Minnesota and South Dakota. And, yes, it's also true that several trillion neutrinos from the sun just passed through your body since you started reading this sentence. Did you feel them?

In Chapter 10, "Science," we arrive at the doors of Fermilab. Is the history of this place real? Did they really discover all these tiny particles and create the Standard Model? Yes, and no. Yes, Fermilab has a long history in particle physics, but it's not the only place; I simplified. Since the 1960s, there were many universities (University of Chicago, Columbia, SUNY Stony Brook, University of Hawaii, University of Illinois— Urbana-Champaign and probably more) as well as other research centers and government laboratories (CERN Geneva, DESY Hamburg, Argonne National Laboratory and probably others). But Fermilab was the premier particle accelerator in the world from 1974 until 1993, (when Congress decided to kill the Superconducting Super Collider in Texas and the accelerator construction at Fermilab—a sad day!).

If you want to get a sense of Fermilab's heyday, this is a fun page: http://history.fnal.gov/botqrk.html. It describes the discovery of the *bottom quark* and has several 1970s-era photos of the scientists involved and the equipment they used. By the way, Fermilab is open to the public with tours available. Batavia, Illinois. Go, and bring all the little quarks with you.

As I write (2017), the accelerator at CERN is the premier location where protons smash into atoms, but that may not last much longer. The Chinese really are building a new accelerator, and it really is named "The Higgs Factory" (who knows how they came up with that?). The information in Chapter 23, "Chinese," is as accurate as I could make it. China is a terrible country when it comes to scientific research because they encourage students and scientists to plagiarize and the Central Committee can overrule any discovery to enforce the "truth." This is not science, it's the classic argument from authority. We'll soon see what the Chinese do with The Higgs Factory. It's expected to go online in the early 2020s and it will dwarf the size of CERN in Geneva. I've heard some physicists say the whole facility may be a huge waste of money because there are now doubts that higher energy will discover anything new. We'll see.

So, when do we leave the real world? Is string theory real? Are extra dimensions of space complete fantasy? Surprisingly, most of this is still reality. String theory has been around for decades and many science fiction writers have relied on it. It speculates that there are additional dimensions of space, ten to be exact. This is far beyond what our simple minds can contemplate, and I decided to just focus on one of those extra dimensions, the fourth dimension, and use the directional names of *ana* and *kata*. These names, by the way, are also reality. Some scientists do talk about pointing in the *kata* direction, which of course we can't do because we're three-dimensional creatures. If you want to read a fun book about dimensions, try *The 4th Dimension* by Rudy Rucker. One of my all-time favorites.

Are there really quantum-sized extra dimensions of space? Certainly, this is where the fiction starts, right? Wrong. String theory is tied to quantum physics because these extra dimensions exist only down at the string level. A string is extraordinarily tiny, so tiny... well, it's tiny, let's leave it at that. It's entirely possible that extra dimensions of space really exist down there, but we have no way of measuring them, so there's no evidence today.

The fiction of this story comes in when Bradley explains to Daniel and Marie that CERN scientists who discovered the Higgs boson also discovered evidence of string dimensions. They didn't. I wish they had. That's not to say that we won't eventually find evidence of extra dimensions. We might. In fact, finding extra dimensions is completely plausible. Some would say it's just a matter of time. I'm in that camp.

Additional fiction comes in Chapter 10, "Science." Dr. Park explains to Daniel and Marie about coherent neutrinos. He says that they've learned how to control the phase oscillation, just like a laser. In the real world, neutrinos do indeed have a phase, and they really do oscillate between phases. That's what gives us the three flavors. But, alas, there is no such thing as a coherent beam of neutrinos locked in the same phase.

The scientists at Fermilab are today conducting several experiments to understand how neutrinos oscillate as they travel. I hope the NOvA team or the LBNF team discovers that neutrinos pop in and out of the extra string dimensions, solving the puzzle about why neutrinos have little interaction with normal matter. Yeah, that might happen.

And then there's Chapter 20, "Collaboration." Nala explains to Daniel all about the expansion of a quantum dimension and the resulting compression of another physical dimension. She tells him that the universe behaves like a balloon. You expand in one direction and it compresses in another. Okay, I admit it, I made all that up. Nala writes the "Spiegel equation" and the "Spiegel graph" on a napkin and tells Daniel it will be as famous as $E = mc^2$ someday. Yeah, I made all that up too. There is no Spiegel equation; in fact, there is no Spiegel.

Chapter 20 and beyond were fun to write. As an author, once you've left the tracks of reality, you can go wherever your imagination takes you. I wanted the story to remain believable, but I also needed the technology to be able to compress space by 99.99 percent or more. It's the only way we humans will ever get to the stars.

Traveling to the stars is ridiculously difficult. The Milky Way is a hundred thousand light years across. Even our arm, the Orion Spur, is ten thousand light years long. Our "local" area, where the star VY Canis Majoris is located (yes, it's a real star), is five thousand light years across. Even with huge advances in our spaceflight technology, we'd need tens of thousands of years to get to VY Canis Majoris. As Daniel points out, a light-speed radio "conversation" would be: "Hi, how are you?" Wait four thousand years. "We're doing well, how are you?" Wait another four thousand years... It's absurd. No civilization would do this. The limit imposed by the speed of light is crippling to both travel and communication.

Which brings me to the main premise of the book. The chance that humans are ever going to communicate with alien civilizations using radio communication is slim, maybe none. Sorry, SETI, but you're not likely to hear anything—ever. We're listening, but *nobody is broadcasting*. We've been searching large portions of the sky and millions of frequencies, yet SETI hasn't yet heard a peep. Why? Possibly there is no one out there; we're alone. Possibly space is just too big, and anyone out there has utterly given up any hope of communication.

But another answer is that radio, or anything based on electromagnetism, is a technology that simply doesn't fit the requirements. Nobody is broadcasting because at interstellar distances, radio is far too slow, and more importantly—they've found some other way.

We'll need to find that way too, a mechanism to avoid the cosmic speed limit altogether. In this book, compressing space was my way, but there are certainly others (quantum entanglement?). For now, this is science fiction, but if we stay curious and keep exploring, we may yet uncover some aspect of the universe that will solve the problem. When we do, I hope we'll find that many other civilizations have figured it out too. It's possible that the galactic conversation is already happening, right now, and that someday it will be our turn to join.

If you'd like more details about the story, plus a lot of pictures that couldn't possibly fit into the book, please go to my web page: http://douglasphillipsbooks.com.

Did you like this story? There's more! (You knew there would be, right?) *Quantum Void* is the next book in the series and is available now. I've included the first chapter below to whet your appetite.

And finally, books live or die on reviews. If you enjoyed the story, please consider writing a short review. It only takes a minute, and your review helps both future readers as well as the author.

Thanks for reading! Douglas Phillips.

# Acknowledgments

Thanks to all the help from authors at Critique Circle, especially Travis Leavitt, Stephanie Cory, Kathryn Hoff and P Mathison. There's nothing like a critique from someone who's down in the trenches writing their own book. Your comments were incredibly valuable in helping me shape the plot and characters, and your ability to consistently locate my numerous mistakes was a humbling (but helpful) experience!

Thanks to my editor, Eliza Dee, who taught me all about novel architecture and point of view. You can read a thousand books, but many of the shared traits among them can still remain hidden until someone else explicitly points them out. Now, I see those structural features everywhere.

Thanks also to Rena Hoberman for the beautiful book cover. I loved it when I first saw it, and I'm looking forward to exploring new concepts for the next book.

Many thanks to my friends and family (John, Phil, Rachel, Jeff, Dave, Jim, Todd, Trevor and others) for your time and feedback on the early versions. I hope you recognize the final story, but if you don't, it was all your fault.

And finally, thank you to my wife, Marlene, for helping to shape the female characters of the story and for putting up with months of me droning on and on about four-dimensional space and Fermilab.

# Quantum Void

Book Two in the Quantum Series

By Douglas Phillips

Text copyright © 2018 Douglas Phillips

All Rights Reserved.

**Eight months after the astounding discoveries made at Fermilab...**

Particle physics was always an unlikely path to the stars, but with the discovery that space could be compressed, the entire galaxy had come within reach. The technology was astonishing, yet nothing compared what humans encountered four thousand light years from home. Now, with an invitation from a mysterious gatekeeper, the people of Earth must decide if they're ready to participate in the galactic conversation.

The world anxiously watches as a team of four katanauts, suit up to visit an alien civilization. What they learn on a watery planet hundreds of light years away could catapult human comprehension of the natural world to new heights. But one team member must overcome crippling fear to cope with an alien gift she barely understands.

Back at Fermilab, strange instabilities are beginning to show up in experiments, leading physicists to wonder if they ever really had control over the quantum dimensions of space.

The second book of the Quantum series rejoins familiar characters and adds several more as it explores the frontiers of human knowledge and wisdom. Of course, it wouldn't be part of the series if it didn't have a few twists along the way!

# 1 Ripples

Nala Pasquier slid the bangle bracelet off her wrist and placed it on the security table. The metal detector at the entrance to Wilson Hall was a new addition, a sign of changing times. Fermi National Accelerator Laboratory was once a place known only to the locals of Chicago, but its relative anonymity had disappeared eight months ago. First contact. Life beyond Earth. In the new era it was hard to find anyone who didn't know about Fermilab, or the secrets of the universe the physicists who worked there had uncovered.

Nala waved to the security guard. "What's my new word today, Angel?" She correctly pronounced his Spanish name, *An-hel*.

"*Descubrir*," the guard answered with a tight smile.

A particle physicist is not easily stumped, but Angel might have succeeded. "Use it in a sentence," Nala asked as she gathered her belongings.

"*El descubrió una mosca en la sopa.*" He crossed his arms, challenging her capacity to learn the language one word at a time. With dark brown skin and a last name that was often confused as Hispanic, most people were surprised when Nala told them she was half Haitian and that French was the language of Haiti, not Spanish.

"Discover?" she asked tentatively. "He discovered a fly in the soup?"

The guard nodded with approval. "*Está bien.* You got it."

Nala laughed. "*Descubrir.* Discover. That's a good word to know in my business. Thanks Angel. *Yo quiero descubrir algo nuevo hoy.*"

"You want to discover something new today," Angel echoed in English. "Your Spanish is getting better, Nala." His pride was obvious.

"I have a good teacher." She waved once more and walked into the building's interior atrium, an open space that soared to skylights far above, mirroring the expansive ambitions of the scientists who worked here.

Perhaps she would discover something new today. Her work in the science of quantum space had advanced by leaps and bounds thanks to some tips from an alien source. It was an exciting time in particle physics, in part because there was still much more to learn. At their core, every scientist is a lifelong student of nature.

Nala took the elevator to basement level three and then descended two flights of stairs even deeper into the Earth. She walked a long concrete hallway and rounded a corner. The sign on the door hadn't changed—*Diastasi Lab, Authorized Personnel Only*—but it no longer took a top-secret security clearance to become one of the authorized few.

Their work with extra dimensions of space was now public knowledge. Government classification had finally been lifted, and Nala was back in touch with colleagues at other labs, former friends that thought she'd disappeared off the face of the Earth. Her stunned friends, even her mother, had been left in the dark for years. *Um, yeah mom, we figured out how to reach into a fourth dimension and compress distances by a factor of a billion.*

Spatial compression had already made unmanned spaceflight obsolete. The stars were now within easy reach for any probe, camera or radio link. Interstellar travel for humans was not yet possible, but one step at a time. Earth was now connected into a vast web of alien civilizations. The future was wide open.

Nala tapped her badge on the security pad and pushed open the door. "Morning, Thomas. Sorry I'm late," she said to the stout, red-haired young man at the lab's workbench. Thomas, her lab assistant, was hunched over a signal generator, one of a hundred electronic components that covered the bench and filled every available shelf and niche in the overcrowded lab.

Thomas looked up with a grin on his bearded face. "Och, you're a wee scunner, you are," The accent was fake, but it was also pretty good.

She pulled a chair close to the workbench and turned on a computer. "That's a new one. Are we Scottish today?"

"For a wee spell, lassie. Perhaps 'til midday lunch," Thomas replied.

"Or as long as you can keep the Sean Connery accent going?"

"Possibly 'til then, aye."

Thomas wasn't Scottish. Or Irish. Or German. He was Russian on most Wednesdays. And every Friday, he became a strange cross between Ricardo Montalban and the swashbuckling Spanish cat from Shrek. A bit wacky, most definitely an oddball, but mostly Thomas was fun. Anyone with a rebellious streak and a touch of drama was okay in Nala's book.

"We'll amp it up a wee bit today, my friend." She settled into her normal position in front of a set of three large computer displays at one end of the workbench. She tapped the keyboard, a panel with gauges appeared on one display and she moved a slider labeled Tau to her chosen value. It was a simple command, but potent, backed by the largest particle accelerator in the United States.

Four floors above in the Fermilab main control room, colleagues who operated the accelerator would be at this very moment awakening the giant machine, inserting protons into its heart, and initializing the powerful magnets that formed the two-mile ring of the Main Injector loop. Soon, those protons would be screaming down a curved pipe at close to the speed of light. Eighty thousand laps every second. Most people had a hard time wrapping their head around that kind of speed so someone had installed a digital counter on the Main Injector tunnel wall, a sort of odometer that ticked once for every one thousand laps. As the protons reached full speed, the counter's digits became a blur.

One hundred-twenty-five giga-electron volts. A beam of protons with that kind of power could burn a hole through your head. It had happened once before in Russia—a visitor who had accidentally peered into an opening with a live beam. The results were not pretty.

Nala and Thomas ran down an operational checklist together, validating system status and checking their lab equipment. Thomas adjusted the alignment of a pink pipe that pointed straight into a clear plexiglass box above the workbench. The box was ground zero for the neutrino beam that would shoot through their lab at near light speed. Thomas placed a compact webcam inside the box and inserted a rubber tube through a hole, the other end of the tube connected to a large tank of nitrogen.

Finishing her checklist, Nala looked up. "Shall we?"

351

"All systems are go for launch," Thomas said, temporarily lapsing into his NASA ground controller's voice.

Nala picked up a handheld radio from its cradle. "Is Cody working today?"

Thomas nodded. "Aye. That he is."

She keyed the transmit button. "Cody, Nala. Got anything flying around the loop yet?" The question was purely a courtesy. She could feel a slight vibration in the floor which meant the accelerator was already spinning particles around its racetrack.

The radio hissed, followed by a man's voice. "Where've you been, Nala? Hell, we've been on standby pretty much forever."

Five minutes late to the lab today. Taunts were just part of the game. "Okay that's enough, smart ass. We're ready down here when you are."

"Stand by." A few seconds later a high-pitched hum reverberated from the overhead pipes—the sound of protons, ramping up to obscene energy levels. "One-twenty-five gig," Cody said. "We're up to full speed. You've got targeting control, but I'll manage the neutrino oscillation."

"Gotcha." She clicked a few times on her computer. "Let 'em fly."

"Protons away."

Somewhere behind a thick concrete wall, a magnetic gate opened and a stream of fast-moving protons blasted through. The particles smashed into their target—a disc of graphite no bigger than a coin. A stream of pions ripped out the other side, decaying in picoseconds to neutrinos and headed straight into Nala's lab.

The background hum increased dramatically to a loud buzz that filled the room. Thomas put on sunglasses, pinched his lips together and focused on the webcam inside the plexiglass box. As the pitch of the buzzing reached an irritating level, a brilliant blue flash blasted from the box accompanied by a loud pop. Thomas didn't flinch.

352

When the flash dissipated, the box was empty, and the nitrogen tube had been cleanly sliced where it entered the box. Even after hundreds of launches, the disappearing act never failed to impress.

"Tau is perfect," Nala said, her eyes glued not to the plexiglass box but to her computer screen. A window popped up showing a live image returned by the webcam, now positioned in another dimension of space.

As it had done a hundred times before, the magic of expanding a quantum-sized dimension forced a corresponding compression of ordinary space. From the perspective of the camera, five hundred million kilometers had just compressed to almost nothing and the planet Jupiter was suddenly within camera distance. The giant planet appeared on cue, beautiful in its color but oddly flat in shape. More like a disc than a sphere, but any three-dimensional object looked that way from quantum space. Compressed, flattened.

"'Tis near enough to spit upon," Thomas said, his Scottish accent returning. He checked another computer screen. "4-D volume looks right. Nitrogen density is 1.24 kilograms per cubic meter—plus the camera. About ten percent higher than yesterday."

Nala pushed away from the workbench and swiveled to face Thomas. "Okay, we're half-way there. A clean expansion into 4-D, brand new space populated by quarks and held in place by HP bosons." Hyperbolic paraboloid or HP bosons were the latest addition to the Standard Model—the parts list of elementary particles—their existence revealed by alien knowledge transfer and confirmed by human science. Precisely how these new bosons shaped space was still an area of intense investigation.

Thomas nodded without comment, and Nala continued to think out loud. "So, now for act two. Instead of letting the bosons leak naturally back to 3-D space, we'll intentionally collapse back to quantum size and monitor for any hints of gravitational waves—or maybe we should start calling them HP waves? I don't know."

"Aye," Thomas replied with a sly grin. "We'll need a new name for a lot of things. Call 'em Pasquier waves. I'll submit the name change to the Academy of Science."

"Fuck off," she said with a glare. "You know my opinion on that arrogant bullshit." Last week he'd proposed the *Nala boson*. The week before the whole Standard Model would be renamed to the *Donut Box*, with each type of quark and lepton changing to Glazed, Sprinkles, Choco and so on. She'd kind of liked that one.

Her fake-glare morphed into a smile and she turned to her computer. "Be ready to monitor the density, my friend. Initiating collapse."

She pressed a key and within seconds the surrounding air wavered like heat waves coming from an oven. Her computer screen wavered too, even the surface of the workbench.

*That's not right*, she thought. They were seeking gravitational waves so weak as to be undetectable by anything but the most sensitive of instruments. A slight tremor. A wiggle. This was a sloshing bucket of water.

Ripples propagated through the air and within seconds had permeated the entire room. The walls, floor and ceiling pulsated in a slow oscillation. Waves penetrated her body making her own bones feel as pliable as everything else. On an intellectual level the unnatural panorama was eye opening but there was no denying a far more primitive reaction, the feeling of slipping off the edge of a cliff. Both her mind and her heart raced.

"Anomaly!" Nala's voice sounded like she was at the bottom of a well. She grabbed the hand-held radio from its recharger and pressed the transmit button. "Cody, shut it down!"

The edge of the workbench pushed into her hip in rhythmic surges as if it were trying to get her attention. The computer monitors hanging on the wall above the workbench deformed like they were sheets of rubber. Then, as quickly as they had started, the waves dampened.

The air calmed, and the floor and the workbench resumed their solid existence. On the other side of the lab wall, the enormous particle accelerator spun down until the loudest thing left in the room was Nala's heart, pounding inside her once-again-solid chest. She leaned against the workbench and took a deep breath.

"Whoa. What the hell?" Any particle physicist routinely dwells in the realm of the bizarre; quantum physics is not for lightweights. But over weeks of experiments, she'd seen no precedent for today's gymnastics.

Thomas stepped toward her keeping both hands on the workbench. "You okay?" he asked.

"Sure, you?"

"A bit queasy."

"Yeah, me too."

They stood in silence for a time. Anomalies are expected in groundbreaking science, even welcomed as opportunities for discovery. But lack of control was always disturbing.

Nala plopped into her chair and turned to the computer display. It showed a line graph that looked like it had just been through an earthquake. "Wow. Tau went crazy there for a minute, even sinusoidal."

Thomas peered over her shoulder. "And here I thought you smarty-pants physicists had this four-dimensional stuff all figured out."

Nala took another deep breath, her heart calming. She glanced back at her lab partner. "Yeah... I thought we did too."

A loud cracking sound caused them both to jump. It came from the plexiglass test box at the other end of the workbench. A tiny light hovered in the center of the box. The light wasn't there at the beginning of the test.

It was a pinprick, nothing more, but far more brilliant than any dot ought to be. Nala shielded her eyes and drew closer. A fine mist slowly circled the point of light forming a disc shape that spiraled inward. It gave the appearance of a miniature galaxy only a few inches across.

"Fascinating," she said.

As they watched, there was another crack and a bit of the plexiglass case broke away. The chip joined the mist to be drawn into the point of light. Another crack split the far side of the box.

"Holy shit," Nala said stepping back. "Whatever it is, for such a little thing it's got some punch."

And then as quickly as it appeared, the light silently faded away. The mist twisted delicately for another turn and then evaporated, leaving the box empty once more.

Thomas stood behind, watching the last wisp of the gracefully pirouetting mist. "Kind of pretty," Thomas said. "But unexpected."

Nala concentrated her stare into the test box, searching for answers. Both the waves and the pinprick of light were anomalies, no question, unseen in any previous test. Were they related? Could they be recreated? The effect would need more study. They could be on the brink of a landmark discovery. A breakthrough.

Of course, it could be dangerous too.

*******************

Buy the paperback for *Quantum Void* at Amazon:
https://www.amazon.com/dp/1973583933

356

Made in the USA
Middletown, DE
14 January 2019